DOC SPEARS **JASON ANSPACH** **NICK COLE**

DARK OPERATOR

DARK OPERATOR **BOOK 1**

GALAXY'S EDGE

Edited by Lauren Moore
Published by Galaxy's Edge Press

Cover Art: Tommaso Renieri
Cover Design: Ryan Bubion
Formatting: Kevin G. Summers

Website: www.GalaxysEdge.us
Facebook: facebook.com/atgalaxysedge
Newsletter (get a free short story): www.InTheLegion.com

JOIN THE LEGION

FREE SHORT STORY

TIN MAN

WHEN YOU SIGN
UP FOR OUR VIP
MAILING LIST

The Savage Wars might be all but over, but that doesn't mean there's peace in the galaxy just yet.

Legion Dark Ops has always been a unit shrouded in secrecy. Tasked with performing covert missions, its kill teams are filled with the best warriors from within the ranks of the Legion.

Kel Turner is one of the youngest legionnaires ever to be selected for Dark Ops. After many battles and trials he is faced with the greatest challenge of his life—operating by himself on a remote planet at the galaxy's edge, a foot soldier for the policies of the duplicitous House of Reason, tasked with solving a crisis that would take ten kill teams to resolve.

Diplomats, spies, shadowy terrorist groups, and an enigmatic general work with and against him as he fights to save a society from itself.

What can one operator do alone, separated from his kill team, fighting a war that has no name?

This lone operator doesn't know what it will take to win. He only knows he's not going to lose.

PROLOGUE

I know a true believer when I see one. I was one myself once.

I know in my heart that I still am.

I've been here since the beginning, selected by General Rex himself at the very end of what most people thought was the end of the Savage Wars.

And I still believe. Fervently. But what I believe in isn't the mission. Not anymore. It's the people in this organization. Even after thirty years, I believe in them now more than ever.

The rest of it? Better not to think about that.

The kid in front of me sits like a granite statue. He looks like they all do when they're selected to come to this unit. I'm not only talking about his physical appearance. It's his bearing. He's coiled and ready to strike, but he has it under control. He's smart. You can tell. He needs to get a new Legion black dress uniform. This one is getting too tight across his chest and shoulders. He's reaching that age when he's getting thick, laying muscle on top of muscle instead of losing weight from all his exertions.

The team coming back from Antione spotted this kid's talent. Gave him good marks. The best. I agree. He's a performer. All the indicators are there of him being a good fit for this unit.

I don't have any doubt that he's the kind we want. The kind that's going to soak up whatever we teach him. The

1

kind that's going to drive himself harder than anyone else ever could. The kind who cares more about the mission than anything else. He'll always put himself last in the equation. The equation we all try and conjure the answer to. How do I crush this?

So, do I tell him?

Do I tell him... it's not going to be what he thinks? Do I tell him that in the end, he's going to question everything he believes?

Do I?

I've tried before. Even the older selectees have trouble absorbing it when I tell them.

Some of them just don't want to believe it.

Some of the them, the selectees, decide to return to their units. What we offer is just not for them. The Legion was already the best fit for them. They were already in the most elite fighting unit in the Republic. They have status, and anyone can see it. There's plenty of camaraderie, regimentation, and of course, KTF.

They ask, "What was I thinking, leaving all that?"

Because this... it's not all that. We're the guys doing the jobs that no one ever hears about. There's no recognition for what we do. And though there's a mystique that, like a siren's lure, draws some to us—those types, they don't stay.

It takes a true believer. To stay.

I've heard us called a cult. Most don't call us anything, because our existence is largely unknown, even within the ranks of the Legion. The difference between us and a cult is that you can leave at any time and we won't stop you. Over the years, we've released many for cause. Better to have killed them. If this is where you want to be, there's hardly anything else in life that'll fill the void in your soul when you're not counted within our ranks.

That's why I'm still here.

It's best to be honest about it all instead of pretending it's about something it isn't.

I'm looking at this kid sitting at perfect attention, and like I always do, I see some of myself in him. I'm older now. I'm here more for what I can do with my brains than with my body. But I still KTF with the best of them. I keep up with the younger guys. Many times, I'm in the lead. It hurts more now than it used to, though. In many ways.

I know where this path will lead them. Him.

So, do I tell him?

"Have a seat, Turner. I'm Sergeant Major Nail."

Firm handshake. The kid's got a big toothy smile. I can feel the electric excitement he's putting out.

Was I like that? Was I? I think I was. It doesn't seem possible now, but I believe that's the truth. I was just like him. Once. A long time ago.

No, I won't tell him. Won't even try. He'll find out on his own. We'll be here to help him through it when he does learn the truth.

Only one thing left to say now.

"Welcome to Dark Ops."

01

Fear welled up in Kel's chest.

Only he knew it wasn't fear. He was amped up and the adrenaline flowed as they left the staging area to start the purposeful movement toward the objective. His armor was comfortable, and comforting. Familiar. Leej armor augmented many of his senses, but often when making a stealthy approach to a target, he felt more comfortable without it, better attuned when he was part of the environment instead of inside the most advanced combat protection system the galaxy had ever known. Inside a shell.

Moving out to KTF with his team and the I-squared troops produced a cocktail of mixed feelings. Excitement and concern about the op, and always the anxiety about not letting anything slip—not letting anyone down—in other words... not failing. Failure. The greatest sin. All of this combined to heighten his performance during any mission. He'd learned most operators experienced the same feeling at zero hour. It was a good feeling.

From a life spent in the crucible, Kel knew this: just about every good thing in life lay on the other side of fear.

Through the augmented night vision inside his bucket's HUD, Kel saw the controlled chaos of the oddly shaped troops gathering into their assigned groups for the assault. In Legion Dark Ops, kill teams like Kel's frequently found themselves working with local planetary militaries and militias. There wasn't enough Legion to go around for the Republic's needs.

"Where's the captain?" Kel heard Tem ask over the L-comm.

"Rigors of command," Tem replied. "He's in the rear with the I-squared kraltan."

"I heard that, jackass."

Of course Captain Braley Yost heard it. That's why they'd said it over L-comm. Jerking each other's chains mercilessly was a constant pastime and one of the reasons the team was so strong. Their team leader was not immune just because he was a captain. There were no distinctions by rank on a kill team during a mission. A patrol might be led by the most junior man on the team, and when it was time to lead, everyone else on the team followed.

"And if either of you wants to babysit the kraltan, be my guest," said Braley.

Non-Republic human forces were indig, short for indigenous. Mostly these were local police or military who need a little help in getting that KTF done and restoring order. In a big galaxy, not every planet had a Republic military presence. Especially out along the edge.

On a planet like this one, Dark Ops often trained indigenous non-humans to provide the killing work that always needed to be done somewhere to someone. Not only did the alien indig have alien cultures, language, and technologies, they shared the same major drawback as the human indig: they were *not* Legion.

Alien races were always twice the trouble. Double that of indig. Indigenous squared. When you said I-squared, everyone knew what you meant and the headaches it implied.

"I'll stay with the command group," Braley said. "The kraltan needs some hand-holding, I think."

"You'll always be our kraltan, Captain Yost," Kel joked.

Kraltan was the local's rank for the leader of a unit of any size. In their culture, there was only leader and follower. Teaching the I-squared that individuals also had to take initiative to be effective warriors was too difficult a concept for them. Rather than attempt to change their host's rank structure, they decided to fight other cultural battles while training the hamsters.

One thing you learned as a legionnaire and especially so in Dark Ops... you can't fight every battle. So just fight the important ones.

The Kylar were a minor space-faring species contained to one main planet on the edge. They traded with other systems along the edge and even the mid-core, and were largely a peaceful species. "Hamster" was a bit of a misnomer. The Kylar didn't particularly look like rodents. Bipedal, short, and covered in a multi-colored velvety fur, they had a humanoid form. Their faces were rather flat and not at all rodent-like, and their teeth were more evocative of a bovine rather than the sharp incisors of their namesake. Some of the Kylar understood Standard, but spoke it less proficiently. This was true of the security forces Kel's team worked with. Yet when time was critical, the hamsters demonstrated they could understand most commands issued in Standard, avoiding the slight delay necessitated by translation.

As far as alien troops went, the Kylar had not been the worst they'd ever worked with. But theirs was not a warrior culture. They loved to burrow and build, plant, bake, brew, and share. That made them eminent hosts, but ones eminently vulnerable to the problem the kill team had been sent to confront.

Other species were now intruding on the Kylar home world, and one species in particular was getting particularly nasty about the whole affair. The zhee.

As usual. They were the galaxy's uninvited and incredibly boorish guests who never failed to make a menace of themselves.

Like the Kylar, the zhee had starfaring capabilities. But whereas the Kylar did not show the proclivity to expand their domain and influence beyond their home system, the zhee were ever the violent expansionists. Only Sergeant Bigg had any experience with the zhee, and he had little good to say about the zealous interlopers now on the Kylar home world and looking to cause harm.

Kel had studied the zhee at length while preparing for the mission back on Victrix along with the rest of the team. A species dedicated to war, the donkey-like aliens had equine faces and odd, claw-like paws. And while their cold expressions in the holopics warned him that here was an enemy not to be underestimated, nothing could replace firsthand knowledge. On Kylar the team learned that quickly. The first week planetside and they'd seen the results of a zhee attack on a Kylar farming village. No one had been spared. Nothing had been stolen. The attackers only left behind smoking remnants, and a declaration scrawled on a wall with a charred Kylar femur bone. Kel didn't need to know the zhee hoof scratch language to read what it said.

Death to all the Unclean.

This wasn't Kel's first tragic sight. He'd seen the reality of war all his adult life. At seventeen, he joined the Legion and reached adulthood in their ranks. But nothing ever affected him the way their inspection of the devastated village did. Kel tried to forget the image of a child's small body, decapitated, trodden upon, her soft form surrounded by crushed toys.

It was the toys that bothered him the most. Because the toys told you everything. It had been a child. Playing. And the killers had disregarded that information and done what they'd done. To a child just playing...

You tell yourself you'll be hard and the galaxy won't change you. But the galaxy just laughs right back in your face and shows you some new horror.

The kill team came to a rapid realization that day: The House of Reason might be many things—duplicitous, fallible, aloof. Many pejoratives could be deployed to describe the political body's boundless inefficiency. But sometimes, sometimes, they got it right.

Sometimes KTF needed to be done to stop the horrors for at least a moment. Sometimes people needed to die so that children could go on playing with their toys in the dirt.

Kill Team Three absolutely needed to be on Kylar.

They stalked through the silence of the night, watching for zhee sentries and doing their best to remind the hamsters that making noise now could cost them their lives. Kel's ears strained for the slightest hint of zhee, whether it be sentries or patrols. They were where they shouldn't be—where the zhee didn't want them; past a southern line that always seemed to move northward as the zhee ravaged more farms and killed more natives in their effort to consume the entire planet.

The five-man kill team had been dispatched to assist the Kylar in dealing with their zhee problem. An initially small and seemingly reserved settlement of zhee were allowed to relocate onto the planet some dozen years ago. In that time their numbers had grown almost exponentially and exploded into what had become the current problem: a foreign invading force seeking to displace the Kylar from their own home planet.

Mass murders of several small rural communities had occurred in the past year, and it was no secret who had perpetrated those heinous acts. The zhee made it known that Kylar communities were no longer neighbors, but inferiors to be removed by any means necessary from the region. The unclean and profane who did not worship the four true gods could not be allowed to exist alongside the zhee. Now that the four gods had blessed the zhee on Kylar, their will must be fulfilled for the planet.

Expecting goodwill and mutual respect from the refugees they had cheerfully welcomed, the Kylar failed to appreciate the destructive force the zhee posed to their peaceful communities. The planet had rarely known war in its history. The government tried its best to negotiate with the zhee, sending its most friendly ambassadors. Only their bloody and maimed heads returned. The House of Reason encouraged patience and appeasement as a means to prevent further violence, and so no restraints were placed on the zhee community. Instead, the planetary government tried resettlement. They sent out long caravans of repulsor sleds and rounded up as many Kylar communities near the zhee as they could, leaving villages and burrows behind to be pillaged and burned at will.

With further acts of savagery against the helpless Kylar, the government eventually accepted the harsh reality of their situation: an increasingly uneasy Kylar populace was demanding protection from a species who wanted them exterminated from their own world.

Finally the House of Reason agreed that some form of assistance was beneficial; most importantly to the Republic, and secondly to the Kylar. The Kylar had some value as a minor trading partner on the edge, and as allies, looked particularly endearing in holovids. It would not do for the core planets to catch sight of bucolic Kylar villages burning. Yet the situation on the planet was complicated, and when problems became unclear, the politicians knew that it was best to do nothing, or, commit little.

The House of Reason in its ultimate wisdom considered the use of Dark Ops legionnaires to be a small commitment.

"Contact..." Over the L-Comm, Kel who was working with the indig scouts spotted two zhee on patrol. "Hold." In one word, Kel spoke volumes. "Braley, I'm going to take these two unknowns."

"Do it, Kel." The next few minutes would determine if they would keep the advantage of surprise or whether they would pay the butcher's bill. "We hear anything, we're launching the assault. Do it right, man. Good luck."

Thanks Braley. Just so long as there's no pressure.

Kel settled his hamsters into the tall grass and told them to wait. Satisfied they'd understood, he crept forward. "BGs," he sent out, indicating the figures were no longer unknowns, but bad guys. Two hulking zhee carrying their blasters like they were operators, but talking loudly in their muffly-huff voices about something. In the dead of the night they acted as though they were the only living souls in a dead galaxy. They wouldn't live long enough to learn from their hubris.

Kel made no sound in his approach to the target.

It wasn't just the armor. It was skill. And when done right, it was a beauty admired by pros, and a terror that frightened those who thought the galaxy was a much more civilized place than it really was. This wasn't combat. This was murder.

Seconds later silenced blaster shots at no less than ten meters, whispers in the dead of night, told the story of what had just happened to the two zhee.

"Splash two," informed Kel. "We're good."

Long pause. Some night wind crossed the grass and caused it to wave.

Then, "Objective rally point next," Braley put out. "Get the hamsters moving."

Kel paused to look at his teammates. They were all large men, made positively gigantic in their armor compared to the Kylar. Tem was the largest, along with their team leader, Captain Yost. Kel, Bigg, and Poul were only slightly shorter. To anyone not familiar with their individual preferences in weapons and equipment, they were indistinguishable in their armor. To Kel, they were his brothers. He knew them by how they moved, not how they looked.

The size difference struck Kel funny as he considered that it was now the big boys of his kill team called in to win the day for their little hamster brothers. The Kylar had zero success in their attempts to contain or deter the zhee from attacking civilian targets. The team had spent months teaching the hamster constabulary basic light-infantry type operations. The Kylar had a remote history of a warrior culture, but it was seen as anachronistic and unnecessary in their era. The zhee had proven that view critically wrong.

The oddly shaped buttstocks on the hamsters' weak, locally produced blasters made them look non-threatening, even comical in comparison to the two zhee he'd just slaughtered. The House of Reason prohibited the export of peer-grade technology to non-peer planets; especially those technologies that had the potential to be used against the Republic, weaponry being main among them. Often, the Legion was prohibited from using their own advanced weaponry on minor worlds for fear that the technology might be disseminated to a potential future threat. In this instance, the House of Reason did not prohibit the Legion's use of any of their organic weapons and equipment. Regretfully, they also did not authorize the commitment of gunships or orbital weapons platforms to the cause. They were on their own.

Kill-Teams were almost always alone.

Only starlight broke through the heavy cloud cover, leaving little ambient light. Perfect weather for the raid. The Team and the Kylar assault force assembled in a wooded clearing on a small spur overlooking a dry arroyo, one major terrain feature away from the target site. A narrow wash continued below them, leading around a ridgeline to a basin where the zhee compound was built on rising ground. Standing with Kel and his four teammates were forty hamsters in light armor and equipment, ready to move on the objective.

The huge, walled zhee compound had grown to house multiple extended zhee families—a tribe—until it became a fixture in the region. The suspicion was justified that much of the violence against local Kylar farms originated from compounds such as this one.

The intent of the operation was simple. Deter the zhee from their aggression in the area by capturing tribal leaders inside their own compound. The zhee organized themselves along family lines with a tribal elder and senior male family members controlling the group. Little happened that the elders did not know about or dictate. Capturing them would demonstrate to the zhee that they were not beyond the reach of Kylar law and its enforcement.

The men would be separated from the women and children and questioned. The large multi-family compound would be searched; weapons and any other dangerous devices would be confiscated, and any evidence linking the recent crimes to this location would be collected. The ability to develop intelligence linking these zhee to other zhee settlements and any intentions to terrorize more Kylar communities would lead to further operations to bring stability and safety back to the area.

Sergeant Bigg broke the quiet in everyone's bucket. "Kel, lead off and get your containment in place. Let us know when you're up."

"On it."

Kel was convinced Bigg had been in the Legion since before topsoil was invented. At times it seemed their team sergeant had literally been everywhere and done everything to everyone. There was little that ever seemed to surprise him, or that he didn't have a plan to put into action when a challenge arose. Kel wanted to be that kind of leej. Now he took the lead with four Kylar troopers. They traveled down the grade of the wash slowly, patrolling silently and paying attention to their surroundings. Tem followed close behind with three squads of troops, followed by Bigg, then Captain Yost accompanying the Kylar commander.

Poul, the team's fifth member, brought up the rear with a slower moving squad of hamsters carting extra gear.

They reached the end of the wash, and Kel halted the patrol at a small spur, their last cover and concealment before the zhee compound. Peering through the brush, he could see a dim light rising from behind its walls just a hundred meters away. He halted the assault force as Bigg and Poul pushed the group into a loose perimeter facing outward, alert for any movement around them.

Days before, Kel had taken several of the Kylar scouts out for a pre-target surveillance of the compound. A half a kilometer on the other side of the zhee compound a wooded plateau allowed observation of the zhee and their small valley. Digging was a natural activity for the hamsters, and on a similarly lightless night, the group quickly dug a small hide where two of the troopers remained for several days and nights. They observed the zhee from their concealment, transmitting images of the donkey-like aliens and their activities to Kel and the team. This pre-target surveillance allowed the team to form a picture of how many zhee were likely in the compound and what their routines were.

The zhee never seemed to be in any state of alert, despite their recent raids on the local Kylar. Whether they were overconfident or just lazy, Kel couldn't say. At each dusk, the zhee closed the large central gates of the compound and retreated behind the five-meter-tall earthen walls, rarely venturing out until the light of the next day. If they were expecting Kylar reprisals after any zhee murder-raids, they showed no sign of being too worried about such.

"Alpha, Bravo, you're up," Kel whispered, releasing his two containment teams.

The hamsters nodded and moved out in silent response, taking a careful route into their positions covering opposite corners of the large rectangular compound. Two hamsters crept left, two more off toward the right. Kel had pointed out to each of the two teams where he wanted them to set up. Concealed by areas of defilade and brush they began laying in the tripods of their heavy blasters.

So far, so good.

The containment teams would observe for any compromise of the party's stealthy movement up to the walls and front gates of the compound. If the zhee detected them from the parapets and opened fire, the only hope for success would be return fire from the heavy blasters the containment team now emplaced. Once exposed and moving across the wide and open area, there would be no turning back for the hamsters. It would be win or die. Not even a kill team could stop that from happening.

The hamsters on containment would also get to eliminate any armed "hoppers" escaping the compound during the raid. When the zhee covered small distances quickly they sometimes used their powerful hind legs to spring away like a kanga, spurring the hamsters to call them hoppers. Kel was always amazed how all soldiers, regardless of species, had a way of breaking down the truth of a situation. Hoppers was a term he would continue to use once they'd left Kylar.

Each team gave him a wave when ready, and he flashed them a thumbs-up back to confirm. The time for slow, stealthy movements was almost over. Kel's heart pounded in his ears and he called in his report.

"Captain Yost, containment is in place. I have eyes on. We still own them."

The captain exchanged words with the kraltan who in turn gave instructions to his subordinate leaders in the low intonation and grunting sounds common to their language. The troopers filed out under Bigg, Poul, and Tem's direction until they reached Kel's position. From here the top of the zhee compound walls could just be seen against the stars.

Kel turned on his external speaker and in a firm voice gave the order.

"Assault, assault, assault."

One of the hamster squad leaders chirped in Standard, "Let's go."

I like this kid! He's ready to do some work! Kel thought.

"Kill them first, kid," he said, unsure if the youngster understood him at all.

Moving at a light jog to cross the fifty meters of open terrain, the scuffle of feet and rattling equipment no matter how carefully secured thundered in Kel's bucket.

Any minute, that gate is going to spring open, or zhee with crew-served blasters are going to spring up from the parapets and light us up, Kel thought darkly.

The parapets remained empty.

The columns moved forward, one leej leading the way to a portion of the wall twenty meters on either side of the closed double gate. On the other side lay a large courtyard flanked by domiciles and common areas. They had watched the holofeed of the compound surveillance for days and had made large terrain models for everyone to study. There would be no surprises.

There should be no surprises.

And yet... there were always surprises.

Hamsters brought forward slim nano-tube ladders and raised them in heartbreakingly slow, to Kel who was moving fast in body, mind and spirit, arcs toward the top of the walls.

Tem and Kel raced up a pair of ladders first while Poul did the same on his side of the gate, the remaining ladder ascended by one of the better I-squared troops they'd selected to join them. Bigg stayed on the ground, organizing the other squads as the troops moved into place, aiming their weapons at the gate as they waited.

Kel reached the top of the wall first. Looking down into the courtyard he saw no movement. Kel whispered and his bucket added a thermal overlay to his vision. It was weak and would not see through the doors of the dormitories facing the courtyard, but confirmed there was nothing alive or moving in the courtyard.

A hamster made it up to the top of the ladder to his left; Tem was on his right. Across the courtyard Poul and several hamsters brought weapons to bear from their side.

"We got them dead to rights," Poul's voice filled his bucket. "I see nothing."

"Same here," Tem said.

Kel pushed his N-22 farther in front of him. He disabled the weak thermal overlay on his bucket vision, favoring the new view as he settled behind the optic of his rifle. Switching to infrared and gradient thermal fusion, he scanned the various buildings around the inner courtyard.

"I see hot images in all buildings. Most seem to be horizontal. Looks like we caught everyone sleeping. The room on the 'three-side'—I'm picking up four or five hot bodies, maybe more, upright and moving around the center of the room. They're not moving toward the door. Don't think they're aware of us yet."

Kel utilized the numeric nomenclature for the compound wall and building directly across from the breach point as the twelve o'clock side, everywhere else in the compound named for its clock location. The tech inside his bucket allowed him to paint the exact target for his kill team to identify, but the simple method, unlike helmet tech, could be counted on in all conditions and was therefore always team SOP.

"Copy," Yost acknowledged. "You ready to wake them up?"

"Ready to drop a squawker now," Kel answered.

From the other side of the compound, Poul took the cue, cranked his arm back and threw an object deep across the center of the courtyard. The cylindrical device continued its arc over the courtyard until it bounced off the door of the dormitory, thirty meters away.

Nice toss, thought Kel.

"Activating," Poul said over L-comm.

The squawker was pre-programmed in the zhee language to issue commands on a repetitive loop, preceded and followed by a shrill, deafening blast.

SCREEEEECH!

"YOUARESURROUNDEDBYKYLARSECURITYFORCES!"

"MOVE OUT OF YOUR STRUCTURES WITH YOUR HANDS UP!"

"STAND IN THE CENTER OF THE COURTYARD AND DO NOT MOVE!"

"DO NOT DROP YOUR UPPER LIMBS BELOW YOUR THORAX OR YOU WILL BE KILLED!"

"AWAIT FURTHER INTRUCTIONS. YOU ARE UNDER ARREST."

"COOPERATE AND YOU WILL NOT BE HARMED."

SCREEEEECH!

The message repeated several times. Kel and Poul watched the courtyard through the optics of their N-22s. Tem stayed on his K-17 carbine and smaller optic, the hamster next to him doing the same, waiting for the appearance of any threat from below.

On thermal Kel could see large and small figures moving within the buildings, clearly females and young offspring, rising and clustering in the dormitories near the doors. Some of the braver ones opened the doors to their buildings, looking into the courtyard for the source of the shrill commands. After the fifth or sixth iteration from the squawker, some of the occupants crept into the courtyard, upper limbs held high, with zhee children clinging to each other and the females.

Kel kept his attention on the building to his twelve o'clock. The same five or six larger figures now moved chaotically about the small room. One hopped to the rear of the building before he lost sight of the hot outline of the body deeper in the structure . After a minute the figure reappeared carrying several cold, black objects about a meter in length. Almost certainly weapons.

"I've got the males in the 'three' building still in place, but it looks like they've recovered weapons," Kel updated them all. The rules for use of force were clear: any armed zhee could be engaged with deadly physical force at any time during the op.

"Looks like the females and kids're all moving into the courtyard," Tem added.

The zhee lived with usually three-to-four-times as many females as males. The males for the most part chose to live segregated from the females and kids, except for special occasions. *Like making more baby zhee*, Kel had thought. Now, he kept up a steady stream of communication with the rest of his team to stay ahead of the breakdown in the plan that would invariably come. Or maybe they'd just get lucky and it would go down just like it did on the sandtable. By the numbers.

"I don't see any males or weapons in the group in the courtyard, and I don't see any bodies left in the dormitories. The males are staying put for right now in 'three.' I'm locked down on the front door."

Kel was focused. If the zhee from building three made a move to the courtyard, he'd be ready. His trigger finger still straight and alongside the weapon's receiver where the safety was located.

First armed zhee I see, I will bring down the hate.

The captain's voice came over the L-comm. "Kel, are we good to breach and pull the women and kids out to the wash point?"

"Yeah, Cap," Kel replied. "I'm burning through their clothing on optics. I don't see weapons and I don't see anything obviously concealed. I think we're good to go."

The thermals on Kel's optic gave him the ability to see through light clothing, barring a few of the synthetic fibers you weren't likely to find outside of the core worlds. The thin, voluminous clothing most zhee wore might conceal a lot to the naked eye, but hid nothing from his thermal vision.

Advantage: technology, Kel added to his running commentary of how the mission was progressing so far.

"Commencing entry now," Braley noted. "Kel, any movement from the 'three' building—if they're armed, smoke 'em."

Waaay ahead of you, boss, he thought but only gave a terse "Roger." The anticipation Kel had felt at the beginning of the op was long gone. Now, he was doing work. Now he was settling in and swimming through the mission like a shark moving water over its gills. The mission was life. And he was living.

Bigg moved forward with several of the hamster troops, slipping toward one side of the gate while troops on the other side waited with weapons at the low ready, watching the breach point for any sudden and unexpected movement.

It was a double gate, with no visible hinges from the outside. That meant that it opened into the courtyard. The gate could be barred from the inside; there could be any number of mechanical locks. They just didn't know.

No matter. Kel knew that Bigg loved breaching. Any barrier. Any method. He loved it all. The opportunity to breach a door made him act like a kid going to his first seamball game.

Bigg motioned two of the hamsters forward. One carried a small cylinder on his back; the other had an L-shaped nozzle in his hands attached by a small diameter hose to the cylinder. Bigg would've preferred to explosively breach the gate. It would've been faster, left them exposed for a shorter period of time, and given them an advantage by helping to disorient the folks on the other side of the gate. But there hadn't been enough time to get the hamsters up to speed on that skill.

Instead he'd focused on mechanical, ballistic, and thermal breaching, wanting to leave them with skills they could put to use immediately and hopefully sustain better over the follow on missions. In this case, teaching them how to use a locally-sourced industrial plasma cutter rather than teaching them to rely on tech they didn't have and likely wouldn't receive from the Republic seemed best.

Starting from the bottom of the left-hand gate just inside of where the hinges would be, the two hamsters ignited the cutter. The tip glowed with purple plasma as a thin line of glowing metal began to melt and separate from the gate. The trooper advanced the tip steadily up the half-centimeter thick metal. They did well, doing just as they had practiced on many varieties of scrap doors during Bigg's breaching classes—not moving too fast as to be ineffective, not moving so slow that the metal in the cut could re-weld. In a matter of a minute the cut reached the top and when there was a sliver of metal left joining the top of the gate. Braley moved up with another squad of assaulters, ready to make entry.

The cut was completed and the torch bearers moved out of the way. Another trooper moved forward quickly with a pry bar and wedged it into the cut. He levered the bar and was rewarded with the appearance of a gap as the gate gave way. Tossing the pry bar to the side, he pushed on the gate with both hands as it dissociated itself from the gate and fell into the compound. The breacher quickly moved out of the way as Braley pointed to the opening, prompting the first assaulter in line to move.

White lights on the hamsters' carbines switched on as the assaulters slipped through the breach point; the first moving immediately left, the next moving immediately right, until everyone moved against the strong wall of the breach point and Captain Yost, standing just inside the gate, could observe it all.

The lights on their weapons illuminated the faces of the bewildered zhee gathered in the center of the compound; many had dropped their arms to gather their young, but no one fired, despite the Squawker's warnings.

Kel nodded approvingly at the hamsters' discipline. If anyone fired there could be a sympathetic response that led to a mad-minute—everyone shooting just because they'd heard someone else shoot. It was known to happen even with well-trained troops, but would be a disastrous way to inaugurate the hamsters' first major operation. Fortunately, that had not happened. Yet.

"Why don't you fancy snipers stay up here?" Tem said over L-comm. "I'm going down to the wash point to help out."

Kel, Poul, and their troops had more than enough advantage to continue the overwatch without him.

"Sounds good," Kel and Poul said, almost in unison.

Tem slung his carbine behind him as he climbed down the ladder. Then, weapon back in hand, the operator headed to the breach point.

Down in the courtyard, the zhee wheezed to each other while the translator device one of the hamsters held barked off commands. If the zhee kept their paws above their heads and continued cooperating, they would not be harmed.

It seemed to be working. For now.

Small groups of two or three females with several children were herded out through the breach point and met by hamster troops, weapons pointed nervously at each group, shaking white lights aimed at their faces. Each adult was approached by two troops, taking control of the female's arms and placing ener-chains around the wrists behind the now braying, kicking zhee's back.

Ener-chained captives were then passed off to another group who escorted the detainee to a holding area fifty meters in front of the compound as they were placed in a sitting position. Depending on how badly they were resisting, those still putting up a struggle were unceremoniously placed face down and ener-chains applied to their legs as well. The young zhee stayed close to the women, crying and trying to hide under the females' robes.

Biggs had once told Kel the little ones were just as likely to kill you as the adults, but that didn't seem the case right now.

A particularly aggressive zhee refused to be cuffed, the wheezes piercing above the low level brays. Tem stepped forward to help. He slung his weapon, then swept zhee's legs out from under her, grabbed the nearest limb and rotated her on her stomach, kneeling on her back while the hamsters cuffed her. The other zhee wailed and screeched, yet no one else seemed anxious to receive similar treatment.

The captain updated the team over the L-comm. "Last few coming out now. Overwatch, how's that 'three' building looking?"

No sooner had the captain asked when three's door cracked open and the barrel of a blaster appeared. Kel and Poul fired simultaneously, the shooter collapsing across the threshold. Blaster fire erupted from deep in the room. A zhee female fell with a shriek, shot in the back where she exited the compound, her arms raised high in compliance .

The snipers had seen the zhee within the building making a move toward the door but hadn't had time to warn the others. Sometimes return fire was a special form of communication all its own. Braley and the hamster assault team sent a torrent of bolts at the building, encouraging anyone within to rethink their current life choices.

Kel had a moment of intuition. "Cap, get those hamster kids and the rest of the team out of the compound. We're going to keep heat on that building."

"Moving," replied Braley, not pausing to discuss the suggestion.

Kel and Poul sent shots deep into the room, hoping to contain the small group of male zhee, who had wisely retreated behind the cover of the wall. A shot left one of their weapons every five to ten seconds, Kel and Poul alternating their suppression of the zhee.

"We have the zhee barricaded in three. They don't appear to be making a move," Kel updated. "Anyone hurt?"

"Negative. We're out of the breach point and behind the walls."

Kel didn't want to turn his head to look behind him to see where his teammates and the hamsters were. Tem, Bigg, and Braley could get things organized without him.

"Do you want me to send some love into that room?" Tem asked, itching to use his energy grenade launcher to likely excellent effect.

Braley paused. "No. Not yet. We need to capture one of these donks." Donk. Kel liked that pejorative for the zhee. "I suppose we can try to talk with them. Kel, want to try a little cross-cultural communication?"

Kel clicked his teeth together three times in rapid succession, activating the translator function in his bucket speaker, pre-programmed for zhee.

"You in the building. You are surrounded. We have your families in custody. They will not be harmed. Throw out your weapons and come out of the building with your hands raised high. Do it now."

"Hey man, you sound like that holovid police drama I watched as a kid," Poul joked over the L-comm.

He ignored Poul and repeated the command. Could they hear him after all the blaster exchange? He wondered if his translator program was doing an accurate job.

"Cap, they're making no move to drop their weapons or leave the building. They're still armed."

Bigg spoke up over the L-comm. "I think it's time to bring up the rats."

The Kylar, though the team jokingly called them hamsters, actually bore little resemblance to their namesake. But their dogs were absolutely the spitting image of theirs. Rats. That is, if rats weighed 90 kilos and had mouths full of razor-sharp teeth.

The rats seemed to be especially xenophobic. Kel loved dogs along with most other animals. But the feeling was not reciprocated by the rats. The first time he tried to get near one without his bucket on, the handler had to use all his strength to restrain the snarling animal. In full Legion armor the rats didn't have any strong reaction to the leejes, but still couldn't be handled by anyone but the hamsters.

Near the kraltan, two handlers and their rats waited. On signal, the handlers trotted forward with the rats, harnesses strained as their handlers wrestled the large creatures forward.

"Rats are ready," Braley spoke.

"Marking now," Kel said. Using his infrared laser, he looped a pattern continuously, painting the wall near three's door with the invisible beam. The infrared spectrum light was visible only to the animals, not to humans. The handlers released them through the breach point. The animals paused for a moment, looked around, saw the laser marking the entrance to the building, and took off at a dead run, covering the distance in a few seconds. Just as they'd been trained.

This is gonna be good, thought Kel.

The rats barreled through the partially open door into three. With his optics Kel could see the rats leap upon a figure, knocking it down while other donks shrieked and brayed.

A figure moved purposefully into the center of the room. On all channels Kel yelled, "GET DOWN," as he grabbed the hamster next to him and tried to encourage him down his ladder.

Ka-*BOOM*!

The noise of the explosion filled the air, followed by a shower of debris and grit. Kel made his way back up the ladder, racing as fast as he could climb.

Braley yelled over the L-comm, "Status check, is everyone all right? Sound off…"

It was obvious what had happened. One of the zhee had an explosive device, most likely something worn to punish anyone attempting to apprehend them. The rats had forced the zhee to prematurely detonate their suicide-homicide device. But the team had planned to mitigate that possibility, and it had happened.

They sounded off one at a time as Kel topped the ladder. Duracrete chunks littered the courtyard and several small fires burned in piles of debris. Poul's bucket crested from the opposite wall, also surveying the destruction. The face of building three gaped wide open, its flat roof collapsed into so much rubble.

"Check your Kylar and make sure the kids on the ladders are okay," Bigg announced over the L-comm.

"What do you guys have up top?" Braley asked.

"Checking now," Kel blurted. "I don't see any movement from three. It's pretty much destroyed. I'm not picking up any signatures in the compound that look like anyone's left alive."

Coming down the ladders, Kel and Poul made their way to where the rest of the team waited. They'd held the lightly armored Kylar outside until the five members of the kill team were assembled. They went first, clearing the area with their weapons raised, collapsing their sectors of fire methodically, looking for any movement or signs of life while keeping the Kylar troops behind them.

When it was obvious that there would be no more trouble from the zhee, Braley left them and walked back to where the kraltan observed the spectacle of the smoking compound. In the distance, the dozens of zhee detainees had stopped their braying and started a guttural, rhythmic chanting that made you want to punch them in the face. The captain quickly reviewed events for the kraltan and agreed it was time to bring the vehicles up and continue processing zhee into custody and transporting them to the holding facility prepared back at base.

They'd been lucky.

Now Kel and the rest of the team walked around checking on all members of the Kylar force. No severe injuries had occurred. Yeah, they'd been lucky. The post-danger shakes took hold of him for a moment, then passed as the adrenaline began to fade.

Later, as the sun rose, they worked for many more hours, trying to render the site safe. They discovered stores of chemicals and other materials that were precursors for explosives. Completed explosives already sewn into vests and belts were buried behind the compound. They opened crates of blasters and collected several datapads. All of these they left for the Kylar investigators to document and inspect as evidence. It would take days to process the scene.

"Be nice if some of their politicians would come and take a look at the mess they created," Kel muttered to Bigg. The guy who'd been everywhere and done everything just gave him a look that said that would probably never happen. And, that the Kylar were definitely in way over their head. One of those looks that only guys like Bigg can give someone who hasn't got tired of asking all the question that are never going to get answered.

Finally it was time to return to the security force's base. They would check their gear, stand the troops down, and start the process of reviewing the events as a team. Once completed, then they could rest.

"Where's Tem?" Bigg asked. No response came over L-comm.

"I'll get him," Kel said and vaulted from the back of the sled. There stood Tem, bucket in hand, frowning at the scene of frozen destruction. His look of resignation said it all.

"Well," said Tem to the still air and the silence. "I guess that's got it done proper."

02

"I recommend we take our afternoon break and resume this council meeting in two hours. Until then, esteemed senators."

The man's manicured finger moved across the lightly glowing button in front of him and a soft chime emanated throughout the room, signaling the session's end.

Before he could stand, his aide was at his side, gathering the senator's datapad and placing it in his ever-present bag.

"Lucius, a word?" a portly, aging man said as he approached, pushing upstream as others moved toward the ornate doors at the front of the chamber.

"Certainly, Thaddeus," said the House of Reason's Planetary Security Committee Chair, Senator Lucius VanderLoot as he rose from his polished leather seat that felt more like a throne to many privileged enough to get so close. "Something urgent that can't wait until the next session, I presume?"

"No Lucius, not anything like that at all. I simply wanted to tell you how much Ceres and I were looking forward to your attendance at our dinner. We have arranged for some... special entertainment... for your pleasure at the end of the evening," the aging senator shared with a smile.

Lucius could easily imagine what Thaddeus was intimating. These rotating get-togethers by the senators at their private estates was a necessary, if frequently dull, part of Liberinthine political life. Most of the exchanges and maneuvers that led to ascent or descent in the spectrum of power seemed to mirror who attended these dinner parties. Each party was an opportunity to display the wealth of your home and convince other power-brokers of the refined cultural sensibility implied by the extravagance of the event.

It was vital to be worthy of invitation, even amongst the elite of the Senate and House of Reason. It was equally vital to attend once included. Absence gave other members, and most consequentially their spouses, opportunity to plot against you. Lucius had no fears in this regard.

No senator would dare harbor such intention against him.

Generations of VanderLoot wealth and connections had led to a hereditary position of responsibility as stewards of the Republic until the VanderLoots came to see that as their place in the universe. Being the head of one of the most influential families in the galaxy came with certain implied guarantees, such as invulnerability from petty intrigue. It helped to know where the bodies were buried.

"I would expect no less from such a grand host and friend as yourself, Thaddeus. Lydia and I look forward to it. Please extend our gratitude to Ceres. I'm sure we will enjoy what you have planned for the... entire evening."

He continued on with his aide trailing behind him, exchanging curt pleasantries with the other council members before taking the path through the outer ring of halls leading to his offices and personal meeting chambers.

His aide rushed ahead to push open the gilded mahogany door and stand to one side as Lucius made his way through the front office. He greeted his public secretaries at their desks, then moved through door after door, each room more ostentatiously decorated than the one before. Finally, he came to his private chambers where his chief of staff waited.

Accius VanderBlanc stood at attention as the senator sat behind his massive desk.

"I thought I was going to have some of those imbeciles murdered on the spot, Accius. I swear half of them should apologize to the oceans that provide them the oxygen they're consuming. It is supposed to be a committee, not a contest to prove who is the foremost cretin in the galactic capital."

"Thank Oba you run the asylum then, sir."

Accius had recently ascended to the position of running the senator's office and public affairs. He had the usual family connections to the VanderLoot dynasty; he'd attended the same academies and institutions as had all the members of the Republic's true intelligentsia. That was an unspoken necessity. It was not possible to serve the Republic without having attended one of the few select institutions of approved learning, implicitly communicating to the elite that you were "one of us."

He'd been raised as one of them from birth, every activity and social function controlled by his parents and extended family to ensure he was known to the best people in the center of the Republic's control center. And of course, there was a blood relation through generations of carefully planned marriages to ensure that power and wealth coalesced.

Accius had attended the Academy for Galactic Governance and after a short stint in the Ex-Planetary Diplomatic Service, returned to Liberinthine and began work for the most powerful man in the House of Reason, some said, in the galaxy.

It was all as had been planned for him, and to Accius, it was all deserved.

"Senator, did the Meridian situation proceed forward this morning? Shall I have the briefers from Ex-Planetary Affairs standing by?"

The issue had been introduced but there was to be more testimony and debate in the afternoon session.

"Yes, have them in the chamber ready to be called forward. I assume you have the summary for me now? I don't like to ask questions I don't already know the answer to." Lucius was well aware of the situation on Meridian. The vote to give or deny assistance from the House of Reason to a planet on the galaxy's edge would be unlikely to have any lasting effect on the stability of the Republic, but might serve as an opportunity for any politician ready to exploit the situation to its most fruitful potential.

Meridian was typical of many planets on the edge. Settled by humans during the earliest part of the Great Leap, it became isolated from its progenitor and because of its distance from the political center of the galaxy remained relatively isolated during the long years of the Savage Wars. It certainly lagged behind the core galactic worlds in many ways, but with the end of the galaxy-wide conflicts seemingly near, it had suddenly reemerged and shown interest in commerce with the mid-core and core worlds.

Meridian was ruled by a feudal system, controlled by twelve families, descendants of the original colonists who maintained large fiefdoms. The families cooperated at a planetary level through a governing body composed of representatives from the twelve ruling families, the Domestic Conclave.

Their export economy was dominated by agriculture. Much of what they offered in trade included crops, foodstuffs, and other goods now thought to have only existed on the progenitor world. The climate and radiation apparently had made it especially kind to the original settlers as their home world crops needed little if any genetic manipulation to thrive there. In essence, the world was a time capsule preserving much of the early galactic explorers' cultures.

Meridian was fascinating in that one regard: its connection to the beginning of galactic exploration and colonization. It was an often romanticized period and was thought by some to be an idealized time in human existence. Once the cruel experiment in pre-hyperspace exploration ended, the exciting period of rapid expansion throughout the galaxy began, and the discovery of new worlds and races captivated holo-vid audiences throughout the Republic. The holo-dramas made the early expansion into the galaxy seem adventurous and mysterious. One popular show, *Star Pioneers*, had run for several seasons, telling the drama of a small group of colonial families searching the galaxy for a habitable world, battling alien races, and fighting to conquer a new home.

Of course, almost nothing like that was recorded as having happened in over a thousand years. The early FTL explorers had some wild times, but subsequent settlements were meticulously surveyed out before colonization was even attempted. Dull science made for poor entertainment and couldn't compete with the fantasy of the earliest part of the diaspora from earth.

Many of the nostalgic products from Meridian were currently popular on Liberinthine and were gaining more interest in the popular culture and media.

Meridian was becoming recognizable as a brand.

A small Republic diplomatic mission had been sent to Meridian years before. The situation that had come to the attention of the House of Reason and the Planetary Security Council, and most specifically to Lucius, filtered through the Republic's diplomatic mission on Meridian.

Relative peace threatened to dominate much of the galaxy for the first time in over a thousand years, the end of the Savage Wars promised to be in sight. Even edge worlds managed to reconnect with the rest of the galaxy and enjoy prosperity through trade. It seemed Meridian would be one such shining star, until recently.

Internal unrest troubled the planet. Generations of social injustice and limited opportunities for those who lay outside the privilege of the twelve families ruling Meridian and their select friends had become the source of resentment among many.

Analysis conducted by Republic political specialists concluded that Meridian and its so-called Domestic Conclave was not barbaric or especially heavy-handed in its daily governance. Universal education and excellent health care, for a technologically hampered world, improved the lives of the masses. There was a press that served a minor propaganda role but did report the events of the day in an uncensored manner; the judicial system allowed for due process; Meridian's economy prospered, and the middle class appeared to be growing with the expansion of off-planet trade; and the large agricultural and labor classes had opportunities to change their station in life through individual effort.

But the winds had shifted on Meridian. Recently, acts of terrorism and protests had disrupted many of its capital cities and their infrastructure. While Republic Intelligence estimated the number of malcontents to be miniscule, their means were primarily violent and had root in ideological protest. The Domestic Conclave responded in an appropriately brutal fashion.

Now they were requesting help from the Republic. Really, as Lucius imagined these primitive supplicants from a backwater world, they were petitioning him personally, a preeminent leader of the House of Reason, to save them from themselves. If he were being honest, which he rarely was with anyone else but himself, he felt unique among all others in his ability to see the complexity of the situation.

"If I may ask, sir, what will be your position on aid when it comes to a vote?"

Lucius considered the question from his young assistant.

"We're related, are we not, Accius?"

A quickly controlled shadow of confusion crossed his face. "Yes, Senator, on my mother's side we share common blood. Your aunt and my mother's aunt grew up and attended school together. They shared weekly victuals their entire lives, so I'm told."

Lucius sighed. "Yes. Lovely ladies both, I remember them well. All right then. Then you are here to further your education after all, and this is your first opportunity to see one of these matters play out as it should. Influence. It's all about influence, Accius. The influence of the House of Reason, and how we achieve that influence for the good of the Republic, are matters that take a lifetime of training and, well, breeding to fully comprehend."

He continued, noting the appropriate attentiveness displayed by his young chief of staff. "Here we have a world with great potential. Certainly, not one ready to be a full member of the Republic, but with great potential nonetheless. At the moment, they've no great benefit to bring to the Republic. Their internal problems are truly no existential threat to the galaxy. But the question you must ask yourself is, How might they someday be of benefit to the Republic and the core as a whole? And, upon answering that question, our next question is, Should we send them Republic Army troops to further their crackdown and restore despotic rule to their planet as rapidly as possible? Well, tell me, young Accius. What say you?"

"Of course not, sir! That would be an enormous commitment of resources and would promote the image of the Republic supporting a brutal, non-egalitarian form of governance over humans," Accius replied. They both knew that the same measuring stick was not applied to alien races.

"Indeed it would. That would be an absurd use of our power and economic resources," replied the veteran senator. "Should we then ignore their request and inform them that due to the reported abuses of their citizens, as well as their history of punishing iconoclasts with death sentences, we are sanctioning and isolating their world? That we look forward to resuming trade with them when they have solved their internal issues?" the senator queried.

"It seems like that would be a popular option with many on the council," Accius observed.

"So, you'd agree that there exists a middle ground, yes?" Lucius allowed his young apprentice to digest his rhetorical question. "As to Meridian's request for technological upgrades, giving them unfettered access to peer-level technology is not warranted. Before we bring a planet on the edge up to a level where they have equal footing with us, we must consider whether they have developed a level of consciousness consistent with that expected by the House of Reason. It would be irresponsible to elevate such a world so rapidly."

Accius nodded in understanding.

"When we provide aid to a planet, we do so in a manner proportionate to their development and their utility to us. You've studied for years to understand these principles. Now you're learning how things are applied in practice.

"We have an opportunity now to exert some influence in this crisis, but it is not necessary to give away the jewels on the first date. My recommendation to the council will be that we do provide them aid. I will recommend, and the council will see my wisdom in this, that the aid be partial and not everything they are requesting.

"Above all, the Twelve Families on Meridian want to maintain the status quo and remain in power. They want to restore order to their society. Therefore, we have an opportunity to assist them, for the good of all peace-loving peoples, and to influence them over time to foster change within their society. Change that will benefit them, and change that will ultimately benefit the Republic, of which they may someday be a member. And with that assistance comes... gratitude.

"We will send them aid—technical aid, military aid, economic aid. But it will be limited. The package we'll design will include this assistance, and of course, that package will be conditional. It will primarily be conditional on their goods reaching the core along with agreed-upon tariffs to the House of Reason. Without committing substantial resources or gaining public attention on the Spiral News Network, we can assist Meridian, get their trade back on track, and keep the focus off the House of Reason. We have tools for just such a purpose." Then to himself he muttered, "I suppose those knuckle-dragging legionnaires will need to be involved..."

"What's that, sir?"

"Enough for now, Accius. I must rest."

After Accius closed the doors behind him, Lucius lay down on the day bed in his private office. He thought about gratitude. And what form that might take. How it would be shaped to benefit him and the House of Reason. Being a problem solver was hard work. Imagining the subtly concealed praise by the holo-journalists on their morning programs as he expounded his role in solving this crisis on Meridian filled him with contentment as he drifted off. His daughter was married to a senior producer at SNN. Many members of the House of Reason had family members or marriages that connected them to the media. It didn't guarantee favorable coverage; they were the media after all. Negative press entertained the masses more so than positive press. However, Lucius hadn't participated in a single unscripted media event in his career. He'd never been caught off-guard or embarrassed by a reporter. Most of the journalists he dealt with were known to him through years of social and family connections.

He would contact his brokers to plan a strategy for future investments in the burgeoning trade from the quaint little world. He relished the thought of the mechanisms he would turn loose, the workings of a giant machine with thousands of cogs, all existing to serve the Republic and the person who controlled them with but a few words.

Cogs of the Republic. The actual mechanisms, who they were or how they did their work, the most powerful man in the galaxy did not concern himself with knowing.

FLASHBACK

Antione Orbit
Republic Navy Frigate _Bellerophon_

How I Went Dark, or, Better Lucky Than Good: the Kel Turner Story

So before we go any further I need to tell you how I ended up in Dark Ops.

"This must be the luckiest week of your life, Sergeant Turner." The lieutenant doesn't say it like he's happy for me. Whatever. The lieutenant isn't going to dampen my optimism today, however short lived. I am feeling lucky. Question is, will I still be alive to feel that way in a week? "Yes sir. It is at that." I stood at parade rest. Think the Legion is famous for its harsh rituals, among other things? Well Legion Reconnaissance's the only place in the Legion where a trooper stands at parade rest for a corporal, a corporal for a sergeant, a sergeant for any more senior sergeant...you get the idea.

Just hearing myself called sergeant feels odd. The stripes were only pinned on me yesterday. Standing in the bay of the Navy ship makes everything a little surreal, too. Talon dropships are being loaded with ordnance. Navy types doing Navy things in a cyclone all around us. The platoon is flaked out in an out of the way corner of the deck. I'd only been back at the unit for a day before we got spun up. Now here we sit. Waiting.

"Walk with me, sergeant," Lieutenant Cosgrove says as he turns, expecting me to fall in step with him. I double-time to assume a position to his left as he walks toward a quiet part of the huge bay. The rest of the platoon return to flop onto their carryalls. I caught Corporal Trumbull's eye-roll as we depart. My assistant team leader can't conceal his dislike of the lieutenant. I hope the platoon sergeant didn't see that. Where is Sergeant Bullock? Why is the platoon leader pulling me aside alone and without him?

Lieutenant Cosgrove is something of a hard ass, even within recon. He's the picture-perfect Legion officer. He's as big as the biggest leej which means in armor, he's a giant. Out of armor his chiseled features make him look like a sports star or a holo-action hero. All that's missing are the models on his arm and pockets filled with endorsement deals. There's a rumor that he'd been drafted for the big leagues but had chosen the Legion instead. Officers don't share personal details, so it was just a rumor, but a believable one.

As my platoon leader finds that quiet spot and halts, I resume the position. I have a pretty good idea what he's going to say. A pep talk about taking care of the men. I'm wrong.

"Sergeant Turner, I didn't ask for you to be in my assault platoon, much less on the pathfinder squad. But I follow orders. CO says you're on the drop, you're on the drop." Unbeknownst to any of us, the plan for the invasion of Antione was well underway when I left for orbital freefall school. Freefall was a whole other level of skill, well beyond the automated low-level parachute descents we were taught in recon operator training. That I graduated and made it back in time to join the unit for the biggest planetary assault in recent history felt like divine providence. Getting my buck sergeant stripes was just the icing on the cake. The cherry on top was being assigned to first platoon as the Alpha fire team leader of the most select squad; the pathfinder detachment.

We'd be the very first onto the planet and preparing the way for the rest of the recon company to seize the spaceport. Then, Repubs would land and Magnus IV heavy gravtanks–with Legion support–would roll over Antione in an avalanche of leej grey and basic green. But first, we had to be the eyes on the ground at the spaceport. Despite what we tell ourselves, the reality is we wouldn't really be the first on the ground. It was a big planet. Somewhere below, the really cool guys were already working, covertly marking targets for orbital strike, sabotaging infrastructure, and doing stuff every legionnaire dreamed about. Or so the scuttlebutt said.

"Sergeant," my platoon leader forms a knife hand and pokes its tip, his middle finger, at my chest. "Everyone is depending on us. You wouldn't be in recon if you weren't the best. But I don't know you. So, I'm asking you. Are you up for this? I know you're smart so don't give me any glib, 'KTF, sir' kind of answer. I need to know."

It took me two tries to get to recon. It's all I'd wanted since I got out of leej basic. I was distinguished honor graduate from sniper school, which got me the nod to try out for my first recon selection even though I wasn't yet 19. I passed, but didn't get selected. My second try six months and a lot of blood and sweat later, I made it. I finished number one in the recon operator course; the same again in orbital freefall school. Now I'd been selected ahead of my peers for sergeant.

His question pissed me off, officer or no. *What the frell more do I have to do to prove I belong here?* "Sir, I'm absolutely ready and committed to the successful completion of this mission," I growled, realizing I'd failed to conceal my irritation. The lieutenant's face grew sour and flushed but before the inevitable dressing down came at me, he was interrupted.

"Pardon me, sir." It was Sergeant First Class Bullock, the platoon sergeant. "We have an updated operation order at the company TOC. We'd best not be late. Sergeant Turner, Staff Sergeant Sung is looking for you." Sung is the pathfinder detachment squad leader and would be the jumpmaster for our drop. Now is when we were supposed to be doing another deck-dive as a team, practicing our actions for the jump. It's not every day you get to go to war by diving onto a planet from the edge of space. Sung, the Bravo fire team leader Sergeant Shuck, and myself had checked chutes and crossloaded equipment so many times I knew where every item was in every member of my fire team's carryalls.

"Thank you, Sergeant Bullock." The lieutenant's displeasure with me seemed forgotten for the moment. "Dismissed, Sergeant Turner." I came to a sharp position of attention and did an about face. Sergeant Bullock winked at me as I trotted off, his head turned so Lieutenant Cosgrove couldn't see. *Sergeant Bullock saved my butt right there. What was that even about?*

I told Staff Sergeant Sung about my interrogation. He motioned me to stand at ease. The pathfinder detachment was rank heavy; we're all at least corporals, so are a little more relaxed than the other squads. "The lieutenant is a good officer. It may have felt personal, but it wasn't really about you. He's just jealous that he's not going to be leading the pathfinder mission. He has to stay with Bullock and bring in the rest of the platoon. If we prove the air defenses are knocked out, they may not even need to jump in after us, they'll just land." It made sense. The hulking young officer was being cheated out of the opportunity to make Legion history by leading the pathfinders in. I'd be eating my liver too if someone else was going to make a combat freefall and I was excluded. If the rest of the company doesn't at least get to make an auto-jump onto the airfield, there'll be some hard feelings. Not as bad as I'd have felt had I gotten back from freefall school to find all of recon deployed without me. That would have been unbearable. Sincere or not, the lieutenant had been right. I was lucky.

"I understand, Sergeant Sung, but it still felt pretty personal. Like he was questioning my ability." I'm not thin skinned, but his words stung a bit. Taking his frustration out on me didn't seem like something a good leader should do.

"It's not about you," Sung reassures me. "Bullock chose you and I agreed. Or else you wouldn't be here. Forget about the lieutenant for now. I've gone through a few platoon leaders in Recon. They always get a little cranky at times like this. He'll get over it once the KTF starts. Come on. Let's get the squad together for another deck-dive."

The squad is on their feet. Corporal Trumbull raises his arms overhead and gives a war cry. Now the bay echoes with similar cheers. I see it too. Everyone's facing the holo showing the fleet spread over Antione, particle beams and neutronium missiles, the flashes of their impacts illuminating the night on the surface.

"Who's going to KTF now? We are!" Trumbull yells, a chant of "KTF, KTF, KTF," starts. I look at Sung. He smiles at me. "Twenty hours of this, and we dive."

03

Kel got out of the shower and readied his duty uniform. There was just enough time to grab chow and make it to the team room and still be ten minutes early. They had returned to Victrix the preceding day and started the morning together with physical training. As he got up to leave the dining facility, he saw Tem and Poul make their way into the mostly empty hall. He acknowledged them as he left, secretly satisfied that he'd beat them to the team room.

He bounced up the stairs to the second floor and placed his hand against the door to the team room. The number "3" above the door stood alone as the only identifier. His DNA was recognized and the door slid open. Bigg sat at his desk typing on a holoboard, looking at the projection from his datapad, as did Braley at the opposite desk. They gave Kel a nod as he passed by and made his way to the next room and the loadout cages.

After Kylar they'd gone from cruiser to dropship and then arrived at the base late last night, but didn't return to quarters until they'd spent several hours accounting for and securing weapons and equipment. They'd had ample time to do most of their gear maintenance on the cruiser, as well as perform an exhaustive after-action review of the last op. Things had wound down rapidly after the raid on the donk compound. In their time together post-mission they had all agreed their time on Kylar had been productive and had generally positive feelings about the hamsters they left behind. They'd turned into good troops. Whether they would remain so for the foreseeable future until someone from DO worked with them again was an entirely different issue. "They ain't bad little guys," Poul had opined on the ride home. "But you know... hamster gonna hamster."

Generally, the issue of the Kylar being able to sustain the skills and methods they had been taught was not centered on the capabilities of the individuals they had just spent months integrating into an effective unit. The hamster security forces had proven capable of adapting and learning new tactics and procedures. No, the success or failure of their program was going to be determined by their government and the security forces command. The kill team had built a program that gave the Kylar the essentials of how to conduct the types of operations that would give them a decent chance of restoring peace on their world. If the Kylar decided against pursuing further operations against the zhee, then the units would be disbanded or sit unused, and the value they'd built would quickly evaporate like snowmelt at noon.

Their kill team had done its job, and stability was now in the hands of the Kylar.

As the team commander and team sergeant worked to finish their reports, Kel, Tem, and Poul organized personal gear and common team gear for the next call-out.

Besides their time spent training and leading the Kylar, they'd gathered voluminous amounts of information about their hosts that was being assembled into the reports as well. Holo-images and location data of all the bases and regions where they'd worked were meticulously recorded. They'd also surreptitiously collected DNA and biometric data on the security forces they'd come in contact with and formed a biography as detailed as possible about all the members of the strike unit they had ushered into existence. If someday one of those individuals took the low road and became a bounty hunter or otherwise participated in acts against the Legion or the Republic, Dark Ops would track them down and deal with them.

Going rogue was not unheard of. Indoctrinate enough people in the ways of efficient violence, and sooner or later some of them would use those skills for bad purposes. D.O., Dark Ops Command, did not like to lose track of those people.

In a more mundane function, the information would also serve to prepare anyone else going out to work with the Kylar.

Enough information to fill a black hole had been gathered and was now in the final stages of being assembled for digestion and then dissemination. It would find its way to a brief with the commander of Legion Dark Ops, Legion Intelligence, and likely the Legion commander himself. Eventually the information would move up through the labyrinthine path to Republic Intelligence. Kel was confident of one thing after participating in many missions like this so far: information went up, but it never came back down.

Braley stuck his head into the team locker area and announced, "We're outta here, headed to the puzzle palace. Don't wait up, kiddies. If we need you, we'll holler. Otherwise see you tomorrow for the a.m. workout."

They had a good plan for tomorrow; they'd get out of the Team Room and head to the range and kill-house. After all equipment was accounted for and maintained, and the paperwork was done, the usual routine post-mission was to the focus on making the team ready to roll again. They liked to start with the basics, ensuring all weapons systems and their operators were functioning perfectly and then working team tactics in the shoot house.

They'd spend every hour they could working all skill sets individually and as a team until they were given their next mission. Orbital and sub-orbital infiltration, dismounted patrolling, vehicular tactics, breaching, urban and mountainous terrain ascent, repulsor and aerial platform gunnery, medical response training; the list was practically endless. Then there were the individual skills that needed constant maintenance. Kel and Poul would peel out additional time to hone their sniper skills; Bigg worked the demo range experimenting with new techniques and products to make his breaching more impressive; Tem focused on data stream intrusion; and the captain would have the most important job of all. He had to keep politicking and working his officer connections to make sure that the *best* kill team in Dark Ops got the choicest missions.

If you weren't training for the next fight, the bad guy was.

A few hours into their tasks inside the team locker and Kel's datalink chimed. Braley. A message scrolled through on his forearm:

> *Kel, meet us in the planning*
> *cell office.*

"Well, boys, I gotta make an appearance over at the head shed," Kel said as he straightened up after moving a case of energy grenades back onto its shelving unit.

Both Tem and Poul stopped what they were doing and stared at Kel blank-faced.

"What?" asked Kel innocently.

Poul was the first to start in on him. "No way! Not again! Why do *you* always get the sweet deals?"

"What are you talking about?" Kel asked, wide-eyed.

"Don't play dumb, Kelkavan, you know exactly what this is about," said Tem.

Once, Kel had let it slip that he didn't like his full name. That had been a big mistake. Tem had immediately blitz-krieg-ed this weakness and tortured Kel for days. Tem managed to fit his name into every conversation until after a while, it actually stopped being annoying and the team tuned him out. He eventually tired of it and only hauled out the Kelkavan-grenade for special occasions like this.

"You're getting selected again for some lone-operator kinda gig," Tem whined. "Once again, you're doing the ho-lo-drama spy stuff, living like a cartel boss on the House of Reason's unlimited credit chip, while the rest of us no-bodies gotta hang around here counting charge packs for our K-17s. Good on you, buddy. I just want to know who you keep losing credits to at the Century Club for them to keep picking you for these little jaunts."

It was true. This wasn't his first rodeo into the galactic bush alone. And at least one of the missions he went on as a lone operator had been pretty cushy while he lived off the credits of the Republic's Ex-Planetary Service, much the same as the diplomats the Republic had stationed on the planet. Diplomats were of the political class, and they did not suffer when posted away from Liberinthine.

"Plus," Tem continued, "why should a guy born and raised on Pthalo get any more breaks in life? Is there some trust fund waiting for you on the other side of twenty?"

Kel didn't feel like going through it all again, denying that he'd grown up in paradise. He had, but he was not one of the galaxy's uber-rich. His parents worked hospitality in the tourist industry. His father had been a legionnaire back in the Savage Wars, and wanted to raise a family someplace safe from the fires of the conflict. Pthalo seemed like that kind of place because it was an intergalactic off network banking haven. There was no way the House of Reason was ever going to allow any conflict to get near all that hidden money.

Kel also didn't feel like rehashing for Tem that two of the solo missions he'd been assigned were absolutely miserable experiences. He'd not only been away from the team and working with no support, the missions were on worlds with conditions that not even Tem would have found memorable except in their difficulty and harshness. Tem never complained about poor meals, sleeping arrangements, lack of female companionship; in fact, he rarely complained at all. Except about the lack of a mission. His friend was one of the most resilient operators Kel had ever known. But Tem would have pitied Kel, not envied him, had he known how bad those stints were. Not every lone mission was a chance at glory.

Tem was a decade older than Kel. He'd come to Dark Ops after rising through the regular Legion where he'd been an assault platoon sergeant before he garnered the attention of Dark Ops. Kel expected Tem would be made a team sergeant and given his own kill team any time now. Poul was between the two of them in age but like Tem, spent a longer period of time in the regular Legion than Kel had before coming to Dark Ops. Kel joined Dark Ops much earlier in his Legion career. He flat out admired both Tem and Poul's time in the regular Legion because that was really where you KTF'd. Turned loose, line Legion units were death incarnate. That invaluable experience helped his friends develop useful leadership skills that ultimately made for a great operator.

There wasn't a cookie-cutter template for a Dark Ops Operator. The unit was tiny, but filled with a wealth of background and experience, even though drawn from an organization as conformist as the Legion. When DO saw what they were looking for in a candidate, they went after them. Even after his years here, he wasn't sure how to define what that certain thing was.

"Aw, it's probably just more questions about Kylar," Kel said, shrugging off Tem's ribbing. "I'll be back in an hour, I bet, but thanks for the good wishes for my overall happiness and well-being to become the Secret Squirrel of the year at the next Legion Ball. Poul, can you finish up with the load-out for the morning? See you, Temostecles."

Kel could hear Tem's voice trailing off as he walked away.

"Least I'm not ashamed of *my* name."

Walking outside in the warm sun and cloudless sky across the quad to the white plasticrete and mirrored window building, Kel's mind raced with the possibilities of why he was being called to the planning cell. He checked his excitement, reminding himself that he could very well be called in for an entirely different reason than a mission. Was there any reason to believe he was walking into an ambush? Had he committed some infraction that they'd confront him with, clap him in chains, and toss him in a shuttle bound for a prison planet? Kel didn't think so, but in the stories told by leejes huddled around fires, there were always ones about just that kind of scenario playing out for some unnamed leej. It could happen. You never knew. Kel checked his uniform before he walked through the planning cell entrance. Moving through the first set of offices, the sergeant major at the first desk pointed to the secure room. Kel put his hand over the panel and waited for the chiming response before the unmarked door slid aside and he entered. As the door closed, he faced the center of the room where Braley, Bigg, and several Legion officers sat around a large table. Sergeant Major Nail was there, watching him as he entered. The senior-most NCO was sitting next to the commander. A chair sat empty with its back toward him as he moved efficiently to the right side of it, ending at attention and delivering a hand salute. "Gentlemen, Sergeant Turner reporting as ordered."

Dark Ops Commander Colonel Hartenstein returned the salute from his seat at the center of the table. He gestured to the chair facing the gathering.

"Thank you, Sergeant, and please relax," the colonel said in his deep-voiced, paternal manner. Never had Kel heard the colonel raise his voice, even under fire. He was always the picture of calm. He'd seen the colonel KTF when necessary. The man knew everyone in his command by their first name and always addressed his subordinates with respect.

Bigg had once said, "There's only one human being I pray wouldn't lose sleep over how to kill me. The colonel." Kel had always kept that in mind as a motivator, feeling that the colonel's eyes were on him.

Kel knew the other DO officers in the room. A member of the Planning and Intel Cell each sat on either side of the colonel, with Braley and Bigg to his far left. With a barely perceptible smile, Bigg caught Kel's eye and let him know that everything was all right.

"I'm due elsewhere and will turn this briefing over to Planning in a minute," the colonel said. "Sergeant, I've gotten the summary of the mission on Kylar. Your team commander and sergeant speak highly of your actions there. Job well done, Kel."

The colonel's praise meant more to Kel than any medal because of the deep respect he had for the man giving it. Respect because of the colonel's combat skills, and how the man treated everyone as his professional equal. He managed to reply, "Thank you, sir."

"Son, there's a small matter we've been tasked with, that you're going to get briefed on. You've been selected for this by the command staff and myself, based on your previous performance in similar situations. The selection has been seconded by your kill team leadership also. If you want this assignment, it'll mean some time away from your team again, also... some unrated time. If that's agreeable, Major Carr will get you up to speed."

Unrated time meant that he would be working independently without supervision. This meant no performance review on his record. Kel didn't care much about the promotion ladder. He intended to remain in Dark Ops for the duration of his Legion career, and in Dark Ops having unrated time on your record was as good as any performance review; it meant you'd been doing something special, even within Dark Ops. It was an administrative tattoo that indicated exactly what kind of animal you were.

Kel looked over at Braley and Bigg, who both gave him the thumbs up.

"I'm honored, sir. Thank you for the opportunity."

An hour later, Kel headed back to the team room. More in-depth briefings and material would come his way the next day and then he'd have a scant three days to prepare before departing.

As Kel walked in, Poul looked up from his datapad. "Let me guess, you're getting the Order of the Centurion. Congratulations. Now even the corpse of Tyrus Rechs has to salute you."

"Nope. But I am heading out on my own," Kel said, trying to not show his enthusiasm.

"I knew it! Whatever. You know... just..." he sputtered with faux disgust and rage. "Whatever, Kel! The rest of the team and I will be just fine without you, Captain Perfect," said Tem.

His friend slouched in his chair, not looking up.

"Actually," Kel drew out the word. "Tem, you've been requested to report to Planning Cell right now." When Kel had finished receiving his brief warning order for this next mission, the major had told him to send Tem along when he returned to the team room. Judging by Braley and Bigg's smiles, Kel guessed that Tem had an opportunity of his own in the offing.

"Yes!" Tem jumped up out of his chair. "Planetary Security mission? You aren't the only one living the secret agent lifestyle, Kelkavan."

Poul slumped in his seat. "Oba, if I have to spend the next six months deploying to Area Doxy for more orbital free-fall practice, I think I'm just gonna lose it, man."

04

As it turned out, Kel and Tem would not be the only ones headed away from the team for a stint. Braley was headed off to the Legion Command and Operations Course, Bigg was going to Operations Cell for the next cycle, and Poul would be farmed out to another team until all five legionnaires would be reunited again.

"This stinks," Poul sulked. "It's like I'm going somewhere too, but I'm not really going anywhere." No one wanted the team to be split apart for any reason, but it was a reality for DO.

Bigg smiled. The next cycle would be good for him. He'd once told the team that he and his wife had not been under the same roof for more than a month at a time since they'd been married.

"When I told my wife that I was going to be in Ops for the next six months, and most likely not going anywhere, we both wondered if our marriage would survive." Everyone laughed. Bigg was the only married man on the team and one of the few in DO. They clearly had found a way to make it work.

"I'm not headed off to any party myself, Poul," the captain tried to console him. "A staff school is about the dullest thing you can imagine, trust me. Besides, when you move down the hall to round out Team Seven, you'll most likely be headed out for something soon. Sergeant

Dari's team is damn good. Don't worry, you're not going to be polishing electrons around here the whole time."

It was true. Dari's team was good. Like all kill teams in DO, everyone knew everyone else, if not from having worked with them personally, then at least by reputation. Team Seven had singled itself out as the team that spent the most time staying proficient at orbital and sub-orbital infiltration. All the kill teams maintained proficiency in that skill set, but as a result of self-selecting to be the team that spent the most time doing so, Seven was generally thought of first when a mission called for that method of insertion. It was a strategy that also frequently worked against them; there were by far more missions that did not call for a covert insertion from orbit by free fall. Seven was often held in reserve by command, waiting for that unique combination of factors to call for an orbital free fall insertion. They stayed home a lot compared to the other kill teams. Being overly specialized could be a bad thing.

"I hear you, Cap. It's just, well, you know how it is."

Kel knew what Poul meant. Life in the Legion was one of consistency and familiarity. Even in the regular Legion you might very well spend years with the same people, becoming accustomed to and even dependent on the patterns you developed with them. That cohesion from familiarity is what built a great fighting unit. It was even more so on a kill team. They were a family.

Finally, Bigg broke the somber mood. "No more boo-hooing, ladies. Three'll be back together in no time. Kel and Tem gotta finish packing. Let's see if they need any help."

Kel and Tem were in their respective loadout cages going through gear. The two had not discussed their mission with each other, though Cap and Bigg each knew the broad strokes of where each was going and what they'd be doing. It was just part of good operational security. There'd be stories to tell after the fact, but no unnecessary exposure of information beforehand. It was simply understood in DO; quiet is best. Period.

One thing Kel did notice about the gear Tem was sorting through and packing into grav containers was he didn't seem to have any restrictions on what he could take with him. He checked all his usual gear, just as if he was going on a call-out with the team for any other mission.

Kel, on the other hand, was briefed that his would be a technology-restricted mission. The planet he was going to, Meridian, had an immurement placed on them by the House of Reason for peer-level technologies, especially information and tech related to weapons and certain quantum manipulation applications.

That meant no blasters and no leej armor.

He understood the restrictions, to an extent. Planets that had a proscription placed on them for trade in current Republic tech were frequently places where the House of Reason had concern that a potential friend could represent an emerging enemy. When aid was given, if the aid contained military goods, it was frequently older Republic tech, or modest improvements to the host's current tech. Even in those cases, it was because the partner planet had proven itself to be trustworthy. The Savage Wars had raged for generations. The House of Reason was intent on maintaining the hard-won edge it had achieved for the Republic. Kel couldn't imagine what the universe would be like if someone like the zhee had tech as good as a kill team.

It would be a living nightmare and a lot of innocent people would die.

A lot of the tech was certainly available on the galactic black market. If a client was willing to pay, there were knock-offs and sometimes even stolen tech that could be obtained, but at a great expense for gear of questionable reliability.

What it meant for Kel right now was that he had some deliberate choices to make.

Blaster was a moniker that everyone used to collectively describe several types of weapons in their arsenal of tools. Some actually were particle beam accelerators. Some discharged blasts as coherent energy in the spectrum of light. Others were combinations of the two. Their energy requirements and ultimate purpose determined the technology used.

Kel wasn't a scientist but knew basic theory. Particles of miniscule mass could be accelerated to fantastic speeds and would smash into any object with tremendous kinetic energy, but at a cost. Blasters took a lot of energy to power. These weapons were used mainly on naval vessels and large vehicles that had the capability to generate and store such vast amounts of power. Defense against these weapons was practically nonexistent.

Most current weapons the Legion used were part directed particle energy, part coherent light energy. The beam had to be focused on the target to be effective. When aiming at a target, the weapon ranged the target and focused the energy at the speed of light before discharging. It was a near instantaneous process. At extreme distances, the light energy could not be made coherent enough to be effective, but within the energy capabilities of handheld weapons, the useable range was still over a thousand meters. Specialty weapons like his N-22 and other sniper weapons extended that range two or three times that distance, but utilized more particle beam effect to do so.

The light energy mechanism inflicted incredible damage on anything it contacted, especially at the point of focus. The weapons were capable of burning holes through biologic tissues in the blink of an eye. Particle beams, however, punched through things, especially living creatures, and created devastating wounds that were deadly no matter where a person was hit.

Regardless of the science behind the tech, he was going to a world where he was kept from using his usual weapons, so for the time being it might as well not even exist.

Meridian was limited to chemically propelled projectile weapons. Kel knew from experience, they were no less deadly than any blaster.

He had such weapons in his cage and trained with them frequently. He picked up his favorite carbine of the type. It used a caseless projectile that contained its own solid chemical propellant, launching a composite metal pill about 7mm in diameter. The projectiles were formed together in a small pack that was expended as the rounds were individually fed into the chamber. Each pack contained about a hundred rounds. It had an electronic ignition system. The projectiles traveled at about 3000 meters per second, inflicting devastating wounds and could even punch through many intermediate types of barriers. The weapon was prone to overheating with extremes of rapid fire, but knowing the parameters of use for the weapon system alleviated that weakness in most circumstances.

When comparing the utility of blasters to projectile weapons, the advantages and disadvantages of each were frequently offsetting. By weight, he could carry more ammunition than he could charge packs to produce the equivalent number of shots. However, blaster discharges traveled at the speed of light. They also traveled in a line of sight, needing no compensation for the ballistic arc caused by gravity's pull. Blaster discharges were also immune to the effects of wind.

So the question was, could he bring his slug thrower since blasters were off-limits? His gear would be traveling with him by grav container and sealed with a purple imprimatur denoting Republic diplomatic status. It afforded legal protection from search by any customs officials at his destination, and his gear would return the same way. However, there was always the unforeseen possibility of something going wrong. He was most concerned about the return trip at the end of the mission. If some customs or other House of Reason functionary decided to exceed his authority and bust the seals, and thought the weapons were in violation of the immurement from his return destination, there could be trouble.

The Legion and DO in particular had a tenuous relationship with the House of Reason. He was on a Planetary Security mission directed from the seat of the galactic government, but that didn't mean that every part of the machine understood that. Yes, DO would get it sorted out eventually and keep him out of trouble, but Kel had learned that the best way to maintain the confidence of his leadership was by not involving them in any problem he could anticipate and avoid, or solve on his own.

Since Kel wasn't one hundred percent certain his advanced slug throwers would meet the letter of the law to take with him to Meridian, he decided to leave them in the cage. He would procure most weapons from the embassy or the host, which would also be more useful in his goal of blending in and assimilating with the folks he was going to advise and train. One large, longer item caught his eye, and without hesitation, he gathered it into the 'take' pile. He might get a chance to use it.

His armor was the other major issue. It was more than just ballistic and environmental protection. With the bucket he had capabilities that improved his awareness and linked him to critical information in a fight, the greatest of these tools being his L-comm. DO armor was a perk even above what the Legion regulars had. Other Republic Forces like the Army and Marines did not even have Legion-class armor. But with no other leejes on Meridian, the loss of the L-comm would not be hyper-critical.

He would bring along some nanotubule garments that he could wear under his civilian clothes while traveling and under the basic armor he would be taking to the planet. The garments would offer him some level of ballistic and impact protection, as well as protection against sharp weapons, spall, and other projectiles from blasts. The material hardened in the impact area instantly as a response to challenge and would even do so against strikes to the material during melee. It wouldn't protect him like his own armor could, but it was much better than being naked.

He selected an armored vest with multiple pockets and attachment points, tried it on for size, and put it in the 'take' pile as well. A helmet rounded out his personal protective gear.

He did settle on a basic handgun for self-defense. It used ballistic technology and also incorporated a bio-electric scrambler that could be selected for a less-lethal application. It had an integral light and holosight. It was unremarkable tech, common throughout most worlds, and small enough to be easily concealable. He had a few carbon blades he would wear that would escape any attempt at technical detection and, when well concealed, might get past a body search.

There were a few other items that would be going with him that not even the savviest Republic cog would recognize if he had to undergo a search on returning home, and that would be enough.

Kel was in his cage, kneeling and sorting gear, when Bigg stuck his head in.

"Hey, Team-Daddy, anything up?" Kel asked noticing the team sergeant's presence.

Bigg smiled at being called that. Kel had been the first to call him that, and now everyone, even the captain, used the moniker from time to time.

"I just wanted to say, Kel, be careful on this one."

Kel frowned. "Yeah, of course. I'm always careful." Kel sensed that this was a different caution than the usual fatherly advice Bigg dispensed on occasion.

"I got a little more info from ops cell and the commander than what was discussed in your initial brief. What I'm saying is, this op has the potential for a lot of attention. You're going to be working with a lot of pols and likely Republic intel folks, more so than on your last planetary security stints. Just remember: protect yourself. These folks will put you in bad positions, situations where things are likely to go wrong, and then blame you for the outcome. So don't trust 'em. Not even a little."

With that, Bigg winked and walked out of the loadout room.

I'll remember that, Kel promised.

One of his last stops was by the med cell for a quick checkup and to get his implant. The small implant behind his left ear would sync with his datalink and gave him hands-free communication through the link in his pocket. It would broadcast directly to his inner ear and detect nerve impulses or subvocalizations to transmit voice. His specs projected holo to his visual cortex through the link and allowed him to access information more efficiently, and provided decent night vision augmentation. It wasn't a bucket, but it would do.

Equipment ready, Kel made the rounds and shook hands. When he got to Tem, he wanted to say something encouraging, but all that came out was, "Hey, don't screw this up."

Tem laughed. "Right back at you, brother. I'm buying when the team is back together."

"KTF," Kel said, walking out the door. Excitement welling, he suppressed a smile so as not to look like a buffoon to anyone who saw him on his way out.

He hopped on the autonomous sled with his grav container and other kit loaded in the covered front compartment, and directed his link to send the sled to one last destination before the spaceport, the sustainment cell building.

He had an appointment and was a few minutes early. As he sat in the waiting area of the front office looking at his datalink, a civilian walked out of a small office and with a smile, motioned him to follow her. "Sergeant Turner, please have a seat," she said as she made her way around to her desk. She was older, slightly plump, and had a matronly appearance in her plain business suit. In a sweet voice, she began what was likely a routine speech.

"Please place your datalink on the desk. I am authorizing the encrypted account for 500,000 Republic credits." She handed him a small two-centimeter-sized square black case. "This is the hard chip with the same credit line. When you reach your destination, I recommend checking it in with the embassy operations center. If your datalink becomes corrupted or lost, the account can be reset."

She placed both hands palm down on her desktop and looked squarely at Kel.

Here it comes, thought Kel. *The threat.*

She would not disappoint.

"Sergeant Turner, by signing for these funds you are accepting the responsibility for them. Your datalink will have an exact accounting of all your expenses. Necessary expenditures for your sustainment and for the accomplishment of your mission are budgeted and authorized. They will be reviewed meticulously on your return." Now her previously sweet, motherly-like voice became as harsh as any Legion drill instructor's.

"This is not a personal vacation paid for by the House of Reason. Any violation of pecuniary fidelity and the regulations of which you have been formally trained and certified will lead to prosecution and likely incarceration on a prison world at hard labor for the remainder of your natural life."

Kel felt dizzy, his mouth parched, and his heart pounded in his ears simultaneously. He could not remember feeling anxiety like this since he was a young leej, finding out what the two-way shooting range that was his first fight had been like.

Everyone had heard stories about DO guys disappearing, making little rocks out of big rocks on a prison planet where they never again saw the light of day, when their datalink was unable to explain expenditures at gambling houses and speeder dealerships. At best, you could have your pay withheld and be sent back to the regular Legion, or maybe dismissed from the Legion altogether. If you were lucky. At worst, you went to a place that was worse than death. That was the rumor.

"Place your hand here, dearie," the mistress of the credits said, a sweet smile back on her face.

Kel was glad to get out of that office and back into his waiting sled, the nervous sweat on his forehead drying in the midday sun.

Taking the hop into orbit to the Republic cruiser *Resolve* was a brief yet turbulent flight due to local atmospheric conditions. He watched the approaching capital-class cruiser get closer until it filled the view though his portal. He'd never been on the *Resolve* before, but he'd been on other Repub Navy ships, including cruisers.

Kel was traveling in civilian garb. Like many other DO missions, the need to blend in with the population and be unremarkable, or at least not look like a legionnaire, was a necessity. Vital in fact. Of course, Kel always wondered what any reasonable person would think if they ran into a DO operator in a major transportation hub. Civilian clothes and long hair or not, a young, fit, and muscular male with scars and wearing clothing that anyone would imagine concealed some kind of weapon did tend to broadcast a certain message. Like standing next to a dangerous animal without a cage between you. Some things were difficult to hide about oneself. But the best covert operators learned to do it. Learned to look human just like all the other humans that didn't have to do the hard things that needed to be done.

Kel preferred a close-cropped head of hair and no facial hair. His hair was longer than Legion regs right now but short by DO standards. He'd considered making the first leg of the journey on Republic Navy vessels in uniform, and then transitioning to civvies for the final hop out to Meridian. Whether that would be a way to better blend in while on the Navy cruiser was debatable.

He was traveling under classified orders that allowed him access to any Republic Armed Forces vessel or facility just by presenting them to the Captain. He decided to travel in civilian attire with longer hair. The Navy was accustomed to shuttling around DO, even if all they knew was that the long-hairs on board were to be left alone.

Kel made his way with his gear, following the crew chief toward the edge of the hangar deck. Civvies or not, when Kel approached the officer of the watch, he paused to set his gear down, face aft, and render a hand salute to the Republic Flag. The Navy master at arms standing watch greeted him and held a datapad up as Kel bounced his orders from his own datalink. The young sailor read them, then squinted to read them again. Straightening, the kid said, "Sir, I need to take you to the Liaison Office, would you follow me please?" The young spacer looked scared. He'd likely been trained what to do in such an event, but it was probably his first time encountering this particular situation. He was doing fine by Kel's estimation. But he was clearly having trouble breathing and talking as they started out.

They made their way through a series of corridors and sharp turns to reach an office where the alert had been sent ahead that he was aboard. A grizzled but sharp-look-ing senior chief stood awaiting him. "I'll take it from here, spacer. Thank you." Kel liked the senior chief immediately. He had a knowledgeable face and friendly bearing that put Kel at ease. "I'm Senior Chief Yeoman Masterson, sir. I'm responsible for liaison on the *Resolve*. Can you bounce your orders to me please? Make yourself comfortable," he said, gesturing to a chair in the cramped office.

The chief read the orders on his own datapad several times. "Sir—" he began.

Kel stopped him there. He'd made the decision to not be standoffish with the crew any more than he needed to be, and treating other service members with respect was important. "I'm a sergeant, Senior Chief, no need to call me 'sir.' I work for a living just like you do."

The senior chief's smile broadened. "Very well then, Sergeant. We will get you and your gear berthed. I as-sume you need to keep everything with you and don't want anything stored?"

Kel nodded.

"Good. You are currently the only person from the, ah, Legion," the senior chief said with a question in his voice, "whom we have on board. As I'm sure you know capital ships have a purposed module for, well, folks like you. It is currently unoccupied. Of course it's built for a whole team, but can be secured solely for your bio-signature during your duration aboard."

Kel kept smiling good-naturedly but made no move to confirm or correct the senior chief's assumptions.

"Otherwise, we have VIP quarters, but they are closer to the command group, operations, and ship's traffic."

"That'd be fine, Senior Chief, thank you," Kel said.

"The XO advised us yesterday that you would be coming aboard. Of course, the CO and XO know you are onboard, as does this office. They understand that your mission doesn't necessitate any change in the operations of this ship, and, uh, since they've advised me that you are not a commissioned officer, I can let them know that you will not be making an appearance in the officer's mess?"

"That all sounds good, Senior Chief."

"It doesn't mean that you may not receive an invitation while you're on board to dine with the captain, you understand, Sergeant?"

"Certainly, Senior Chief. That's very kind. I plan to take most of my meals in the module as I have a lot of work to do during the trip," Kel said, hoping to communicate his desire to stay sequestered while on board.

"Of course, Sergeant. Why don't we get you settled then?"

The senior chief insisted that a spacer take Kel's gear and follow them to the module. They got several long looks from spacers on the way, and any that were too obvious were redirected by a "Carry on, Spacer" from the senior chief.

They reached the module, where a Marine stood guard at the entrance. Inside was a relatively large room with a small area denoted by a table and six chairs to his left, a sitting area on his right, viewscreens on the walls, and a hallway between the two areas leading back to a series of individual quarters.

"Pick whichever stateroom suits you. We'll key the module entrance to you. I've sent your datalink my contact and also the mess steward's link. You can have meals delivered here, but," the senior chief hesitated, "I'd be honored to sponsor you to the chief's mess, if you'd like. You won't be bothered there and, well, it would be a pleasure to have you."

Kel smiled. "Thank you, Senior Chief Masterson, I'd be honored. Like I said, I have a lot of work to do, but I promise to take you up on your kind offer. One other thing. Usually we have access to the gym, can you bounce that info to my link?"

"Of course, Sergeant..." He trailed off.

"Call me 'K,' Senior Chief."

Kel took the first stateroom on the left. It had a set of bunks, a small retractable desk, a toilet, and a shower. Two full kill teams could berth here. It was likely repurposed for other visitors when not in use by Dark Ops, but for now it was all his.

After unpacking, Kel settled down in the common area with his datapad linked to the viewscreen on the wall. He had a lot of studying to do to prepare for the mission to Meridian. There were volumes of information about the planet—its history from the time of its discovery until its settlement and colonization, its physical and political geography, the culture and social structure.

He delved into what was known about the organization of the current government, the public administration and legal system as well as their law enforcement and public safety functions. There were biographies about key players in the government at planetary and local levels.

In particular, Kel researched all he could find concerning the Meridian security forces. There was little enough to read about their military and nothing at all concerning specific individuals in positions of leadership. While it was interesting to read about the climate and rainfall statistics of the planet, it would be more useful to him to know what number and type of armor and artillery units they had, what kind of arms they currently utilized, and who the military leaders aligned themselves with politically. Anything concrete about the situation he was walking into would be great to have running on those background apps inside his mind before he actually walked into those situations.

Some ruck-humped Legion sergeant back in Recon had taught him that the desire to win was important, but the will to prepare was everything. Kel had lived by that bit of wisdom ever since it had been given. And he'd never regretted it. Not once.

He'd just read the same page three times before becoming aware he wasn't absorbing any of it. There was just too much and most of it didn't seem to be helpful. He knew a trick to focus.

He opened a blank screen and typed. "What is my mission?"

He concentrated on this for a while before answering. He had an open mandate. He was the first Republic military adviser to Meridian. What he learned and the relationships he built there would help define the planet's future with the Republic going forward.

His first mission was that frighteningly simple.

He wrote, "One: Assist Meridian in ending civil unrest." That alone was a tall enough order. He was just one man. By himself he could not run an intelligence or counter-terror program. But he could *assist* the Meridians in doing so, only better than they were doing it now. By building rapport with the local forces, advising them how to improve their tactics and ability to fight the insurgents, he could accomplish the mandate of his mission.

Which Meridian forces were appropriate for his attention? He still did not know.

He looked at the files he'd been slaving over. They were all but worthless. For his efforts he felt no better informed. Under the first mission he wrote a sub-heading, "Learn who the enemy is." He could not help the Meridians find, fix, and finish the enemy if no one knew who they were. It was a developing situation. Information about the threat was lacking on his side of the galaxy. He would look for opportunities to identify the threat once he was on the ground. If not through the Republic Intelligence presence at the embassy, then by working with the Meridians.

Next he wrote, "Two: Assist the embassy preparing for civil unrest." The embassy would have a regional security office and people responsible for just that. In his experience, most ex-planetary missions were not prepared for that level of danger, physically or psychologically. Since Meridian had traditionally been a sleepy backwater where not much happened, the security office was probably small; maybe just one or two individuals. Kel would offer his expertise to help them prepare for the safety of Republic diplomats and their families planetside. He had never been to an embassy that had not appreciated help from a legionnaire to evaluate and improve their defenses.

Kel would be on the planet for six months. It was a long time away from the kill team. Finally, he wrote, "Three: Maintain personal readiness as an operator." He would have to continue his own training and preparedness. He would have to be sharp to deal with threats while on the mission and would need to be ready to return to his kill team fit to fight having not missed a step. If he got back after however long he was away and Bigg wanted to PT them into the ground... then he had to be ready for that. As he looked at the three missions he'd just written down, the weight of it all settled on his shoulders suddenly. The task was immense. He was being thrown into a maelstrom and he couldn't do it all.

He sat there for a half a second, failing.

Then he reminded himself of something Bigg said. "An operator isn't an operator because of big muscles. Operators are operators because of big brains." And brains in the head beat blisters on the feet.

That's what it meant to be an operator in DO.

The next morning, Kel hit the gym. It was several decks below and when he got there at 0500 ship's time, it was largely deserted. He spent the first part of his workout running in a gravity chamber. He started at 1 G and a level surface for the first ten minutes at a moderate pace to warm up, then increased the gravity as he also increased the inclination of the plane for another twenty minutes. In the back of his mind, he could hear Tem joking that running promoted cowardice. He'd certainly spent a lot of time in the Legion running, but it was not the best exercise to get you ready to KTF.

He finished by doing some linking motions on the mats—bear walking the matted area of the gym, then doing walking handstands back and forth as many times as he could from one end to the other until he tucked into a roll and stood. He did a few other circuits back and forth, until enough people entered the space to make things crowded. There'd been a few spacers filtering into the gym after he'd started, and he caught many of them staring at the new face in their gym as he did his routine.

That'd be enough for right now. He wanted to get back to work and he'd be interspersing exercise throughout the next twelve hours while he studied, so it would not be a sedentary day.

Once he got back to his studies, Kel settled into his planned routine. He took a couple more meals by himself in the module and continued to wade through thousands of words of research.

Kel reassessed his earlier judgement concerning the quality of information he'd been given. It was not worthless. He was forming a rudimentary picture of the Meridian crisis. Civil unrest appearing in any society was a symptom. Folks rarely took up arms and tried to murder their fellow citizens unless they had a reason.

The twelve families of Meridian had maintained a system that rewarded complacency and doled out a share of freedom and wealth to those who played along with their plan for society. Their closed system had created the problems they now faced. It seemed simple to Kel.

The flip side of the coin was simple as well. It was summed up neatly in one of the intelligence summaries he'd read. It was undoubtedly one of the incidents that had prompted the Domestic Conclave to ask for Republic assistance. In the capital city of one the major continents, the terrorist forces had raided a primary school attended by the children of many members of the regional family.

Terrorists held a classroom hostage and murdered the teacher in front of the children, then issued a statement that the institutions and agents who perpetuated the plutocracy of the 'Twelve Families' would be destroyed. After the authorities closed in, ransom was demanded with the children to be exchanged for freedom. The crisis was managed by the planetary police forces. A shootout occurred during the exchange. The result was the deaths of all the hostage takers along with more than a dozen children. The report was horrific. Many of the details important to him were missing — details that would allow him to form an accurate idea of what went wrong, and how he could prevent a disaster like that from occurring again.

The House of Reason's rationalization for interfering in one planet's affairs versus leaving another to their own devices sometimes perplexed him. Regardless, he was a legionnaire. More than that, the most elite of legionnaires. He would perform any mission to the best of his ability or die in the attempt. Beyond that, there was an important final rationalization for his peace of mind, one much simpler. Right and wrong. Whatever social injustices had driven the unrest on Meridian, terrorism and the murder of innocent civilians was evil. Pure and simple.

That's my mission. Do what's right, and come home with pride. With my shield, or on it.

That he could do.

Kel needed a break and had linked Senior Chief Masterson earlier to ask if the offer to join him at the chief's mess was still open.

The Navy ritual of separate dining areas for officers, senior, and junior enlisted dated far back. Kel had spent some time around the Navy during his career, hitching rides with the Legion to different destinations, but he was always there with a large group of fellow leejes. They were fed in separate messes during extended travel on naval vessels.

This was a first for him, dining with the Navy. He knew by reputation that dining in the chief's mess was a big deal. He entered the mess and looked around to find that Senior Chief Masterson was already rising to greet him, waving him over to an empty chair near the head of the table where he sat with four other chiefs.

"Gentlemen, meet our guest, K," the senior chief said as Kel took his seat.

"Thank you for the invitation to your mess, gentlemen. I'll try not to ruin the linen," Kel said, noticing the white tablecloths, silverware, and Ellurian blue crystal water glasses.

"K, the food is usually pretty decent. A steward will be with us in a minute and we'll get started," his host told him.

Kel was used to cafeterias and buffet-style eating in the Legion. In the garrison, taking a tray and waiting in line to be served portions, or to scoop out something yourself, was a way of life. He only now thought about its institutional nature as the table stewards brought salads and appetizers to their table.

A soup course was served, followed by the main course.

"Rindar steaks from the mid-core are on the menu tonight. I like mine a little rare. If yours is overdone, please say something," Senior Chief Masterson whispered to him.

After dessert and kaff, his host explained to him how the mess system worked in the Navy. The chief's mess had a separate procurement from the other messes. They stocked from the best that any planet or station of call had to offer.

Kel was impressed. While it didn't make him reconsider being a legionnaire, he certainly admired the lifestyle the Navy had to offer. Of course, being locked up in an interstellar metal coffin did deserve some special considerations, he supposed. Good chow was likely the best perk these spacers had.

Kel's routine on the ship for the next week followed the same pattern. He kept up his physical training out of necessity and boredom, and continued to absorb as much material about Meridian as he could from his studies. He knew that he was going to have a steep learning curve once he got there and hoped the embassy professionals would help fill in some of the blank spaces for him and speed his acclimatization.

Each night, Kel joined the senior NCOs in the chief's mess. Nobody broke the unspoken protocol to ask Kel who he was or what he was doing. He enjoyed their company and was satisfied sipping his kaff while listening to the chiefs' chitchat about their day, the comical things that happened with their young spacers, and how they solved problems. He was impressed with their thoughtfulness and how they applied their experience to solving those problems, being in charge of many technical and systems-related tasks that took large teams of individuals to control. Kel smiled and laughed during the conversations, and truly was appreciative for their acceptance and courtesy.

One morning Kel arrived at the gym a little later than usual to find a squad of young Marines on the mats doing some basic combatives. Their squad leader, a young corporal, shouted encouragement as they played a game where two Marines tried to wrestle each other out of a five-meter circle outlined in the center of the mats.

As Kel walked over to a resistance station, one of the Marines said loud enough for him to hear, "Who in the seven nebulas is that freak?"

A squadmate elbowed him in the ribs, and their corporal said, "Hey, give me two more in the circle," to regain their attention. Kel recognized a couple of the kids, having seen them on watch outside the module. One of the other Marines whispered something to the loudmouth, then both turned their attention back to the circle.

Kel started his workout and was developing a good ache when he noticed the young corporal standing next to him. He appeared to be nervous and was waiting for Kel to pause before speaking. Kel stopped his motion.

"Hey, Corporal," Kel said with a smile on his face.

"Sir, I hate to bother you, but..."

"That's okay, Corporal, what is it?" Kel wasn't sure what to expect next.

"Well, uh, I was starting to work with my squad on some things, some knife stuff, and I wondered if you might have anything you could show us?" the young Marine got out.

Kel didn't know if he would've had enough guts to make such a request when he was that kid's age.

"Sure, Corporal, I'm glad to help if I can." Kel walked to the mats to see the group standing in a loose circle, all holding practice blades in their hands and looking somewhat nervous.

"Why don't you show me what you've been working on and I'll see if I can offer any suggestions?" They were practicing basic thrusts and parries with training blades, trying to perfect what they had learned in basic training. Paired off, one Marine took turns thrusting into his opponent, closing the distance and planting the blade into the other's abdomen. They did the same thing with overhand strikes to the upper chest, then slashing to the face and neck. They practiced parries with the knife, attempting to fend off the other's attack. After observing for a while, Kel had something to say.

"It looks like everyone is doing a good job. I find it usually helps no matter what I'm teaching to start with the basics. Do you have a live blade?" he asked the corporal. The large Marine went to his bag and retrieved one of the Marine-issued personal protection blades, a standard design going back to the origins of their service. Kel removed the blade from its sheath. Some of the Marines looked apprehensive.

"Don't worry, I'm not going to do anything screwball. All training has to be safe. That's a necessity. When you are a leader and are training your own squad, never forget to treat them the way you would want to be treated and to teach them what you wish you had known at their stage."

Everyone relaxed a little. Kel continued. "How does a knife cut? There's an edge and there's the tip. Most of the motions you're practicing emphasize use of the tip. That's good. But, how do you cut with a knife?" It was a rhetorical question, but Kel could see he had their attention.

"Knives cut with the edge and the edge needs to move across whatever surface you want it to cut." Kel took the knife and placed the edge of the blade deep against his palm. Kel pressed the blade directly into his palm and he heard several of the Marines wince and suck air in through their teeth. Kel made a point of pressing very hard, then took his hand away to show everybody the blanched indentation the line of the blade made against the skin of this palm, but that there was no blood. Then he repeated the same demonstration, placing the edge of the knife against the side of his own neck. Again, he had their attention as their eyes widened and he heard more wincing. Kel pulled the knife away. "See, no blood, no cut.

"Now, if I attempted that while drawing the blade as I pressed," he made the motion in the air, "we'd have a different result." Kel saw several heads nodding.

"So, learning to use the knife in a way that takes advantage of the target you are offered gives you more options. If my opponent is armored over his thorax, it doesn't matter how hard I thrust or stab, I'm going to be ineffective. All humans and every alien species I've encountered are universally constructed much the same way: the nerves and the important vessels are located toward the inside of the extremity. If I draw across the inside of the arm or thigh, I'm more likely to injure a major artery and even the nerve if I go deep enough."

Kel handed the live blade back to the corporal who returned it to his bag, out of the training area. With a training blade he demonstrated on the corporal several different types of draw cuts across the arms and legs and how to set them up. The Marines paired off and practiced. Kel worked with the corporal and when the kid was doing well, the two of them walked around to each pair, observing and complimenting, and where necessary correcting what the Marines were doing.

Kel showed them a reverse grip, how to close within an opponent's grasp and use the knife hand to strike, and how to cut both inside and outside an opponent's reach. He was having fun. They were great young Marines and, looking back later at his time on the *Resolve*, the little gym session became a highlight of the journey.

The last night before reaching the station, Kel dined with the chiefs in their mess. At the end of the meal Senior Chief Masterson announced to the group that 'K' would be leaving the *Resolve* the next day. The chiefs all shook his hand and wished him good luck. Kel was humbled by their well wishes and thanked them for making him feel at home. Kel never wanted to be anything but a legionnaire, but that didn't mean he didn't respect the difficulty and demands of the other services' missions. Experiencing life aboard a capital-class cruiser made him think about the complexity of the Navy and their mission and appreciate the individuals and tasks required to make things happen.

Kel went back to the module for the last time and checked his kit. He planned to rise early the next morning, ready to depart as soon as the *Resolve* berthed in the large station.

The next portion of the trip was not going to be so easy. Kel lamented a skill he would be relying on, one which he sorely lacked.

Why didn't I take theater in high school? He sighed in his rack, unable to enter a peaceful sleep during the last of the night watch.

I can do this.

05

Orion Station was the major hub for this sector of the galaxy. It served as a port of call for the Navy as well as for commercial transportation across the mid-core and out toward the edge. Its large permanent population served the station and a never-ending circuit of ships coming and going, vessels as varied and numerous as the stars themselves.

Leaving the military sector, Kel headed into the station proper and after a block into the concourse, was as good as invisible among the other inhabitants. He'd been here before and was somewhat familiar with the layout of Orion Station. His link provided the physical plan, broadcasting routes to his specs as he traversed through the crowded station. First he made his way to the trade zone where he rented a locker large enough to secure his gear, and then concentrated on finding a café with a booth to sit at and access the holoweb.

As he sipped his kaff, he scanned the open net, looking at listings for current berthings and expected arrivals at the port and terminal, checking commercial transport as well as bulk cargo haulers. While he knew it'd have to be flat out lucky just to find a ship traveling directly out to Meridian from Orion Station, Kel started by looking for those parameters on the off-chance he could easily solve his travel dilemma that quickly. Optimism was an overlooked virtue in the military, one Dark Ops operators had to embrace. Especially when they were outnumbered, surrounded and low on charge packs. Any ship that had Meridian listed as a port of call would likely be returning there eventually. How soon, was another question altogether. Kel didn't want to spend a month on the station waiting around for transport out to his backwater destination.

His search didn't turn up any ship with a destination of Meridian listed, and there were no ships listed in berth along the docks now having come through Meridian. Kel had been afraid of that. He clicked his tongue and stared off at the concourse for a moment, putting together a new plan. One that would get him out to Meridian faster than later.

He was going to be doing things the hard way. He couldn't get the information he needed on the open net. He was going to have to get creative and do some research, and that would be a more time-consuming task than he wanted to tackle sitting in this café.

He did a quick search for a cheap place to hole up for what he hoped would not be more than a day or two. The place he found was not far from the café and was decent enough. No frills or perks but a small private room with toilet, shower, and a bed. He had one bag with him and what he carried on his person, which was his pistol, knives, and datalink. *Might as well get comfortable, could be at this a while.* He tossed it all on the bed and got to work.

He was not as talented as Tem at working the data stream, but for what he needed it would not require a lot of specialized skill. Much of the situation he now faced had been anticipated, and this was a common problem for DO—how to get where you needed to be. In fact, they were specialists in all manners of moving from point A to point B. The algorithm Kel opened allowed him to enter multiple search parameters, and prompted further refinements as he accessed more and more data. His data-link and its intrusive abilities tapped into the information core of the port terminal's scheduling system, allowing it access to the history of routes and manifests of every vessel that had ever passed through Orion Station. Kel was only interested in current and planned routes.

Ships that had recently traveled from Meridian were placed in a separate category. Analyzing the routes and their frequencies, the pattern established by most vessels hitting Meridian on a frequent basis, it appeared that none would be likely headed back there anytime within the next couple months.

No good.

Now came the next best avenue of research—ships traveling near Meridian that, if the price was right, might divert and deliver Kel to his destination. There were incentives Kel could provide such a ship besides a straight exchange of credits that might entice the right crew into accepting the commission.

The algorithm let him search stores of information on the declared and undeclared financials of those vessels, sorting them into potentials for his ride out to Meridian. Finding a candidate that did not have multiple destinations already declared meant they were looking for contracts, trying to pick up some delivery work at their destination that would carry them to another with a full hold.

Finally, Kel had a candidate. Sitting off Orion Station awaiting a berth was a private freighter that had visited Meridian in the past two years and whose next declared destination included only one planet, within a relatively short hyperspace jump from Meridian. The only technically illegal part of his work on the data stream was snaring financial statements. *If you don't get caught, you ain't done nothing wrong* wasn't a valid justification in his opinion but, in some cases, it was a default philosophy for an operator. It allowed him to develop a picture of a family-owned merchant vessel, barely making ends meet as they worked the edge, trying to fill their holds with whatever would pay at the next destination. They were expected to berth at 0800 the next morning.

Kel began mentally rehearsing for his new role as he imagined meeting the captain of the *Callie's Dream*.

The next afternoon he sat at a table in one of the restaurants near the terminal, waiting for his guests to arrive. A couple entered the restaurant who fit the description Kel imagined of the captain and his purser from the *Callie's Dream*. They were a husband and wife team, dressed in gray ship's coveralls, thin and somewhat gaunt. He had a head of dense black hair and an expressionless face; his wife wore her dark-red shoulder-length hair tied behind her head and had a pleasant, pale face and complexion.

Kel waved them over and stepped out of the booth to greet them. "Hi, Captain Yomiuri? I'm Tamford Nielsen, from the Republic Trade Mission." He bounced his official credentials to the Yomiuri's links through his specs.

The man took a second to look at the datalink in his hand and then extended his hand to Kel." Jim Yomiuri. This is my wife, Caroline." Kel shook her hand and gestured for them to sit.

"So, Mister Nielsen, you said you were interested in the *Callie's Dream*? You have some cargo you need transported?" Captain Yomiuri looked reserved and even uninterested in the concept.

Mrs. Yomiuri spoke up quickly. "Other than travel to Meridian, you didn't specify what cargo you had to move. We'd need to know what that's going to be before we get started with negotiations."

Kel had been using the Nielsen cover for all exchanges since he'd arrived on the station. Most transactions left some trace of identity, and his link backstopped his story perfectly. The intel cell had established this identity to match Kel's biometrics as well as register the cover with all Republic governmental agencies. No one could penetrate the cover identity, including investigators within the various Republic intelligence services; it was a real identity. The diplomatic mission on Meridian only knew that Nielsen would be arriving. The Republic Intelligence asset stationed with the embassy and the ambassador would be aware of who he was and that he, Kel, would be arriving at an indeterminate date in the near future. The rest he would work out once he got there.

"What I'm hoping you'll agree to is, I think, a decent opportunity for you," Kel began. "I am the new Republic trade negotiator headed out to Meridian. You're familiar with it, yes? I have the plenipotentiary power on behalf of the House of Reason to establish a new trade agreement with Meridian. The Republic is interested in increasing trade with that world and finding a way to regularly bring their goods in to the core."

The Yomiuris were suddenly very attentive.

"I'm looking for transport to Meridian to begin my mission but also need a ship that can take an immediate shipment of goods from Meridian back this way to be received for shipment to Liberinthine." Kel had authorization to leverage such a deal once he got to Meridian, knowing that the trade counselor at the embassy in Meridian had been alerted of just such an eventuality.

"So, you have no cargo to carry to Meridian. We're not bound for Meridian," the captain said curtly. "That detour would be an expensive proposition for the Republic. With no freight to transport to Meridian, traveling there empty makes it doubly expensive for us, meaning doubly expensive for the House of Reason." Mrs. Yomiuri placed her hand on her husband in a subtle way meant to evade Kel's notice. It was a tell.

"I understand that," Kel reassured them. "I have the ability to make the trip equitable by authorizing a captain's commission on the portage of the goods and their delivery back to Orion Station. The freight has buyers waiting on Liberinthine and I have a provisional contract with another carrier who will accept delivery from the station. The cargo primarily contains goods that are to be disbursed to wholesalers in the capital by auction. Because the commodities from Meridian are part of a rising market, the futures being traded on this shipment are expected to reach a record. While there is risk involved and the potential commission on the sale of the goods is not a guarantee, the potential for what may be a substantial profit exists."

This was different than a pure exchange of credits. Hiring the captain of the *Callie's Dream* to simply carry him to Meridian would not be cheap. However, the cost to the House of Reason through this venture would involve no outlay on the front end for the Republic, and only minimally reduce their profit on the back end. The brokerage house managing the auction of the goods from Meridian was a front business run by Republic intelligence. Few ventures of this type happened purely on the back of the Republic taxpayer. RI had ways of paying for things that involved legal business.

The captain looked at his wife briefly and then asked the important question. "How much is the commission?"

Kel smiled. "I can offer you 1.5 percent." One and a half percent of the potential value of the sales of the freight could total close to a million. Or it could just barely cover their costs. It was a risk for them. But given the picture that Kel had put together of their family business, he had a feeling it was the best offer they'd seen in a long time.

The two of them took in a few breaths before Mrs. Yomiuri answered. "Well, certainly we need to do some research and we'd need you to provide a projected manifest and breakdown of the goods."

Kel expected no less.

"We are planning to pull out tomorrow. We have a contract to fulfill making a delivery to Calcarion." Calcarion was a mining planet; though it had a breathable atmosphere suitable for most life forms, it was otherwise inhospitable and barren. If not for its mineral wealth, no one would ever visit there. Virtually anything needed to sustain life had to be shipped in, with too few residents to justify terraforming or much self-sustainment beyond hydroponics and vat grown protein.

"I'm bouncing the manifest awaiting on Meridian and a detailed breakdown of goods now. I've also included some market research. I'm sure you'll want to do some more analysis yourself. I also think it's fair to tell you that I need to investigate other potential carriers. This offer has a time-sensitive aspect. I'm sure you understand." Kel got up to leave. He knew he was being abrupt, hoping to force a reaction. The Yomiuris both stood as well.

"A moment please, Mr. Nielsen?" Mrs. Yomiuri said, shooting a glance at her husband.

"Of course." Kel left them at the table and made his way to the entrance of the restaurant. He waited there as the two talked in low tones, not gesturing or giving away any indication of emotion. After a minute they walked to the entrance where Kel stood, hands folded in front of him.

Captain Yomiuri appeared anxious as he said, "Well, Mr. Nielsen, we think your offer definitely merits investigation. We are returning to our ship and are going to consider your offer. We need a few hours. May we contact you then?"

Kel extended a hand. "Of course. I'll be waiting. Good day to you both," he said and turned to leave.

He understood their situation. They needed a good run and Kel's offer had the potential to be just that. Kel knew their financial situation; they ran on a low margin of profit and were likely one major repair away from insolvency. The captain's low-level irritability conveyed some of that desperation, as did his wife's eagerness. Not immediately leaping at his offer made Kel respect them; it indicated their professionalism. Had they leapt at his offer without question he would have been suspicious of their desperation. A family-run venture like the Yomiuris' was also more likely to be a ship that offered a safe passage; there were lots of star-haulers who never arrived at their destinations not because of theft of their cargo, but rather misalignment of hyperdrive coils or other maintenance issues that meant the vessel simply never reappeared from hyperspace. A captain was far less likely to tolerate an unworthy crew or vessel when it carried his own kin.

Though Kel gave no indication of this to the Yomiuris, he did not intend to search for another ship. Instead he returned to his room to train for a while and relax. He was confident that the Yomiuris and he would be traveling together soon.

Kel had no sooner finished his workout than his datalink chimed. He put on his specs and answered, seeing the two senior officers of the *Callie's Dream* through the link.

"Mr. Nielsen, did we catch you at an inconvenient time?" the captain asked.

"Not at all, sir," replied Kel, though not giving the Yomiuris the courtesy of a visual link, "just in the middle of several tasks. Have you considered my offer?"

The captain let his wife speak. "We have. If you would bounce us a copy of the contract, we'd like to review what we discussed, and you can make your way to the *Callie* for a tour."

Kel smiled to himself. "I'll send it over now and will be on my way. See you then." He cleaned up and packed, checked out, and made his way to the port. If the proposal was accepted, he'd get his grav container from the locker and bring it to the *Callie* after the contract was signed and registered.

The *Callie's Dream* was an atmosphere capable freighter that had a gross tonnage of about 30,000, meaning she had about 100,000 cubic meters of storage volume for cargo. Containers could be secured to the hull in multiple configurations, increasing the carrying capacity substantially, but rendering her limited to micro-gravity operations. She was about as big as an atmosphere capable ship could be made. Kel could see the blocky, utilitarian construction of the freighter through the viewport at the gangway. She wouldn't win any beauty contests, that was for sure.

Kel found the Talon dropships he spent much of his life in to be sexy in their design, sleek and dangerous-looking, fast and powerful to fly. Freighters like the *Callie* reminded Kel of a rectangular box with forward external features that resembled an afterthought by the engineers who'd designed her—*Oh yeah, I guess the crew needs somewhere to live.* Knowing how crews felt about their ships he'd keep those opinions to himself while on the *Callie's Dream.*

He chimed from the base of the gangway and was greeted over his link by a crewmember. "Mr. Nielsen? I'm Deck Officer Tan Yomiuri. I'll cycle you through and meet you at the lock." The gangway was secured to the ship in its berth, but airlocks sat at both the quay entrance and at the ship for foot traffic. A larger berth for bulk and container cargo was located farther aft but was only used when loading operations were carried out.

The lock opened and Kel made his way across the tunnel-like ramp to the exterior hatch of the ship which opened once the quay hatch sealed. Tan Yomiuri stood waiting. "Please follow me to the wardroom," he said as the exterior hatch sealed and the interior hatch retracted to reveal a small corridor running fore and aft along the interior hull. Making their way forward, he was led into the small wardroom where Captain and Mrs. Yomiuri waited with several other crewmembers.

"Mr. Nielsen," the captain said, "welcome aboard. Let me introduce you to my crew and family. My wife and ship's purser, Caroline, you've met. My first officer on the flight deck is my brother-in-law, Eric Sullivan, Caroline's brother. Deck Officer Tan Yomiuri is my brother," he said, pointing to each as he went. "Tan's wife, Aggie, is our bo-sun. Behind you," he gestured to a short, wide-shouldered man with thick gray hair, and a similar-looking female version of him just behind, "is my uncle Yoshi, the ship's engineer, and his wife, Meiko."

Meiko beamed. "Just call me Auntie Meiko, everyone does."

"The rest of the crew is predominately family as well. We all have children on board who work as spacers and deckhands, even those still studying have duties. Have you ever been on a family merchant vessel before, Mr. Nielsen?"

"No sir, I have not."

The captain gestured for Kel to sit with him at the small table. The rest of the family stood where they could, as the engineer and Auntie Meiko took either side of the door, looking in from the hallway.

"Though I am the captain, we make decisions as a family and all adults have voting rights on the ship. We've been discussing your proposal and have a few questions."

His first officer spoke up. "Potentially, this could be a very lucrative contract. A captain's commission is an unusual opportunity. We've never seen one on the *Callie*. A lot of the goods from Meridian seem pretty ordinary. Why the generosity of the offer?"

Kel had studied the narrative well, designed by the intel cell to give him enough background to make his role as a trade negotiator plausible. Kel didn't enjoy working in other identities. He liked jumping out of dropships, breaking expensive things, and shooting bad guys. That is, he liked being on a kill team. They were his family. If Kel had wanted to play make-believe, he would have joined Repub Intel. Nonetheless, it was necessary for this part of the mission, so Kel described things as he understood them. Though his cover was a deception, the contract and the futures market on the goods from Meridian were real. The best type of cover story was a true one

Kel explained how nostalgia and the cultural perception on Liberinthine was driving a market for the goods from Meridian. They'd surely gleaned as much from their own research.

"There is a time-dependent factor to capitalize on the current trend, because right now that's all it is, a trend. Whether it will be a sustained phenomenon or not, only time will tell. I've been given the authority to exploit the situation, but the risks must be mitigated. There may be large, dedicated runs to Meridian if the market holds. Right now, investors are not willing to invest the up-front costs to do so. There's also a political investment occurring on behalf of the House of Reason, the desire to develop a greater diplomatic relationship. Essentially, a couple of dynamics occurred in proximity to one another that have made this the time for the Republic to act."

The group seemed to consider this.

Leaning forward, Caroline Yomiuri said, "I've run the numbers. Based on what data Mr. Nielsen has provided and what we've found, the risk seems minimized and the potential for a strong profit exists. The contract is guaranteed by the House of Reason, not some private equity 'promise-now-deliver-never' group. My vote is yes."

"Then I'm going to call for the family's vote," the captain announced. He looked at each person in the room, and one at a time they offered their "Yes."

Satisfied, he turned back to Kel.

"Mr. Nielsen, if you'll sign, we can register the contract in the port, get you berthed, and leave the station early. We'll save another day's fees, that is... if there's no objection," the captain asked Kel.

"I have a small errand to run but I'll be back within the hour, Captain."

"Crew, make ready to get underway."

Kel was back aboard with his sealed grav container in less than an hour. One of the junior crewmen guided him to his stateroom after taking the case to a small container room and strapping it down.

"Sir, you're welcome to use the wardroom or the adjoining galley at your pleasure. Otherwise, your stateroom is about the only other area on the ship for your use during the voyage. I'm needed elsewhere, if there's nothing else?"

Kel had thought about it already. "After we're underway, would it be possible to find space to exercise? I just need a small area, like any open area in the cargo bay."

The crewman scrunched his forehead as he considered the request.

"I'll ask my uncle Tan when I get the chance. I'm Ochio, by the way. Dinner is at 1700 hours in the galley. I'll check on you later, sir."

Kel settled into the stateroom. There was a bunk and a small bathroom. There was enough room to walk sideways if the bunk was down. Otherwise with it folded up, a small desk could be lowered and a chair levered out from the wall as a workstation. The trip to Calcarion was supposed to take four days, and after the *Callie* offloaded her cargo, with any luck, they'd be in orbit around Meridian within another week.

He settled into his bunk and put his specs on, scanning yet more data from the area study on Meridian while thinking about what he was going to find when he got planetside.

A few hours later the first officer chimed Kel's stateroom, inviting him to the wardroom for dinner. There was a place for him at the table beside Caroline.

"Hello, Mr. Nielsen. Settled in all right?" she asked, briefly looking up from her datapad.

"Yes, ma'am, and thank you," he replied.

"We eat in shifts around here. If you're ready, let's go next door to the galley and we'll get a tray of food and make our way back here to eat." She led him through a curtained threshold at the back of the room into the galley. Kel had thought he'd heard the high-pitched voices of children, coming from the galley, and he'd been right. Two tables each had a few teenagers and younger children seated around them.

"The galley serves as their classroom in the afternoon after morning duties are completed, and is also the social area after the evening meal," she explained. The young crewmembers were eating or playing games on their datapads, conversing with each other, happy and at ease.

"Which ones are yours, Mrs. Yomiuri?" Kel was curious to know.

"Ochio is my oldest. His sister, Tara, is on duty in engineering with Uncle Yoshi." Ochio had the fair complexion of his mother and the dark hair of his father.

"Let's see what Auntie Meiko has for us. The kids take turns helping with galley duties. We all take turns with the kids' school lessons. I have a class to teach tomorrow that I need to brush up on tonight. Physics was never my strongest subject, but getting the kids ready for their standardized exams has made me better at it than when I was a student myself."

"See one, do one, teach one," Kel said.

"What's that?" she asked. "I've never heard that before."

Kel felt stupid in the unguarded moment. Anyone with a military background would have heard the saying. He'd said it reflexively.

"Oh, I've just always heard you don't really know a subject until you can teach it," Kel recovered.

"That must be true," Mrs. Yomiuri agreed.

They grabbed trays and moved toward the open window to the kitchen. This Kel could relate to. The chief's mess on the *Resolve* was an experience, but this was more comfortable to him. Auntie Meiko's face brightened when she saw Kel. "You are a growing boy!" she said, looking Kel up and down. "Give me your tray. You need extra portions. Auntie Meiko knows what a growing boy needs!"

Kel blushed and thanked her. "That's very kind, ma'am."

"You call me Auntie while you're our guest on the *Callie*, you big strong boy!"

Kel laughed. "Yes, m... yes, Auntie," he got out.

"You go enjoy," she shooed them back to the wardroom.

They sat and ate, talking between bites. Mrs. Yomiuri asked Kel about life on Liberinthine, and he lied about what living on the Republic's capital world was like. He'd visited there once. He had not been impressed. The same things that seemed extraordinary or important to the political class inhabiting the planet were the kind of things

Kel could not tolerate—masses of people flaunting their wealth and connections, making one appearance after another at all the right places with the right people. He preferred the life of a legionnaire. He tried to make it sound convincing while trying his best to not appear to be as much of an ass as the people from Liberinthine came across in Kel's experience. The captain walked into the wardroom from the galley and sat across from Kel.

"Settled in, Mr. Nielsen?" asked the captain.

"Yes, Captain, and thank you."

The captain looked at Kel and paused. "Is this your first time on a family merchant vessel?"

The captain had asked him that this morning while berthed at the port. The captain was sending him a subtle message, trying to perceive something about Kel. Kel had noticed something else telling. The portions that the captain and his wife had on their trays was much less than half of what Kel had been apportioned by Auntie Meiko. Kel's observation of the adult crew was that most of them, especially the captain and his wife, looked emaciated. Kel began to put together a clearer picture of the family's financial situation, and what impression the captain must have of him in his persona as a trade negotiator from the House of Reason.

"It is my first time on a family merchant ship, Captain, and it is an honor. Your crew, well, your family, have been very kind and gracious, sir," Kel said, hoping to convey as much respect as he could. Before the captain could say anything else Kel continued, "I'm embarrassed by how much your aunt insisted on feeding me, sir."

The captain looked disconcerted. His wife took up the conversation. "We run on a thin margin, Mr. Nielsen. The children are our priority and we would never do anything to cause them privation. The adult crewmembers, we, well, we take smaller portions of food. Many of us skip the lunch meal altogether, you know, so the children don't have to," Mrs. Yomiuri stammered.

The captain put his hand over his wife's, taking the lead back. "Mr. Nielsen, please don't think ill of us. It's not always like this. Most of the time our runs have been quite profitable. We have been under some duress lately. I'm sure that to someone from the center of the Republic we must seem quite pitiable..."

Kel held up his hands. "Please, Captain, Mrs. Yomiuri. Firstly, please call me... Tamford." Kel had to think a second to remember his cover name. "I understand perfectly. I appreciate your taking me into your confidence. Hopefully, we're going to turn things around for you with this contract. In fact, I'm confident of it," Kel said, trying to sound upbeat. "As for the meals—"

"Forgive me," the captain interrupted him. "That was not my meaning. You are our guest and I never meant to imply that you had to worry about your meals here on the *Callie*. My aunt would be disappointed with me if she knew I'd made an error in courtesy like that with a guest."

"Please think no more of it," Kel assured him. "Folks from the House of Reason can be a bunch of stuck-up gasbags, but I'm not that sort of person. I specifically looked for a family venture, and I'm glad our paths crossed. I hope when we're done, you'll feel so as well."

The captain smiled for the first time since Kel had met him. He hoped he'd helped them understand that while onboard their ship he would treat their family with respect and not like a perfumed diplomat expecting aristocratic treatment. If he were in their shoes, he'd probably have the same misgivings about him traveling with them. They were clearly accustomed to transporting cargo; having passengers was not a part of their regular service, much less a functionary representing the House of Reason.

Kel shook each of their hands and begged their leave to return to his stateroom. He dropped by the galley window to thank Auntie Meiko for the wonderful meal. She beamed with pride as Kel left before he blushed again.

It seemed to Kel there were always opportunities to do the right thing. The best operators he'd ever known were not just useful in a fight; they seemed to be capable in any situation. He thought about the Yomiuri family. These people were truly living on the edge. Kel went to bed that night thinking about the things he was grateful for in his life and wondered how the rest of the team was doing.

Kel arose the next morning and dressed in some loose-fitting clothes and shoes with a good gripping surface and made his way aft toward the cargo hold. He'd gotten a message from Ochio that said:

> *Deck Officer Yomiuri here.*
> *Uncle Tan said there's space*
> *in the cargo hold you can use*
> *anytime. Just check in with*
> *whoever is on duty. Ochio.*

Tan Yomiuri was on duty in the cargo hold. Kel found him with a datapad in hand, checking the restraints on a large container, tethering it to the deck. The cargo hold was immense. It was divided into bulkheads, with a large central opening through each. The sides of the hold abutting the hull had enormous racks where many containers were shelved and tied down. The central hold contained rows of different sized crates and containers, some of them stacked to nearly the forty-meter height of the hold.

"Hey Mr. Nielsen, Ochio said you were looking for a little room to do your thing?" Tan asked.

"Yeah, if that's not a problem," Kel said while scanning the huge space that was the hold. "Anything I need to be cautious around?"

"Not particularly." Tan shrugged. "What did you have in mind?" Kel told him. "Doesn't sound like a problem. If you find a container or tie-down that doesn't seem solid or taut, please let whoever is on duty know. The buckles are all self-tightening and have monitors on them, but we still do manual checks on all of them each duty rotation. You can imagine the hazard loose cargo can pose, especially when we get ready for orbital entry. If you notice something like that while you're doing your thing, it'd be appreciated."

Kel promised he would.

He moved into the central area of the hold where there was a natural four-way intersection between stacks of containers. He limbered up by doing a simple routine of movements, squatting, jumping, push-ups, and flutter kicks. After he felt his core get warm, he moved toward a stack of containers he'd been eyeing since his arrival. The base container was ten meters on a side and a little more than two meters tall. Stacked on top of this was another similarly scaled container, leaving about a handbreadth of a rim exposed on top of the base container. Similarly scaled containers were stacked higher up, reaching to about twenty-five meters.

Kel stood close to the wall of the base container and leaped to get a finger grasp on the rim, swung himself up to the ledge created by the next container in the stack, and performed the same maneuver, again, and again, until reaching the top. A bulkhead crossed just over the top container, a narrow lip of the beam sculpted into the bottom of the bulkhead, designed to allow for mechanical attachment of winches or other mechanisms to aid in the placement of cargo. Kel eyed this for a second, then leaped again to grasp the lip of the bulkhead. Grasping both sides of the bulkhead, he traversed the hold, hanging from the bulkhead, moving one hand at a time across the hold, until he was over another stack of containers a few meters below. He dropped on to the top container, and scaled his way down the short stack, until he reached the deck, running back to his starting point at the larger container stack and repeated the climb, traverse, and descent several times.

He could see Tan and some other members of the crew watch him for several minutes. At one point it looked like Tan was going to say something to him, and seemed to think better of it before returning to his inspections.

Kel found a space on one of the container shelves along the hull where there was a gap between containers barely wide enough for Kel to fit, and leaped up a half meter to grasp the rounded bar of the leading edge of the shelf and did as many pull-ups as he could. When he felt spent, he dropped to the ground and did more flutter kicks, returning then to do more pull-ups. After ten iterations of this, Kel felt he'd done enough for the morning. Walking out of the cargo bay Kel saw Tan and said, "Everything seems secure. Thank you."

The deck officer gave him a reserved smile.

After breakfast he complimented Auntie Meiko's cooking again and told her to please not include him in the afternoon meal preparation, saying that he normally didn't eat lunch.

"I don't know how a growing boy can stay strong skipping lunch, but if you change your mind, you just let Auntie know." She'd made Kel laugh again with her kind manner.

Making his way to his stateroom he saw many of the teens and children in their ship's coveralls headed to the galley, he assumed for lessons. He passed Mrs. Yomiuri as well. "Time for class?" Kel queried.

"The younger kids have self-directed study run by the older kids. Classes don't start until after lunch. Wish me luck," she said, heading toward the forward compartments and the bridge.

Shipboard routine passed like this for the next several days. There was pleasant conversation in the wardroom each evening after dinner with those not on watch, and Kel went to the cargo hold to work out once or twice a day. He studied and did what he could to keep himself active in his stateroom.

He learned that the *Callie's Dream* was a second-generation venture, started by Captain Jim and Tan Yomiuri's father. The brothers had grown up on the ship, and now their own children were doing the same, as were the other members of the spacefaring family. Where once the crew was only partially family, now the crew was essentially only family by birth or marriage. They had a home world that they took extended vacations on yearly, Callie's World—sometimes because business was slow, sometimes because business was good and they could afford to enjoy the extra time planetside. Kel had wondered about the children and whether they were going to grow up exclusively on the ship. They'd told Kel that the children made planetfall at each destination to experience what they could; it was part of their education. Otherwise, the yearly vacation on their home world was the longest stretch they spent as ground-pounders.

The evening before arriving in orbit around Calcarion, the captain briefed Kel about the events of the next day. "The Calcarion Mining Consortium has a spaceport. The consignment of goods that we carry, however, has a destination for a site closer to one of the new mines, essentially on the other side of the planet from the spaceport."

The landing site closest to the destination was not a fully constructed duracrete spaceport; it was an improved surface but not a commercial field for repeated use by spacecraft. There was a survey registered that included a recent update filed by another merchant captain. The survey indicated the field could handle the mass of the *Callie*, but there was always risk utilizing a rough landing field. If the ship was damaged in any significant way due to the surface of the landing zone giving way, the *Callie* might never lift again. It would be a death sentence for their family run business.

Calcarion had significant mineral wealth. Most of the rare ores were utilized in the building of hyperspace coils and other esoteric applications. At some time in its history, the planet had seen significant volcanic activity. Its crust was riddled with jagged mountainous chains and glaciers covered its poles. Fossil evidence indicated that early life forms never developed beyond their primal stages, poisoned off by some ancient extinction event. The mineral deposits and their value had been long guessed at, but only in the last hundred years had it been exploited.

They were headed to Alpha Site, an area that represented the next phase in development of the planet's resources. Everything had to be shipped to Calcarion. Their manifest held notations of rock boring lasers and sonic earth movers as well as stored foodstuffs and equipment for closed system farming and vat grown proteins. The site apparently had a population of nearly a hundred workers.

"You're welcome to use the jump seat on the bridge if you'd like to see how a landing like this is done, Tamford." The captain had been quite friendly to Kel the last several evenings, even though it was obvious that the risk of the impending landing troubled him.

"Thank you, Captain. I wouldn't miss the opportunity." He could never tell the captain that he'd made many orbital and suborbital free falls, seeing the approach to a planet's surface in a very up close and personal way with nothing between him and annihilation but the thin barrier of jump armor.

Riding in a jump seat would be like the first day of a three day weekend.

FLASHBACK

How you Get There is Half the Story
Over Antione

The ramp of the Talon is open. Sung stands at the edge. Most of the release point calculations are done by the Navy, but we're taught that a jumpmaster can never delegate the responsibility for any aspect of a jump. The Navy won't bear the mark of failure if we don't arrive at our target. It'll be ours and ours alone. Sung has the plot of the drop zone telemetry holo'd from his forearm data link as he compares it to his visual ground indicators. From 100 kilometers above the surface, there's a lot of room for error.

"Slide south five," Sung says to the pilot.

"Roger, Legion. Sliding five south." The pilot is experienced enough to know not to argue with a jumpmaster on a combat dive. Sung spent hours with the Talon crew going over the flight plan. He let Shuck, Trumbull, and me tag along to take part in the planning. Fifty more drops, I'll get my chance to go to jumpmaster school. Shuck is nearly there.

"Maintain track and altitude." Sung turns to face us in the pax compartment where we're splayed out like awkward mannequins in the troop seats. "Six minutes. Stand. Up," he says in staccato emphasis. Carryalls between our legs. Our N-16s secured to our sides, exposed and ready to lay hands on as soon as we touch down. Freefall compatible armor—the FCA—the essential layer of flight control surfaces and attitude jets worn over the armor on our arms and legs. Finally, the massive parachute containers on our backs. All combine to make us inflexible as durasteel girders as we help each other stand. Even with the grav decking turned down, our bulk makes us as graceful as capsized turtles struggling to right themselves.

Things would happen methodically now, in a way we all anticipate and depend on. The commands Sung will give us are already an oath lasered into our brains.

"Check life support. Check control surfaces. Check navigation." Any failure of a system to show green or the jump control program in our buckets to read anything but *Active*, and a jumper would have no choice but to peel out of formation and take the shameful ride back to the frigate. For this drop—an actual combat space dive—for anything but a life support failure, I'll go ahead and risk it. I'm sure the others would do the same. I don't have to make that call. My systems are all good.

"Move to the ramp." We were exiting in two sticks, me leading my fire team on the left, Shuck on the right with his. We'd follow Sung off the ramp into oblivion in about...

"One minute." My heart pounded. Pushed near the edge of the ramp just behind Sung I could see the planet surface for the first time. On both sides of us, tiny dots that are formations of bombers careen off the atmosphere, dropping air-denial munitions. The chaff in the upper atmosphere and the surface bombing from the ships in orbit should disguise our presence. Should. As I hear the thirty second warning, I forget about the chaos in the envelope around Antione and focus on the edge of the ramp. The dark planet rolls by under my feet.

"Go."

I step off and arch my back. I do what they taught me and make like a frog. Everyone tells you to relax, that it's the secret to falling stable. That's sure true for sub-orbital work, down where the atmosphere is dense enough to stabilize your fall. Up here, the FCA has to do it all. My bucket shows the program controlling the attitude jets is working. I know that because I'm not in a spin, but it's reassuring to see in my HUD. My drogue chute deploys and I pay attention to the altimeter. *93K.*

There isn't much I can do now except stay alert and fall. The master jump program is controlling and coordinating all our FCAs, and has given us a nice, even spread between jumpers. The sword icons in my HUD show me that our sticks have formed into a loose arrowhead, Sung in the lead between Shuck's team and mine. *70K.*

I'm still stable, so I go ahead and activate the rear view in my HUD to check on the team behind me. Trumbull's bringing up the rear, trailing left. I can tell it's him. He's short and wide at the shoulders. Equipped for freefall he's almost a perfect cube-shape. We're all together. My HUD shows us in optimal position, but there's nothing like confirming it visually. *50K.*

It's night. There are spotty areas of illumination below, which amazes me. Who wouldn't turn out the lights when they're being bombarded from orbit? Where we're headed though, it's dark. Not black, not in my bucket. The spectral augment lets me see as though it's daylight. The spaceport is a huge duracrete plain, sitting in a bowl of short hills and a few taller peaks. I can see the shapes that are machines and spacecraft on the duracrete between the hangers. It's a commercial port. The militia is down there somewhere waiting in defense. No matter. In a few hours, they'll either be dead or hiding. Nothing will stop us from seizing the spacefield.

I can feel the resistance from denser atmosphere and get the warning icon I'd been anticipating. I make myself arch a little more and relax my limbs. *30K.* We've been falling for three minutes. At ten kilometers the parachute containers will deploy and we'll take the slow, silent ride to the surface floating under the massive canopies.

The canopy activation warning flashes. I check on the camera to make sure there's plenty of separation between me and anyone around me. The HUD confirms we're all clear and I feel myself get heavier as my feet fall below me and the tug of the canopy slows my fall. I look up to see the huge air foil above me. Oblong and beautiful. For the first time the silence is broken by Sung.

"Guide on me."

The virtual projection of the flight path in my bucket shows me everything in a way that makes me wish I saw the world this way permanently. Our drop zone is marked by an orange cross. The compass heading is highlighted. The ground features are enhanced in a faint green outline. If only you could see everything this way, you'd never get lost. You'd never be in doubt. Doubt is the killer.

Sung is at the tip of our formation. I follow his path and do the same maneuver with my canopy, taking a serpentine path to spill some altitude and not over shoot our drop zone. The rear view in my HUD shows the sky behind me filled with oval shapes, passengers suspended below by the invisible shroud lines, oscillating gently beneath.

Sung flares his canopy and touches down lightly. I do the same as the ground rushes at me and the tone of the ground proximity warning buzzes in my bucket. I touch down gently and simultaneously key the canopy container release and ignore it falling off my back as I reach for my N-16 and the belly band holding it to my side. I'm able to do this as I step out of my carryall straps without tripping. Prone, I push my weapon out in front of me and strain to see movement or any hot shapes in my HUD. Nothing. We stay like this for another minute.

Over the squad channel Sung speaks. "Rally on me."

I key the fire team channel on L-Comm. "Alpha, on me." I make sure that the nanites are consuming the canopy and its container as it all disappears into dust. I get my carryall on my back and stand. "Head count," I say as I double check everyone's PID in my HUD. Trumbull, Howard, D'antonio, Pabon, Yamazuki, and me. "Wedge up," as I take the point, the rest forming up to trail to my rear. Shuck is a hundred meters on my right, moving his team with us toward Sung. We've landed together, without injury, undetected. We're a kilometer from the edge of the spacefield. I feel proud. But I remember the admonition. *Freefall is just a way to get where you want to go. It's not the mission.* Now we're ready to start our mission.

My elation at being alive and on the ground is ruined as a sun ignites above us and we all instinctively drop to the ground. A flare or a flash drone is overhead, exposing our nakedness in the open. Blaster fire comes at us from two directions. "On line, on line," I say as I choose a spot and unleash fury. Controlled chaos is an understatement. No matter how many times you train for it, it's always different from a simulation bot shooting at you. Sung gets us moving. Shuck's team is bounding, moving in short rushes as we continue to lay waste to everything. The light above extinguishes. Someone fired a drone-hunter and killed it. Trumbull has the launcher. Must've been him.

Now it's our turn. "Alpha ready. Rush," I say as I jump to my feet and dash forward. A scraggly bush is my goal and I reach it in three seconds as I fall prone and bring my N-16 to my face and send more bursts at the rocky outcrop on the hill where I think the fire came from. Time to move. We repeat this again, and again. There's no return fire and we hold ours in response. Still moving forward, now up the rise, slower than before, alternating between Shuck's team and us.

Soon we're there. I see bodies around the rim of a fighting position. "Grenade," I say as I toss one into the depression ahead of me. The purple and white flash lights the hillside briefly. Debris is still raining as I stand. "Assault," I yell as the team moves on line with me to crest the last small rise. The grenade was probably unnecessary. Three charred bodies in militia uniforms, the mangled remnants of their blasters leaking plasma, adding to the smoke filling the depression. They had us dead to rights.

"Alpha, Bravo, status," Sung asks. Shuck's team silenced an unmanned autoblaster, probably controlled by the guys we just barbecued. Sung takes me and my team up the slope to investigate ahead and set a blocking force. Trumbull is on the fire team channel. "So much for the silent part of swift, silent, deadly." Our motto. Pabon is with him. "Looks like the rest of the company is gonna get their wish." He's right. There's nothing to do now but get ready to bring down the Goshawks for a full drop on the field. We have to take the spacefield the hard way.

Shuck converges on us and we both continue our report to Sung. No one has been hit. A miracle. "Turner. You and I are taking Alpha and we're taking the west slope. Shuck, get Bravo up on the east. Start marking anything that looks like an auto turret or gun emplacement. We're going to get one good run on it all by the Talons before the drop. Get the beacons locked for the Goshawks first. If we buy it, at least they'll have the grids locked in for the approach. Let's do it."

We expect another militia firefight with every step. Orbital bombardment continues to harass the surrounding area. Maybe it succeeded in concealing our little firefight? Maybe it had the militia hunkered down and scared to move?

Sung is giving the situation report to the TOC in orbit. The rest of the company will be jocked up and loaded on the Goshawks, waiting for the word. When they get it, what happens next will be the definition of berserk.

06

Navy pilots were nonchalant in their duties, even with particle beams scorching past them. The atmosphere on the bridge of the *Callie* was tenser than Kel had experienced. He settled into the jump seat, attached his restraint, and otherwise remained unobtrusive, one of his specialties as a sniper.

The captain and his first officer went through their checklists obsessively as they prepared for entry into the planet's thin atmosphere. Heat generated by the powered descent obliterated their vision through the viewscreen. Though not creating as much friction as a true free fall descent, familiar gold and red flames appeared in the periphery of the display.

The *Callie* encountered little turbulence as she navigated from her sub-orbital altitude across the planet, coasting across the northern hemisphere following a latitude north of the equator. Just shy of the terminator and crossing into night, the man-made structure of the spaceport and other whitish duracrete masses could be discerned even from this altitude. Their pristineness stood out in stark contrast to the barren waste that was the rest of the inhospitable rock. As the captain piloted the *Callie*'s descent, large mountain ranges rotated into view stretching from the north and the south to the equatorial flats. Piercing navigation lights sprung to life, forming a geometric pattern at the base of a diminishing mountainous range where a massive flat area dominated the landscape. Daybreak commenced as they descended to their target, the orange light making the surface more inhospitable than the darkness successfully concealed.

The pilots kept up a steady banter with the ground controller, using jargon he could not decipher until the landing zone filled the viewscreen. Tension rose on the small bridge. Ships without huge debts protected their ship for future contracts and avoided unimproved landing fields like this one.

The floor vibrated as the massive landing gears deployed below them. The co-pilot checked visual monitors and systems indicator panels, ensuring gears and repulsors worked in unison. For a brief moment it was a storm of noise and violence and Kel could feel everyone collectively holding their breath at this most dangerous of moments. The moment of landing.

The *Callie's* forward motion arrested as the ground drew closer and closer until the ship rocked slightly as it touched down. The pilots continued to sit under power, waiting for an indication that the landing surface was going to accept the weight of the freighter. Kel held the additional minute of silent anticipation with the men before the pilots removed their helmets and shook hands, big smiles infecting their faces. Kel grinned too. It had been as slick a job of piloting as he had ever witnessed.

"Crew, prepare for ground operations," the captain announced over the IC. It'd be forty-five minutes or more before anyone could exit the ship, waiting for thermal dissipation to cool the exterior of the hull. Kel unstrapped and shook hands with the captain and co-pilot before following them aft, still the silent strap-hanger.

"Eric, do you want to update the survey of the landing site after things cool off? Best to get it done early," the captain told his brother-in-law.

"On it," the co-pilot responded.

He had become familiar with the deck officers and the bosun as well as the rest of the family working the cargo bay. Kel had volunteered to help, and was invited to attend the unloading but was politely asked to please stay out of the way.

What must have been the full complement of family was in the hold, minus Uncle Yoshi the engineer, no doubt tending the ship's engines after the stressful burn into the atmosphere. It delighted Kel to see the teens and children, datapads in hand, the older commanding small robots to methodically remove tethers from container stacks, the younger spacers practicing the manual tasks to prepare loading machines. Container cranes slid out along gantries from their storage points along the hull.

A siren sounded as the bosun, Aggie, monitored the lowering of large stern and port ramps, the unpleasant orange light filling the hold, the taste of ozone from superheated air around the hull wafting in. The captain and his wife departed, no doubt to meet the ground committee and arrange for the off-loading. Kel remained behind, impressed with the efficiency of the crew, still entertained by the sight of the school-aged children preparing for the task of offloading.

Through the portside cargo bay doors, the outline of a sloping mountain range, jagged and flinty sprang from the horizon. From the same direction rose a trail of dust. A convoy of vehicles approached.

The first vehicle pulled up. Repulsors shut down, the large flatbed settling as dust rose and fell, coating everything in yellow tinged grime. Three men got out of the rear cab and made their way toward the ship. The captain and his wife waved and moved off the end of the ramp to meet the strangers halfway. The small gathering shook hands all around and not long after, more repulsor flat-beds arrived at the landing site. Several large wheel-pro-pelled trucks towing empty container carriages pulled up behind them.

The adults moved from the hold down the ramp to meet the group. Kel could see them discussing what must be the loading plan, and then dispersing into differ-ent groups to move onto the ship and inspect the cargo.

Kel stayed for a while, watching as the work to dis-tribute the containers commenced in earnest. Loaders moved from the massive hold, down the ramps, carrying one container at a time to the waiting flatbeds and car-riages. He hated shirking work, but it had been clear they considered him in the way. He could continue to gawk, or do something. He made his way down the aft ramp, sur-veyed the landscape, and broke into a fast, rhythmic pace toward the tallest peak that had first caught his eye.

He returned two hours later, ready for water and rest. The unloading progressed, the flurry of activity temporarily slowed as the crew awaited the return of the next iteration of trucks to cart away the mountains of remaining con-tainers. In the galley the crew ate in shifts, inhaling their meals to make room for more diners during the natural break in off-loading activity.

Kel smiled back as Auntie Meiko forced a sandwich into his hand and gestured for him to go sit. The unload-ing continued throughout the rest of the day and night. When Kel rose before sunrise the next morning, curiosity drove him to the cargo hold to see it approaching empty.

With the container stacks removed and the shelves barren, the space looked even more enormous than it had when full. During yesterday's run the massive ship was never absent his sight. It was truly a leviathan, nowhere near the size of a capital class battlecruiser, but impressive nonetheless.

The verbal commotion grew louder as he found himself naturally drawn to its source. Aggie and the captain's daughter, Tara, stood at the bottom of the ramp with two of the miners who gesticulated menacingly at the young ladies as they yelled.

"You tell your purser and captain that it is *on* the manifest, but it isn't in any of the containers. It is *your* responsibility to account for it. Tell them we will be *back* and will be performing a full search of your ship until we find it," the older, fatter miner said. He and his lanky partner got in their vehicle and raced away in a cloud of dust just as Kel arrived.

"Trouble?" he asked.

"Yes," said Aggie. "That was the chief of mining operations. He told us the boring machine they're depending on was shipped without the charge packs. They're apparently proprietary and there's no substitute. The machine is useless without them. He's telling us they're listed on the manifest but that they haven't found them in any of the containers. The manager's accusing us of losing their goods. I tried to explain that isn't possible and that the containers are sealed by the shipper, but that didn't satisfy him. He's telling me they're going to return and search our ship. Maybe he thinks we stole them? I've got to tell the captain," Aggie told him, tears forming in her eyes. Tara looked shaken as well and followed her aunt into the ship.

Trouble was coming. He returned to his room to dress for the day, his plan simple. *Better to act, than react.*

Kel stopped by the wardroom. The adults were crowded in and around the small space as Aggie and Tara retold the story they'd told Kel. The men flushed, some of them clenching their fists. Some looked sheepish, a look he recognized from the faces of weaker men, but never a legionnaire.

The captain spoke with the gravitas the threat deserved. "Everyone, calm down. Tan and I'll go talk to them. This is just a misunderstanding and I'm sure we'll be able to solve this peacefully. Just in case, I want the ramps up and secured, except the fore-port ramp. Women and children stay in quarters. I want the crew doors sealed from the hold to the operation and living areas. The rest of the men I want in the hold, ready if I signal. Everyone knows what to do. Now, let's move."

"Captain," Kel said, catching him in the corridor. "It might be safer to seal the ship and discuss this over link."

"No," he dismissed Kel's suggestion. "There's a chance these miners could try to harm the ship. Mr. Nielsen, I suggest you stay in your stateroom."

Kel said nothing but followed the men into the hold area. He stayed out of the way, watching as the ramps were closed and sealed, save the forward most ramp where the men stood, watching the rising dust clouds of approaching vehicles.

The captain and Tan moved to the bottom of the ramp awaiting the arrival. Kel moved to stand just behind them. The captain turned to speak but caught himself, Kel's grin stopping him short.

"Sir, I have some experience in crisis negotiations. If there seems to be a point where you're not having a favorable result, I'll offer to intervene on your behalf."

Before the captain could object, the first vehicle flared in a cloud of dust too close to the bottom of the ramp, two trailing vehicles peeling to either side to form a crowd perimeter. The fat miner got out of the driver's side of the lead vehicle to stand just forward of his door. A passenger exited but stood behind his door, rudely concealing most of his body and hands. The occupants of the other vehicles did likewise. Their actions screamed "threat." Kel did not see weapons. Yet. That everyone stayed close to their vehicle door told Kel that they had weapons within arm's reach inside the vehicles, waiting to be retrieved should their leader order.

"Captain Yomiuri, you have our property. We will not pay any ransom to you pirates—'cuz that's what you are, that or incompetent. Give us what you owe or we'll seize your ship for failure to complete the contract," the grizzled fat man yelled gratuitously, only a few meters away.

"Mr. Thell, I can assure you neither is the case. As you well know, all those containers are sealed and—" It was a futile effort on the captain's part.

An arm jutted at the captain, a single pointed finger stabbing out. More yelling accompanied it. "Then we're gonna make a thorough search of your ship and its contents and satisfy ourselves that you're not takin' advantage of us. If we can't find our goods, then we can work on the assumption that you aren't a crook but you're just incompetent. Either way, we will have our satisfaction." Looking back at his men for approval, his fellow miners yelled encouragement as Kel saw one of the men reach into the cab of his vehicle.

Kel leaned forward. *This is going to get out of hand. The time is now.* He drew his pistol in one smooth motion and fired. Kel placed a single shot through the windshield nearest the man at his far left. The slug penetrated the glass, arresting the man's motion toward the open cab and the weapon that surely awaited. His eyes moved to where he wanted the next round to go—the windshield of the driver's side, near the shoulder of the standing occupant, aware of the man's right hand resting on something in the vehicle.

Kel's eyes darted to the lead vehicle where he repeated the same pattern, his pistol following his eyes, finishing with the vehicle to his right.

Six shots made one continuous roar. The miners stood frozen. They weren't as stupid as he first thought them. Kel finished by turning his pistol on the leader.

"Mr. Thell, is it? Let's all calm down," Kel kept his voice mild, contrasting the moments preceding. "I will kill the next man who tries to reach for a weapon."

The silence he received told him his communication was effective.

"Mr. Thell, you and your men get back in your vehicles and move out. Now. I won't tell you again."

Kel's intervention had lasted less than two of his heartbeats. It was all the part of his life he needed to donate. Two heartbeats. Nothing more.

Wordless, the miners tumbled into their vehicles and reversed course back to the mountain range, clouds of the sick, yellow dust swirling behind them.

"Captain," Kel said, watching the vehicles race away, "I think we should make haste to depart."

The captain didn't respond. He met Kel's eyes, his mouth frozen as though the power of speech evaded his control. Kel returned the pistol to its holster and put a hand on a quavering shoulder. "Sound good?"

The captain stared at Kel with wide eyes and mouth partially open. "Yes, Mr. Nielsen. That sounds very good."
After the *Callie's Dream* was underway in hyperspace, Kel went to the cargo hold to work off the rest of his adrenaline. He said hi to Ochio as he passed the small office, startling the young man with his greeting. He wasn't far into his workout when the captain, Caroline, and several members of the crew approached.

"Mr. Nielsen, uh, Tamford, can we talk about what happened?" The captain stood at the front of his entourage, the others cautious in their postures. *Oh boy, they're afraid of me now.*

Caroline stepped around her husband. Her smile quelled his fear. "I watched the whole thing on the monitors. I've never been so frightened for my husband and my family in all my life. Those men were going to seize our vessel. Our home! Thank you, Mr. Nielsen."

Kel raised his hands palm forward. "I'm as glad as everyone that it turned out well."

"Would you really have killed them?" Tan blurted in a jumble.

Kel tried to appear pensive before responding, but he'd formulated his answer long ago. Every warrior had. "Once those men threatened violence against your family, they surrendered any right to gentle treatment or any further attempt to resolve the conflict by negotiation. Yes, had they shown any further intent to do you harm, I would've killed anyone who posed a threat to you."

He let those words and their impact rest on them for a moment. It was clear he'd hit them where none of them wanted to be hit. Hit them with a truth few, and especially those who lived in small controlled conclaves like a family running a freighter operation, liked to admit... that the galaxy was a hard and dangerous place where the strong preyed upon the weak.

If they thought there was no one to stop them.

Everyone remained silent. The captain broke the somber moment. "Normally, any passenger with arms is required to surrender them to the bosun until they reach their destination. Being a diplomat, I never thought to ask you or demand to search your luggage. I guess we know that in this particular case it was good for all of us... that you were armed."

"Don't you maintain arms on this ship?" Kel asked, surprised. "Neither you nor Tan were armed going into this situation?"

The captain shrugged. "Yeah, we have some short-range blasters; they're safer to use on the ship than projectile weapons or regular blasters. They stay in the arms locker. Our drill for these situations has been to arm up with high pressure hosing and pipes. If Thell's gang had tried to board the ramp, the crew would've pummeled them."

Kel considered this. "Of course, if that group of idiots responded by shooting, you'd have likely ended with dead or wounded in addition to having the *Callie* impounded."

The captain nodded in agreement. "It would seem so."

Kel tried to steer the course of the conversation in a positive direction. "Well, maybe that's something we can talk about, Captain? How to have a better plan for the next time?" The captain nodded affirmatively as did the other members of the crew, as if slowly awakening from a dream to decide it was time to face a reality they'd been trying to ignore.

The captain looked back at Kel. "Thell's vigilantism is going to cost him. I sent a report to the mining consortium before we left orbit, detailing the incident from our perspective. I also promised to register the incident with the Republic and the Spacers League. It may lead to a proscription against merchant vessel traffic to the planet. At a minimum, it will significantly raise the cost of shipping to Calcarion. It may leave them with only small fly-by-night operations to ship with. Most of those outfits working the edge are sketchy operations to begin with. I doubt any member of the Spacers League will take a contract with them again. The consortium will have to decide what to do about Thell after this incident. You killing him may have been the kindest way out for him."

Dinner was excellent that night. Everyone had large portions and Auntie Meiko seemed in her element, fawning over Kel and refilling his kaff whenever it ran low. After dinner the captain and Caroline invited Kel to their private quarters. It was a deck below the main level and in a part of the ship Kel had not visited.

Kel had imagined that the crew and their families all lived in a stateroom similar to what he occupied. He was pleasantly surprised to be ushered into a small apartment with a cozy sitting area of couches and chairs with a large vid screen on one of the bulkheads, colorful floor and wall coverings, and soft lighting filling the comfortable space. The couple's two teenage children, Ochio and Tara, joined them as they sat and chatted about the different destinations the Yomiuris had visited over the years and what had stood out about some of them. Finally, Kel asked them about their home, Callie's World, and what it was like. Kel had never known anyone from there.

"It's home, what can we say?" Jim Yomiuri sighed. "We're lucky to have been born there." Tara swiped a holo to float over them as her father narrated. "About half of its surface is covered by shallow seas. The weather is mild where we live, close to the equator. It's lush and green and not crowded. Our family plot goes back a dozen generations and covers several hundred thousand hectares. There's not much industry or agriculture, though. The biome is difficult to adapt to earth-common plant life, but there's nothing harmful to humans there. The arable areas and modified crops and livestock provide a living, but the only way to really earn a living is off-planet, so that's what most families do, ours included."

His wife smiled and nodded. "It's what I think of when I think of home. At least, after we've been out for so long. Spacers like us are a strange lot, Tamford. A few months home, and the stars'll call us back to the *Callie*. Two homes, one calling us from wherever we are not, you understand?"

The Legion was his home. While he could understand Caroline's perspective, he couldn't relate. At least, he didn't think he could. As he sat comfortably with the Yomiuris he felt a warmth, a glow from them. They were special people. Could he ever imagine such a quandary, longing to be where you were not? There was only duty and the Legion for him.

Kel had to dodge many of the queries they sent his way. The best tool for evasiveness was to return question for question. He plied them all about themselves. Kel's subtle but friendly sparring sent a message that was being received by their patriarch. Jim Yomiuri gently restrained his family's questions as he steered the conversation away from Kel. The captain was putting it together and was helping. Kel knew that he knew. It was best not to ask the pleasant stranger too many questions.

After several hours Kel begged his leave and thanked them. He'd really enjoyed their evening together. Before taking his leave, Caroline asked, "Kel, would you be willing to teach the students something while you're with us? I know all the children would be interested in learning from you."

He thought for a moment. "Hmmm. Well, how much do the children know about first aid?"

"We try to go over some on a regular basis. Do you have some training in medicine?"

Kel grinned. He'd been through the Legion's independent medical tech course and usually ended up serving as the team medic. "I actually went to school to study medicine before I switched to trade studies. The diplomatic service also makes medical response a mandatory course at the academy before being sent to a posting. I'd be happy to review your medical kits and do some basic teaching if that sounds good to you?"

Caroline looked at her husband for agreement. "That would be really helpful. The kids would love to hear anything from someone new."

Kel looked at the captain. "Jim, if you're amenable, maybe tomorrow we could talk about some of your defensive measures?"

The captain sighed. "I think it's time. I'd appreciate any input you have. Until then, thank you."

Kel shook everyone's hand and said goodnight.

He was confident he could help them in both areas and do so without compromising his cover. At this point in the journey, he wasn't overly concerned about being blown. The cover as a trade diplomat would continue to serve him, but once he was working with the security forces he'd revert to his role as operator.

This part of the mission was exhausting. He didn't feel cut out to be a spy. He couldn't wait to get operational. Everything until then was just killing time. Preparing for the show.

The next day began with a quick workout and breakfast, then Kel went to the small infirmary to evaluate what supplies and equipment they carried. They had a lot of the essential equipment—a portable Medcomp analyzer, nanomeds and gels, auto-tourniquets, an artificial intelligent airway, as well as an autosynthesizer that could manufacture small quantities of meds.

He checked one of the ship's emergency med kits. It had the basic equipment necessary for the types of injuries that would be seen on a ship: medicines and nano-dressings for burns, pain meds and means to halt bleeding from crushing injuries and other trauma, nano-tubule autosplints for fractured limbs, and other small items for first aid. All quick solutions for the most likely injuries a spacer might face while working on a cargo ship.

This gave Kel a good idea of how to tailor his instruction to the students that afternoon. He jotted a few notes on his datapad until the captain walked in and handed him a fresh mug of kaff.

"What do you think?" Jim asked. "Anything glaringly missing from our med stock?"

"No, it seems you're well provisioned. I'm looking forward to working with the children," Kel said.

"There's any number of skills that a spacer needs, Tamford, especially on an operation like ours where we're essentially alone. It's not like being in the Republic Navy where help is only a bounce away," the captain said.

It was a probe. And though it wasn't clumsily, it was hard to miss. The captain telegraphed he thought there was more than met the eye about their passenger.

Kel didn't take the bait. "Have you given any thought as to your defensive training?"

"Yeah," replied the Captain slowly, as though not sure how to proceed, only that he must. "How do you want to start?"

"Well, the first step is understanding the anatomy of a fight. If you agree, I'd prefer to start with some lecture time to introduce some of these concepts to you all."

The captain nodded. "Sounds good. We're all spacers but no one here has a background in the military or security forces," he said, shooting Kel a look. "With no cargo to chaperone, duties are limited right now. How much time do you need to prepare for your talk? Can we start this morning?"

Kel nodded. "That'd be fine, can we use the galley in about thirty minutes?"

"Definitely. We'll see you there," Jim said, standing to make the arrangements.

Thirty minutes and some change later, Kel soon stood at the front of the galley with most of the adults and some of the older teenagers sitting around the dining tables, all turned to face Kel with expressions ranging from interest to concern. They were a serious lot, thought Kel. Which was good, for what he was about to teach them was indeed serious. Very serious. Ochio and Tara sat up front with their parents.

"I've been asked," he began, "to talk, a little, about personal defense after what happened on Calcarion. I think there are some valuable lessons to learn from that encounter." All eyes were riveted on Kel. It turned out the whole crew had watched the encounter unfold from their viewscreen monitors. They'd probably discussed it and what it made them feel during the quiet moments that were the life of flying a starship between worlds. By their stillness, Kel knew they were taking this seriously. They knew some change in the weather had come to their lives, that nothing would ever be the same again.

"Let me say some general things about a fight, and a gunfight in particular," continued Kel. "As you know, avoiding confrontation is the best strategy of all. Being aware of your environment and what's going on around you is extremely important. If you can anticipate trouble, it's easier to avoid." Heads nodded all around.

"But I'd rather talk about some concrete concepts and assume we're in a situation where a fight is unavoidable. There's a triad that we talk about that contains the three basic elements of how we succeed in a gunfight. One is marksmanship. The second is weapon manipulation. And the third, and most important, is mindset.

The silence was thick enough to cut with a flick knife. Kel made sure all eyes were focused on him.

"Marksmanship is the ability to hit your target. Even with a blaster at close range, an aimed shot is better than an un-aimed shot. It's not who shoots first, it's who hits first that counts. Learning the fundamentals of how to shoot accurately is an essential.

"Weapons manipulation is the next leg of the triangle. How to draw the weapon from a holster or concealment; how to move with the weapon safely; how to engage multiple targets; how to reload or recharge the weapon—and there are other skills—that's what we mean by manipulating a weapon.

"The most important is the last: mindset. Some people are not born with the 'mean gene.' If struck, their immediate response is not to strike back. Some people who are well versed in the first two elements simply find they are incapable of pulling the trigger when confronted with a living threat."

There was the look of surprised contemplation on more than a few faces.

"Mindset can be taught and aggressiveness improved with training, but some people just can't overcome their lifetime of socialization to not harm another being." Kel looked about the galley. More wide eyes and rapt attention.

Uncle Yoshi raised his hand. "Kel, how did you know those thugs were going to get violent? You moved so quickly. How were you sure they weren't just going to keep talking loud like hot plasma rising but not do anything?"

"Good question," Kel replied. "Part of it is intuition as well as training. The intuition part is this: intuition is nothing more than the ability to make a rapid decision based on a limited number of facts. I've been in similar situations before. So I had a pretty good idea of which way things were going to go."

Everyone leaned forward in their chairs as Kel said this, anticipating a war story. He'd have to disappoint them for now. There were more important things to discuss to make his point.

"The other part is training," he continued, sure that he had them now. "Learning how to recognize human and alien pre-assaultive behaviors helps to anticipate when a situation is going to go very bad. Assessing someone's facial expressions and their body language is important. In the case of our encounter, Mr. Thell and his gang were demonstrating their hostility to us with everything they did. Thell's speech was agitated. He as much as promised us that he was going to board the ship. Thell established his intent to force his gang's will upon us almost immediately in the confrontation.

"So, intent is an important aspect of establishing the presence of a threat. The next is establishing the means. There were more of them than us by twice the number. Even if they had no weapons, they had the means to do harm to us by numbers alone. Or at least, to try and do harm to us." Kel smiled. "Another thing. They stayed so close to the cabs of their vehicles, rather than approach us with open arms to talk, that alone told me that they most likely had weapons hidden. Those weapons may have been blasters; they may have been pipes and hoses like you carry in the hold. At that point, it was irrelevant. They had demonstrated to me that they were in possession of the means to do us harm. And that they were willing to."

Kel thought a few data cores were warming up in the room.

"Finally, they had the opportunity. They were not threatening the captain over the link; they stood right in front of us, near enough to close the distance from a handful of meters. If they had threatened us over the Alpha Station link, they could not have been an immediate threat. By being so close to us and demonstrating their intent and means to harm us, the opportunity was established by their presence."

Kel paused, seeing he still had their attention. "What's the first rule of a gunfight?" No one volunteered an answer.

"Have a gun!" Kel answered to a few laughs. Some of the tension in the room was relieved.

The captain raised his hand, attempting to get everyone back on tract as was the Captain's prerogative. "Tamford, what's the next step in our education then? We need to break and get everyone back to their duties and get ready for the children's afternoon schooling."

Kel answered with another smile. Then, "I think later we should evaluate your arms locker and start spending time on the other two elements—making sure everyone can manipulate the weapons correctly."

Kel spent the next several mornings of the trip with the adults and older teens in the cargo hold, familiarizing them with their weapons. They had a half dozen low-power hand blasters. He first showed everyone the basic features of the weapons and drilled into them how to remove the charge packs and dissipate any stored charge in a safe manner for practice.

Marksmanship fundamentals and actual target practice came next. It was a lot of material to cover in the four days they had remaining together before arriving at Meridian. He taught them how to correct malfunctions when they occurred and how to reload new charge packs efficiently. He covered basic principles of how the weapons incapacitated a threat most effectively, and tried to improve upon their mindset.

It's a start. The teenagers were more adept at the physical learning, while the adults had lots of questions about the circumstances that might lead to the need for self-defense. His answer was always the same. "You'll only regret the times you're not ready."

It was a start.

He spent afternoons with the kids, teaching basic med lessons, much as he'd review them with the team. He started by showing them diagrams of the human anatomy and tried to talk about how the body worked without scaring the younger children. Talking about bleeding, burns, and broken bones in a way that was not frightening to the children turned out to be an easy task. Living the life of spacers, the kids had grown up with the knowledge of the potential dangers that existed on a ship. In some ways, the kids had already grown up fast. More than a few had haunting remembrances of injuries and emergency situations they had seen during all their combined flight time between worlds.

During each session they discussed different injuries, how to evaluate an injured shipmate by inspection and touch as well as how to also use the portable analyzer and follow its prompts to treat any bodily insult. He showed them how to use the auto-tourniquets to stop bleeding and the nano-gels that could be applied to any wound.

On the last day he had the students pair up, one older and one younger, and tested them a group at a time, giving them a scenario and the injuries they were to treat on their simulated patient, Tara. At first, he felt guilty and hesitant that he made the simulated wounds so bloody with the practice aids. Tara assured him they'd be fine. By the end of the morning, Kel felt satisfied with even the youngest kid's abilities. Far from gun-shy, now they seemed almost eager for an emergency.

Kel spent every evening with the Yomiuris in their family quarters. It turned out the Yomiuri teens were older than Kel had estimated. Ochio was nineteen and was studying for his deck officer's exam. Tara was almost eighteen and was still deciding what her next level of certification would be.

"I'm thinking about studying more medical modules and maybe trying for a corpsman certification," she told Kel one evening.

"I think you'd do great," Kel encouraged. "Every ship needs a good medic, and no matter what else you do, it's knowledge that will let you help yourself and others the rest of your life."

On the last night before arriving at Meridian, Kel was turning in, just having packed his grav container he hoped for the last time until heading back to Victrix. The door chimed. He opened the compartment door, surprised to see Tara on the other side.

"Uh, hi, Tara," Kel stammered, unsure what to think.

"Hi, Tamford. I was just coming off watch and thought maybe you might want to, you know, talk for a while."

Talk. Her long hair was let down and framed her face. She seemed much older than the child he'd initially taken her for. She was perfect. Panic gripped him, a strange flutter in his chest. It wasn't her beauty, or the opportunity. It was how he'd been blindsided. He'd never in his wildest thoughts considered a moment like this on the journey.

"Wow, uh, I'm afraid I have to turn in, but thanks," Kel said in a rapid-fire expulsion as he stepped back and simultaneously keyed the door.

No way that just happened, Kel thought. A thousand mental images filled his head, most, but not all of them terrifying. Kel had done high altitude and oxygen deprivation training. He'd done micro-gravity combatives where some of the evolutions included slow depressurization of the compartment, simulating shipboard combat without armor or supplemental oxygen. The feeling of slow asphyxiation was horrible. Kel could easily imagine the sensation of his capillaries bursting and blood boiling before it froze, his eyeballs shattering as his lungs exploded while Tara's father, the captain, watched him through the porthole of the airlock, frowning as he ejected Kel from the ship into the black void of space.

07

Kel was ready to depart early the next day. He hoped no one on watch had taken notice of his late-night visitor. Surely there had to be a monitor observing the corridor outside Kel's stateroom. Nothing happened, but the potential for misinterpretation of the encounter worried him. He did not want to destroy any goodwill he'd built up with the Yomiuri family.

Once again, he was offered the honor of riding the jump seat for the descent through the atmosphere of Meridian. Kel had a great view of the mountainous continents and silvery seas below. He'd studied the geography and easily spotted Argolis, the largest continent. Spanning the equator and protected by oceans on three sides, it held the seat of their government, the Domestic Conclave, in the continental capital, Tiryns, where they would soon land.

During their holding orbit Kel contacted the Republic embassy and started the process of confirming his arrival as Tamford Nielsen with the office of the chief of the diplomatic mission, which in this case was the ambassador from the House of Reason. Kel read the man's biography; a career diplomat who'd spent a lifetime in appointments around the edge, separated by long periods on Liberinthine. There was very little of note about the man's record that stood out. To have received an appointment as an ambassador to a planet so far on the edge hinted about several possibilities. He was well connected enough to merit an ambassadorship, but was either seen as a potential challenger to a seat of power in the House of Reason and so was banished, or was incompetent, and had been sent someplace where he could do the least harm.

Either way, Kel tried to be invisible to the embassy functionaries when on missions like this. It was best to not gain the attention of the political class. It was unlikely that Kel would have much contact with the ambassador. But still, it was good to know who was in play. You can't enjoy the game without a program.

Landing at the spaceport in Tiryns was uneventful but nonetheless interesting to Kel, like every drop. Making planetfall with a viewscreen in front of you instead of in the back of a dropship made the event far more enjoyable. If there was no one waiting to shoot at you, so much the better. Incoming fire tended to focus one negatively. It was nice to just sit back and enjoy the show.

Tiryns was a large city with a half million inhabitants, making it the largest population center on Meridian. Not big by core standards, but big enough to conceal trouble. The spaceport sat several kilometers from the edge of the urban areas. Using his datalink he did a topographic evaluation of the capital on the way down, noting several areas that could represent military-type bases. None of them were particularly large.

Much of the surrounding area looked to be agricultural. The city sat landlocked near the geographic center of the continent, between two mountain ranges running north and south, effectively dividing the continent into thirds.

He still puzzled over the intelligence summaries describing the organization of the security forces. Some of it didn't make a lot of sense to Kel. It made him think the analysts didn't necessarily understand the material either. Hopefully things would be clearer once he got on the ground and could get some briefings directly from the embassy team.

Almost as they touched down softly, Kel received a message that he would be met at his ship by someone from the embassy. As the ship sat cooling and the ticking noises of contracting durasteel abated, it was time to say his goodbyes to the Yomiuri family. The overture was fading. It was time to get to work at last.

"I'll be moving directly to the trade mission to start finalizing the terms of the shipment with our local officials, and I or someone from the mission will be contacting you by the end of the day," Kel said, shaking the captain's hand at the boarding airlock. Kel would make it a priority to get this done and get the Yomiuris on their way as soon as possible. He would be glad to turn this task over to the trade mission officials and step away from playing the role.

Some alarm bell whistled for attention as one of the main drives began to vent across the landing pad, sending about great clouds of steam.

"I expect it will be a busy few days for you and the crew," he commiserated to the captain, who waited with him watching the hustle and buzz of the crew about their jobs.

"It will," the man replied with his usual stoic economy of words. Then, "I can't thank you enough for your help with, well... I just mean to say, thank you. I hope our paths cross again."

Kel didn't know if their paths ever would cross again, but he hoped so, too. Right at that moment he really did. They had treated him as family in the short time they'd spent together. It was hard to imagine he might never see them again. Easier to just tell himself he would. "I feel the same way. Thank you for making me feel welcome, Jim."

The enclosed staircase hovered into contact with the hatch, sealed, and settled into place on the dura-crete below.

Kel felt anticipation building as he bounced down to meet the hot surface. The captain called out over the groan of the cargo ramps lowering aft of them. "You're not really a trade representative, are you?" he yelled.

The captain pinned him with dark eyes long used to watching the instruments of interstellar crossing. Trying to find what was known and true to make another cross-ing between all those gossamer-connected worlds that was the galaxy as a whole.

"If I can be of help, let me know," was all Kel said, and made his way into the bright sun reflecting off the landing surface of the spaceport. And shortly thereafter he was gone, the work of preparing a freighter for another long haul began in earnest.

Kel waited only a few minutes before a ground speeder neared the ship. A grinning, dark man got out of the driver compartment and made his way over to Kel, waving as he walked. "I'm looking for Mr. Nielsen."

"You got him," replied Kel. "I'm Nielsen."

"Pen Abaascus, embassy operations officer. Let's get your gear loaded up and we'll get going." Kel had only the few small bags and his sealed grav container. They placed them in the front compartment then both hopped in the cab. "Let me get us out of the spaceport and we'll head into the city and go directly to the embassy if that's all right with you. We'll get you settled in your house later."

"Sure, sounds good. How far to the embassy?" asked Kel.

"Should only take us about thirty minutes this time of day. It can get pretty congested at peak hours. You couldn't exactly describe this place as efficient." The man laughed softly at his own joke. "When we get in, we can go to my office. I'm next to the regional security office, and I assumed you'd maybe want to start there?"

That sounded good to Kel. He didn't want to talk about his mission or identity out in the open.

"Sure, then I should probably check in with the trade mission." *And get to the military-political liaison*, Kel thought to himself.

"No problem."

Kel immediately switched to observer mode, gathering impressions about the capital and its world. As they made their way past hangers and terminals to the security gate, there were no bots out and about. Yet, things appeared clean and in decent repair. Nothing looked particularly modern in design, but nothing appeared dilapidated or neglected, either. Only a handful of smaller craft sat on the duracrete landing zone, nothing near the size of the *Callie*.

A high security fence surrounded the spaceport, and several security vehicles with rear-mounted heavy weapons cruised the interior perimeter of the large field.

At the exit, two gray uniformed and armed men waved them through on their side, while a vehicle coming from the other direction was halted at the checkpoint. Several of the gray uniformed troops surrounded the vehicle, examining the vehicle contents and running handheld scanners around the exterior of the vehicle. The driver sat looking uninterested in the whole production. The troops were armed with pistols and what looked like compact subguns.

"There've been several bombings in the past week around the capital," explained Abaascus as he pulled away from the checkpoint. "No injuries, just random kind of stuff. Kids with bombs, I guess. Nothing has happened at the spaceport. I think even these Meridian Eleftheria wackos think it's important enough to leave alone while they try to overthrow the twelve families, or whatever it is exactly that they're trying to accomplish."

"Meridian Eleftheria?" Kel asked.

"Yeah. There's graffiti all around the university area, and they seem to take credit for just about every bombing or old lady's missing pet on the planet. Whenever there's a student protest, there's always signs for them. They kind of appeared on the scene in the last few months, and man, the number of bombings has jumped since then. No power disruptions here in the capital, but some of the coastal cities have suffered a bit."

This was important information. Information that was completely lacking from his area study and the most recent intelligence summaries he shipped out with. He knew he'd be standing under a waterfall of information the next several days, trying to get oriented.

It was time to soak all that up.

They made their way to a major thoroughfare leading into the center of the city. The road had two lanes and was separated by a central green section with trees and landscaping. Other roads led into and off the main highway, with drivers accelerating and decelerating to avoid collision with other vehicles making unexpected turns on and off the faster moving road. There was a mix of some repulsor vehicles with a larger proportion of wheeled vehicles of all shapes, colors, and sizes.

Even at major intersections there didn't seem to be signals to control the flow of traffic. Several times Kel was certain he was about to see a collision when at the last second the drivers swerved to avoid a crash.

Noting Kel's attention to the chaos on the road all around them, his driver commented, "Yeah, it's a little crazy driving around here. It's best to drive like they do—point your vehicle where you want to go and accelerate. You'll get used to it."

Larger intersections had roundabout traffic circles with a raised central hub where huge spreading branches and thick leaves topped tall trees with bare trunks. Nearby, several green uniformed officials stood beside a parked official vehicle. As they drove around the circle, Kel could see on the side of the vehicle a language he could not read below an emblem, and above it the words *Transit Police*, in Standard.

The sidewalks and public areas teemed with people moving about their daily business. The residents appeared healthy and active. Lots of preschool children with their mothers and people interacting with what must be their neighbors, laughing or arguing. Most were uniformly dark, like the olive-brown color many spacers get from exposure to radiation from too much hull-time on a ship.

They all had dark hair to match their complexions. Kel hadn't seen one blond head the entire drive so far. With Kel's sandy hair he thought it might be worth considering a bio-cosmetic color change. It would make him stand out less. And that was easily done.

As they slowed near a congested area, Kel spotted a small gathering in front of a mercantile center. Another official vehicle with different coloration and an emblem on the side was parked on the sidewalk as two blue uniformed officials armed with pistols talked with an agitated older gentleman, maybe the storeowner Kel guessed. The older man gesticulated wildly and the officials calmly listened. Kel couldn't read the words over the emblem on the vehicle for the angle at which it sat as they drove by.

"I've seen, like, three different types of security forces since I've been on the ground," Kel noted. "What's the story with that?"

Abaascus kept his eyes on the road as he explained. "Yeah, there's three basic types of cop here on Meridian. There're the Transit Police, the guys in the green uniforms. They seem to have responsibility pretty much like the name suggests. They maintain order on the roads, do some checkpoint security on the highways as well.

"Then there's the House Police, the guys in the blue uniforms. They do property crimes and some crimes against persons stuff.

"Then there's the National Police. They were the guys manning the spaceport in the gray uniforms. They are an entirely different deal. If you're just a regular guy and get mugged, the House Police are who you go to. If you're related to one of the Twelve Families and anything happens to you, bam, straight to the National Police you go."

His explanation paused as he put both hands on the controller to jog sharply to avoid a collision, then continued without commentary on the incident.

"They seem to be the guys who handle the internal security and have more of a paramilitary function, I guess you'd say. They do investigations, and they take over from Transit or House on anything major. The system's confusing, but it seems to work for them," he added while making another jog around a slower vehicle.

"What about a standing military presence? I read about their planetary army, but there wasn't a lot of organizational detail." Kel was still in the dark after reading everything available from the intel summaries. He was prepared to work with anybody, but there were significant differences between working with cops and working with the military.

"Yeah, they've got an army," answered Abaascus. "It isn't very big. The guys from the military-political section will have more to tell you, I'm sure. So will our RSO. All I can say is I rarely see any of their planetary militia guys around."

There was a pause as they came to another roundabout and Abaascus navigated them through the chaos of vehicles crossing multiple lanes through the radiused turn. "Truth is, the Families really do run everything here. That's what I've observed. There're different laws for the regular folks than the aristocrats. Family connections here mean everything.

"The National Police is run by the Kyrgiakos, the patron family of Argolis, and probably the most powerful on Meridian. There're two other prominent families on Argolis, but the Kyrgiakos dominate the center of the continent and control most of the industry and agriculture.

They most definitely run Tiryns," he said while looking at Kel and raising his eyebrows to make the point.

Kel continued to draw on his training as a critical observer as they made their way through the capital. He did not get the impression that this was a city under siege. It looked like these people were out living their lives and going about their usual daily activities, regardless of any class struggles supposedly grinding things to a halt.

"The local cuisine here is superb compared to most places I've been posted. I can show you some of the better restaurants in the clear zones where you can get an excellent meal. Some of them aren't too far from the university and at lunchtime the view ain't too bad, if you know what I mean. I don't go over there much since the student protests have gotten routine. Almost every day now it seems."

Kel nodded. "How long have you been on planet?"

"About two years. I'm stationed here with my wife who works at the embassy in the management office. She's the one you can thank when you see your quarters. We're both career ex-planetary diplo-corps. We met in the service. It was a nice, quiet posting the first year or so. Now... here's our turn." Abaascus looked over his shoulder and raced their vehicle into a small gap between two vehicles, forcing his way between them, then quickly darting onto a side street.

They slowed to approach an open area between several converging blocks of buildings revealing the embassy compound. The three-story central building had its façade covered by a shimmering lattice of mesh hanging from the flat roof encompassing all sides of the building. On one side Kel could see where a portion of the façade between windowed floors was charred and pocked. Blaster fire.

"Yeah, that happened last month," Abaascus said, catching Kel's look. "No one was injured, but putting up that field was expensive to get done quickly. Local contractors, you know?"

The protective energy field would be somewhat effective at dissipating weak particle energy weapons but would never defeat anything military-grade. The area study had emphasized that Meridian had low-grade military technology. The damage had to be from some repurposed industrial particle beam cutter, improvised and used expediently by the attackers.

"If they're all pissed off at the Twelve Families, how is attacking the Republic embassy going to get them help reforming their crappy system? Makes no sense. I can understand why they're cracking down harder on these crazies," the man finished as they pulled up to the entrance of a walled compound.

The gate slid open slowly in response to their halt, and a black-uniformed local peered out at them. The gate opened wider and three of the black-uniforms came out to scan the vehicle's exterior. Then the guard on the driver's side smiled and waved them through.

There were so many blatantly obvious errors in their security procedures—allowing a vehicle to approach the exterior embassy compound so closely before inspection being one—that Kel began a mental checklist of what he would do to improve the physical security and procedures of the entrance checkpoint. He'd likely need to scrap the whole thing and start over.

He'd mention it to the RSO.

They pulled into an open parking space between the two dozen assorted vehicles parked inside the walled compound and got out. "Let's leave your stuff in the speeder," Abaascus said. "I'll be taking you to your quarters later when you're done here for the day."

Several of the black-uniforms milled about the open parking area, the entrance to the flat building at the end of a walk lined by topiary. *The typical touches of the upper crust at the expense of the taxpayer,* he mused. A crude fence ran atop the walls and parapets of the surrounding buildings, hasty attempts to improve the physical security of the compound. All ineffective by his first impression.

Kel followed Abaascus to an office marked *Operation and Management* where his host gestured to a chair for Kel to drop his small bag.

"Let's go across the hall and I'll introduce you to the RSO. You'll like Bell. He's a good guy."

They walked across the hall and through another small administrative office to a door marked *Regional Security Office.* The door was open and the room dimly lit. A small man sat behind a desk studying his datapad, looking up as Abaascus knocked on the open door. "Hey Bell, got a second? Someone new I want you to meet."

The thin man rose from behind the desk, extending his hand as Kel stepped through the threshold into the small office. "Bell Lee, I'm the RSO, pleased to meet you."

Finally, time to get to work, Kel thought as he met the man's hand and introduced himself, properly for the first time in too long. "Kel Turner, glad to meet you, too." It was nice to be able to drop his cover name at last. They knew who he was and where he was from. It was always a relief to be with professionals and not have to do the awkward, "introduce yourself without really saying where you're from," kind of thing. They knew who he was. Sort of.

"Come on in, guys, and close the door," Bell said. There was one chair and he gestured Kel to it while Abaascus remained standing. "Get you something, Kel?" Kel appreciated the gesture but he was ready to get to work.

"No, I'm good, but thank you."

Bell hesitated a moment. "This is my first time working with one of you guys. If there's anything I can do to help, then that's what I'm here for."

They spent the next half hour answering Kel's questions about recent events. Bell mimicked Pen's opinion that until a year ago things had been peaceful. The occasional act of political violence or bombing against state institutions had been known to happen, but the frequency had skyrocketed in the last few months. The attack on the embassy happened a month ago. Sporadic small arms fire had peppered the main high-rise on the compound, followed by the blaster bolt that had damaged the façade. There was no attempt at an assault on the compound.

"I didn't notice any Marine presence." Kel had already known that there were no Marines assigned to the small Republic mission. It was a tactic, asking a question you already knew the answer to. It took advantage of a person's vanity that they knew something you didn't and got a subject talking. Right now, everyone he met was a subject for questioning.

"No. We use local contractors for security. They're mostly ex-Meridian police or militia. The ambassador's protective detail is former National Police. Decent guys. Maybe we can convince you to spend some time with us?" Kel would accept the invitation. Security here was poor, but it would be an error to think he was looking at the cause of it. Most of the time, the institutional inertia of the diplomatic corps was to never want to appear threatening or potentially hostile in any way to the host planet. When the security situation degenerated, the diplomats were satisfied with half measures and what amounted to the ostensible presence of physical security rather than a truly effective plan for prevention and protection. Kel imagined the uphill battle the RSO was likely waging regarding such issues.

"Absolutely. Anything to help. I imagine it's been a one-man show to get security up to speed around here?" Kel said.

Bell looked relieved. Someone finally understood him. It was that look. And Kel had seen it before. "I knew you guys were cool," he said referring to Legion Dark Ops, without explicitly summoning the demon. "But that was a quick study. Yeah, the ambassador and the military-political guys think some more uniformed guards and a little tanglewire are all we need. No one got hurt in the last attack, right? So, let's not overreact. We don't want to offend the Meridians. The ambassador even thinks if we upgraded security too much that it would only invite more attacks. That kinda guy, if you read what I'm saying? I'm not working alone, though. Pen here has been a great help and is the fella who actually makes the construction and the physical improvements happen."

Abaascus chimed in, "Hey man, my wife works here, too. I'm invested in getting this place safer in a huge way."

Bell spoke with care to not spook Kel by asking too much at their first meeting. "We've got more improvements planned. Maybe I can pick your brain about those, too?"

Kel was glad to. He understood only too well the nature of the problem the RSO was facing, trying to make the diplomats understand the potential threats developing on Meridian.

They chatted more and Kel got better informed about the situation on the planet and the capital. It was always that way. You could only read so much. Then you had to listen. And after that you had to go see for yourself. After another half-hour Kel brought it to a close. "I think I'd better check in with the military-political section and let them know I'm on the ground. I also need to check in with the trade minister and get some things officially turned over." He shook Bell's hand again and promised to see him later.

Abaascus escorted him through the institutional corridors, past bustling offices on the ground floor to the multi-story building housing the diplomatic staff. There was a sudden demarcation in the décor and appearance of the interior. A polished white stone with glimmering crystal flecks tiled the corridors, reflecting the indirect lighting concealed along the edges of the ceiling. Art from around the Republic's worlds decorated the walls, including holo-portraits of Liberinthine political figures past and present.

Pen led him to a lift where they continued up to the next floor and through a door which required Pen's bio-signature to open. Beyond that, a smaller lobby with several secretaries, all with blonde hair, sat at a large reception desk. Pen waved to one as he moved them forward.

"Karin, this is Mr. Turner, just arrived and here to report to Counselor Sun. Kel, I'll leave you to it. Bounce me if you need me to guide you around. I'll just be hanging loose in my office." Abaascus moved closer to Kel's left ear and whispered, "I'm sure you've endured worse." Kel had dealt with the political class on every one of these types of missions. He had a good idea what to expect next.

The secretary escorted him through another signature-accessed door to stand in yet another small office where a thin, twitchy man in a dark suit stood by the side of his desk, hands folded in front of him, standing between Kel and an open doorway.

"I'm Mr. Gravin, *Chief* Minister Sun's private secretary. The *chief* minister will see you now. Follow me please." The way he continued to emphasize *chief* Kel knew was meant to place him at a position of disadvantage. *It's not more impressive than general or colonel to me, buddy. In fact, team sergeant is a tougher title to earn.*

Behind a large ornate desk sat the minister. He was a portly, late middle-aged man with thinning hair and an expression that Kel thought reminded him of faces he'd seen in horror holovids. The expression he wore was not human. Maybe he'd learned the mannerism from dealing with too many alien races. His eyelids were open abnormally wide, and Kel did not see the man blink.

"Please have a seat. That will be all, Gravin. The door please," he said as his private secretary left the stately room. Many pieces of high-end art decorated the walls, and several sculptures stood near the bank of windows overlooking a part of the city, the shimmer of the protective screen just beyond.

"Kel Turner, sir, reporting on arrival from—"

Before Kel could continue the man cut him off.

"My title is Chief Minister. I've worked very hard for that title and believe I am due the courtesy of you using it."

Kel waited for the man to continue. He did.

"I don't like the Legion and I especially have no use for Dark Ops." His mouth pinched like the words left a sour taste. "I don't even know why you are here. The situation on Meridian is a political crisis, one which we have well in hand. Not a military one."

Here it comes, Kel thought, *the "I see in color, you see in black and white" speech.*

"The elite of the Ex-Planetary Service like myself have trained for decades at the finest schools in the galaxy. I could be a department head of any university on Liberinthine just for the asking. I report directly to the House of Reason and my name has been considered for senator many times.

"The nuances of the situation on this planet are simply beyond your grasp, Legionnaire. I have spent three years here advancing the cause of the Republic and the House of Reason at great personal cost. I am sure they have excellent reasons for sending someone like you to this mission, but," and now he rose to his feet with some difficulty, "I will *not* tolerate any *outlandish* behavior or barbarous attempts to *ruin* the diplomatic atmosphere we have established. I simply will not."

The man collapsed back in his chair, flushed.

Kel didn't react. Being a Dark Operator meant being invisible. When working these types of missions, it was always best to get the mission accomplished in the most silent, professional manner possible. Self-aggrandizement was a sin in DO. Kel had been taught the best way to maintain the confidence of his leadership was to make as few waves with the political class as possible while going about your business with efficiency and extreme lethality on demand. This was likely going to be the exception to Kel's usual way of starting a mission.

Kel had been sitting at attention, a calm look held on his face during the chief minister's brow-beating. Now he put on his murder face.

His voice dropped low and hard, his countenance cold as En Shakar. "Chief Minister..." Kel rose to his full height, his hands now on the man's desk, leaning toward the fat man. He spoke softly. This forced the listener to be attentive. "I also work for the House of Reason."

He let that sink in.

"Senator VanderLoot expressed extreme interest in your section's role in the current situation. He is most anxiously awaiting my involvement in the matter."

The man's florid face drained of color.

Kel turned and strode toward the door, then paused. "I will endeavor to make my presence as unobtrusive as possible. I hope when my mission here is over that I may report to the Planetary Affairs Council your personal... spirit of cooperation?"

Kel didn't wait for the minister to speak. He just made his way past the private secretary and to the outer lobby.

Screw him. Kel had a difficult, potentially dangerous job to do here, and if he was not going to be able to count on the embassy for full support, he'd fight back now instead of later when he might not have the time to have a pissing contest. Playing hardball had been a minimal risk. Kel knew the chain of command as well as the structure of the House of Reason, and knew who Senator VanderLoot was as head of the Planetary Security Council. He was also equally sure the senator had no idea who Kel was. Dropping his name was a gamble, but a calculated one at that. And, it was a small one. From the edge the minister would have no rapid ability to contact Liberinthine, and likely the grand senator couldn't care less about some diplomat posted to the ass-end of nowhere.

So why not roll some dice and maybe put up a win?

Kel also understood how to see things from the minister's perspective. A mid-twenty-something muscle-head who is generally responsible for breaking the enemies' expensive things and stacking bodies could be perceived as having only one mode: kill.

After all, we are called kill teams. No one outside of DO knew that, though. Dark Ops was a classified organization. While their existence was known in some circles, little about them, their size, or their organizational structure was public information. It irked Kel that the minister prejudged him and did not give him a chance to demonstrate his quiet professionalism.

The relation between the Legion and the political class was complicated. Sun had to be aware what that relationship was. The Legion had the right—the responsibility, really—to utilize Article Nineteen to check a true abuse of power by the House of Reason, and hold a coup. At some level, the chief minister should have wanted to avoid a hostile relationship with the Legion, much less DO. Why make enemies where they didn't exist?

He was about to make his way to the lift when a disarmingly friendly middle-aged woman with a huge smile walked toward Kel and extended her hand. "Are you Mr. Turner? Pen called me and said you were in the section. I'm Jacee Eller, I'm first secretary of the military-political section. Why don't you follow me and we'll go sit down and have a kaff?" Her kind manner put Kel at ease, especially after the hostile few minutes he'd just had. Abrupt contrasts between moments of sudden violence followed by the need to refocus and adopt a new mental posture were common in Kel's life. He felt grateful for this opportunity to reset over a hot cup of kaff.

Jacee made small talk, inquiring about his trip, as she led him to a small alcove and poured them both a cup. A moment later, sitting across from each other in two comfortable chairs she got down to business.

"So, did Sun make an ass out of himself or was he a good boy today?"

Kel screwed on a smile. "The former, I'm afraid."

Jacee laughed. She had shoulder-length salt and pepper hair, and homey curves. "Don't take it personally. He's been left out on the edge a long time. He tends to exaggerate his importance. He's harmless, but I wouldn't go out of my way to aggravate him."

That was not his intent, he assured her. "I hope to be as invisible as possible while I'm here. In fact, I doubt I'll even be on the embassy grounds much once I get settled and can start working."

Kel looked about the office. Its décor told Kel much about its occupant. Framed holo-images of alien settings, Jacee posed with faces from around the galaxy hung on the walls. Multiple plaques memorialized her accomplishments, and small mementos from different cultures decorated the desk between stacks of chips and several datapads. Jacee had likely been a diplomat for decades, serving the Republic on worlds like this her entire career. Kel's attention was drawn to a small photo of her and a legionnaire wearing a colonel's insignia on his dress blacks. She looked happy in the picture.

"Mr. Turner, I'm actually going to serve as your liaison here—"

"Please, call me Kel."

"And I'm just Jacee, Kel." She smiled broadly again. "I've done this with DO before. The situation here has changed dramatically in the last six months. I'll get you up to speed with what I think is relevant, and then we'll plan out the week to get you out and about and acquainted with the local players."

They spent the next hour talking, with Kel mainly listening and occasionally asking questions. Jacee described the Meridian Eleftheria as a domestic resistance group whose base seemed to be composed of the young student population. They had only recently announced their existence after several successful bombings of capitals around the planet.

Between the ride in from the spaceport and his introduction to Bell, and now Jacee, he had more useful information than he'd built up from studying the whole way here. *But that's how it usually is*, Kel thought.

Jacee concluded their meeting by telling him she'd bounce him later with an itinerary after she'd made some calls.

In the lobby, Kel found Pen waiting for him.

"You mentioned you wanted to go to Trade before we got you settled in?" Pen said. "Let's do that now."

Kel met the trade minister, a true professional. He had the contract Kel had bounced him from orbit and assured Kel his local agents would be working to fulfill its terms and get the *Callie*'s hold topped off and on her way.

"This actually comes at a fortuitous time," he told Kel. "The last major shipment off Meridian had buyers bidding on the contents before the shipment ever reached Liberinthine. The local warehouses and wholesalers are predicting a rising demand in export, and the result has been increased production around the planet. Our economy is expanding rapidly, and the anticipation has the suppliers and wholesalers anxious as they step up their productivity. Our projections are showing more goods than we have off-planet carriers."

That was great news, thought Kel to himself. The Yomiuri family had been kind to him, and he was concerned about their finances. He'd feel great about having a hand in improving their quality of life.

"Minister, I need some help and don't know where to start." Kel explained in broad detail the situation. "I consumed many of their supplies and they were already running on a tight budget when I joined them. How do I help replenish their stores to make up for their inconvenience? I don't know anything about merchant ships or shipping." The minister used his link and one of his assistants came to the office to retrieve Kel.

The trade assistant heard Kel out in his office and had a suggestion. "There's a ship's chandlery near the spaceport. It would be a straightforward matter to outfit your friends with local goods for their mess. They usually have recommended packages depending on the crew size, duration of the voyage, how fancy you want the food, and the like. I'm Ramer. If you need something else, let me know." He bounced Kel the contact and Kel thanked him and left. His plan was to surprise the Yomiuri family with the delivered goods to further thank them for their hospitality. Yes, Kel had gotten them out of a tight spot and had given them additional help by training them, but he felt close to them and also a little sorry for them, too. If he could do something kind for them, he'd like to.

As part of the captain's contract, the captain had the right to use some of the cargo for crew provisions. Kel also knew that Captain Yomiuri would most likely not do so. They would want to maximize the potential profit of whatever would be delivered for auction at the final destination, no matter how miniscule a portion of the goods it turned out to be they would use. He'd seen they were that frugal.

On the way out of the Trade section, another office door opened and a fit gentleman with gray at his temples stood in its doorway. He nodded at Kel with pursed lips and Kel returned the gesture, the man turning into his office. Kel had seen multiple large holo-screen projections running on all the walls save one, where a physical map of the planet was projected. The door said *Trade Analysis* beside the bio-key pad. Kel stored this information for later use.

Kel found his way back to the embassy operations office where Pen Abaascus sat at his desk. "Hey, it's near quitting time, partner. Ready to see where you're going to lay your head?" Kel agreed it was a good time to get settled. He'd had a productive first day at the embassy and had a lot of preparation to do. He also was starting to feel hungry.

"Oh, can we stop by and see Bell for a second on the way out?"

They went across the hall and found Bell ready to leave as well.

"Bell—weapons. I have my basics, but I'll need a rifle and a basic load-out."

"That's no problem. Do you need it right now or can you get by until tomorrow?"

Kel assured him tomorrow would be fine.

Pen drove them several miles up into the shallow hills. The increasingly glitzy residential buildings indicated a steep rise in the economic indicators for the area. Some of the homes occupied entire city blocks, surrounded by their own walled and tall-hedged enclosures, with gates blocking their drives. Others seemed to contain multiple houses in a compound designed for extended family living. Many of the residences had armed guards, some uniformed, some in local dress, milling about the entrances.

The wealthy were taking security seriously.

"They call this area the Hills," noted Abaascus over the straining engine noise as they climbed up twists and turns alongside armored compounds. "It's where the upper crust and the pols in Tiryns tend to live. Welcome to the elite, my friend."

Pen pulled up to one of these walled residences, the adobe walls partially obscured by the tall, bushy-needled trees surrounding them. At the double gate stood a black-uniformed guard, the same as Kel had seen at the embassy. Pen pulled up and lowered the window as the guard looked in.

"Hello, Mister Pen. Coming in?" the guard asked in lightly accented Standard.

"Yup. This is Mister Kel, the new resident."

Kel leaned forward and smiled.

"Okay, we've got him on the list." The guard signaled the gate to open and Pen drove them into a stone-paved courtyard with several speeders parked in a corner shaded by large trees.

"Come on and I'll show you around!" Pen said, not trying to hide his enthusiasm.

A covered walk between flower beds led into a courtyard surrounded by three two-story houses and a single-story central building adjoining two of the houses. The roofs were tiled and ornate; flowering vines grew up the sides of the light earth-colored walls. A portion of the courtyard was sunken, and a small pond and waterfall filled one side.

"See why we call your new digs 'the palace'? Yours is the one on the far left. The other two with the common space adjoining are occupied by a guy from the communications center, a Republic Army guy, and a guy from the trade mission, Ramer, I think you met him today. Let's go introduce you to the house staff."

Pen led the way into the single-story building where there was a spacious sitting area with plush lounging furniture, and an adjoining dining area with a table large enough to seat eight or more people.

Standing at the entrance to the kitchen was a short, plump, dark-haired woman with a kindly look about her. "Eirene, this is Mister Kel. He's the new resident I told you would be arriving. Eirene is the cook. She makes three meals a day for you guys but leaves after the noon meal every sixth day, which they call Kronos, and doesn't return until breakfast the start of the next week, Luna. There's also a pair of housekeepers Eirene will introduce you to. They take that same day-and-a-half off to spend with their families, so you're on your own for meals and the like when they're off."

"Dinner een one hour, Meester Kel," Eirene erupted, smiling.

The apartment was impressive. The ground floor contained a living room and small kitchen and dining area. On the upper floor was a huge master suite with large closets and a bathroom with an ornately carved local stone tub and shower.

"Hang loose and I'll grab your stuff. No worries," Pen said without waiting for Kel to object.

Kel's head swam a little. This was what most guys were jealous of when they knew a DO teammate was going on a planetary security mission. Living with diplomats always meant first-class living. Even the lowliest member of the diplomatic corps lived in luxury, all paid for by the good citizens of the Republic. Diplomatic missions on any developed world, especially a human world, secured local housing and selected those that tended to be like this one: extravagant. Citing the need for security they preferred to contract housing with walls and privacy.

Kel was impressed. Previously he'd had one sweet mission where the living was pretty good whenever he wasn't in the sticks doing KTF stuff with the locals. He had been in the field for weeks at a time but had enjoyed the time back at the house they set up for him. He shared it with several other DO guys working similar stints, but only one or two guys used the place at the same time. This was a whole new level of breakball-superstar living. He'd take holos of the place to show Poul and Tem when he got back, otherwise they'd never believe him. He could imagine them eating their livers out, howling in jealousy when he showed them the opulent design and grand size of the arranged housing.

Pen brought his stuff to the entrance of Kel's apartment and told Kel he'd see him in the morning. "I'll swing by after breakfast and get you. One of the vehicles parked outside is for you, but why don't we wait until tomorrow to get that sorted out, okay?" Kel had no objections.

As Kel unpacked, he tried to concentrate on getting ready for the challenges ahead, but between his hunger and the events of the day, followed by winning the interstellar lottery that was living in this house, he decided to shelve any other preparations until tomorrow.

He met his housemates already sitting at the dining table where an empty place setting awaited him. He recognized Ramer from the Trade office and they shook hands again. "I thought we might be sharing the palace together but didn't want to say anything in case you had other plans. Kel, this is Gren Matson, he runs the communications center at the embassy." Soon Eirene brought bowl after bowl of food to the table, and motioned for the men to start serving themselves.

"I gotta say," Gren began, "I've been a lot of places. What Meridian might lack in up-to-date tech, they make up for in their food. And there's some mighty fine companionship to be had around here." Laughing, the man winked at Kel.

Kel smiled but didn't reply. He had a mission to perform and wasn't thinking about entertainment. But as a legionnaire, good food combined with large portions did more for his morale than any long-haired companion might.

Kel dug in. The meat was broiled to perfection, falling off the bone when Kel cut into it. There were steaming piles of sliced sweet root, and a mix of several vegetables lightly sautéed, some with a sweet taste, others with a deep, earthy flavor. Kel ate several plates and his appetite gained the attention of his dinner companions as well as Eirene as she came to check on them.

"You big strong boy, you eat like real man," she said. "You like Mama Eirene cooking? I gonna cook for you till we find you good Argolis wife, maybe Peloponnese girl. You like?"

Kel laughed out loud as did the two other men. "No, Mama Eirene. I only want to eat your cooking." The woman laughed loudly as she slapped him on the shoulder.

"Ooh, you hard like stone!" She said something in her local tongue then, "Too much work all the time. I gonna fatten you up." With that she departed for the kitchen and Kel could hear her singing in the kitchen.

After saying his goodnights, Kel went to his quarters and collapsed on the giant bed, still dressed. He'd only meant to rest his eyes.

Boom!

A deep rumble jolted him awake in the night. The explosion had not been close, his subconscious told him. No need to be alarmed or come up ready for action. Nonetheless, he grabbed his pistol as he rose up from the grand bed he'd been sound asleep on, returning it back to its holster under his shirt.

There was a small balcony overlooking the courtyard. He couldn't see anything from this vantage point. He needed a better view. The balcony wall was decorated with small protruding stones and flowering vines clinging to the estate's walls. He had enough ambient light to identify a route and scaled the wall the three meters to reach the low pitched roof, easing himself up over the edge as he trod lightly on the crimson clay tiles.

On the roof's peak, he scanned the horizon. Toward the city center he could see a small fire and smoke rising from a lighted area, faint sirens wailed in the distance. Of all things, what he felt was relief. Relief, and gratitude. He had a mission. There was a fight coming.

You think this is the real deal? Setting off bombs around civilians? He said to an unseen foe. *I'm going to show you what real is.*

FLASHBACK

First, You Gotta Win the Fight
Antione

"Rapier one, how copy?" Sung had been busy registering targets for the Talons and communicating with the lead pilot. We'd identified a dozen suspicious sites from the ground that evaded detection by the intel analysts in orbit and were even missed by the drone reconnaissance before the invasion. Between our two vantages, we also found three mobile ground to air defense pods concealed by revetments of stacked shipping containers and stealth netting. There is no substitute for eyes on the ground.

A new voice in our buckets. "Warhammer three, we are locked. Inbound. ETA four minutes." We find a depression on the reverse slope, still overlooking the field. Shuck reports his team has done the same from the eastern side. I check on the team. There isn't time to dig graves. Everyone finds a bit of cover. The closest registered target is only three hundred meters away. Definitely danger close. If the Talon crews are good, it won't be an issue. But even a good crew can make a mistake if they're flying evasively, trying to avoid ground fire. It won't be the blaster cannons that will get us, it'll be an errant 200-kilo plasma bomb. Sometimes the guidance AIs get confused. I knew everyone felt the same as I did, though. There was no way we were going to miss the show.

I am not disappointed.

Two pairs of Talons come in from our backs. No sooner am I aware they're overhead than the field and the surrounding slopes ignite in a supernova. The incongruity of how it occurs is dreamlike. The Talons cruise at a reduced speed, so slow it looks like you could hit them with rocks. The rate of fire from the cannons' controlled bursts in a dozen different azimuths happens in the blink of an eye, and repeats in a never-ending light show as the birds fly their track across the field. The plasma bombs strike select buildings at the end of the run, just before the birds break into a high speed bank and disappear at the velocity I'm accustomed to seeing them fly at. It's instantaneous destruction at its most precise.

"Warhammer three, run complete. Climbing to angels-five and staying on station," the lead pilot tells Sung. The Talons would be circling high above, on call for close air support, waiting to rain more death. Held in abeyance. The airspace over the field would soon be occupied by another.

"Roger, Rapier One. Excellent effect on all targets. Stand by for on-call CAS acknowledged." Sung breaks comms with the pilots. I'm listening on the command channel the same as he is. There's been a constant buzz over L-Comm, almost impossible to keep up with, but through the roaring waterfall of voices we all know what's coming next. Our drop zone beacons show an active link with the inbound aircraft. "Alright, Alpha, Bravo," Sung says. "Time to move up and get eyes out. Anyone still down there, we're all the company has to keep them suppressed. Let's do it."

I'm already on my feet. "Alpha, up. On me." I take off. I already planned our route and the team knows what I expect of them. There's a trail leading to where more high ground gives a better view along the west slope about 500 meters ahead. It's not time for a deliberate patrol. It's time to run like death is on our heels. The terrain is rough and I feel my ankles and knees grind as I pound the earth, each footfall reflecting the unyielding ground back to me as I keep up my dead run.

"They're on track," Sung says, panting. I know he's somewhere behind me. Finally, I reach the narrow plateau below the military ridge I'd been eyeing. I want to look back for the Goshawks, but won't tear myself away from my task as I throw my body prone and scan over my rifle below me. The spot I picked is good. We're high enough to see well. We're farther up the field, but nowhere near the main port where one of the hangars burns wildly.

I key up my HUD and try some different spectral combos as I search likely spots for a team of militia to be hiding with a heavy blaster, ready to shoot our guys as they exit the birds. My lungs burn like the fires around the field, but through the shifting flames and their shadows I spot nothing moving. My own breathing deafens me.

"The Talons creamed 'em," someone says over the team channel. Howard? "If they were smart, they hightailed it out of there and into a deep hole a long time ago." Yamazuki? "Stay on task gentlemen," I remind them. "Eyes out." Sergeant Sung drops beside me. "They're here."

We all look south. It's impossible not to.

I'd been monitoring the launch of the Goshawks over the command channel, a perk of being a squad leader. I knew they'd been dropping out of orbit from the time we first got our beacons aimed at the spacefield. I'm not ashamed to admit I wouldn't trade places with the rest of the company. Orbital freefall is a wild ride. I don't mind heights or the openness of space, so I find space diving liberating. It's tight spaces I hate. Crammed into the back of a 64-passenger Goshawk is a suffocating feeling, even in armor. The autocanopies are small and tight on your back but just large enough to keep you from being able to sit upright. Instead, everyone rests on the carry-alls attached to their chest. You're literally wedged in one at a time by the loadmasters, facing the fuselage jump doors, packed so tight that it's only your armor that prevents injury.

The Goshawks are nothing more than flying cans full of vacuum-packed leejes whose purpose is to race them to battle under eye melting G-forces and deposit them like hail stones from a hundred and fifty meters above the target. It's the absolute fastest way to put legionnaires on the ground, immediately ready to fight. I disliked it immensely.

The two birds carrying the rest of the company would have raced down into the atmosphere at speeds rivaling a blaster bolt. If that wasn't enough to make you hope your nausea nanoimplant was up to date, the bucking, nap of the earth flight to the drop zone would make your insides feel like paste. What I saw now was the only part of the flight a jumper looked forward to. I always prayed to Oba for the arrival of that final sharp climb as you popped up violently, levelling off as the doors retracted and the feeling of weightlessness rewarded us as we jumped from the coffin of the Goshawk.

The lead Goshawk just popped over the hills and levelled off as it slows and passes in front of our position. The jump doors are fully retracted and leejes pour from both sides of the craft, emptying from tail to nose. Canopies billow to full inflation for a moment before square panels open and close in a pattern of flickering tiles, steering the suspended jumper straight down. Trailing behind and slightly higher, the second Goshawk with its absurdly elongated shape and wings fully extended drops its payload, littering more leejes into the air.

I unconsciously count as the first of the jumpers exit. By the time you exit and reach 'five-one-thousand' in your head, if the repulsor assist pack on the parachute container doesn't fire to give you that critical lift, you'll never remember you didn't reach 'six-one-thousand'. Six seconds. Six seconds from the time you jump until you're on the ground. When it's you under that canopy, six seconds is all the time that exists in the universe.

We're all silent as we watch. I felt the rush as though I were with them, the sensations of an autojump as familiar as the feeling of air in my lungs. "Time to go," Sung said. "They may need CAS and it's still our job to support them." Across from us, Shuck's team is already on the move.

Trumbull takes point as we form a loose wedge to patrol along the slope. Below us, the company is formed into platoons and moving to contact, spread out across the field in a travelling formation. The mounted platoon should be landing soon with the fast attack vehicles and Mk 2 heavy blasters. There is no fighting. Yet. "Turner," Sung said from behind me. "Let's make for that ridge with the comm tower. It'll give us the best view." Another half-klick ahead is a weather sensor site and what was probably a hypercomm generator. Or what's left of it. We'd made that a target just in case any militia were left on site guarding the communications relay. It was a legitimate target. As we got closer, the wreckage proved how accurate the Talons' gun run had been. Twisted durasteel and melted plasticrete is all that's left of the site.

I have D'antonio and Yamazaki. Trumbull went with Sung and the rest as we split up to clear around the site. The blockhouse is slagged. It was too small to be anything but a housing for equipment, not a bunker for troops. From the head of the landing field there's blaster fire. A lot of it. "They've made contact," Shuck says from somewhere across the spacefield. "Small arms fire's coming at them from the port management section." I guess that should have gotten a plasma bomb as well.

"If you can see it, you direct the CAS for a gun run," Sung tells him. I stay quiet. I know he's busy, breaking into the company net to coordinate with the closest unit on the ground before he hands the ball over to Shuck. Sporadic fire breaks out from somewhere else on the field below. I can see only reflections of blaster bolts off one of the hangars in the distance. I can't pinpoint where it's coming from. The nearest elements of the company are still too far away for it to be much of a threat to them. The defenders sprang their ambush too early.

Everything happens at once. A bolt whizzes past me from my left and I drop as more fly overhead. D'antonio and Yamazaki crawl next to me as we return fire in the general direction. I wiggle behind a craggy projection for a little cover. Now I see movement a hundred meters downslope. Vague human shapes. Three. More. But they're cold, not hot in my bucket. They're using some kind of spectral camo tech. It's a counterattack by the militia. A bolt disperses white fire on the rocks just above my head, sparks raining on me. I stay low and click onto the HUD view slaved to my N-16. Forget about using the weapon optic. Time to cheat. Looking at the HUD, I raise my arms to align the reticle on the shapes and start firing. The guys are doing the same. Bodies drop. Quiet.

"Sung, you guys okay over there?" They're on the other side of the slagged blockhouse out of our view, though we're separated by only a dozen meters.

"Sung's down," Howard says. "I need help."

"Stay on your gun," I tell him. We're in the middle of a fight. "Trumbull, what've you got?"

"We're good. I didn't see any fire coming at us except from your side. Howard, Pabon, get on line with me. Turner, we're going to assault. You ready?"

Time to finish it. "Roger," I say. "Assault." I pop up and start lurching down the slope. *I'm up. I'm seen. I'm hit.* I drop behind a mound and roll left to see around it. D'antonio and Yamazaki are a fraction of a second later as they hit the ground. No one's shooting at us. We keep rushing, a few meters at a time. Hitting the rocky ground hurts, even in armor. "Trumbull, anything?" I pant after I drop to the ground again. He, Pabon, and Howard are somewhere off to my right.

I hear his strained voice. "No. We're about on line with where I saw you drop them. I'm tossing a grenade over there."

"No," I say, hoping I've stopped him. "I can't see you; you can't see us. You could be tossing it right at us." I couldn't see them over this irregular, rock covered slope. I knew they had no idea where we were.

Trumbull grunts. "Okay. Fair enough."

"We can't be more than another rush or two from them. Stay put and fix them. We're going to finish it from this side." Or so I hoped.

"Got it," Trumbull tells me. "We'll be your base of fire. On you."

"Last little bit, guys," I tell my men.

"Let's go!" "We're death dealers," I hear from them both.

"Ready. Rush." We're on our feet. To our right, Trumbull and Howard are sending blasts downrange. As I run, I can see the bodies heaped below me. I put some unaimed blaster fire ahead of me, then slow to make it count. Where my shots contact the human shapes on the ground, nothing moves. It looks like we'd already been successful. "Trumbull, move to us," I tell him. On my left, my men push wide and we all come onto the scene together.

We close on a group of dead men. Trumbull, Pabon, and Howard meet us and in pairs we check bodies and take weapons. These militia wear some kind of baggy camo layer over their uniforms, draped from their heads down to their feet making them look like giant amoeba.

"We'd better tell the company the militia is using tech to defeat our night vision," Trumbull says. "Yes, we will," I tell him. "Let's get back to Sung. He wounded?" I ask.

"Sorry," Howard says. "I kind of did a stupid back there asking for help when he got hit. He's dead." "You sure?" Yamazaki asks before I can tell them Sung's readout in my bucket is flat. "Yeah. His head's gone."

08

"Hear that explosion last night?" Kel asked his breakfast partners.

Eirene served up another feast that morning. The two other embassy men joined him, still in bedroom dress and unshaven, saying little as they poured their kaff. By this time, Kel had completed his morning exercise routine, showered, and dressed for the day.

"Explosion? I didn't hear anything. Couldn't have been too close. We've kind of gotten used to them. Besides, there wasn't any alert from the RSO office, so it couldn't have been too significant," Gren said, blowing steam off his kaff. "Let's eat."

There was a type of fried egg wrapped in a light, fluffy pastry, bowls of fruit, and a thickened milk sweetened with a reddish fruit. There was plenty of hot kaff and fruit juice as well as bread with jelly and honey. Oba, he was going to have to watch himself or he'd go back to the team so fat he wouldn't fit in his armor!

Not long into breakfast Pen showed up. "Morning, gents. Just some kaff for me, Eirene, the wife and I had breakfast. Ready to get going soon, Kel?"

"I have an errand to run back near the spaceport. I need to tie up a few loose ends before we get the day going. Is there time to do that?" Kel asked.

"Yeah. I'd better get that kaff to go. We can make good time there and back at this hour if we leave now." Kel and Pen grabbed a mug to go and made their way out.

Pen drove the speeder as Kel took in the sights of the city at its early morning hour. Traffic was sparse. It seemed business didn't start until later in the day.

"There was an explosion in the city center last night," said Kel over the roar of the engine. "I looked for mention of it in the local cast but didn't see anything."

Pen nodded. "That's common. The national communication ministry hasn't had time to sanitize it for release yet. I heard it, too. Bell will have more info this morning. So, you met Jacee? Great lady, huh?"

Kel agreed.

"Yeah, she's something, all right. She was married to a Legion colonel." Pen took his eyes off the road to make eye contact with Kel to see if there was a response. "I guess they're divorced. I've seen her with a few under her belt at embassy parties. Be careful. She gets ahold of you, I bet she could crush your bones!" he said laughing. Kel remained silent.

"Pen, when I was leaving the trade office, I saw an assistant there, I guess he's the trade analyst—"

"Yeah, he's Republic Intel. Don Snyder, or so he's called," Pen said bluntly. "Nice guy. Keeps to himself. I suppose you need to see him?"

For the moment, Kel declined. He'd meet with him when the time was right. He appreciated Pen's forthrightness but didn't want to discuss more with him. Pen was the operations manager for the embassy; he wasn't part of the military-political section or read-in to Kel's mission. In his experience, in most small posts on the edge there were few secrets about comings and goings in the embassy. He wondered what had already been circulated about him throughout the small diplomatic community. No more needed to be circulated by Pen or anyone else.

"I'll see him at some point," was all Kel said.

They rode in silence as Pen drove them to the outskirts of the spaceport and into a warehouse area where they found the chandlery. Row after row of large warehouses lined the wide road, freight and repair businesses all located in close proximity to serve the spaceport trade.

The sliding gate covering the entrance was just being retracted as they pulled up. *Symopolous and Sons* the sign read. Tangle-wire topped the perimeter fence and a vehicle gate jutted from the sides of the main building, enclosing a large yard full of stacked containers and warehouse buildings, lifters, and sleds.

The interaction was simple. Kel told the proprietor what he was after. Mr. Symopolous, Kel guessed since the man did not introduce himself, knew the *Callie* was taking on cargo and had contacted the purser to offer his services. "They have not put in any order. Who else can they use? We're the only chandlery servicing this port," the man said in unaccented Standard.

He bounced Kel a listing of the packages and prices for what Kel had outlined. Fresh provisions that could be used immediately or put in stasis estimating three-meals-a-day for approximately ten adults and ten children. Kel reviewed the options and prices for the different package contents. He was not familiar with many of the words, some of them transliterated into Standard from the local language, giving names for foodstuffs Kel didn't recognize. Pen was helpful as he knew most of the items, and Kel tried to pick an assortment he thought the crew would like and that Auntie Meiko would appreciate in her galley.

Kel gave his instructions to the man, with the promise to make clear to the purser that the bill had already been paid, and including a link saying, *Thanks, from Tamford.*

Mr. Symopolous shook Kel's hand and thanked him for his business.

"Do keep us in mind if you have further use of us. I've included my business link for your convenience."

Kel checked his link. A listing for *George Symopolous, Chandler,* now appeared in his contacts.

Not far into their return journey Kel took out his data link and after a minute of searching said, "Let's take a detour on the way back."

"What'd you have in mind? It's not... going to be something I'm going to regret, is it?"

Kel smiled. "No. I want to drive as close as we can get to the site of last night's explosion." Planetary police had sent out no security update to the embassy staff. Just the useless 'No security warnings' for the morning's group RSO message. As the security officer, Bell should've received advisories from the local police and in turn passed that on to the staff, if for no other reason than to influence a person's route to work. That the police had shared no intelligence after last night's bombing was telling to Kel.

"I'm no legionnaire, man. You sure this is safe?"

Kel laughed. "Look, I promise I wouldn't do anything to put you in harm's way." Kel projected the likely epicenter of last night's event on his datapad and was now bouncing that to the vehicle's nav. "Anything doesn't look smooth, we'll tank it and head out. Good enough?"

Shrugging, Pen altered their course, taking them deeper into the city.

The streets were still not alive, and as they got closer to Kel's best guess about the location of the blast, he could see a street blocked by two House Police vehicles. "Pull up to the next intersection. I'm getting out. If you have to move, circle back to this spot. I will meet you in thirty minutes. If thirty minutes passes and you don't hear from me, head back to the embassy." Before the man could respond, Kel was out of the vehicle moving on foot.

He put a cap on he had borrowed from the alcove outside Eirene's kitchen to disguise his hair; it probably belonged to one of the gardeners. He'd already started growing out the facial hair above his lip; it seemed all the men here wore large, bushy mustaches. Tonight, he'd take the time to bio-tint his hair dark.

He took a route around several blocks to what he mentally projected as being the site of the bombing, moving just fast enough to match the morning city pedestrian traffic.

After a few redirections in his route, he saw it—more official vehicles blocking the streets around a walled building. *House Police*, the emblem over the gate declared.

Through the decorative gates at the walled entrance, he spied the damage to the front of the police station. The double doors leading into the building were askew from an explosion; rubble and structural steel were exposed around the entrance wall. Numerous gray National Police officers congregated in small groups, conferring with each other and directing the blue uniformed House Police to evaluate the scene.

Kel didn't pause, but continued to walk past, planning a route back to his drop off point.

Interesting. A police station had been the target of last night's bombing. The incident had been suppressed in the local news feed and the embassy left in the dark.

Why, he wondered, and by whom?

Sitting in Bell's office an hour later, Kel related his observations. Bell was also troubled by the lack of information on last night's bombing.

"It's happened before. The Transit and House Police have been hit. The responses have been to shut down protests at the university. Sometimes they've brutally dispersed the crowds, but no fatalities. I guess we'll have to see what the response to this will be." Bell shrugged. "These protestors are smart, though. They've never directly attacked the National Police. My intuition tells me if that happens, we'd witness a bloody crackdown on the next Eleftheria protest. Send a strong message. Those National Police guys don't mess around."

"Why no alert to your office from the local liaison?"

"That's what I'd like to know. It's not the first time we've been left out. Still, I'm going to ask our National Police guys what's up."

Kel agreed. Censoring news of this nature was an indication that the state felt vulnerable. Trying to contain the information so as not to generate enthusiasm for any would-be bombers hoping to do the same did have some merits, not that Kel approved.

"I've got a meeting with Jacee in a few. Can we hit your arms room?"

Bell led him down to the end of the hall to a room with a security door with a retinal and DNA scanner access. He led Kel into a small space only a few meters deep and as wide, with racks on the wall from floor to ceiling.

Kel started inspecting the arms on the racks. There were several K-17s. It irritated Kel; he was specifically proscribed from bringing his own K-17 because of the export-tech restriction on Meridian, but it was fine for the embassy to have them on hand. Typical. Kel decided to skip them anyway; he'd already seen what he was hoping to find, and it would most likely be on par with what the local forces would be using.

A Stonewell-5 sat on the top rack in front him. Kel pulled the carbine down and examined it. It was a projectile weapon, firing a caseless solid chemical propelled 7mm round, not quite as advanced as his slug throwers back in the team room, but an excellent weapon regardless. It fired from a detachable magazine and unlike his more advanced rifle of the same class, did not disintegrate the magazine during the chambering process; the rounds needed to be loaded into the magazine and the empty magazine removed before a new one could be seated.

The magazines held 80 rounds and were extremely tough. Many older weapons had excellent operating systems, but their magazines failed to feed well, making the weapons all but useless. One of the reasons the Stonewell-5 had been around so long with so few essential design changes was that it was reliable from almost its immediate introduction. They were found on virtually every human world, even when greatly advanced weapons like the K-17 existed.

The short-barreled carbine had no optical or heads-up holosight. Kel had brought some of his own favorites, anticipating that this vital link in the weapons system would be lacking when he got to his destination.

Kel then noticed several subguns in the rack closest to the floor. He examined the one he selected, a Collins Needler. Needle guns served a niche role, even when they were novel technology. The needle-like projectiles could be accelerated to several thousand meters per second by the silent magnetic coil drive, and a magazine carried 500 of the sleek pills. The separate charge pack could power about a half a magazine's worth of needles, so the need to carry several packs to power the projectiles was as necessary as the projectiles themselves.

It made for a small package, with the stock collapsed it would easily fit under a heavy shirt or jacket. The projectiles caused devastating wounds at short ranges, and their small mass coupled with frangible construction meant that the rounds didn't over penetrate, but were ineffective against armor and other barriers. The accuracy fell off greatly after a hundred meters or so, but were still effective at stopping a fight at those longer distances, provided you hit the intended target. The magazines were pre-loaded and disposable, and he could fit three of them in a shirt pocket.

It was a weapon that could be improved upon, and was by later designs, but for personal defense and close work, it was adequate. It would never be his first choice as a weapon, but beside the carbine and his pistol, it would serve.

Kel rummaged through lockers to find magazines for both, charge packs for the needler, and 7mm rounds for the carbine. He found plenty, and settled on two cases of a thousand each of the 7mm to start. He'd sign for more as needed.

There were several small, concealable grenades, both energy and fragmentary explosives, that he laid aside. They fit in a pocket and carrying one of each could be done with little externally visible indication; nowhere near as powerful as what he would carry on his leej armor, but ideal for concealment. Being adequately prepared to deal with one or two assailants was always a concern in an urban environment. Crime existed everywhere, besides the terrorists he'd be hunting.

"This will get me started," Kel told Bell, who'd been watching. "I'll drop by at the end of the day to cart this stuff out if that's okay. Where do I sign?"

Bell grinned. "I'll bounce you the form."

"Are you checked out on the K-17s?" Kel wondered. *They have them, but can they actually use them?*

"Sure. Well. Familiarized. I haven't actually shot one in a while. They're really here for worst-case scenarios. An invasion into the compound, you know? They're on the tech proscription for the planet, so I try not to take them to the NP Headquarters' training range and flaunt it."

Kel agreed that was smart. "I can check you out on it and we can always use the sims program. You can get most of the important training done dry without ever blasting a thing. Slug throwers are much harder to use. If you're keeping current with that," Kel nodded to the pistol obvious under Bell's jacket, "the K-17 is easy enough. Based on my little recon this morning, I think the threat level is elevating. Preparing for contingencies is important now."

Kel was still concerned about the poor physical security at the embassy. An earnest attempt by the dissidents to raid the embassy would be difficult to repel with the current measures in place.

"Bell, one other thing. I didn't see any heavy weapons. No auto-blasters or heavy blasters. What's the plan for a siege on the compound?"

Bell's shoulders sagged. "Good question. I asks, but I no gets."

Kel understood. "We'll figure something out then. Check you later."

After entering the tower to meet Jacee in her office, Kel found her exiting the elevator in the lobby.

"Ah, just the man I was looking for," she said. "Let's take a walk." She led the way around the lift shaft to another hall down to a security door. She identified herself through a vid screen, and the door opened to reveal an office corridor. They continued down the hall, passing an open door where his palace roommate, Gren, sat at a desk composing on a datapad.

"Hey roomie, slumming with the hired help? Hey Jacee," he said grinning. Kel could see the closed door behind Gren with a security module around it. The vault must have contained the embassy's hypercomm equipment, as well as the other more mundane comm and technical gear necessary for information transfers through the embassy. He'd learned that Gren was a captain in the Republic Army but had many advanced degrees and spent the last several years at diplomatic postings as a comm specialist.

"Hey yourself, Captain Matson," Jacee said, raising her eyebrows in a mocking fashion. "Check yourself for any extra limbs growing from your back today?"

Hypercomm fields had historically caused severe mutations in biologic tissue, making the occupation of communication specialist hazardous and brief. Thank Oba, those issues had been solved generations before.

"Nothing to report from back there, but I might have something interesting to report growing elsewhere."

"Beast!" Jacee laughed as she took Kel farther down the hall to the last office. It was a quiet office with several desks occupied by administrative workers. Jacee led him to one and the man sitting at the desk silently held out his hand to Kel as he and Jacee approached. She looked at him, "Kel, bring up your link. We're going to get you the host accord package as well as a physical hard copy. A lot of the security forces you may encounter will not have any kind of data device."

An accord package gave an extra measure of protection to the operator on the host planet. It wouldn't shield him from any of the planet's law or obligations to conduct himself as a guest, but if he got into a jam and was questioned by the police or military, it would keep him from being arrested. It was a part of the aid package the House of Reason authorized, a requirement to ensure an operator had protection from the host-planet security forces. Sometimes, the House of Reason knew what it was doing when they threw their weight around the galaxy.

"The package is now on your link," the tech said after a few taps on his datapad, "and contains the separate authorizations from each of the host security forces, signed and authenticated by the commanders of the Transit Police, House Police, Militia, and most importantly, the

National Police. The card," he it held out to Kel, "has the same info in holoform for anyone without a data device. They're both locked to your biometrics and DNA... for both identities. Just set the identity when presenting it. I'm sure you already know that."

Kel did know how to change identities on his link instantaneously and effortlessly. He could do it by sub-vocal command. Unless something unexpected came up, he wasn't planning on using the trade mission identity again.

The tech continued, "The text is in Standard and Meridian local, and identifies you as advisor to all of these security agencies, authorized by the respective head of each force, and ordering the person reading the accord to assist you in any way possible and not to detain you. It states you are authorized to carry special weapons and may not be searched." The tech looked up at him. "Don't rob any banks."

Driving back to the palace was his first experience on his own in the city. He would have to get familiar with it and the sooner the better. His specs displayed route information but as he explored the city, he found much of the information incorrect. It was not yet evening and traffic was getting dense. A turn down what on his specs looked like a major thoroughfare between residence complexes turned out to be a staggered maze. Abandoned sleds and other debris blocked parts of the route. Previously concealed men came out of their hiding places to stare at him.

Bad neighborhood, Kel thought as he halted to reverse his course down a neglected street. A wheeled vehicle raced behind him and halted to block his path. Kel reached for his pistol as another suddenly pulled out, concealed from behind a mass of rubble to block the street in front of him.

Ambush!

The first threat was a man with a rifle exiting the passenger side vehicle in front of him. Firing through his own windscreen Kel sent a blaze of shots at the man. The glass webbed and exploded with an explosive *krish*. Dust filled the cab as Kel kept working the hole he'd created in the glass and drilled the man to the ground.

Kel ducked and crawled across to the passenger side door and pushed it open. He tossed the small grenade sideways toward the rear of the vehicle and waited for the explosion before following it out.

Assault! his brain screamed as he tucked and rolled to his side to see underneath his own speeder. The first human forms he saw he lit up. Two bodies fell as he continued his barrage.

Move! He turned to the vehicle in front, the driver now running to escape what he'd correctly presaged as his turn on Kel's killing floor. The man was unarmed and Kel tracked him for the few seconds until he ran out of sight.

Kel reloaded and looked around. Scanning. What spectators had been present were now gone. He keyed his specs with his implant. "Pen, get me help. Check my location. I'm in a vehicular ambush and need assistance."

To his credit, the RSO responded without question. "I'm rolling immediately. I've got your location. Help is on the way."

Kel moved on the first man he'd killed and kicked the rusted rifle away from the prone body. The man was not going to rise again, large exit wounds in the man's head spilled their contents out on the ground. Behind, the two bodies showed similar results. In the distance, the odd sirens of the local police grew closer. Kel holstered his pistol and found his accord holo and raised it over his head with his hands.

The first vehicle to arrive wasn't a police unit. A grey sedan with tinted windscreens floated up and the fit man he'd seen in the Trade Analyst office stepped out.

"Hey," the man said. Kel waited for more. It didn't come. He lowered his hands.

"Hey, yourself," Kel responded, still feeling the high of combat and a little euphoric.

"Need any help?" Kel knew this was the Republic Intelligence officer, Don. The man remained by his vehicle, reserved and unperturbed.

"Oh, just a little gunfight. Nothing I can't handle." The sirens preceded the sleds by a second as they came to a bouncing halt behind the sedan. "But maybe you could help me with the locals."

The man nodded. "Can do." With that, he turned to cut off the Transit Police officers as they hopped out of their sleds.

Pen pulled up with a small convoy of guards, dismounting at a run to join the scene. "What happened?" Pen blurted out as the protective detail guards dispersed around them. Sirens wailed and crime scene holo border went up fast. Suddenly hidden neighbors were coming out to spectate now that it was safe.

"Caught in an ambush is what happened," Kel said, annoyed at himself. "Hey, that's Don, right?" he gestured toward the man still talking to the police.

"Oh yeah," Pen confirmed. "How'd he get here so fast?" Kel wondered the same thing. Had the RI man been following him?

"This bad neighborhood," the police sergeant said in pidgin standard. "Many students come from these ghettos. Many ME from here."

Pen looked at Kel. "How did you end up here?"

He shrugged. "Exploring my environment."

The next day Jacee drove him on a new route through the city. The building density thinned out and small agricultural plots filled in the spaces between what looked like factories. They stopped for lunch at a small villa and were seated in a picturesque hanging garden overlooking a tranquil pond surrounded by old willow trees. Like much of the city's architecture, the café took advantage of the mild weather of Tiryns. The gunfight yesterday was not forgotten, but didn't diminish his ability to appreciate the beauty around him now. He could shift in and out of a state of combat readiness instantly because he never completely relaxed or lost awareness of his environment. When you were the only one you could rely on... then you could never really let down. There was no one else out there to watch your back.

"We're going to make several stops around the capital," Jacee announced after the waiter left with their order. "I've arranged introductions with the heads of the various security agencies. The state militia is headquartered on the southeast coast and we'll get you introduced out there another time.

"The militia is primarily responsible for coastal security and is more similar to naval infantry, I suppose."

Jacee's descriptions revealed she possessed an excellent understanding of military and security organizations. It impressed him.

"There is some anti-piracy action that requires brown-water navy capability, and that's what they do. The militia has little presence in the interior of the continent. They're not a very family-influenced organization, whether as a by-product or result of not having a large force with much power."

She continued. "First we're going to meet with General Stereopolis. He runs the House Police. His family is likely the second most powerful on the planet. Geographically they dominate the politics of the west region of the continent. Their headquarters is near here. So far he's been cooperative, and effective in his role as the top cop."

Jacee's breakdown of the functions of the different security forces was a little more nuanced and detailed than Pen and Bell's had been the day before, but there was no contradictory information coming at him. So Kel felt he was getting a pretty solid picture for now. The closer he got the more things might shift as they came into focus...

"Then we'll head to the south side of the city to the Transit Police headquarters. By numbers, the Transit Police are the largest force on the continent. General Alkady is from the Chokalany family, who pretty much politically control the east coast of the continent. They are not considered to be as powerful or as well-connected as the Stereopolis clan. Alkady is a flirt of the first class and I adore him," she said. "He's utterly charming, but it's his control of the transit system and goods which keep him and his family in favors and kick-backs that are key to their position on the Domestic Conclave.

"I have the day planned so that we finish back toward the center and at the National Police headquarters. Gavros Kyrgiakos is the general of the National Police." A frown appeared on her previously beaming face. Its presence made Kel sit up straighter as she sighed before continuing, a burden settling on them both.

"We have to be careful with him. I've dealt with the man for several years, and we've never developed a friendly interaction.

"He is well-placed within his family and there's no question that his uncle, Ayorba, is the most powerful man in the Twelve Families. He chairs the Domestic Conclave." Jacee paused again as she tried to explain the political situation to Kel.

"Everything on Meridian is ruled and administered from Argolis. Yes, the Twelve Families are all represented on the Conclave, and each family is the local power in their own regions and continents, but Tiryns is the seat of the planet.

"The National Police are national in name only; they are truly a planetary organization, and Gavros is head of the security apparatus for the whole megillah.

Kel chuckled. He hadn't heard that phrase since his dad had passed away. It always struck him funny. He never learned where it came from, but he knew what it meant. He thought.

"The Twelve Families are organized like a criminal enterprise, and the National Police especially so. Gavros has subordinate commanders in every country. They're loyal to their own regional clan, but Gavros is the chief-of-chiefs. Is this making any sense?"

Kel nodded. He understood why the area study had been such a mess, focusing on most everything except the security forces organization. It was a complex dynamic.

"What I'm saying is that Gavros is the most powerful man on the planet. He personally controls the largest effective armed force, not just on Argolis, but the whole planet. And as far as I can tell, he is not interested in the Republic's help whatsoever."

They continued to talk over lunch and Kel refined the subject to talk about recent violence.

"I've read all the intelligence summaries of the past year's terrorist incidents. By far, most of them are in Argolis."

Jacee agreed. "Tiryns has the central university, and students from all over end up here. The movement seems to be student-based. The kidnappers from the school-hostage incident were from three different regions, but no clear connection between them has been revealed. None of them were from Argolis. The bombings, the targeted attacks, now the hostage incident—they all indicate an organized group with excellent support. We're not getting a lot of information from the National Police." She shrugged.

Kel thought a minute. "What does our trade analyst have to say?"

He received a wink. "I'll arrange for you to meet tomorrow."

"We've kind of already met," he said, thinking about the timely appearance of the man after his ambush. "But a real introduction would be nice."

She made another frown and tilted her head. "Kel, I'm familiar with what DO does. I represent the House of Reason's position. They want the security situation resolved and trade undisrupted. You have a mandate to assist as you see fit. The question is... what is that going to look like?"

Kel rubbed his chin for a long moment before responding. He was going to play his cards close to his chest until he knew her better. "I'll let you know when I know."

They spent the next few hours traveling to the headquarters of the two smaller police organizations, meeting with their generals and staff. They were short meetings, but beneficial. Each general welcomed Kel warmly, and it was his impression that their warmth was a result of the excellent relations Jacee had developed with each of the men. By the end of the second meeting, Kel knew the locations and organizational head of the two forces, and had the personal contacts of the general's staff to coordinate any future visits.

Kel made it clear that he was there to assist the security forces on behalf of the House of Reason. That meant assessing their operations in order to offer advice on improvements in tactics, techniques, equipment, and support that the Republic supplied. Kel was here to personally assist Meridian in restoring order to their homeland. That Kel had the ability to recommend aid and financial assistance through the embassy caught the attention of the heads of the two different agencies and was positively received, he thought. Nonetheless, other than establishing goodwill, the two organizations had little to offer in the way of advancing his mission.

As the late afternoon sun set, Jacee drove them to their final appointment at the National Police Headquarters. The NP Headquarters compound covered ten or more blocks near the city center. It housed the planetary HQ, the regional base for Tiryns, as well as the central training base for the NP. Behind fences they passed the many barracks of the training command. Classrooms and ranges as well as large fields full of troops performed physical training around the compound. Kel looked through his specs at a topographic map, confirming that this was one of the sites he'd seen from orbit and had marked as a possible military base. On the ground, it certainly appeared to be more of a military organization than anything Kel had yet seen on Meridian.

Jacee pulled up to an ornate gate, manned by well-disciplined troops in gray uniforms with what appeared to be new Stonewell-5s and sidearms. The guard looked over Jacee's credentials, then directed them through the gate.

They parked and walked toward an august building topped with the seal of the National Police. Between large wreaths of gold were two rifles crossed over a short sword, and curving Meridian script around that. The wreath was decorated with bolts of lightning superimposed on each side. *That looks like most any emblem of a special operations force,* he thought. *Lightning bolts and swords were always a dead giveaway. These guys don't see themselves as cops.*

Marble steps led past stone colonnades and a two-story entrance. There a pair of officers waited, gesturing for the couple to follow as they made their way up a sweeping staircase up to the lobby. At the far end stood another pair of large wooden doors. Guards opened the doors, and Jacee and Kel followed their escort into an outer office. A male secretary stood at attention beside his desk.

"The general will see you now." Without waiting for a response, the officer pulled the office door open and stepped to one side, gesturing for the two to enter.

General Gavros Kyrgiakos stood awaiting them. Several of his subordinate officers stood by him in a line, guiding them toward a short table surrounded by chairs.

"Meez Eller," the general said in heavily accented Standard. "Please come sit. I am pleased to take this meeting."

Pleased or not, the dark man did not smile. At their two earlier meetings their hosts had each warmly embraced Jacee and made small talk while they sipped tea together. The atmosphere here loomed like a heavy storm cloud promising thunder.

"I have little time today but want to meet your new associate."

Kel remained at attention as he introduced himself. "General, I am Kel Turner. Pleased to be at your service." Kel would not offer his hand until the general did the same. The general did not.

The general looked him up and down like an NCO inspecting a private last into formation, then gestured to the chairs. "Let us sit for a minute before I must depart."

The general waited to speak until they had all sat and his officers moved to flank him. "You are well after ambush yesterday? No injuries?" Kel wasn't surprised the general knew about his fight.

"None, sir. I'm fine. Thank you for asking."

The man gave a tight-lipped smile. "We are working on the problems in those neighborhoods. Well, what do you have to discuss with me today?" he asked, abruptly leaving the subject.

Jacee took the lead. "General, this is the advisor the House of Reason has sent at the request of the Domestic Conclave. He is our specialist in counterterrorism and operations in—"

"Ah. Yes." The general fixed Kel with his eyes. "You are Legion then. Yes?"

Kel nodded once, saying nothing.

"You are Dark Ops also. Yes?"

Kel nodded.

The general stood. "I cannot stay. I will send for you, Meester Kel, yes?"

Kel nodded. He and Jacee stood as the general stood, the large man departing with his officers through another door as their original escorts gestured to them, leading them back through the offices and out of the building to their vehicle.

As they were escorted out, Kel was already consumed with thoughts about the stout man he'd briefly met. The general had made some assumptions about him, and Kel confirmed them. He doubted that Jacee would have promised the man his own Dark Ops legionnaire when alerting the general of the impending aid package from the Republic, or at least not in so many words. But the general had communicated much to Kel already.

Once in their vehicle, Jacee turned to Kel. "He talked to you. And he's going to send for you. That's a good start."

Kel guffawed. "Glad you thought so. It felt like I was being sized up."

"Of course, you were. He's sending for you? What do you suppose he'll want you to do?" Jacee rejoined.

He kept his suspicions to himself. Whatever the general expected, it probably wouldn't be safe, comfortable, or easy.

My specialty.

09

Kel arose early and worked out. He was the first to eat breakfast and was loading up his vehicle and driving out of the palace gate before his housemates had even awoken. Eirene clucked disapprovingly when she saw Kel's new hair color.

"Your hair so beautiful. Why you make like farmer this color? Your hair color of the gods. You make girls cry with your gold hair. Now, meh!" She shrugged her shoulders. "But—Eirene still find you good wife."

Kel had spent the evening before inspecting his new weapons and preparing for his morning. It had bit him hard not having his rifle at hand when he drove into the ambush. Stupid. He knew better. The grenades came in handy, though. *Explody things always come in handy.* He'd replenish his supply later.

He had an ambitious plan for the day. He'd been short-changed on training once they'd returned from Kylar, and he refused to neglect his skill maintenance any longer. Bell gave him the access codes to the National Police range, which the RSO and his security guards used for their own training. Kel had no trouble getting past the main entrance and into the range area. The officer on duty at the range control office made small talk with Kel and he received assurance that it was fine for him to use the range of his choice. Most of the ranges had only twenty-five or fifty meters of distance for training. Kel would require a hundred meters to best confirm the function of his weapons.

He parked and moved his gear to a covered area and selected the Stonewall-5 Carbine to start with. Last night he had laid out the gear he'd brought to Meridian, especially the different electro-optic options he had for aiming systems. He'd selected a compact viewer-style optic to mount on his new primary weapon.

Sighting systems that linked to the bucket of his leej armor were the most versatile. He had no bucket on this trip, so everything else available gave combinations of features with advantages and disadvantages. Holosights worked well, but they emitted visible light. They could be linked to his specs and forego the physical projection, but if you didn't have your specs, you were right back to the same problem: creating a ready target indicator for any opponent. Not good.

True optical sights were the next option. They demanded physically mounting the weapon into your shoulder so that its aiming mechanism was accessible to the shooter's line of sight. The one Kel selected had the option of multiple ranges of magnification, range finding ability, and ballistic solutions based on the range to target. It was small and weighed only 100 grams.

It mounted easily on the Stonewell, and Kel ran a diagnostic program on the system through his datalink. Placing a laser guide in the chamber of the gun he aimed the rifle and by pressing a button the sight aligned itself to the mechanical center of the bore. Now he had only to zero the optic so the point of aim and projectile impact were the same at 100 meters.

He'd placed several targets downrange at the 100-meter line in front of the high earthen berm of the backstop.

He now assumed a prone position, getting comfortable with the weapon as he selected a two-centimeter square to aim at.

He had his datalink next to him and his specs on. The two devices worked together to allow him to vocally input changes to the elevation and windage adjustments of the optic, zeroing it to the rifle effortlessly.

Now he fired a group of five shots, slowly, deliberately, pressing the trigger at the bottom of his respiratory cycle after exhaling, sending a round down range during the pause at the end of each slow breath. One larger hole appeared at the center of the small square.

Kel removed the magazine, checked the chamber, and put the weapon on safe. Kel's link had captured information about the velocity and aerodynamic properties of the projectiles he'd just fired. He reviewed the data and accepted the inputs. A screen showed him a table of drops the projectile followed on the polynomial curve of its gravity-influenced trajectory out to 1000 meters. Kel again accepted the inputs. He wouldn't get a chance to confirm them today, but in his experience were so close as to never be the difference between a hit and a miss on a man-sized target.

Kel moved down range about ten meters from the targets. A twelve-centimeter box was the object of his attention. His optic's line of sight sat six centimeters above the line of the bore. This was crucial. Sighting at the top of the box, Kel fired several rounds, satisfied to see the rounds impact the center of the black-outlined box. At any distance closer than about fifteen meters, the mechanical offset of the sight above the bore had to be considered or the bullet would impact the same amount low. If aiming at a small target like the brain, failing to compensate for the mechanical offset could result in failure.

People just didn't stop doing what you wanted them to because you shot them. Not even with a blaster. Not always. With a slug launcher, you had to put the pill into the part of the anatomy that would end the fight. That meant you had to know where to aim—exactly.

Satisfied for the moment, Kel rummaged through his gear and came up with a sling for the carbine. He attached it to the weapon and placed his left arm through the large loop. He moved through multiple positions, moving the weapon muzzle down, muzzle up, letting go of it with both hands, moving it to his back, and finally back to the front, gratified to feel the sling automatically changing length to provide the proper tension and control around his body.

Finally, he had a small module to place on the front of the handguard that contained several wavelengths of lasers and visible light for illumination and marking. It was a simple matter to zero the device to the weapon, repeating a similar process as he had done for the optical sight. Satisfied, he breathed a sigh of relief. It was a laborious process, an enjoyable one, but a task nonetheless. Only now did he feel confident the weapon was ready for use.

Did my pedantic obsession keep me from having the rifle when I needed it? It still ate at him he hadn't simply made sure the critical mechanisms were lubricated and loaded the weapon for his trip to the palace instead of delaying until he could do his *perfect* preparation of the weapon. Pistols were a poor weapon for killing. It had worked out, but only because he was better than his assailants.

Let it go. I'm alive. They're in the dirt. Do better next time.

He repeated similar technical routines for his needler, his pistol, and finally, put his attention on the only long-arm he'd brought with him from his team room cage: his Braughton. The 'Big-B' was Kel's favorite non-blaster weapon. As a sniper, it was a joy to study the ballistic math that ruled its ability to reach out and touch any target he could see, even at a distance of several kilometers.

It fired an 8-millimeter solid projectile that weighed 20 grams at a hypersonic speed of 1500 meters per second. The large projectiles still followed the laws of physics and the lateral trajectory was affected by wind, especially at extreme distances, but the magic combination of speed and aerodynamic projectile design seemed to negate those effects almost magically.

The weapon pleased Kel whenever he held it. The optics package allowed him instantaneous information to the range of a target and the solution to allow a hit without input from Kel. The short-wave invisible laser read the direction and magnitude of all the winds from the muzzle to the target and adjusted the lateral deviation of the round. Kel needed to calibrate the firing solution for the gravity of Meridian and could do it here at the 100-meter range.

Firing a few rounds, the data from the groups allowed the program in his link to make the necessary measurements and calculations, and after reviewing them, he accepted them. It would be satisfying to confirm the data at an extended range, but that would not be possible today. In all his time as a sniper, he'd never been let down by the predictive algorithms of the ballistics programs. Even when hitting a planet cold, the environmental data provided by the Intel Cell prior to a drop had always given Kel accurate data and, most importantly, first-round kills. Even so, nothing made him as confident as doing things the old-fashioned way and confirming his data at actual distances. The way he'd always done it.

I will never fail because of lack of preparation. I am the weapon. Not the computer.

Having Big-B made him feel complete. It was certainly his favorite. He doubted he'd even get the chance to take it out again on this trip, but he felt better having it with him on the planet. He felt less alone with it. His mind drifted during the sublime concentration of the work, and laughed to himself at the passing mental image. Some leejes marked themselves. He never considered marking his body, always thinking that someday, he would find his way into the secret world he now owned. Or, owned him. You couldn't be a covert operator with a big Legion sword on your arm. Sure, tats and body-mods could be removed, but he'd always secretly kept his eyes on the prize, even before he knew its name. Dark Ops. If he ever did get a tattoo, he knew what it would say, written in red across his chest.

With a rifle in my hands, all things are possible.

Finally, Kel felt like it was time to start training. Ensuring his weapons and gear were functioning perfectly had been a necessary and even enjoyable part of the morning, but did not qualify as training.

Kel had his nanotubule garments on under his clothes. He put on his helmet and noticed that it was not unlike those he'd seen the National Police troops wearing. His was made of a solid exofiber construction that could stop virtually any projectile and would even dampen the blast effect of many energy and chemical explosive grenades. He put the armored vest on his chest and back, the material joining front and back to each other by a seamless tech, and attached several magazines for his S-5 to the front. His pistol rode in an adaptive holster on his waist. He found a med kit and attached that to the armor as well. There'd be other small items he would add later, but this would serve for now.

First, he squatted and jumped, repeating the act several times to make sure his gear did not bind or interfere with extreme movements of his body. Everything seemed comfortable and functional.

Picking up his S-5, he took a deep breath and sprinted the 100-meters to the berm and back. Once at the starting point, he turned and facing downrange he brought the gun in front of him. He drew a magazine from his chest, inserted it into the carbine, and felt the gun auto-cycle to chamber a round. He brought the gun to his shoulder and fired five quick rounds. He then dropped into a prone position, fired five more rounds, then rose to a kneeling position and fired five more. With little conscious thought he returned the weapon's selector to the safe position, rose, and took off at a sprint for the target line again.

He repeated the drill several more times until seventy-five of the 7mm rounds had been expended. He paused to inspect his marksmanship. All rounds were within the confines of the black box, save one outside the line by only a bullet's diameter.

That's where the sight was when I broke the shot, so that's where it went. Next time, wait that extra millionth of a second, Kel coached himself, disappointed at his less than perfect performance. He still had to train with the other weapons. After a sip of water, he started a new drill. Soon he lost himself to his exertions and time ceased to matter.

Kel was feeling satisfied. He packed up but left his armor on. On the slow drive to the ranges he had passed

an obstacle course. Almost every form of military training forced trainees to run an obstacle course. The Legion
certainly had. They had some value, Kel admitted, in that
having to negotiate obstacles of different heights and difficulty did build confidence and identified potential weak-
nesses. There were no troops on the course. Kel hadn't
asked permission from range control to use the area, but
thought taking advantage of its availability wouldn't create any problem.

He parked near what seemed to be the beginning of
the course, looked at his link, and started a timer. In his
armor he sprinted to the first obstacle, a series of pro-
gressively higher walls that by the last one, Kel had to run
and leap to just get a fingerhold on the upper ledge to pull
himself up and then drop to the other side. A series of ladders and ropes led to higher levels on a high tower and
back down, followed by a low crawl through some drain-
age pipes and then under tanglewire. Obstacles where
after a five-meter rope climb the player had to swing up
onto a large log only to walk on the top of the sloping surface down to another rope for descent to the ground were
particularly challenging in his armor. There were a multitude of other obstacles, not necessarily difficult ones, but
designed to make the player use their upper extremities
as well as their legs to negotiate them.

Kel sprinted back to the start and checked his time.
Now that he knew the obstacles, he thought he could beat
it, and started again. He repeated this twice more. By then,
the sun was high in the sky. He had seen troops moving
about the compound all morning in the distance, and now
seemed to be gathering for what must be the lunch hour.

He took his gear off and was storing it in the vehicle when the range control officer pulled up next to him in a NP speeder.

"I got tired just watching you," the man said to Kel. "No one use that obstacle course hardly no-more. Is all good?"

Kel assured him it was.

"I hope it was okay for me to use it," he said. "I didn't ask, sorry about that."

The man waved off his concern. "Is fine. You use whenever."

Later as he drove off the compound and entered afternoon traffic, Kel checked his link. He had both hands on the controllers and was finding Tiryns traffic challenging. He read a message from Jacee while drivers around him swerved in and out of their lanes.

Meeting with Don in an hour.

He hoped no one would mind his appearance as he gunned it for the embassy. He had questions to which he needed answers.

Kel cleaned up as best as he could before stopping by Bell's office to tell him everything went well at the range.

"No problems. You take your guys out there much?"

Bell gritted his teeth. "Not as much as I should. I had a program of training and semi-annual weapons qualification for the security force, but it's pretty much turned into just getting everyone out at least twice a year to prove they can shoot. The ambassador's protective detail is more disciplined and are out at least every couple of weeks. In fact, I was hoping the end of this week you could come out with us and help out."

"Consider it done," Kel said, and headed over to the tower to make his meeting on time.

On the way out of the elevator, he saw Chief Minister Sun and his assistant, Gravin, walking in the other direction. The horrified look on both of their faces was priceless, but Kel sheepishly grinned like a pouncing vulpine as he walked by. *Of course, I'd run into them. And looking like this!* he thought. He had no reason to feel embarrassed about working hard. *And I even cleaned the sink in the first floor fresher up as best as I could after scrubbing off the grime. What more could these perfumed princes expect?*

He entered the trade office and walked directly to the faux analyst's door, chimed, then stood back and waited. The door opened and Don Snyder gestured Kel in. The many vid screens Kel had noticed the other day were off, and Don held up a warning finger as he walked to his desk and waved a hand over his data pad.

"We're shielded." The man stuck out his hand. "Don Snyder. Pleased to formally meet you, Mister Turner. The other day didn't really count, I guess. It wasn't the best place to make our acquaintance." He invited him to sit as Kel set the record straight on just using his first name.

"Fair enough. I'm Don. Getting settled?"

"I am, but there's one thing that has me unsettled and I'm hoping you'll know the answer. Who's behind Meridian Eleftheria?"

Don smiled for the first time. "That, my Dark Ops friend, is the question."

Kel stayed the rest of the afternoon, pouring over reports, viewing holovids, and learning what connections the intelligence officer had strung together about the ruckus of the past several months. After sharing all of this, Don gave Kel some insight about the workings of the diplomatic mission.

"I brief the ambassador on a regular basis. Have you met him yet? He's harmless. He's a career diplomat and this is probably his last posting before retirement. Don't be surprised if he tells you his kidnapping story. As a young diplomat he was posted on a planet where the local alien chieftain kidnapped him for several days and ransomed him for favors. The embassy had gifted some goods to a rival, and the chieftain felt slighted. The Koobs grabbed young Marlo and kept him in a cage for a few days. They didn't harm him and everything turned out fine. I bet that was forty years ago, but he still tells the story as the most significant event of his life. If you meet him, you'll hear it. He'll feel it necessary to prove to a legionnaire that he was a tough guy when he was younger."

Kel knew the type.

"Anyway, I'll give you the same rundown I keep giving the ambassador."

Don explained that until a few months ago, no one had even heard of Meridian Eleftheria. Student protests at the Tiryns University had started in earnest only this year but really picked up steam the last few months. They had a list of social grievances: income inequality, opportunity inequality, no participatory government—things Kel did not think unreasonable, and the protests had not been violent.

Bombings occurred in many of the planet's capitals. Banks, revenue departments, Transit and House Police stations all favorite targets. The acts were all accompanied by demands for the oligarchy to accept general elections else future violence increase, ME taking the credit. About the same time, their logo, the raised fist, became popular as graffiti around the university, on banners, and even clothing.

Two months ago, one of the largest natural fiber co-operatives was burned to the ground. Whether it was arson fraud by the owner or an actual act of terrorism, ME took credit.

"We have zero open channels with the National Police," Don said. "I get what they decide to share with me, but that's not been much. I have a liaison in their investigative branch, but his role's more to discourage the flow of intelligence. The answer is always the same, 'matters of state security.'

"It boils down to this: the NP are responsible for state security and the NP, from the head on down, do not trust the Republic and do not want our help. The Domestic Conclave asked for our assistance, hoping to get access to tech. Since that is not happening, they don't seem too amenable to authorize Kyrgiakos and the NP to open up the flow of info."

"Do you have sources or agent nets formed?" Kel asked. While he didn't expect Don to lay out his agent payroll, he did want to know if the intel man had any independent information coming in.

Don shrugged. "I would not call them highly developed. I do have a source in the NP close to the investigation division. I can't say I've gotten much use out of him for the money I've paid. Yet.

"I do have sources in the student community. They're not ideologues, they're just people on the fringe who can tell me what the protest organizers are saying. It's a lot of egalitarian philosophical stuff, not anything that reveals hard-core terrorist inclination. The 'Students for Democracy' organization feels there is a cultural and hereditary connection to a popularly elected form of government. They spend a lot of time talking about the roots of their ancient society and how the Twelve Families corrupted that when they founded Meridian.

"Then came the school hostage incident on Peloponnese. This was a pigasaur of a different color. Obviously, to have planned and coordinated a kidnaping like that took more than a day or two for some casual acquaintances to put together."

"What responding agency handled the rescue attempt?" Kel asked, still irritated such basic information was not addressed in any of the summaries.

"It was National Police, but it was the locals, not Kyrgiakos' special boys." *Special boys.* Kel expected the NP would have some form of anti-terrorist unit.

"My guy at NP tells me he expected heads rolling after the fiasco, but strangely enough, nothing. This is a culture where they *always* find someone to blame. My guy says there was an investigation, but it was inconclusive at best. NP has a specialized team here at the headquarters that's supposedly the unit tasked with all high-profile responses. The situation went hyper critical before they could fly in from Tiryns. We all know what happened then—the locals botched it."

Hostage rescue was one of the most difficult tasks imaginable. What Don told him filled in a few of the blanks, but not all of them. The incident still bugged him. He'd file it away to reexamine later.

"I still have more questions than answers about ME. I don't know who the players are, how they're organized, or most importantly, the source of their support. Bomb-making materials and weapons require money and know-how, and the Students for Democracy do not seem the likely source for that.

"I'm looking at all possibilities. I haven't seen anything to lead me to believe that it is being supported offworld. There are no exo-religious or other exo-ideological elements to this. If they were building zhee temples, cloistering their females, and drinking fermented horse milk, that'd be a clue." They both laughed.

"Other possibilities," Don continued, "are that it is part of a power play by one or more of the families to gain an advantage. Most of the attacks have been on this continent with almost weekly incidents here in the capital."

"What have the responses been by the security forces?"

"No crackdowns. Yet. The Transit and House Police block traffic and try to confine the protests to the campus. There's only been one incident where they deployed anti-riot tactics. Stunners to disperse the crowds, and only because the students started vandalizing buildings and vehicles. My sources say that the violence and property damage were caused by criminal opportunists looking to cause trouble, not the protestors.

"The NP have raided a lot of residences and farms around the country, looking for bases of support and trying to gather intel. My guy tells me they've been unsuccessful so far. I'd rate his reliability as low, however."

Rating a source of information as Level 1, 'proven reliable,' all the way down to a Level 5, 'known liar,' was important in considering the information the agent provided. It sounded like Don had assigned a fairly mediocre rating to his NP source.

"The NP are working this alone as far as I can tell, and it's entirely possible that they aren't sharing information because they don't want us to know they haven't had great success.

"I'm continuing to work on developing sources wherever I can. Honestly, before this so-called popular uprising, most of my efforts were invested in profiling the Twelve Families for future exploitation. We have a small mission and we don't have much in the way of assets. I'm probably going to be getting more help soon. This has caught us off guard. For right now, it's basically you and me. There's some overlap in what we do, but you have a full-time job here yourself."

Kel considered this.

"I don't need to run my own agents but I will be sharing all the intelligence with you that I get," Kel assured him. "We may be getting a break soon. I will keep you updated. I may have something happening soon that will get me closer to the NP."

"What's that?"

"I'm thinking that General Kyrgiakos wants to see how his Dark Ops leej plays."

10

Before Kel left the embassy that day he stopped by to see Bell. He pulled him over to Pen's office to be able to confer with both of them about some concerns he'd developed while getting his feet on the ground.

"I've been thinking about a couple of things. Our vehicles are all thin-skinned. If the threat level continues to increase, we need to think about getting our vehicles armored. An ambush on one of the diplomats or their families is looking more and more likely."

Bell answered. "The ambassador's limo is the only vehicle in the fleet that's fully armored. We've been talking about that though."

The two seemed a little defensive after Kel pointed out yet another potential weakness in their security. He was hesitant to proceed, but pushed ahead anyway. He mentioned some other ideas about improving the physical security around the embassy. His recommendations wouldn't be hard or expensive to implement. They first needed to extend the area of approach around the compound to prevent an explosives-laden vehicle from detonating right at the compound gates.

They needed to place a checkpoint and barricades farther out where the guards could scan and search vehicles before letting them proceed, and then screen them again before letting them into the compound.

"We've been lagging in getting our physical security improved, that's for sure," Bell admitted.

Pen grunted. "You're right. Still working on it. We can show you what we have drawn up. Work is scheduled to start on that next week. I also have some ideas where we can get the vehicles upgraded."

It was a start. Kel didn't want to stomp on their toes or make them feel he was the bull in their china shop, but he wanted them to feel an urgency to move things along. They asked for his help. They were going to get it. Based on Kel's afternoon with Don, he wasn't hopeful that the situation would deescalate anytime soon.

Kel started the drive back to the palace, anticipating whatever Eirene had planned for the evening meal, when his link chimed him. He had his specs on and allowed the comm to go through. A major in a National Police uniform was on the other end of the link.

"Mister Kel. I'm Major Todalin, General Kyrgiakos' assistant. The general is requesting you meet us for a practicum tonight. Shall I tell him you are available?"

A practicum? "Yes. I am available at the general's convenience. Will this be conducted at the National Police headquarters? I can be there in thirty minutes."

The major shook his head. "No. I'll bounce you the location. The security detail at the gate will know to expect you. They'll search you and your vehicle, just to prepare you."

Kel frowned. "I'll have all my weapons and protective gear with me. Is that a problem?"

"Not at all. The general expects you to be ready to work."

The major disconnected, and a second later Kel received the location grid for the meeting.

Ready to work, huh? Practicum? Is that a different way of saying training exercise? Or is it code for smoke the new guy to see what he's made of?

Kel jinked his speeder, narrowly avoiding the repulsor that dodged in front of him and the lane of gridlocked vehicles to his right. The late afternoon traffic was chaos, an endless stream of repulsors abruptly weaving in and out of nonexistent lanes all around him. He took his time and eventually arrived at the given location—an industrial area with large fenced off warehouses filling either side of the two-lane street. The shadows stretched long as the sun dipped behind the peaks of the rusted roofs.

Kel slowed as he came to a compound whose chain-mesh fencing was interwoven with a solid green material, preventing any view into the compound. It wasn't as effective as a field distortion barrier. He got glimpses into the compound through the many small gaps in the slats, windowless warehouses and large open areas of pavement on the other side.

Outside the checkpoint office a guard in a nondescript brown jacket and loose black pants stood by the sliding gate. No weapon was obvious but Kel's intuition told him the man was armed.

The guard approached the driver's side and looked over his dark glasses down at Kel.

He presented the small accord holo before the guard could speak. The man took the holocard, examined it, looked at Kel for a second before telling him, "Pull inside just past the gate and then stop your vehicle. You'll be told what to do. You must be searched before proceeding farther. Please follow instructions."

Without waiting for a response, the guard moved to the small office, spoke a few words, and the gate opened just far enough for Kel to pull his speeder through. Several men armed with subguns waited for Kel, motioning for him to pull all the way forward, then to turn off his vehicle. Kel did so. The gate closed behind him.

Two men approached Kel's side of the vehicle. Two more appeared, one posting behind Kel's shoulder, another on the passenger side.

"Sir, we're going to search you and your vehicle before you can come on to the compound."

"I informed Major Todalin that I was armed and carrying protective gear," Kel replied, keeping his hands visible on the controllers. The guards were dressed casually like the man outside the gate, all with long hair and beards. None wore uniforms. *Likely NP operators*, Kel thought.

"That won't be a problem. Leave any personal weapons holstered and we'll move any gear or weapons in your vehicle as we locate them. Step out of the vehicle."

Kel did so, and the two men nearest him escorted him a few steps away. The man gestured for Kel to raise his arms and searched him from head to toe, locating each of Kel's personal weapons. Then the man produced a datapad and scanned Kel's body, looking for molecular explosives as well as more mundane devices.

Meanwhile, the other two operators tossed Kel's gear, noting the weapons, ammunition, and other equipment, including holding up the energy and fragmentary explosive devices to show their partners.

Satisfied, the guards placed his gear carefully back in the speeder and pointed. "Let's leave your vehicle here for now. Follow us." Through the front door of a nondescript commercial building, the general and Major Todalin stood to one side. They were engaged with another older man with thick black hair, graying at the temples, with a bushy salt-and-pepper mustache, the three of them deep in conversation.

Kel waited to be recognized, and after a short moment the major turned to Kel and waved him over. This time the general extended his hand out to Kel as he neared. "Ah, Meester Kel. I am glad you could take time to meet. Major Todalin you have talked to, yes?"

Kel extended his hand to the major and was met with a firm grip.

"Meester Kel, this is Colonel Graviakis, he is the commander of the Hoplites. You know Hoplite, yes?"

"No, forgive me," Kel replied, "that's not a word I'm familiar with."

"It will be our pleasure to teach you," the colonel said as he shook Kel's hand.

"Gavros, now we can begin," the colonel said to the general, who nodded in return. "Tonight the general is going to be participating in an exercise with the unit." He smiled at General Kyrgiakos. Kel was picking up that the Hoplite commander was eager. "Grab your gear and weapons. There's always the potential for trouble when we're out in the city. Can't have you not able to fight back, no? Meet us through there. Can you be ready in five minutes?"

Kel assured him he could. Kel went back to his vehicle and donned his protective vest and helmet, grabbed his S-5 and made sure he had several magazines. He trans-

ferred his pistol from its concealed location to the exposed mag attachment at his side, and double checked
his load out.

They didn't bring you here to kill you. So far so good,
Kel told himself. *Whatever this is, it'll be interesting.*

He returned with his full kit and joined Kyrgiakos and his
men in the garage bay. Several dozen of the bearded men
like those who had searched him were gearing up and
checking weapons. A large repulsor truck painted as a
commercial hauler sat nearest the exit doors. In the cargo compartment Kel could see it was lined with benches.
One group of troops loaded their gear into the central aisle
as others took seats.

Next to it was a smaller repulsor vehicle with a windowless cargo container on the bed. It also appeared
nondescript, like any commercial vehicle Kel had seen
about the city.

A third vehicle, a wheeled truck with sliding cargo
doors on both sides trailed the others. Standing next to
the open door, the major and General Kyrgiakos waved
Kel over to them.

The general gave Kel a once over, examining the individual items of gear on his body as well as his weapons.
"Okay, you look ready for work. We are evaluating hostage
rescue tonight. We will move to target staging area. We
have kill house in other compound we use for training.
Negotiators are on-site talking to hostage takers. Other
Hoplites are role players. Site is secured by our uniformed

officers. We observe. As commander, I will participate but Colonel Graviakis runs his Hoplites. That is plan."

Kel nodded his head. *This I like, knowing the plan.* He was curious to see the Hoplites work. The vehicle Kel rode in with the major and general took the lead, slowed to make sure the other vehicles were following, then drove out into the city. There was no conversation and Kel asked no questions. *Silence is the universal language of the professional.* When the time was right, they would tell Kel what he wanted to know without his having to ask.

They kept a discrete speed through the city and after only a dozen kilometers entered an area similar to where they had departed—a quiet sector filled with large factories and warehouses. No residences. The evening streets stood empty.

He knew they had arrived when he spotted another fenced compound, this one topped with tanglewire. Past the gate, dozens of buildings were arranged to replicate a small city. This was an urban training site. A large one. Some of the buildings were facades. Some appeared to be fully finished structures.

He stepped out after his hosts as the larger trailing vehicles took diverging paths past them. Knowing that the Hoplites were practicing a hostage job, he knew what the set up likely was. One truck pulled parallel alongside a two-story warehouse, concealing its presence behind the building. The other rolled slowly by, turning to proceed farther down the mock city street and out of sight.

"Let's move up to the house and get good view, yes?" the general looked to Kel for understanding.

"After you, sir," he said, slinging his S-5 to his chest. As the general walked deeper into the compound, Major Todalin broke into a trot to move ahead of them. The general gave a short laugh. "They are all worried, you see. Must be same in Legion? No drop the baby in front of the boss, yes?" Kel gave a short chuckle in response. It was a funny saying.

Kel examined the different structures as they went. Durasteel doors were hung in large metal frames constructed to take the abuse of breaching practice. It simplified the replacement of the doors as they became damaged in training. It was an environment very familiar to Kel. In fact, it reminded him of their urban training site back home and even rivaled its size.

They proceeded two more well replicated city blocks until they veered toward a large roofless building. The major awaited them and spoke into his throat microphone on their appearance. "Gavros is on station. We're heading up to observe the crisis site."

They walked up an external staircase to where a catwalk skirted the perimeter around the entire second story. Lights from the taller surrounding buildings projected a faint light into the open space below. Looking down from the catwalk, the space was divided into rooms of varying size and shape; some of the rooms containing furniture that replicated offices, some residential bedrooms and sitting areas, some typical factory workspaces filled with what looked like rusted machinery providing different obstacles and barriers to travel and vision. It was all very familiar to him. *This could be one of our shoothouses.*

They moved along the railed walk until they reached a corner room. Furniture was randomly strewn around the room, some of the pieces turned on their sides. The middle of the room was dominated by a square table with a single chair facing the door. There sat a man, his hands and feet bound, his mouth taped, and three-dimensional targets of men holding pistols surrounding him. The targets were positioned against the live role-player, leaving no more than a few finger breadths between the man's head and the targets surrounding him.

The restrained man struggled against his bonds. He wore the gray uniform of the National Police, but no protective gear. His muffled utterances were incomprehensible, but believable for a hostage in fear for his life. Sweat shone on his forehead and his eyes darted about wildly. *This guy takes his role-playing seriously,* Kel thought. Role-players acting as the hostage takers paced about the room.

Kel keyed his specs to night vision and saw the other two men on the catwalk drop thick visors down from their helmets. The major nudged him and pantomimed him bouncing something to Kel's link. He clicked his implant. The communications of the exercise's participants came alive.

"We can get you what you want," a voice said. *Negotiators.* "It will take some time. It would help if you would..."

"Help?" he heard the dual voice of a role player on the floor below him echo through his implant. "If you goats wanted to help you would've given us a real democracy generations ago."

Over the next hour Kel watched and listened as the exercise continued. The hostage negotiators talked to the hostage takers, going through their full inventory of tactics, trying to keep the hostage takers talking as they listed their demands and their intention to kill the hostage if they didn't receive full cooperation.

The hostage takers were having fun. Kel had played the part many times himself. It was fun trying to fluster the negotiators by making outrageous demands for gourmet food or luxury vehicles to see how the negotiators responded. It was training for them as well, not just the men preparing to rescue the hostage.

But there was a difference. Kel found that negotiators universally viewed the need for an assault by the hostage rescue team as a failure on their part. Kel could never see it that way. Some people could not be negotiated with; armed hostage takers were not rational people to begin with. There was one way to deal with them. And it was summed up in three little letters. KTF.

His hosts hadn't spoken to him. Kel trained his attention on the goings on below him. At some point, the negotiators would inform the rescue team that the hostage was about to be killed, and the exercise would culminate in the rescue action. He hoped it would be soon.

The major bounced another feed to Kel. This one linked automatically to his specs. A live feed from a small autonomous drone that had crawled or flown in, too small to be obvious to the occupants, showed him the eye-level view. He was impressed with their use of the tech they had available. It was not as slick as his own nano-sized inquisitor drones, but he gave them an A for effort.

Finally. Some action. In his ear, the rescue team leader asked for more distractions to be initiated. The NP vehicles posted in a perimeter several blocks around the kill house had been sporadically activating sirens throughout the exercise. Now they increased the frequency of their distractions.

Kel observed teams of Hoplites approach outside. From two different directions, multiple teams flowed toward the shoothouse in complete darkness and total silence. One group at the far end of the house worked at an exterior door to gain silent entry. Whether they electronically or mechanically opened what was surely a locked door, he couldn't tell from on the catwalk.

He strolled farther down the catwalk to peer at a ten-man element moving through the building, and followed their advance as they stopped at an intersection of two hallways—now near enough to view the door outside the crisis site.

He continued his stroll to the other side of the house as the general and Major Todalin stayed put. Below, other teams had placed explosive charges on more exterior doors, and moved to a ready position. Kel walked back to his original post and directed his attention to the crisis site as the negotiators intensified their pleas with the hostage takers. Outside the room, three rescue team members padded down the hallway. Kel saw two of the men work to place a long strip against the door on the hinge side. Whether it was explosive, a plasma cutting charge, or an energy charge, Kel didn't know. He grinned in the dark, knowing he'd soon find out.

The breachers made their way back to the intersection where the rest of their team waited around a corner, dispersed evenly on both sides of the corridor.

After several minutes of silence Kel heard the general say in his broken Standard, "Good job, negotiators. Your job done. Time to proceed with exercise. Colonel Graviakis, you have control." The general looked toward Kel and pointed down at the center of the room where the hostage made utterances in a high-pitched strain. He gave a thumbs up. *As if I'd be looking anywhere else.* The three hostage takers moved behind a large freestanding wall. *A ballistic barrier.* Kel had noticed it earlier. *Nice to know they're not reckless.*

The voice of the Hoplite commander, somewhere out of sight, filled his ear. "Teams, give me a ready." Colonel Graviakis was most likely located with the negotiators at the command post.

The team leaders from the two assault teams outside each answered with a "ready assault one," "ready assault two," and lastly the rescue team waiting to pounce from around the corner of the crisis room chimed in with a quiet, "Ready rescue."

Though only observing, Kel felt the rush of adrenaline as he heard the colonel's voice. "This is the commander. Stand by for long count. I have control, I have control."

After a second's pause, the voice continued.

"Five, four, three, two—"

The charge on the door to the crisis site ignited in a huge purple shock. *Plasma charge*, noted Kel.

"—one."

The two exterior charges erupted in loud, white flashes. *Explosive charges.*

"Rescue, rescue, rescue."

As soon as the rescue team had fired their plasma charge, they moved with precision to the threshold, arriving to find the door already fallen into the room. One of the men tossed a stunner in and it exploded in a frenzy of purplish bolts and shrill whistles as the assaulters entered the room. Kel paid rapt attention to their tactics.

The first man moved left through the door, clearing his corner as Kel would. A millisecond behind him, the second man through the door did the same in the opposite direction, correctly ensuring there were no threats along the entry wall or the corners. The next men moving into the space alternated directions, none of them moving deeper into the room than a step off the wall. As they entered the room, blindingly bright white lights from their S-5s illuminated the space. Shots rang out in a rapid, even cadence from each of the shooters as the hostage squeezed his eyes shut to escape the blinding lights aimed at him.

"Going long," he heard the assaulter in the far right of the room yell out as he made his way along the wall and into the far corner, aiming his weapon and light deep into the room looking for more threats. The lights threw long shadows on the floor and walls. *Could any artist ever capture the eerie beauty of this,* he waxed philosophic, not for the first time witnessing such a show.

The assaulters moved to the hostage, whose eyelids remained clenched though the shooting was over. He shook so hard that Kel could see his jerking twitches from the catwalk.

Kel diverted his attention from the room to the rest of the house and moved along the catwalk to observe the actions of the two assault teams at work elsewhere. From two different breach points the teams worked clockwise through the structure, clearing each room rapidly and efficiently. He listened to the communications between the team leaders and watched as the men nearest a threshold or intersection dropped a small glowing marker on the ground, indicating to anyone outside that the space had been evaluated and cleared.

Kel walked back to his vantage point over the crisis site in time to hear the general say, "End exercise. I'm coming down."

In his implant he heard the colonel say, "On my way." *It must be tough to be in the command post and not with the shooters. Thank Oba I'll never have to worry about that.* That burden was for officers. *Old ones at that.* In his heart, he felt he would never be that old.

He followed his hosts back down the stairs, weaving past the individual assaulters held up securing their rooms to reach the crisis site. The general slapped the shoulders of most every man as he passed them, saying something encouraging and complimentary as he went.

The rescue team had their visors raised, the white lights from their carbines pointing at the floor splashing light into the room and illuminating everything up to head level, leaving faces dark. Even so, white teeth reflected behind smiles. The general walked directly to the hostage, ignoring the gagged man's noises as he inspected each of the three targets. The three hostage takers were no longer behind their wall, and were inspecting the targets as well, grinning with approval.

Colonel Graviakis walked in, moving directly to the target arrays himself. Kel too made his way there, curious to inspect their marksmanship. Multiple sharp-edged holes alibied each target, centered around the upper half of the heads on each.

The general pointed to the hostage role-player, looked at one of the assaulters and snapped his fingers. Two of the assaulters slung their carbines on their backs and moved to the bound man in his chair. Grasping the armrests, they lifted the man and chair amalgam and carried him out of the room, still bound and gagged.

Why didn't they cut him loose? Kel wondered.

The colonel turned to the general. "Gavros, anything to comment on?"

General Kyrgiakos shook his head. "No. You'll get no reward from me. That is what I expect of you."

Everyone laughed, the tension of the moment broken.

The general looked to Kel. "Let's hear from our Dark Ops friend. Anything to say?"

"No sir, not at all," Kel replied. "That was very well done." He meant it.

The colonel took over again. "All right. Team leaders, get the house reset. We're going to run it twice more. Assault One, you'll rotate into rescue, then Assault Two will get a turn. We'll only run the rescue; we're not going to play the whole thing again with negotiators." The colonel communicated the same to the negotiators, dismissing them until tomorrow's after-action review.

The door to the room was carried out while two other men brought a new door from outside and began mounting it to the frame.

"Meester Kel?" the general said out of his vision. He snapped to face the man.

"Meester Kel, you would like to sit in the chair?"

Here it is! Kel knew this was a test. He'd been expecting it. Challenges like this frequently came up when working with indig. Would the legionnaire eat the favorite local delicacy? It was usually some part of the animal that would be discarded except in times of famine. Would the legionnaire drink the local drink? It was usually an aperitif that tasted like something distilled in a rusty trash barrel and burned like fire going down. Would the legionnaire climb their favorite scaling wall without an ener-harness, like the indig did? Would the legionnaire cook off the energy grenade, only throwing it at the last second, as they did? The permutations were endless.

They were all important tests; tests that, if passed, built trust with the host. Failures inevitably crushed the fledgling relationship.

Kel did not hesitate.

"Thank you. I'd be pleased to."

The room was reset and a chair placed behind the square table for Kel. He took the seat, removed his helmet, and leaned back as the Hoplites moved the three targets into close proximity of Kel's head, just as they had for the last hostage.

Everyone filed out of the room except for Colonel Graviakis, Major Todalin, and the general. Kel shifted his eyes to the catwalk and saw the three hostage takers above him, grinning.

"Meester Kel. No move," the general said as he turned toward the door, the last man leaving.

"Remember," he said over his shoulder. "No. Move."

Several minutes passed before the three officers reached their spot on the catwalk. Not long after he sensed motion outside the door and knew the rescue team must be placing their plasma strip-charge. Had there been sirens screeching, the distractions would have prevented him from noticing any activity outside the room, the breachers' tread was that stealthy.

After another minute he heard the countdown commence. At *three* he closed his eyes to avoid being blinded as the charge went off. He felt the concussion and opened his eyes just in time to see the stunner tossed in, and again closed his eyes. Through his eyelids the purple light burned his retinas. He opened them to see the third and fourth assaulter moving through the threshold as rounds zinged past his head.

Pretty cool, Kel thought. The only time he felt rounds whiz past him were when people were trying to kill him. They did not train this way in the Legion. Too much opportunity for disaster. Plus, it proved nothing, in Kel's opinion. Nevertheless, it was another opportunity for General

Kyrgiakos to have killed him had that been his intention. It clearly was not.

Kel turned in his chair to track the assaulters on their tasks. "ENDEX," he heard in the general's booming voice from above. Kel stayed seated until the general and his crew appeared, smiling as they walked over to Kel, pointing at the holes in the targets all around his head.

"Very nice, Meester Kel," the general said. "Come, let's go up top and see one more." He turned to the colonel and in a disgusted tone said, "Get stupid back in here."

Again on the catwalk he saw two men bring the gagged man back into the room, still secured to the chair, and set the room and targets up again.

Oba, this guy must've done something really bad to deserve this, Kel guessed.

They watched the next run and to no one's surprise the "hostage" remained unhurt, still squealing and making an effort to defeat his restraints. Targets were inspected. Approval was given by the big chief.

"General, are you satisfied with tonight's performance?" The colonel looked to Gavros Kyrgiakos, head of the security apparatus of the entire planet.

"Yes, Colonel. They are yours."

The colonel addressed the Hoplites and soon the team leaders were giving instructions as they once again carried out destroyed doors and replaced them with new ones, ready for their next use.

Kel followed the general out of the structure to where their conveyance waited. The smaller of the repulsor trucks pulled up behind them and as the rear doors opened, two Hoplites exited the kill house carrying the man bound to the chair.

He saw them make a concerted swing and, one-two-three, heaved the chair—man and all—into the back of the truck. He winced as he heard the landing, certain it produced injuries in the role player.

Kel sat in the rearmost seat next to the major, the general up front beside their driver, a uniformed NP officer. After they were on the road a few minutes, Kel decided he'd restrained his curiosity as long as he could bear it.

"Major," Kel said in a low voice. "If it's not rude to ask, who was that man in the hostage chair?"

The general overheard and turned in his seat to look back at Kel.

"Kark him!" The general snorted a laugh before he continued. "I start this unit twenty-five years ago. I was first commander. I become general and must pass command to next generation. To be Hoplite you must be selected and prove worthy. This man, he try and use family connection to become Hoplite." The general snorted again.

"Spiriakos. Bah. He think because his father is head of his family he can pressure my uncle, head of Domestic Conclave, to force me take his son into unit. I say, 'sure no problem' and take him. I think pretty soon he get idea he not wanted here and quit."

Gavros' toothy grin exploding beneath the bushy mustache told Kel all he needed to know.

He liked these people.

Kel thanked the general and the major for the night's activities. As he turned to depart the general stopped him.

"My men report to me when you are on NP training range. They are impressed. I think we can work together, Meester Kel. Tomorrow is party at my home. You will attend."

More than a mere invitation, that was an order.

"The party start at 1600. You be there at 1400. Understand? Major send you grid. Goodnight, Meester Kel. Rest."

11

"Why you must work so late, Meester Kel?" Eirene asked as she poured him more kaff at the breakfast table the next morning.

"I was making some new friends, Eirene."

The woman cackled at this. "You be careful. Big boy like you can get hurt with too many girlfriends. Girls here very jealous."

He'd received the grids from Major Todalin and checked the route. The location was about an hour north of the capital, close to the foothill country. He had a few hours to kill before starting the drive north, remembering the general's very specific instructions about when to arrive. There were some tasks he could accomplish at the embassy. He dressed for the morning with an eye to avoid a repeat of his slovenly appearance yesterday—as though he'd just come out of a hot house—which he had.

Thirty minutes later, he walked into Pen's office. Pen divided attention between multiple documents floating over his datapad. "Hey buddy, late night last night?"

"Yeah," Kel admitted. He'd skipped the morning PT session but felt stiffer as a result. "And an interesting one. Find anything out about our vehicle problem?"

"There's not a commercial source for armor to upgrade the vehicles, but there are sources for some composite plating that should offer decent ballistic and blaster protection. I'm arranging to get some samples," Pen said.

"Great news. The sooner you can get them, the sooner we can test them."

Kel moved on to Bell's office. Kel closed the door behind him and sat down to relate last night's activities to the RSO.

"Wow. That's... impressive. No one has made any kind of inroads like that with the Kyrgiakos inner circle. So, you joined him and his Hoplites for their training, and now you're off to party with them? Sounds like the intel guy is going to be eating his heart out."

Kel didn't mention that his next stop would be to brief the 'trade analyst' Don Snyder.

"Still up for training with the protective detail tomorrow?" Bell asked.

"Will do. See you there." Kel wanted to evaluate the protective detail. They might already be highly competent and need no significant mentoring, or they might be a disorganized circus. If they could benefit from his mentoring, he'd offer.

Kel made his way through the tower lobby waiting for the lift to the Trade Ministry floor. The doors parted and out walked Chief Minister Sun, accompanied by a small flock of diplomats leading a short, stocky man with curly gray hair whom Kel recognized as the ambassador. He had yet to meet the man but recognized him from the many portraits around the embassy.

Ambassador Marlo Givens was surrounded by sycophants stepping over each other in attempts to grab attention, when the group paused to look intently at Kel.

So much for being invisible, he thought.

One of the men whispered something in the ambassador's ear. The older man's face lit up and he moved out of the cloud of attendants to approach Kel.

"Mister Turner, is it? A pleasure to meet you. Welcome to Meridian. I apologize for not meeting you on your arrival, but I understand Minister Sun greeted you on our behalf."

Kel thanked the ambassador as he stole a glance in the direction of the chief minister, secretly pleased to see the man squirm to avoid Kel's eyes.

"Yes, Ambassador. It is an honor to be of service to you and the House of Reason."

The man's face brightened even more from his already wide smile.

"The pleasure is ours. Hopefully when my busy schedule allows, we can find time to sit and get acquainted. A legionnaire of your qualifications, why I'm sure you have many stories to share. I'll have you know, though, I'm no stranger to adversity myself. As a young diplomat, I was once kidnapped and held ransom by a Kublar chieftain, and it was no mean feat of diplomacy and firm character to reach a settlement for my..."

An assistant leaned forward to whisper again in the ambassador's ear, breaking the man's concentration at the height of his tale. "Yes, oh, I suppose you're right. Duty calls, Mister Turner. Do let my office know if you are in need of anything we can do to support you," he said, as he and his swarm of sycophants continued their journey. Kel had bounced Don earlier without response. He tried the door to his office and waited a few minutes before composing another short message.

Made contact with General Kyrgiakos.
Initial impression favorable. I think he
wants joint cooperation. Second meeting
tonight. Can I update you tomorrow?

He checked the time and decided he might as well start his drive north.

The drive was pleasant. In the rolling, hilly countryside above the capital, Kel sped past large fields and grove after grove of manicured trees tended by farmers. The road curved as it ascended, and between rises Kel glimpsed a large complex of buildings on a plateau to his west, with an imposing citadel dominating the rest. It was stark white, carved out of the surrounding bedrock. Huge columns surrounded all sides and a long colonnade led to a grand entrance.

Is that the Pa'artenon? he wondered. He'd check it on his link when he had time.

Not long after, he came to a section of the road where ornate gates marked private drives leading beyond, and soon to the grid he had been given.

A National Police uniformed guard checked his identification, smiled, and activated the gate from his vine-covered guardhouse. The drive led around a cut-rock face to open before the vast grounds of a massive estate.

Wide stone steps led up to a palace fronted with elegant columns supporting a portico. On either side of the stairs, fountains fed waterfalls descending into reflecting pools. Hanging flowers, vines, and ornamental trees flourished in lush colors. Everything looked perfect.

Kel floated into a parking area farther around the bend and left his speeder beside two other vehicles. No one appeared, so Kel decided to walk up the stone stairs to find the entrance.

Large double doors awaited deep under the portico and as he approached, one of the doors opened and a middle-aged woman in a house staff uniform greeted him. Kel checked the time, he was two minutes early.

"Mister Kel, the general is waiting for you in his study. Please follow me."

Kel followed her through a grand hall and into a high-ceilinged room that opened to a huge patio with a view over a garden and ponds. The room was filled with house staff setting up long tables and rearranging furniture, busy preparing for the reception.

She continued past the gathering room to an ornate wood door and knocked before entering. A large study ringed by couches, hanging art, and statues of the human form filled the space. A stone fireplace that had clearly held many fires burned behind a desk where the general stood awaiting Kel.

"Come sit with me, Meester Kel. What can Sofia bring you?"

Kel begged off any refreshment and followed the general's invitation to sit. He stammered out a compliment on the home and grounds.

"Yes. My family has been here since the beginning. This home is very old. I do not live here all the time. I live closer to capital with my family, but I enjoy coming here. It is special place to share with my Hoplites and friends," he said gesturing to Kel.

An antique clock ticked on the mantle as Kel remained silent, waiting for the general to lead the conversation.

"What do you think of our performance last night?"

Kel had thought about that on the drive, anticipating the very question.

"Sir, I was impressed. Hostage rescue is without a doubt one of the most difficult and demanding missions. You have developed your capabilities highly to achieve what you demonstrated last night."

"Thank you, Meester Kel. I am curious. How would Dark Ops do differently?"

Kel shrugged.

"It's not that we would necessarily do anything differently. We do have some better technologies that make the work easier, but as far as *how* we conduct that type of mission, our tactics and techniques are similar."

Hostage rescue was a mission his team trained on frequently, as it required the same skill sets that would be needed for most any raid or urban assault. He'd only ever participated in one actual hostage rescue, but he'd done it hundreds of times in training.

Once on Qulingat't the job had been to recover an asset who had been part of their information network. The spy's activities had been revealed by his injudicious display of wealth—his reward for guiding the team to caches of weapons—and he was grabbed by the local crime gang. His mate had come to their camp and had made the case, albeit in a difficult manner given their race's cultural penchant for speaking indirectly and diffusely. Eventually they understood and she led them to the kidnappers' local hangout, really nothing more than a small gathering of their strangely secreted saliva and mud huts. Bigg and Braley made a quick decision to end the crisis and remove the criminal threat that had been abusing the local population. That operation was probably less complex than many raids he'd been on—like the zhee compound they'd hit on Kylar—but Kel considered it one of their successes as a team.

Kel described for his host some of the tech they used for surveillance, distraction, and breaching, but did his best to illustrate that the tech was a minor enabler in those type of operations. Assaulter skills were the foundation of hostage rescue and in Kel's opinion the Hoplites did well.

The general seemed to consider this for a minute. He rose and moved to a small table holding several decanters and containers, and returned with two glasses, handing one to Kel. The general remained standing as he downed the small glass of clear liquid in one gulp and gestured for Kel to try the same.

Kel sniffed it curiously, found it to be pleasantly aromatic, and threw it back. Kel as a rule did not drink. He had no objection to drinking; he simply rarely did. It was part of his discipline to maintain readiness. No matter. He would never refuse to do so and sacrifice an opportunity to bond with his host.

It burned going down but was silky smooth at the bottom of its travel and not unpleasant. The general smiled.

Kel felt slightly emboldened as the liquid warmed his insides.

"General, I've read about the incident at the school and the deaths of the children last month. Can I ask what happened?"

The man's shoulders dipped slightly.

"That was tragedy, Meester Kel. I feel the weight of it every moment." *He looks like it. Maybe I should have held off. That's why I don't drink. Me and my mouth.*

The general must have felt like discussing it. He went on to give Kel a thorough brief on the incident. He explained that the Hoplites were loading out to make the sub-orbital hop to Peloponnese and take command when the incident prematurely reached its climax.

Negotiations were failing, and the teachers had already been executed. Meridian Eleftheria would start killing children if their immediate demands weren't met. The local NP Special Reaction Team had tried to halt the movement of the hostage takers as they transferred from the vehicles to the aircraft. That's when the shooting started.

It went badly.

When it was over, all of the hostage takers were killed, but so were twelve children. Three more died later of their wounds. Stories still popped up in the local feeds about the surviving families who'd lost children in the tragedy.

"Each National Police division has tactical special response unit. They go through same selection as Hoplites and are all trained in same manner. Why it went so wrong? We continue to look for answers."

The two men sat silently for a few more minutes. Kel knew to keep his mouth shut. The general rose and took Kel's glass and poured them two more drinks. He followed the general's example, this time sipping slowly.

After some silence the general turned to Kel.

"My uncle and Domestic Conclave ask for Republic help. I only want help from one source. I sent for you. I need Dark Ops."

Kel was surprised by the admission. *Gavros requested military advisors from the Republic. How did Gavros know about Dark Ops? And by name? Through Jacee? Was it Don?*

"I am ambivalent to more diplomats from Republic. The people from your embassy I do not like. Jacee is competent bureaucrat. I do not need bureaucrat. We have plenty already. Meester Kel, you have official accord, yes?"

Kel showed him the accord from his pocket link. The general went to his desk, retrieved a small item, and handed the small black object to Kel.

"This is National Police Investigator *aspida*. Carry it at all times. I want that you work for me. No one else on

Meridian should interest you. I am asking your assistance during this time of crisis."

Kel didn't know the word but looked at the insignia in its carrier. It was a small badge with markings similar to the NP seal; a sword and bolts.

"I wish you to work with Hoplites. I also wish you to visit NP special response teams around Meridian. Transit, House, all are subordinate to National Police. You spend time with us, you spend time with only group that matter.

"There is more bad time coming. We come closer to next Domestic Conclave gathering. I have more problem than I have trustworthy people. Hoplites must stay ready for next crisis. I think you can help with all."

Kel took a breath. This was not what as he was expecting. It was quite a bit more. General Kyriakos was giving him access to the entire planet and the cooperation of the National Police. *I think the rapport part of my mission is finally showing results.*

"Yes, General. I'd like to help."

The general reached out to shake Kel's hand. "You must call me Gavros, Meester Kel. I am the chief, the boss. You say my name, everyone know who you mean. There is only one Gavros."

They talked more about the security situation. Kel listened to Gavros' assessments about the ME and felt comfortable to ask more questions. Gavros held up a finger to pause Kel, then placed his nearest hand over Kel's resting forearm.

"Kel, first I have another matter I wish to discuss."

I'm kind of glad to be done with the meester thing, honestly, Kel thought.

"I have daughter. She is wonderful girl. She is soon to start university." He paused a second to see if Kel was following along with his discussion.

"Her dream is to go to Liberinthine and attend university in capital of Republic. You can make this happen for her, yes?"

Kel looked the general in the eyes and nodded. "Yes. We can make that happen."

When Kel had first been accepted into Dark Ops there was a long period of initial training. The majority of it was not the physical culling of a selection; legionnaires were selected for DO because they'd already been through those extensive processes. Most of the training was exposure to new concepts, familiarization with the best technologies and equipment. Orientation to a bigger picture of things. "Need to know only," type-things.

He remembered the day he'd sat in a secure room with two other leejes for a briefing from an unidentified individual in a tailored suit. Republic Intelligence. No one had to go through the unnecessary and clumsy step of introducing the briefer. Some things went without saying. That's how it was.

The briefer spent two hours as Kel and the others were *read in* on several programs run by RI. Classified programs. When they were done, Kel couldn't help but feel that his favorite holoaction and spy dramas from childhood had been permanently ruined for him. Most of what he'd previously thought mystical became ordinary.

Kel was able to promise Gavros that he could get his daughter accepted to a university on Liberinthine. Dark Ops may have been at the Republic's beck and call, but when Dark Ops needed a favor done, the Republic made it happen. There was a program for that. Its mechanisms were the mundane stuff of everyday business, mechanisms greased by social ties, loyalty, and of course, money.

Most of the Republic's governmental structure was composed of analysts and bureaucrats. Within that pool were people with the same social, school, and family ties. The same strata of society intertwined throughout the administrative halls of the universities.

Among those powerful admissions officers were personnel on the payroll of the Republic. Money alone did not motivate them. It was a deeper confluence of motivations. When an old school-friend, someone from *that* government agency—"you know which one"—called you to ask for help with the admission for a "friend of the Republic, someone important to us," it took advantage of several instincts.

Firstly, the person asking for the favor was usually an old friend. You'd been in the same club or organization together. You'd clinked glasses together at all the right parties. The person asking for the favor was not a stranger. It wouldn't do to let him down.

Secondly, here was your chance to reaffirm your loyalty to the Republic. *They wouldn't be asking if it wasn't important for the Republic in some way, right?* you might think. This appealed to your sense of loyalty and patriotism. And here was your chance to participate in something that was, well, secret.

Lastly, you were paid. A modest contribution, a sort of retainer for just such an eventuality, appeared annually in your bank account. There was usually a significant bonus for the successful placement of each candidate. Tax-free income was the best kind. Legal, tax-free income.

It was a successful program that offered an enticement for the cooperation of susceptible persons to exploit the gathering of intelligence.

And it was a program that Gavros knew of.

"Yes. We can make that happen." He wondered again, *Did Jacee or Don float that enticement to Gavros, or did he just assume it could be done?*

Gavros smiled.

"The party will be starting soon. I want you to enjoy yourself, Kel. I have much to do."

Gavros checked the time. He stood behind his desk and leaned over to open several drawers. One at a time, he produced thick binders, a datapad, and several chips that he laid on the desk. He keyed the datapad and moved from behind the desk.

"I must go greet guests. I wish for you to stay here and be comfortable. I will come and retrieve you in two hours, yes?"

Kel nodded and Gavros left the study, closing the door on his way out.

He moved to the desk and began examining what Gavros had left behind. The datapad was unlocked. Kel flicked through file after file of intelligence summaries, holo recordings of what looked like interviews and suspect interrogations, and more.

The binders contained printed documents and still images. The chips Kel examined with his link, and he found more of the same—raw data from the National Police's investigations of the ME for the past year or more.

I'm giving something, he's giving something. But what am I getting for it all? He was now in the confidence of—as Jacee said—the most powerful man on the planet, and inside the organization with the most crucial role in stopping the crisis. Kel wondered as he scrolled through the opened trove of information.

Have I just become his ally or pawn?

"Come, Kel, time to eat," the general said from the doorway. Kel had returned all the materials on the desk to their neat piles.

Gavros led him into the great room of the house. The tables he'd seen previously were now draped with colorful spreads, crowded with trays heaped with delicacies. He recognized many of the Hoplites as he moved into the room; some raised their glass to cheer their Dark Ops comrade.

"You are our guest, Kel, make yourself at home with us. Eat and drink!" Gavros gestured around the room.

Music spilled into the room from a band on the patio. The instruments made a pleasant if somewhat twangy sound, at times reaching a fervent rhythm.

Women in various states of dress danced on many of the tables while others moved through the gathering of men, flirting with the Hoplites. Some of the Hoplites were engaged too fervently in eating and drinking to pay notice to the twisting beauties moving in and about them.

He stopped to admire the sights. Having been all over the galaxy, he felt appreciative that he was from a species with two sexes, identifiable by their many secondary characteristics.

Kel took in a big breath and headed to one of the tables, eyeing a large rack of sizzling meat that he could smell from across the room. *This might be a long night. Best to provision myself!*

As the night wore on and the moon rose high, Kel decided to make a quiet departure. The noise of the party rose to a pitch as the jovial Hoplites downed drink after drink. *Yes, time to go.*

After making his goodbyes, Kel drove down the slow, winding road back to the city, the stars glittering above its skyline.

He'd traveled for twenty minutes when he approached a blind curve cut through a hillside with rising ground on both sides. Vehicles were stopped ahead of him for a length of approximately ten cars. Kel wondered if there had been an accident and thought about pulling to the shoulder to see if he could assist anyone injured.

What's that? Kel made out a pedestrian in the road, menacing vehicle occupants with a rifle. He'd been feeling drowsy. No longer.

Kel had his S-5 draped across the passenger seat with the muzzle down. Killing the lights of his vehicle, he grabbed the carbine and raised it, viewing through the optic as he bumped up the magnification. Keying his specs to night vision, he identified multiple individuals with weapons, gesturing at the vehicles they had halted in both directions. Kel slid his body to the passenger side of the vehicle and carefully exited, taking his carbine and reaching behind the seat to grab his protective vest, donning it quickly.

Kel moved to the shoulder slowly, scanning through the optic of his weapon as he strained to form a picture of the situation. *No doubt about what's happening here.* He keyed his link and bounced Major Todalin from behind the speeder.

The visual popped up in his specs.

"Hello, Kel—forget something?" the major said grinning.

"Major, I'm about ten kilometers downhill from the estate. It appears there is a roadblock and it is definitely not security forces. I see multiple armed males halting traffic and removing people from their vehicles."

The major sobered up instantly. "Can you tell how many?"

Kel was about to answer when gunshots fired. He peeked around the vehicle through his optic. On the bank of the opposite rise, two bodies lay prostrated, gunmen behind them, weapons pointed down at the still figures.

"They're executing victims. Send help." He closed the link and moved farther right toward the embankment. Ahead, standing halfway up the rise was another gunman, bathed in the lights of the vehicles at the lead of the halted column.

Kel scanned around as much as he could. Using his best stealth to ascend the embankment, he could see the front of the column. Two men moved up the middle of the road toward him. He did some quick math. Two gunmen still menaced the figures splayed out on the opposite embankment, while another gunman on the opposite embankment looked toward Kel.

Only one thing to do.

Kel moved the selector of his weapon as he allowed the reticle of his optic to settle on the man opposite him. Kel saw the man open his mouth and raise his weapon just as Kel broke his first shot. He was cognizant of seeing his sight rise slightly with the recoil and he saw the man fall. Later when he played it back in his mind, he recalled the image of the man's upper chest exploding.

Kel snapped his eyes to locate the gunman on the right embankment as the man also began to turn toward Kel, confusion showing just as he reacted to the impact of Kel's next shot. He took the extra millisecond to allow his reticle to settle on the man's chest. The man fell as Kel sent two controlled shots at the man's upper torso. Likewise, Kel later remembered the light patch on the man's shirt, a pocket perhaps, where Kel held the reticle each time he pressed the trigger.

His S-5 had little report or signature in the dark in its suppressed mode.

Crouching, Kel ran along the bank, searching for where he had seen the two gunmen execute the passengers. Ahead, the other gunmen were moving down the column, yelling into the vehicles that their victims had taxes to pay, unbelievably oblivious to the deaths of their two friends at Kel's hands. Their boisterous attempts to intimidate the civilians worked in Kel's favor.

He located the moving gunmen first. They stood relatively close to each other, no more than a meter apart. Kel started on the left and put two rapid, controlled shots into the first man's chest as he drove the weapon right and immediately did the same to the other gunman. He prepared to follow up with more shots, but saw the men drop almost instantly.

He lowered his weapon slightly and scanned, looking for movement, when gunfire cracked. Rounds zinged through the air, impacting somewhere behind him. Kel burst down the embankment to lower ground. He'd been exposed for some time.

Moving along the row of repulsors, he kept the vehicles between him and the remaining gunmen where he'd last seen them. Passengers cowered in the vehicles he passed, some of them uttering screams muffled by glass as they saw him. *Shut up. I'm here to help*, he silently implored.

Kel knelt, canting his weapon to allow him to get lower and see beneath the green repulsor wagon that held the yowling passenger he'd just startled. *I'm about to give you a reason to really yell, lady.* Somewhere ahead was the assailant who'd just shot at him.

Old-fashioned soft wheels screeched on pavement and Kel sprang up into a run to see one of the gunmen dive into a vehicle. Its driver pointed the vehicle downhill, struggling to keep the vehicle straight as they attempted to speed away past the oncoming vehicles halted in the other direction.

Kel sighted in on the vehicle and its passenger compartment, sending as many rounds as he could at the fleeing transport. His efforts were rewarded with the sound of the windscreen shattering but soon lost sight as it screeched around a bend in the road and was gone.

Kel took a breath and looked around to make sure there were no other assailants. Several people had gotten out of their cars. "Remain in your vehicles for your safety!" Kel yelled, but only a few complied.

He was about to bounce the major again when from behind, several vehicles raced toward him. Hoplites, recognizable by their unkempt appearance, protective gear, and weapons hung on and out of a small caravan of speeders careening downhill at him. He raised his hands over head as men leapt from the vehicles, weapons raised at Kel.

"There're multiple bad guys down on both embankments and in the road," Kel repeated several times until he saw Colonel Graviakis approaching, motioning him it was okay to lower his hands.

"I shot at least four of them, but I haven't dead-checked them or put restraints on any."

The white lights on the Hoplite weapons turned the small valley into an early dawn. They moved in formations along both sides of the line of halted vehicles. One group found the two men Kel had dispatched on the road, removed their weapons and restrained them. Other teams worked the embankments and did the same with the gunmen Kel had downed, as other members of the unit moved ahead, searching cars halted from the other direction.

Kel gave a description of the vehicle and the two male gunmen who'd escaped. The colonel barked a command and two Hoplite vehicles stuffed with operators sped down the sloping road in pursuit.

Soon Gavros appeared and joined Kel as he inspected one of the corpses. Young. Scraggly beard. Thin and unmuscled. *Were these ME's best? Were they just hoods out robbing citizens?* He hadn't seen Gavros pull up, confident that he could leave the security to his friends while he inspected his work.

"How many, Kel? Five, six against one?" Gavros asked. "Time for your report."

Kel gave an account of what had happened to Gavros, the colonel, and several of the other Hoplites now gathered around him. Producing his link and projecting a holo, he showed the encounter as recorded by his specs. A Hoplite stepped forward and pushed a water pouch into Kel's hand as he answered questions. "How did you get the drop on them?" "Did they react quickly to your shots?" "Did any of them give you a good fight, or was it just target practice for you?" All were good questions. Most he didn't have a succinct answer to.

"Just lucky," was his final summation.

They remained on site for several hours until the sun rose. Vehicles from the National Police and the other security units responded as did a medical hover. One of the gunmen Kel had shot was still alive. Two Hoplites accompanied the wounded man with the medicos as the hover lifted off for the capital.

The two civilians on the embankment were dead. None of the other passengers had been harmed.

Kel walked the entire scene with Gavros and the colonel for hours. Finally, as the investigators bagged the bodies and took the last holos, Gavros folded his arms.

"This was ME," he said. "We didn't have to wait long for those more bad times, Kel."

It was the start of Kel's fourth day on Meridian.

FLASHBACK

Gee Lieutenant, I Get the Feeling You're Not Genuinely Happy for Me
Antione

I was flaked out with the squad in some shade, my bucket off. After 48 hours of continuous fighting, we were getting our first chance at a little shut eye. Sergeant Shuck is squad leader now. Trumbull stepped up to take fire team Bravo. Recon company cleaned up the last bit of resistance on the spacefield even before the mounted platoon could land. At daylight, Pachyderm drop ships began depositing grav tanks and basic Repub infantry battalions. Elsewhere on the planet, we were told, companies of the Legion were already landed and hard at it.

I dozed in and out, too exhausted to really sort out the images playing in my head. We'd pushed out from the spacefield to secure the adjacent city and locate pockets of resistance. We were moving out before the armor landed. Recon takes the lead, don't you know? It was slow, methodical clearing. We found pockets of militia concealed amongst the civilian population. Not big enough to push us back, but enough to slow us down. We at least had our mounted platoon by that point. Our squad encountered a pretty big militia strongpoint and we called up a FAV and hit them with the heavies. They were dug in to stay. Then we got some assist from a Talon to flatten the whole building.

The militia were every bit the crazies we were warned about. They'd bunkered in an apartment complex. What did they think was going to happen to the civilians living there? We cleared what was left after the Talon's pass, but there wasn't much we could do. I'm trying not to think about it right now. I got it, but I didn't get it. Their own citizens were expendable to them.

I was glad the basics were taking over. Let them do the rest of the grunt work, crawling behind the Magnus IVs. Even as whacked out as the militia are proving to be, not even a fanatic would stay to die-in-place seeing those multi-turreted behemoths roll through the city. Those grav tanks were the best tool for the job and would probably prevent more civilian casualties anyway.

I'd just gone completely unconscious when someone kicked my foot. "Sergeant Turner." I come alert to see our platoon sergeant, Sergeant Bullock above me. I start to rise but he waves me to stay down. He takes a knee and pulls his bucket off. "How're the men?"

"We're good, Sergeant Bullock. Ready to get back at it." I check the chrono on my forearm. I'd been out for an hour.

"Good. Meet me at the company CP once you get yourself together. Take your time." I take a pull from a hydration pouch and put my bucket on. The rest of the squad is out cold. I don't see Sergeant Shuck. Pabon is snoring loudly, his head cocked back at an acute angle on his carryall. I leave mine where it lies. No need to take it with me to the CP. I pick up my N-16 and head out. I'm still a little groggy and not even curious about why the platoon sergeant woke me.

I have no idea my life is about to change forever.

As I get to the command post, a restaurant with the windows knocked out by overpressure from a grenade, Shuck passes me on his way out. "Hey, good luck Turner. See you soon." He makes it sound like he's going somewhere. "Where you headed?" I ask. "They need me in second platoon. You're taking the squad." Second platoon had lost three leejes last night, including a squad leader. He explains. "Our squad isn't going to have any more freefall missions this campaign, so we're getting cannibalized. At least, I am. Hope we get back together once Antione is over. We've got orbital jumpmaster school to look forward to." We clap each other on the shoulder and he takes off.

So, I'm squad leader now? I think as I walk into the CP. The CO, Captain Hardinger, is seated at a table covered in sooty linen, three buckets resting on top. Sergeant Bullock and Lieutenant Cosgrove stand in front of him. I assume rigid attention and wait to be recognized. "Sergeant Turner. Front and center." I take three large steps into the room and pop to attention in front of the CO. "Sergeant Turner, reporting as ordered, sir." I don't remember being told I would be reporting to the CO, but it doesn't matter now.

"Stand easy, Sergeant Turner," the CO says from where he sits. "Pop your lid. I'll make this brief. Good job on the spaceport." He mentions the firefights and Staff Sergeant Sung. He compliments me on my tactical problem solving and small unit leadership during the city clearance. I'm waiting for him to tell me I'm taking the squad. "We have a special tasking. It may involve freefall insertion. It may not. You're taking over the pathfinder squad and being detached to another element. Ground force protection for...Silver." He says silver with a capital "S". I can hear it. I have no idea what Silver is. "Or, it's whatever they tell you your mission is. Do you understand?" My silence conveys I don't.

Lieutenant Cosgrove looks like he's fit to be tied. His lips are pursed so tight they're blanching. "Sir?" Sergeant Bullock requests permission to speak from the CO. "Go ahead Sergeant Bullock." The CO looks relieved.

"Sergeant Turner. There are parts of the Legion that don't officially exist, you understand? Covert. Activities. That's what Silver is. When they need extra muscle, they ask for it from us." Now a crystal energizes and the light goes on. During recon operator training there was a briefing that mentioned something about this. I repeat the hazy memory of the bullet point on the slide.

"Support of special activities, gentlemen?"

The CO nods. "Just. So." The lieutenant looks about to burst. Now I get it. He's jealous of me. Again. The CO stands. "Sergeant, I know you will represent Legion Reconnaissance with the professionalism I expect of you. Don't let us down."

I snap to attention. "Swift, silent, deadly, sir."

I'm dismissed. I'm to get the squad together and move to the spacefield. A Talon will be waiting to take us to our new assignment. Outside I'm putting my bucket on as I feel the hulking presence of Lieutenant Cosgrove. He leans down to put his bare face next to mine.

"There's no way you know how lucky you are, Sergeant." There's no anger in his eyes. He reminds me of a kid who's dropped his candy on the ground. "Don't frell this up."

Sergeant Bullock walks back from the CP with me to tell the squad. I ask him if he ever worked with Silver. He smiles. "I did," and left it at that.

Eyes are wide. Mouths are open. Sergeant Bullock doesn't raise his voice or make threats, not that he ever does. Everyone understands what he's telling us. "What you see and do on this mission, you won't speak about it. Understand, leejes?" Everyone nods soberly. "Just do what's expected of you. It's a special opportunity. It's because you're all the best. Best in the Legion." He's proud of us.

We top off charge packs and stuff carryalls with a few rations, hydration pouches, and more charge packs and grenades. I have everyone grab extra AP mines. Our breaching tools made it down from orbit with the mounted platoon, but we haven't picked them up yet. Probably sitting in a grav container on the airfield. I suppose Silver will get us what we need for whatever mission awaits. An hour later we're on the duracrete looking at a Talon spiral down to land in front of us.

The ramp lowers while in the air as it completes its final rotation and touches down. Off the back hops a leej. I guess it's a leej. He's in no armor I've ever seen before. It's like comparing a turbo speeder to a tractor. We're wearing the tractor. Riding high on his chest is a carbine length blaster with an energrenade launcher tube underneath. A hand blaster sits on his waist. His chest is covered with charge packs and strangely shaped grenades. A vibroblade handle protrudes from a sheath. Nothing is from the inventory of the Legion we're in.

He sees us and ambles our way. I am mesmerized.

"You my recon squad?"

I'm unsure whether to come to attention. I pop to parade rest, as do my corporals. "Sergeant Turner and pathfinder squad, first recon platoon. Sir." I add the last, unconfidently.

He chuckles. "Call me TA. Get on the bird, men. We've got work to do."

12

"Man, what happened to you?" Kel's roommates asked as he walked up to the breakfast table later that morning. If twarg wrestling was a thing, Kel supposed he must look like a champion. Weary and disheveled, he was ready for a kaff and a hot shower. Then bed. But first, he had to get through the entire day ahead.

"Oh, just been working." Kel didn't feel like rehashing the night's events with his friends. He was only interested in breakfast and kaff.

Eirene appeared to fill Kel's cup and without saying a word, placed a hand on his back and patted it.

Kel felt better after the large meal and went into the kitchen to bring his empty dishes to the sink. He gave Eirene a hug and thanked her. She smiled, her eyes damp with tears. She was becoming one of Kel's favorite people.

I'll get all the sleep I need when I'm dead, Kel told himself as he loaded up his gear and drove to the range to meet Bell and his protective detail. But it'd be okay. He had only slept a couple of nights since his arrival and had not worked out in two days. He'd pop a stim tab later if he needed it.

He checked his link to see that he had a message from Don.

Bounce me when you can, it said. *I can meet anytime today.*

Kel sent him a message back, saying he'd meet him at his office in the afternoon. Kel's intelligence coup was a priority, but so was helping Bell with his protective detail. Being the only operator on the planet meant having to manage multiple critical tasks by himself. Already he felt like he was falling behind.

The next time Meridian needed help, Kel would definitely recommend that several kill teams be sent. There was only so much one man could do. Even for an operator. Kel met Bell on the range as promised to help him train the members of the ambassador's protective detail.

"Thought you might like to know," Bell told him in low tones, "I got an alert from the liaison this morning that there was an incident north of the city. ME killed some civilians along the north highway. It's a big deal because that's an area where a lot of the aristocrats live. Seems like the ME were trying to collect 'taxes.' Didn't go so well for them though."

Kel laughed. "Yeah, I was there with the Hoplites and General Kyrgiakos."

Bell raised his eyebrows. "And?"

"That's about the size of it. ME murdered two civilians and were probably going to do more of the same before I got involved. They got one guy in custody in the hospital and are on the trail of another two who escaped."

"Wow. That's a big deal. As far as I know they haven't had a lot of live suspects to interrogate."

Changing the subject, Kel asked if they could get the day started. Focusing on evaluating the protective detail would take his mind off last night's fight. He won. But it easily could've gone the other way. *I was outnumbered, big time,* he realized, over and over again after the incident. *Is this going to be a theme for my time on Meridian?*

A small part of him wished he'd said no to the lone operator mission.

He stayed with them for the morning, coaching where helpful, giving them some new drills to try, but all the time anxious to get to the embassy to share the intel gathered from the night before with Don. After handshakes and compliments to the men of the detail, he excused himself, accepted Bell's thanks, and took the dodging path through traffic to the diplomatic complex and Don's office.

He found Don leaning against his doorway, waiting.

Kel held up his link. "I think you're going to like this."

Don slaved the files to the multiple screens. Kel remained quiet as the intelligence officer swiped through file after file, holo after holo, picture after picture.

"Kel, how did you get all this?" Don was clearly impressed.

He gave a blow-by-blow of the past two days, ending with the events of the early morning hours on the highway. Don asked few questions during Kel's re-telling. Instead, he stared intently, his silence prompting Kel to continue at any pause. He finished with the live terrorist being evacuated off the scene.

Don's eyebrows elevated and stayed there. "There's a lot to analyze here. Good job by the way, if I failed to say so."

I wonder if that hurt him, admitting to me I've gotten more in a few days than he has all year. Now Kel knew he was tired. He never boasted, even to himself. "Don, I've got to be honest. I'm spent. I need about a day's worth of sleep before I'm going to be worth a damn for much of anything."

"I'm sure. No problem. Look, tomorrow is the weekly rest day. The embassy closes as well. Why don't you come over to my place in the afternoon and we'll eat and spend some time sorting through some of this together. How's that sound?"

Not as good as sleep does, Kel thought, but only said, "Great. I'll see you tomorrow then."

He crashed hard. He awoke confused to find twelve hours had passed and that the sun was rising on the next day. *Guess I needed that!* Neither Gren nor Ramer had stirred yet, leaving him alone in the courtyard to work out after which he wandered into the kitchen to find his roommate Gren, looking like he'd had a late night.

"I made kaff. There's a full pot. You were out cold when we tried to get you to go to dinner with us."

Kel got ready for the day and then began his next routine: checking his weapons and gear. It was a myth that slug-launching weapons needed to be stripped and cleaned regularly. Weapons like the S-5 did need some maintenance, but holos that showed the hero snaking out the bore of his carbine and disassembling the weapon daily were ridiculous. Checking that the weapons were mechanically sound and functioned was what was most important. The experience of bringing his weapon to bear and hearing *click* instead of bang was unthinkable. Last night would have had a different outcome had his weapon not functioned flawlessly.

It was paradoxical that the more complex blasters required less maintenance and were less prone to failure than the bullet launchers. While the weapons generated massive amounts of heat, they experienced no stress from the explosive combustion of chemical propellants and suffered from little mechanical wear. While Kel missed his K-17, he did not feel under gunned with the S-5. He finished by inspecting his personal protective equipment and then his datalink and specs. Now he felt ready for the rest of the day's tasks. He'd meant to do these things last night, but his desire to close his eyes had won out.

Kel made his way downstairs to his own quarters' sitting area and found a comfortable spot on the couch to do some reading. He didn't want to start working with Don not having reviewed as much as he could. He imagined Don would probably have spent their time apart tearing into the information with zeal. Kel did not want to be unprepared.

He started by trying to sort the material into coherent groupings. Gavros had given him a massive data dump. One part of the material was information about the National Police itself: its composition, strength, budget, locations—the works.

There was a section on the Hoplites. There were communications codes, bios on its members, lists of equipment and weapons, and more of the same budget statements as for the rest of the NP. *I thought those boys were well funded, but wow. By percentage, DO might not have that big a piece of the Legion pie.*

It gave the potential for a complete picture of the entire organization. *Gavros really came clean and opened the books for the Republic with this. It's almost as if he's trying to show how above the board he and his organization is.* There was a lot of graft and corruption in local government around the galaxy. If there was something rotten about the books of the NP, an analyst could pick it out of this mess of numbers. *Why?*

Looking now at the volumes of reports on the numerous incidents involving ME, Kel started a new document and attempted to form a chronology of events.

Kel was not a trained investigator. Last year he had been through the DO operations and intelligence course. Beyond refining how to plan operations, it delved into how intelligence was gathered and clandestine operations were carried out. It also reinforced the basic structure and staff of conventional units. Order of battle was essential. DO had to organize and train entire armies by themselves. Bigg had done it several times in his career, both with human and non-human allies.

They also taught him the science of gathering tactical intelligence—from questioning suspects and prisoners, to then being able to analyze that information—a critical skill. In many of their operational environments, they had no sources for information other than what they themselves developed. Meridian was proving to be a similar example. *And sometimes incomplete intelligence is better than flat out bad intel. A kill team doesn't have the capability of a room full of RI analysts, but at least if we develop our own intel, it hasn't been filtered or subject to a group consensus before being disseminated down to us.*

A rapid operational tempo demanded access to information as quickly as possible. He'd first gotten to observe this process five years before, when he was still with Legion Reconnaissance. The long campaign on Antione, in which he and his I&S platoon had been among the first to fight, had given him his first glimpse into the world of Dark Ops. It had changed the course of his life.

A month or more into the planetary offensive, Kel and his platoon had been detailed to provide ground force protection for a DO kill team. It was his first glimpse into the black world within the Legion. After a month of watching how they worked, Kel knew that's where he wanted to be. The five operators were conducting missions in an isolated region of the planet and the need for more 'muscle' was provided by Kel's unit.

His first experience with the kill team was providing containment on a series of raids they'd conducted for the purpose of gaining intelligence. The team would start the operation with a target housing a potential source of information. The I&S platoon provided the external security for the objective and also acted as a larger fire element if needed.

What Kel remembered about that first hit was that after no more than thirty minutes, the operators were giving Kel and his platoon a fragmentary order for another immediate mission, and after passing off the prisoners to the Repub Army MPs, they were moving out to another target.

That process repeated three more times on that same mission. Kel and his squad mates marveled at the operators' tireless glee at moving higher and higher up the chain of organization. They'd recovered caches of arms and explosives, and hard intelligence which led them to a sizeable compound and the enemy leadership.

In one day, the information chain they'd followed led them to the source of much of the resistance in that sector.

Kel remembered as the kill team called in an orbital strike on the compound. In a blink of an eye, searing missiles transformed the enemy into an impotent pile of biologic waste.

The acronym one of the operators had explained to him became a large part of Kel's analytical process: D-A-R-K.

Destroy the enemy with precision and violence of action.

Analyze and exploit from tactical questioning and gathering of intelligence.

Rehearse and plan follow-on operations.

Keep up operational tempo.

In practice, it was a much more complex process than what the acronym implied, but like many simple tools, it served a purpose to orient a tired, strained mind when analyzing a complex situation during the fog of battle.

Reflecting on this, his first glimpse into how battlefield intelligence was developed by the pros, a part of him seethed. He had a long standing resentment against RI. So did most of DO. For good reason. Every kill team had at least one negative experience with the spooks of RI. Don might prove the exception that changed his attitude. He was going to keep an open mind. But how Don ended up first on the scene after his ambush in the city still puzzled him. The best he'd been able to come up with was, *he was following me.*

But why? floated around his head, as the holo copies of the documents Gavros gave him beckoned. It was time to stop daydreaming and get back to work.

He started by taking the incidents and trying to place them in chronologic order. He didn't concentrate on the types of acts or the methods used, he just wanted to organize the occurrences chronologically. Later he could organize things by region, methods, and the results.

He checked the time. He'd already been at it for several hours and decided to close up and head to Don's. It was also past lunch. The two men had important work to do, and part of the promised agenda had been food. *P for "plenty" is what I'm looking for.*

"Nice, huh?" Don said when he caught Kel admiring his personal combat grav-sled. Panthers were slick vehicles. They were civilian manufactured and Kel saw them around used as armored rescue vehicles by police, sometimes on the Spiral News Network as background when the story involved blood and bodies. They were standing in Don's residential compound surrounded by serious guards and a serious wall. Kel approved. "You could say the Republic gives me more assets for my personal protection than the diplomatic mission does for theirs, yes?"

"I can see where that'd come in handy. Nice," Kel agreed.

"I'm the sole tenant," Don said, gesturing around the two-story compound as he led Kel up the stairs to his quarters. The mercenary protection force watched Kel ascend the stairs with their boss. These soldiers were the real deal—large, armed, and alert. Not the uniformed rent-a-cops the residences maintained.

The home was as lavishly apportioned as his own, with large comfortable sitting areas and a huge adjoining kitchen and dining area. Halls led in multiple directions to what must have been multiple bedrooms.

A beautiful dark-haired woman appeared from one of the other rooms and made her way to where Kel and Don were standing.

"Kel, this is my girlfriend, Stefania." Don explained she was a student at the university finishing her studies before starting medical school.

"I'm going shopping for dinner for the three of us," she said. "Any special requests?" Don assured her they'd be pleased with whatever she chose and she soon departed.

"C'mon," Don said after her repulsor drove away, "let's go to the back room and we can get some work done."

He led them to a comfortable sitting area with couches and screens on the walls between landscapes depicting hills and lakes from around Tiryns, actual paintings rather than holo-art.

"There's a field active so we can work securely. Before you ask, yes, Stefania is one of my sources on the campus, but she's also my girlfriend. She knows I work at the embassy, but she knows my trade analyst cover. You don't have to worry about mentioning anything mundane concerning the embassy around her."

"What did you tell her about me?"

"That you were a trade assistant; same as your official cover."

He was the intelligence officer, so if Don thought having a national in his house presented no risk, Kel didn't feel in a position to judge him.

"Your security detail and your Panther?" Kel said, referring to the combat grav-sled below them. "How does that jibe with being in the trade ministry?"

Don shrugged his shoulders. "She's a great girl. She knows not to ask too many questions."

They got down to business quickly. Kel was interested to hear what Don thought about the plethora of documents.

"If you were getting paid by the page, I'd say you'd earned enough to buy a home on Pthalo. Again, nice going."

Don made motions over a datapad and passed around holo projections in front of him until he had the order he sought. The first thing Kel noticed was the material he'd struggled to organize himself was in a chronologic timeline. The material Gavros gave them contained many events previously suppressed or concealed from the embassy, not to mention the public. Now they were neatly grouped.

"Wow. I'd just started trying to assemble a timeline out of the raw data before I got here."

Don smiled. "We have programs that do all that. I let my pad review everything and sort the events. Took about a minute."

Kel didn't feel stupid for trying to do the same thing manually, he felt stupid for not having considered that the intelligence officer had the tools to do it rapidly and efficiently. "A lot of new intel in that package, huh?" Kel said, referring to the many incident reports not made available to them previously. "They were holding a lot back from you. How's it feel?" Kel teased the man. He had to know how DO felt about RI withholding intel from them. Kel instantly regretted his jibe when Don frowned. *Yikes! I'm in the man's home. Be polite!* He tried to recover. "Just kidding, Don."

To his credit, Don laughed. "Don't think it's all one-way, Kel. We have a few prejudices about you guys, too."

Kel changed the topic as seamlessly as he could. "What about the Useful Narcissus?" Kel said, using the official name of the program that rewarded acts of espionage with placing the relatives of spies in duranium-league schools on Liberinthine.

"I sent the package to my people, and my secretary will be doing the rest of the formal processes through our cultural office. You were right to accept the request. This is the proof it paid off," he said gesturing at the floating documents. "Big time. I've never had the opportunity to use the program myself, but this is exactly what it was designed to produce. Not bad for a knuckle-dragger." Kel figured he deserved that. If Don could dish it out and take it, maybe he wasn't the reptasaur Kel suspected.

Don took him on a tour of the material, much of which Kel had at least skimmed already. Seeing it organized and broken down into categories was helpful. Connections between acts and methods were demonstrated by another projection, modeling the data in three-dimensions and showing the links and the statistical probability of the purported connections based on the data. It was impressive.

"My early impression is that Meridian Eleftheria is not a grassroots revolutionary movement," Don continued. "I think it's likely there's a well-established faction behind this, using the student freedom movement as a cover for another objective. It's also likely this is inter-family driven. One interpretation is that someone is trying to overthrow not the Domestic Conclave, but rather the Argolis-centered dominance of the DC. Another analysis of the data could lead one to suspect that perhaps the removal of the Kyrgiakos family as the de-facto head of the DC is the goal."

Don went on to illustrate what factors within the data led him to consider that theory.

The majority of acts had occurred in Argolis. That alone was not strange; Argolis was by far the wealthiest and most developed region on the planet. It was also the seat of the planetary government as well as the home to the central university. It had the largest population of any of the Twelve Family's holdings on the planet; that proportionately more attacks had occurred there was not surprising.

Don went back through many of the separate incidents and took the time to unpack what was known about the perpetrators, the victims, and where links occurred. Don made a compelling case. Even in incidents like the school kidnapping, which occurred on Peloponnese, there were distinct, if distant, connections between the victims and the Kyrgiakos family.

All the families had some amount of intermarrying on the planet. None of the known suspects had any familial relation to the Kyrgiakos. Excluding crimes against government and banking institutions, any incident involving crimes against persons—like the school kidnapping—involved victims who had close familial ties to the Kyrgiakos, rather than all Twelve Families.

"That's a hugely non-random finding. The NP must have already recognized this pattern. I didn't see any summary coming to that conclusion in their material," Kel noted.

"That's right. Gavros must have his own analysts looking at this material. I think he held that back from us. I think he wants us to use the raw data to come to our own conclusions."

Kel considered this.

"Maybe so. But what's the next step? What do we share back with Gavros?"

Don held up his hands.

"Hold on there, Legionnaire. We," Don pointed to Kel and himself, "are not sharing anything. We can't make a decision to feed information to Gavros, even if we think he's already come to the same conclusion. The planetary team's got to decide what to do about this. I'll brief the ambassador and his team. Then they'll have recommendations that will be floated to the House of Reason.

"If we prematurely confirm Gavros' fear that there's a conspiracy by another family to oust the Kyrgiakos from power, we might be pushing the strongest man on the planet into more than just fighting the ME. He might start a war against the other families.

"We can't decide who to support at this stage. The ambassador might see things very differently from how grunts like us see this thing, much less the House of Reason. Think about it."

Kel was conflicted. On one hand, Don had a point about not unintentionally sparking an inter-family war. On the other hand, it all struck Kel as the typical way RI made intel disappear into the labyrinth of politics. The only thing Kel knew for sure—he was way in over his head.

"Great. Gavros gave me all this information, knowing what we'd do with it. Now what do I do?"

"Right now, just keep being the good little legionnaire. Help him kill some bad guys. Go evaluate his tactical teams around the planet. If it helps him improve the NP's abilities, it's helping fight the crisis. That's your job. Besides, shooting bad guys is what you like to do anyway, right?"

They heard a knock on the door and Don closed the holos before killing the field as Stefania leaned into the room.

"Are you men ready? Dinner awaits."

They ate well. Afterward the three sat in the living room and Kel exercised his best protection against having to delve into his cover story—he asked the young lady as many questions as he could.

"My parents are farmers," she said with a disarming smile. "They always encouraged me to study, and I did well in school. My examination scores guaranteed me a spot in the central university, and my parents wouldn't hear of me going to a lesser school." Her Standard was nearly flawless. "I'm still not sure I want to be a doctor, but my scores have been high enough that it's been suggested to me by my advisors for so long, it would seem wasteful of me to not at least try."

Kel found that interesting. In any society, doctors held a place of respect. She was a farmer's daughter and the first generation of her family to attend the university. She was likely to become a doctor. To Kel, it did not seem opportunities were being denied her in society.

Kel wanted to ask her about the unrest this past year and what she'd observed on campus, when she stood to excuse herself. She said by way of apology she had to study for an important exam and said good night as she shook Kel's hand. She kissed Don on the cheek and asked if the two would be working late.

Don assured her not.

"I think you may have hit the mother lode, Don. She's a great girl."

"We can find you one too, Kel. Stefania's got a lot of cute friends."

Kel couldn't imagine himself in the role of boyfriend on this mission.

"Thanks, but no thanks. I'm a little busy these days."

"Suit yourself but take it from me, don't wait too long. There's more to life than duty. I should know." Kel considered Don's wisdom for a moment, then filed it in the "disregard" section. Duty was all he knew and all he wanted to know.

Keeping with the post-dinner atmosphere of light conversation, Kel felt Don relax, and the two started to talk about themselves. Kel knew it would be a breach of professionalism to ask probing or personal questions, but he was curious about the path that led Don to this career. Don told his tale in a general way.

"I was a cop. I had a twenty-year career. Most of that time I was an investigator. I did homicide and major crime investigation. Did a stint as a hostage negotiator and with the technical surveillance unit in my agency. I never married and didn't have a family. In my spare time I got an advanced degree in alien cultural studies. It was just something I was interested in.

"I guess my path here started in earnest with a smuggling case I was working. It involved a lot of financial analysis, tracing sources of credits, stuff like that. Turns out the case crossed over to some other investigations being looked at by RI. I did a little work with some of their people, nothing dramatic.

"When I was about a year out from my twenty-year retirement, I was approached. They asked me to meet them for a sit-down. I kind of guessed what it was about. Apparently, I'd done a decent enough job on that smuggling case that I'd gained someone's attention, and here I am fifteen years later.

"It's not a bad life. You'll never get rich, but you could do a lot worse."

Kel had suspected that Don was not one of the cultured, Liberinthine elites within RI. He was a producer, a worker. He wasn't afraid to get his hands dirty. He'd stepped in to handle the local police right after the ambush. Kel now understood why he had that impression; Don had been a cop all his life.

"What about you? I've worked with DO before. You're on the younger side to be one of their operators, if you don't mind me saying. That alone tells me there's something that made you stand out, even among legionnaires. You win the Order of the Centurion or something?"

Kel laughed. "No, it was nothing like that."

In Kel's mind, he wasn't anything special. He'd always just been lucky.

"I was selected for Legion Reconnaissance early. I'd done well as a sniper and was allowed to try out for Recon selection a couple of years before I should have been eligible, I guess. They needed guys. Anyway, I guess you'd say that was my gateway. It took me two tries to get selected before I made it. After that, I lucked out with my timing.

"The Antione campaign was being planned during my first few months in Recon. I'd just completed SO/OFF school when we got the warning order for the invasion," referring to the Legion's Sub-Orbital/Orbital Free-Fall school, pronouncing it 'so-off.'

"My platoon was among the first onto the planet. We did an orbital free-fall infiltration and did the reconnaissance that let the rest of the company seize the spaceport and start the first wave of the invasion.

"After a while I was part of a unit that got detailed to DO, and like you, sometime later I got a call for a sit-down and here I am."

The two men clinked their glasses to that.

Don asked Kel about the roadblock incident. "You seem none the worse for wear. I was never a gunfighter like you, but I've been in a few scrapes. We always had mandatory time off, followed by required psych counseling, stuff like that. I admit I was always a little shaken up after a fight. You..." Don let the question trail off.

Kel shrugged his shoulders. "No. I mean, I feel fine. It's just part of what I do. Another day at the office, you know?" Kel meant it.

A red light flashed on Kel's link. It was a bounce from Major Todalin.

We got 'em.

13

Back in the Hoplite compound, Kel made his way over to where Gavros, Colonel Graviakis, and Major Todalin sat in the ready room, surrounded by three of the team leaders.

"Ah, Kel. Good news," said the colonel. "We have the location of the two gunmen who got away the other night. The vehicle you shot up was found abandoned. Our techs got some DNA. No matches though.

"The gunman you shot isn't talking, but his criminal record—he's no student dissident. Strong arm robbery, assault—all violent crimes. His known associates are from a neighborhood near where the car was found.

"We've had everyone working those neighborhoods and a few hours ago one of our detectives got a tip from an informant that several guys with guns were seen in a residence. Our surveillance team's set up in a house across the street. They confirm at least four males with weapons. We think it's worth hitting."

The colonel continued to the rest of the room, "Karl and Kostas are with the surveillance team," referring to two of the Hoplite snipers, "and are waiting to bring us up so we can get a better look."

The colonel went over an abbreviated operations order for the group, identifying critical tasks for each of the teams. The plan was for the colonel and his team leaders to make a stealthy visit to the surveillance house and evaluate the scene, then backtrack to a staging area about a mile away where the rest of the force would be readying.

Kel felt himself getting spun up. *This is more like it. Let's take the fight to them.*

They formed into a caravan and took a slow course through the city, encountering little traffic as they rolled toward their staging area. Men checked the gear and weapons during the cramped ride, and Kel joined them.

You can't check your gear enough when your life depends on it, he reminded himself.

Soon they pulled up in a wide alley behind a large grocery and mercantile area, a location where a line of trucks would not be out of place. In the darkness there was nothing out of the ordinary about the vehicles.

The colonel grabbed Kel and took two of the team leaders with them in one of the smaller, nondescript vehicles. They rode quietly, weaving through several neighborhoods to arrive at an unlit parking area. They followed the colonel on foot through several alleys, staying in the shadows cast by the surrounding buildings.

Pausing under the shadow of an overhanging roof, the colonel checked his link and pointed toward the rear entrance of a two-story structure in front of them. A door opened on the rear of the building. A dark figure appeared in the threshold, showed himself slightly past the door before he stepped back, completing the recognition signal that the visitors should now advance.

Kel brought up the rear as they walked casually across the alley and into the house, closing the door behind him quietly. He followed the men upstairs where a pair of darkened rooms at one end of a small landing were crowded with men. Black drapes were tacked into place over the windows. Through a small cutout was a camera on a mount, sharing its projection to datapads being held by the huddled men.

The colonel stepped out to one of the rooms facing the rear of the house. Whispered talk between the surveillance team and the Hoplites buzzed behind Kel as he strained to listen while looking over the shoulder of one of the men, watching the images on the pad. Across the street sat the target house, the rooms lit but blinds drawn. Kel compared the live image to his recollection of the overheads they'd seen and started to formulate a plan for how he would conduct the assault.

One of the team leaders, Andreas, tapped Kel on the shoulder and motioned to follow him back down the stairs. The two Hoplite snipers, Karl and Kostas, were carrying their sniper rifles and gear into the front rooms, setting up to provide overwatch. The assault was clearly going down.

"We've got what we need," the colonel whispered to Kel. "Time to get back." The colonel led, reversing their route through the dark and back to their vehicle, waiting until several blocks had passed before he instructed the team leader.

"Okay, Andreas, tell them we're on our way and to get ready."

In the dark lot, they found the force standing outside their vehicles. There were now several marked NP vehicles pulled alongside the group and uniformed officers mixed in with the Hoplites, sipping kaff. As they got out of the small car, everyone converged on the colonel, Gavros included.

"We're a go," the colonel said just loud enough for the whole crowd to hear. "Our eyes can't tell us much about where suspects are located in the house. They tried to send a drone in. No good." Kel regretted not having an inquisitor to loan them. The miniscule sized drones could go anywhere. "Andreas, lead off with your team. Let me know when you are at your last cover and concealment. Let's do it."

Andreas and the other team leaders loaded up with their teams while Kel joined with the colonel, Gavros, and Major Todalin. They took the last position in the order of movement, the marked police vehicles remaining at the staging area for the time being.

Kel had no disagreement with their plan. Two parallel streets accessed the front and rear of the target house. The assault teams would make a stealth approach on foot from both front and back, with the rest of the force staged on the vehicles just around the corner. It was far enough away to make it virtually impossible for anyone within the target house to detect the armored vehicles full of armed men, and close enough for them to roll the rest of the Hoplites onto the target in seconds once the hit kicked off.

Teams would simultaneously breach and enter from front and back, with a ladder team making entry into the second story from the rear of the building. The rest of the force would then race to the target in the armored vehicles. If there was resistance, the armored vehicles would serve as a hardened point for retreat and from which to fight, and would also serve as casualty collection points. The assaulters in those vehicles would be trailers, brought into the structure as needed to clear, handle suspects, or to simply help perform secondary searches of the building. *Not everyone gets to kick a door on every hit,* he mused. *But every job is important.* Of course given the choice, he'd take being first in, every time.

The marked police vehicles would cordon off the block and prevent travel into the area of the operation, as well as document witnesses. There was also a chance that any auxiliary supporters trying to leave the area, especially any non-residents of the neighborhood, could be identified in the subsequent investigation.

If it would only run just that way, for once, I'd appreciate it, was his silent prayer.

From his seat in the rear of the speeder he watched the two lines of assaulters carrying their weapons and tools, moving to their last locations of concealment before making their way around and down the two right-angle streets to begin their approach to the target.

He neither approved nor disapproved. It was a complex plan with many moving parts, and there were opportunities for them to be compromised on their movement to the house. The other alternative was simple: drive the two armored vehicles directly to the breach points and start the assault from there. That relied on a swift movement to maximize surprise, the problem being there were few ways of disguising the noise of heavy trucks in this small, cramped neighborhood.

In either case, if they were compromised then the raid would become a barricade job. Multiple armed assailants in the structure shooting at the Hoplites in the middle of a crowded neighborhood had catastrophic potential.

There was never a perfect answer and the points of potential failure in this plan, virtually any plan, were numerous. The only failure was the failure to be aggressive. The Hoplites didn't lack in that department. Now Kel would see if they had more than just that when it wasn't just a rehearsal in the shoothouse.

The armored vehicles waited, engines running, with armed men standing on the runners, holding onto a side-mounted railing. Kel and the officers each found space to do the same.

"This is Team Leader Red," he heard the team leader Andreas' voice. "Standby for short count. I have control. Ready. Ready. NOW."

Ba-BOOM. Charges at the front and rear of the house detonated simultaneously. Kel's ride lurched forward for the short run to the target house, the teams dismounting as the vehicles were not yet at a complete stop. The momentum of the huge armored trucks propelled the men into a run before their feet hit the ground.

Kel looked up in time to see a flash of a distraction device from the second story. The ladder team was still ascending to the second floor, the second-story window shattered and pulled out of its frame with a wicked medieval-looking pike which now lay on the ground. Men went through the window one after another.

A single operator stood holding the threshold of the first-story entrance. By now the first assaulters had been inside for less than a minute.

Kel strained to hear shots fired but knew he might not hear suppressed shots, had there been any. If the gunmen had fired, he would have heard it. It gave Kel a slight ease. He would have felt best being inside the structure with the first assaulters, though.

People shouted inside the house. After a minute, the operator holding the threshold motioned for them to proceed into the house. Kel followed along, passing the trailer teams outside protecting the perimeter.

The rear door led into a small kitchen and dining area. Immediately to the right was a sitting room where over the shoulders of several of the operators, Kel could see a man proned out on the floor, his feet and legs restrained. Kel followed the leadership element toward the front of the house into a wider sitting area where many of the operators stood. On the ground lay another man, on the floor, restrained, but missing half of his face. *Guess even with my implant it's tough to pick up suppressed fire from outside.* Blood and brains covered a portion of the wall behind where the man had been sitting, a rifle lying on the couch with its magazine beside it, the weapon having been cleared by one of the operators already.

The three officers stepped around another uninjured suspect on the ground, restrained at his wrists and ankles, being searched by the Hoplites. Kel didn't follow yet, taking a moment to watch the Hoplites carry out their suspect control. *Good cover on the head. Good use of angles for the other operator to search the suspect. Not bad.*

A small landing led to stairs, where more of the Hoplites traveled down and out the front entrance to the street. The colonel came down the stairs, saw Kel and smiled, pointing up the stairs. Kel paused to allow another few Hoplites to descend before he made his way up. Several smaller bedrooms and a bathroom radiated out from the landing, operators leaning against the walls and smiling at him as he followed Colonel Graviakis. *I know that feeling. The fight's over. None of us got hurt. Suspects in custody or dead. It's a good feeling.*

In a front room, Kel noted another man dispatched by the Hoplites, lying on the floor in his underwear, restrained, evidence of gunshot wounds to his chest and head, and a rifle lying nearby. It appeared to Kel the man had been in bed when the raid commenced, and he'd been moving toward his rifle when he was surprised by the assaulters. *Even dead men get cuffed.* They were doing it right.

In a back room Gavros and Major Todalin stood over a scraggly, quaking man restrained in a low chair, protesting and stating repeatedly that there had been a mistake, and that he was innocent. They looked up at Kel and motioned him to follow, leaving a pair of Hoplites to guard him. Outside they found Colonel Graviakis with Andreas, the Red Team Leader.

Gavros shook everyone's hands. "It is good. It is good," he said, followed by a flurry of the Meridian language that made everyone but Kel laugh. "I tell them next time do better or they hang. In our language, it is much funnier."

"Gavros," the colonel said. "I'm going back in to continue the secondary searches with the trailers. We'll await the transport to collect the prisoners. Everyone else can leave. We have the uniforms for security. Hopefully, Franc's investigators can get something useful." The colonel turned to leave.

Leaving? He thought. *Why? Now's when the real work starts.* This was an opportunity. *Time to speak up.*

"A moment, colonel. Can you tell me what's going to happen now?"

It was Major Todalin who answered.

"The suspects will get taken to the investigative division and questioned. We'll continue to secure the crime scene and let the investigators evaluate what they find. Hopefully in a few days we'll get a clearer picture of who's who."

They're making a mistake.

"Gentlemen," Kel said, "we might be losing an opportunity for a follow-on hit right now."

The three officers frowned. *Time to win them over.*

"We have two live suspects," Kel continued. "If we start the questioning here, we might get a lead on another part of the ME network. We could exploit that intel immediately. If we wait for a traditional interrogation to occur, every minute there's a chance that another ME safe house will be moved, and suspects go further underground."

Gavros looked receptive. "I ask you here for help. You come long way. Okay. What do you suggest, Kel?"

"Question the suspects here. If we get something, we can roll with the team to another hit tonight. Maybe more."

Gavros said something to his two subordinates in Meridian. The colonel responded in the same sing-song language. They both looked to Major Todalin who nodded. Switching back to Standard for Kel, Gavros continued. "Yes. We are bringing the investigators here immediately to begin questioning."

The colonel departed to tell his team leaders of the change in their normal post-action routine as Kel followed Gavros and the major to the first floor. Two Hoplites stood near the dead body, and two more guarded the live suspect. In the rear the restrained suspect had been hoisted into a chair, a hood over his head, still and silent. Major Todalin shook his head at them and pointed up to the second story.

They made their way upstairs to see a similar distribution of the men throughout the second-floor rooms, and back to the live suspect, similarly restrained, hooded, and in a low chair. This man, rather than terrified into silence, protested his innocence, promising to talk in exchange for his freedom.

The major gave a thumbs up to them. It seemed like an obvious place to start the next phase of the operation.

The general turned his hands palm up toward the suspect, offering the man to Todalin.

Gavros leaned over to Kel and whispered. "Todalin is masterful interrogator. We will start now. No wait for my investigators."

Major Todalin removed the hood. The man flinched as if anticipating a slap.

"It's all right, my friend, you are not going to be harmed." The major repeated this several times as he used his body language and calm voice to soothe the shaking man. "What is your name?"

The man needed no prompting and began talking at a rapid pace. "I am Grigorio, this is my house. I did not know these men. I was told to give them shelter and hide them for two days and that they would be moved. That's all I know. I thought they would kill me!"

"Who told you to hide these men?" the major asked.

"My cousin. He shows up with these two, tells me I have to hide them. Tells me not to leave or go outside, and that they are in trouble, and the police are looking for them, all of that stuff. Then this other guy shows up, brings them more guns.

"This other guy starts bossing me around in my own house, telling me everything is my duty for the freedom of Meridian, all that stuff. I tell them, 'You gotta get out of here, I don't want nothing to do with that,' then they tell me to behave and they'll be gone in a couple of days, or else they gonna kill me."

The major told one of the Hoplites to find another chair. The major now sat with the cowering Grigorio.

"Are you thirsty? Here, drink." The major placed a pouch of water to the man's lips and held it while he took several deep swallows.

The man continued without prompting. "I'm never in trouble my whole life. My cousin, he's crazy to get me mixed up in this." Looking around wildly at the large men standing around him, the man's voice cracked as he blurted, "I never hurt nobody in my life!"

Kel stifled a laugh. He found the man believable. His attempts to protest his innocence were convincing. He knew it could be an act, and the frightened man's cultural cues would mean more to the major than they might to Kel. Now the man became a fountain of words.

The major pressed his questions. Grigorio went on to describe the other men. Evidently, the two gunmen who escaped the vehicle stop the other night were the two men now lying dead in the other rooms. The live suspect restrained and remaining quiet downstairs was likely the "other guy" sent by Grigorio's cousin to assist the situation.

Major Todalin asked some personal questions of Grigorio, calming the more he talked about himself. Todalin used this moment to change the tone of his questions and leaned in like a sandlion about to pounce.

"Grigorio. This is a very serious matter. The two men hiding in *your* house, are wanted by the National Police for murder. They're Meridian Eleftheria. Hiding two murderers—terrorists—in your house, makes you guilty of aiding the ME. That is a crime against the Domestic Conclave. You know what that means if you are convicted, right? The death penalty for you and all your family."

The man broke into shuddering sobs, snot pouring down his face as he protested his innocence over and over, pleading for understanding.

Todalin moved away to pull Kel and Gavros close. He asked the general, "Do we want the cousin?"

"Yes. Offer him deal to spare his life."

The major nodded. Retaking his seat in front of Grigorio, Todalin waited for the man to stop sobbing.

"Grigorio. We would like to believe you. This looks bad. You were not armed and did not try to resist. That is the only reason you are still alive."

The man wept louder.

"General Kyrgiakos has agreed to make a recommendation to spare your life if you cooperate with us."

The sobbing man's eye widened. "Yes, yes! Anything, anything!"

The major made his case for the man to reveal all he knew about his cousin. With no further prompting, the man spouted information faster than the major could ask questions. "Okay, Grigorio," the major patted the man's shoulder as he stood. "I think you just saved your family's lives." The man sputtered gratitudes as Gavros pulled the major and Kel to him in the landing. "Do you want to question the suspect downstairs?" Todalin shook his head. "We have the address for the cousin. We can act on that now, don't you agree?" Kel let it be known he did.

The general pulled his link out of his pocket and typed briefly. "Good. Then it is time for action. The other one, we let Franc's people have." Standing on the porch awaiting were Colonel Graviakis and the team leader, Andreas. Gavros briefed the two on the rapidly evolving developments and ordered the colonel to get his team ready for the next mission.

This is how it's supposed to go. He felt a small sense of accomplishment. *Now if there's some way I can get into the fight and stop being the advisor.* He wasn't the chieftain, or the Koob. Small victory or not, he was just an observer.

Observers were useless.

It had been a little over an hour from the assault to now loading up to move to the next objective. Gregorio's cousin, the radical, lived with a girlfriend in another crowded neighborhood not three kilometers from their current location.

The decision was to do a rolling assault on the house to generate what surprise they could with the goal of overwhelming the occupants. Grigorio's description of his cousin was convincing for his involvement in ME. He had been a university student and was always critical of the Domestic Conclave at social and family gatherings. Several years into his engineering studies, his parents became distressed to learn that he was no longer interested in engineering and planned to change fields to study political theory. He had no criminal record, but Gregorio told of his cousin bragging about his new friends, about receiving training in weapons and explosives. He'd tried to convince Grigorio to stop being a slave to the DC and join him and his new friends.

If ME had surveillance on Grigorio's house, the next target might already be abandoned. Or, they could be headed into a bloodbath. They'd find out soon.

There was only a front street accessing the residence. The house backed up to a rock-cut cliff face with a tiny yard in back. There would be no high-speed avenue of approach for the raiders from the rear, or avenue of escape for the suspects through the back of the house.

They would do a similar two-story assault through the front of the house, with another team entering through the ground floor rear door. Kel rode again with the general and Major Todalin, the major driving and Kel sitting in the front passenger seat. The general sat in back, looking at a drone feed from high over the address they moved toward. Kel picked up the feed in his specs. More of the same narrow streets led into the winding housing development where the target sat.

The column of vehicles paused on the route, everyone watching their pads to see the live view from the single occupant speeder they'd sent as a scout to check the house.

Kel looked at the major's link with him, seeing the view from the scout as it floated slowly by the target house, panning right to show the home. Only dim lighting was visible through the curtains of the main room.

They heard Colonel Graviakis by link. "I recommend we assault."

The armored vehicles sped toward the house, men clinging to the sides. Hoplites leaped onto the duracrete street, a line of operators moving toward the front door as another line moved along a narrow path to reach the rear of the building. A ladder team trotted ahead, some type of animal hide secured to the legs to dampen the sound of its friction against the house. It struck Kel as an odd mix of the modern and primitive. They reached the face of the home and raised the ladder against the façade. A man held the ladder against the building as another ascended, carrying the long tool he would use to remove the second-story window.

The battering ram crashed against the door. Purple electricity flashed as an operator tossed in a grenade, the bang and flash still echoing as the team flowed through the doorway.

Glass rained from above and the operator at the top of the ladder raked the border of the windowsill, shaking loose more large shards, then tossed a distraction device into the room and lit up the darkness.

Shouts, thumps, and crashes came from the back of the house. No gunshots yet, but someone yelled, and a woman's scream came from within.

The eerie glow of weapon lights illuminated the interior of the house, bouncing from wall to wall. Gavros and Todalin stood beside Kel watching the display. Colonel Graviakis was the next to enter the structure, passing two of his operators holding the front room as he walked deeper into the house.

Five more minutes passed as the call went over the link for the general to enter. The three men were met by the colonel, and proceeded directly up the steps. In a back bedroom with several operators spread throughout, were two naked figures on the floor, restrained at wrists and ankles, with hoods over their heads. In a corner was a rifle. On a shelf above the headboard of the bed was a pistol and an old-fashioned durasteel fragmentation grenade.

One of the team leaders spoke to them without raising his head or moving the muzzle of his weapon off the backs of the two restrained suspects. "They were otherwise occupied when we came in. They never made a move toward the weapons. They were definitely not expecting company."

Muffled protests from the two prostrated suspects penetrated through the hoods. He followed the men as they inspected each of the rooms on the second floor, until proceeding down the stairs and down into a well-lighted basement.

Kel was astonished at what he saw. On the walls, workbenches were covered with circuitry and wiring. Buckets of marbles sat under the bench; other buckets were filled with nails and metal debris. Proton batteries sat stacked on shelving. This was a bomb factory.

"Engineering student, huh?" Kel said aloud. Everyone nodded. As Kel looked closer he appreciated with more detail each item and its potential lethality.

A feeling of dread filled him as he sensed more than heard motion behind him. A man with a knife drove downward toward his neck. Kel stepped forward and outside the man's plunging arm, rather than away. He met the arm, turned his hips, and let his opponent's motion carry the knife past. As the man lurched backward to regain his balance, Kel moved with him, now controlling the elbow and hand holding the knife, folding them back toward the man. What he did next, he did out of reflex. As the blade reversed course, Kel guided it across the edge of his attacker's throat. A bright fountain of blood sprayed out and Kel bobbed his head away to avoid the thick jet.

He followed the man to the ground, pinning his chest with his own as the red river pulsed out onto the floor. The man spasmed, and rough air escaped his mouth. Kel's sense of his surrounding environment expanded again, but he stayed on top of the slowly dying man, aware of the yelling of his friends and the crush of their bodies around him.

The man was all but dead. Kel picked the knife up and stood. Hoplites took his place, rolling the man over roughly and placing restraints on his limp arms. He saw where the man had appeared from, a disguised panel pulled back into a small concealed room.

"Are you all right, are you all right?" the voices screamed as they placed their hands on him. He felt strong. Impervious. His body vibrated.

He couldn't help but grin. "I think you missed one."

Was I really whining to myself about being an observer? Ain't no bystanders in a gunfight, he'd once been told.

Or a knife fight either.

Outside, the tinge of color appeared in the sky. It would be dawn soon.

More vehicles arrived on the street. Uniformed officers escorted residents from the surrounding homes as explosive technicians descended on the house to render the site safe for search by investigators. One of their medics insisted on examining Kel. He didn't fight the request. He knew how it was to be the medic and responsible for everyone's well-being.

Colonel Graviakis and the general moved to where Kel was being searched for injury from head to toe. The medic was thorough. Kel approved.

"How is he?" Gavros demanded.

Kel answered for the medic. "I'm fine. What's next?"

The colonel took Kel's cue. The mission had not ended, and it was time to continue working. "General," he said, "we've gotten what we're going to get from this operation.

I don't anticipate getting any actionable intelligence from this scene anytime soon."

Gavros chuckled. "Yes, I think that is enough for right now. Let's wait to see what interrogation brings. Keep everyone on standby." He looked at Kel. "You sure you are well?"

"I'm ready to get back to work. I might need a shower, though."

Gavros' pursed lips conferred approval, perhaps even admiration. "Your suggestion to interrogate on site is good one. Is this what Dark Ops does?" Kel assured him it was. "We must reevaluate investigations. From now on, we will immediately interrogate suspects during these operations against Eleftheria. Take this as command directive and begin planning, gentlemen."

The group broke up and Kel followed the major and Gavros to the vehicle they'd arrived in. As they floated away in the repulsor, Kel replayed the night's events. After once more assuring his friends that he was fine, he asked, "Major, I've read about the laws on Meridian regarding acts against the Domestic Conclave. Is it..."

The major cut off his question. "I know what you're going to ask. No one has been executed for such things in a hundred and fifty years, and it's been generations before that when a whole family was executed as punishment for such a crime. Yet the laws exist and everyone learns about them growing up. Still, it was somewhat of an empty threat to wield against that idiot Grigorio."

The general let out a deep breath. "Yes. But I tell you, if we do not solve this crisis soon, my uncle and rest of DC may make that kelhorned law a genuine threat again. It's only a matter of time."

FLASHBACK

If You Love Killing, You'll Never Work a Day in Your Life in the Legion
Antione

"We all put our skins on one leg at a time. We're leejes, too. We've all been where you are. We're not supermen. We just know a few more tricks." I'm all ears, just like everyone else on the squad as we listen to TA brief us, buckets off. The Talon is at hypercruise. We could be headed to the other side of Antione for all we know.

"Turner," he says to me. "No one will tell you how to run your squad, but if one of us has a suggestion, you might want to take it, got me?" He's got a bushy beard, like the locals wear.

"Yes, TA." I decide to use the name he gave me like a rank. "TA, can you tell us where we're headed? What's our mission?"

"No prob," he assures me. "We're headed south to the secondary capital. We're going after CLEs." Critical leadership entities. It meant we'd be on a manhunt. "The thugs running the planet have gone to ground. We're tasked with rooting them out and bringing them to justice. Capturing the leadership may help convince the militia there's nothing left worth fighting for and keep us from having to flatten the whole place."

That would mean urban fighting. Hitting safehouses. Well-defended positions. I start to think about how to organize the squad. Howard's the next senior corporal. He should take a team. I'm evening out the roster for my two fire teams when TA interrupts.

"Hey. It'll be fun. I promise." Maybe he's misread my deep thought as worry. "Sure thing, TA." I try to sound casual. "We're looking forward to it. It'll be a great learning experience for us. Really round out the squad after our orbital freefall to take the spacefield."

TA cants his head at me. "We heard about that. No one's done a combat space dive in the Legion in a few years. What a rush." He sounds sincerely complimentary. I think about it. "Yeah. I guess it was at that."

Yamazaki's found a new love interest. The Mk29 is a medium blaster. While similar, this one is shortened and has a thicker cryo sleeve. He's putting it to good use on the armored sled that just raced into the intersection. After another controlled burst, the engine housing vents plasma and the repulsors fail. The forward momentum sends the nose plowing into the duracrete as it skids to a halt.

D'antonio is at his side and kneeling, already bringing the single tube M7 launcher off his back. It barely finds his shoulder before he lobs a grenade at the sled. Purple flashes mix with vaporizing metal as the armor disintegrates into slag and secondary explosions in the cab turn the interior into a white furnace. Threat eliminated.

"Nova, Nova, Wolf three," I say over L-Comm to the team in the house. "Another armored gun sled just tried for the compound on the red side road. We stopped it.

No further resistance currently." They'd have heard the explosions and be wondering. Our Talon dropped us off about a klick out and was now elsewhere in a holding pattern, waiting. It's never a good idea to use your ride out for close air support. If it gets shot down, you're walking.

"Rog, Wolf," Papa Bear replies. "Keep it up. About five minutes more and I'll pull you in and we'll call for the bird to pick us up." Papa Bear was clearly their senior sergeant. He was older than the rest of the team and the special operators all looked to him for approval. Zero, who I heard the others call, "sir," once in a while, must be an officer. He seemed to take direction from Papa Bear just like the others though.

"Copy, Nova." They'd been in the compound for twelve minutes. It sounded like they'd recovered the target and were collecting as much material from the site as they could before we split.

"Trumbull," I broke channels. "What's happening on green side? The team says about five more minutes until we fall back to the yard." It was an industrial part of the city and the compound we were holding was a repulsor repair yard. It was surrounded by a security fence and the yard was filled with vehicles stacked on racks, waiting for parts or repair. Garages formed an "L" in one corner and a residence sat opposite it. The property was surrounded by roads and other industrial buildings.

"We're good over here," Trumbull said nonchalantly. He'd settled down since the initial action. "Nothing since we anchored those two sleds on the corners." When the breaching charges went off in the compound alerting the outside security that we were here, he and his fire team obliterated the checkpoint vehicles and guards, just as we did on my side. Until then, no one had a clue we were even here. TA said he had a good feeling about this site holding treasure because of the presence of such heavy security. It seemed reasonable. Trumbull was a little amped up when he made his report after the first engagement. Now, he almost sounded bored.

Once we had our target, almost immediately we headed out and the plan was put together in the air. Papa Bear's op order had been thorough, but casual at the same time. "We'll make our way in on foot. Get us containment on the yard perimeter. Once we start our assault, someone will get the word out they need help."

"Keep them off our backs," Zero made clear. "We have a job to do inside. We can do both, but it'll go faster if we don't have to divide our attention. If it looks like a threat, err on the side of violence of action and eliminate it early."

The leej with the bright red beard, Warchief, grinned at us. "You all like your new toys? We're giving them to you for a reason. Use 'em." Most of us had K-17s now, just like them, except for D'antonio who stuck with his N-16 but added the single launcher M7 and two bandoliers of grenades to his load. "I see the advantage, but call me old fashioned," he explained. "I like separate weapons for blasting and grenade launching." TA was the first to back him up. "There's a lot to be said for personal preference. Use what you're most comfortable with."

Like TA had forewarned, they didn't tell me how to do my job. The last member of their five-man unit, the quietest and least expressive of their group, went by Provo. Of all of them, it was what I thought was probably his actual name. "Turner," he pointed to a holo image of the compound and the surrounding blocks as we cruised in the Talon. "I know you know this, but I'd put you here. This intersection is where I'd bet any reinforcement will come from. You can control your fire teams best from here and be on location for what will probably be the heaviest fighting. Plan accordingly." It was a suggestion I would take, and not just because it was how I'd already determined to do it. The few days we'd spent with these guys had only increased my awe of them.

"Wolf three, Wolf three," it was Papa Bear. "We're coming out of the residence. I've got nothing on the drone. You agree we're clear to bring in the bird?" I checked with Trumbull before I answered. "Roger, Nova. All quiet." Even though the overhead drone didn't show any militia headed at us, Papa Bear was like me, a believer in eyes on the ground.

"Pull back inside the fence. Get a good head count because we're going to be pulling out of here at FTL."

"Trumbull, get in the yard and set security from the green side. We're moving now."

"Rog," I heard back as I tapped my guys. I led the way to the fence. This side had not been breached yet. I pulled out the torch and passed it through the woven plastite like it was water as the guys faced out at the street. "Let's roll." Soon we were weaving between the racks of cars to reach the open central yard. One of the operators, it looked like TA, stood in the middle of the yard, his arm extended overhead holding a beacon.

Behind a shipping container the rest of the team stood around three hooded and enerchained forms. Two of the shapes looked smaller, like females. "Turner, give us a hand," Papa Bear said as he saw me. I patted Yamazaki and D'antonio on the shoulders and they trotted off, leaving me to watch the way we came.

I felt the repulsor hum in my chest and a vibration in my teeth as the Talon magically appeared above the rooftops then rotate as it descended, the nose a meter in front of where TA stood. Impressive. "Bring it in," Papa Bear said over L-Comm. I took a last look in front of me before I trotted to the tail, then spun about, searching for signs of danger. "Last man," I felt a tap on my shoulder and I ran up the ramp to start counting bodies. I laid hands on each of my squad as I counted to myself. "Head count correct, Papa Bear."

"Lift, lift, lift," he said as we gained altitude, the ramp closing as we banked and sped away, me grabbing an overhead cable to keep upright. Looking around the pax compartment, my guys were in jump seats, fists pounding armored chests, the guys high with combat adrenaline and the thrill of success.

On the forward bulkhead, the three prisoners are locked in their jump seats in four-point harnesses, hooded heads bowed. The operators are on their feet, apparently unaffected by the G forces that make me sway as I walk forward. At their feet are two satchels of sharp shapes; datapads and memory cubes.

"Good job, Turner. You and your men," Papa Bear says as we level off. "I never had a doubt," he hammers me on the chest. "Recon never drops the ball." Does that mean he used to be one of us before he became... one of them?

Provo, Warchief, and Zero kneel as they start to sort through the bags. Provo takes a cube out of one and sits, producing a datapad from his carryall and opens a holo over his lap. TA stands next to me. "Have everyone eat something and check weapons and gear. It may not be too long before we have something."

Have something? I'm getting the sense that there's another hit coming. TA senses my question. "What? You didn't think this was it, did you?" I admit to myself I did and shrug. "No way little leej. We're going to do this all night. I promised you it'd be fun, didn't I?"

14

He'd accomplished a lot in his first week on the ground, but it had been hectic and taken a toll. It was a welcome relief to get regular sleep and to be able to work out again each day. After a few days he felt recharged and sharp again.

At the first opportunity he updated Don on the outing with the Hoplites and their success finding the engineering student-turned-bomb-maker. Kel had tried to meet with him immediately after the Hoplites' recent successes, but the intel man was unavailable. Kel wrote it off. Don never reciprocated and gave him any detail about how he spent his days, but he assumed Don had work all over the planet, same as Kel did.

"Don't let this go to your head, but you've had a helluva first week," Don praised. Kel couldn't let that go easily. "Did that hurt, admitting that?"

Don rolled his eyes. "Keep it up. We're still no closer to having a complete picture of ME. When do you start your tour of the other National Police tactical teams?"

"Soon. I feel a little conflicted about it, though," he admitted. "I mean, I'm all about helping them respond to terrorist incidents in their respective backyards, but it seems like the really important work is right here in Tiryns."

Don was more enthusiastic about the assignment from Gavros than Kel was. "Don't be. I think it's got potential to produce good intelligence about ME activities elsewhere on Meridian, as well as give us better insights into the NP, if you know what I mean. They're more of a secret police than a law enforcement agency."

Don didn't share what had kept him out of the capital the past few days and Kel didn't ask. It was enough for Kel to know that the man was doing *something* that got him into the field, also working on solving the crisis.

He visited with Jacee in the military-political section to update her. A lot had happened since he'd last checked in with her. The highway tax collector shoot-out, the missions with the Hoplites, almost getting stabbed; he left out all those details but she had apparently already heard about his actions, and asked him point-blank about the incidents. So, when called out, it was best to stand tall. Jaycee listened to his abbreviated details. She sighed. "I know you're a big, bad legionnaire and all, but take it easy, will you?"

Kel wondered how she had such detailed information. "How'd you hear about those scrapes?" *It could only come from someone in the NP. Gavros? Not one of the Hoplites?* Jacee smiled. "Just take care of yourself, okay?"

And why would Jacee let me know that she *knew?*

Kel remembered Bigg's warning about the pols, that they would hang you out to dry if you were a convenient scapegoat.

"Who's telling tales out of school to Jacee about me?"

The rest of the week remained quiet. Few incidents occurred, not only in the capital but planet-wide. *Maybe*

the worst is over, Kel thought, knowing that was wishful thinking. He spent that time helping implement some of the physical security improvements he, Bell, and Pen had talked about, and even got to test some of the armor upgrades for the vehicle fleet.

Kel's housemates and he spent his last day in Tiryns relaxing around the palace. After Kel's morning workout the three men made a large breakfast together and lounged until the early evening. The weather had remained predictably perfect during Kel's short time on Meridian; he'd never needed extra layers and what precipitation had fallen seemed to occur briefly during hours of darkness. The weather on his day off had been no different.

For the evening meal the embassy communications officer Gren, and the trade expert Ramer, made the case for them to introduce Kel to some local culture. His two friends had a back-and-forth discussion about where to dine; each offered the potential merits of an establishment before the other man dismissed the suggestion over an important flaw, until finally, a sudden consensus was reached.

"Socrates' Garden it is," Gren exclaimed. "Dining and entertainment at its finest."

Gren drove allowing Kel to appreciate the early evening's quiet and minimal traffic. The trip was not a long one, and soon they pulled up to a circular drive where a pair of valets dressed in sandals and robes opened their doors and greeted them.

"Gren, it's not a good idea to let someone else park your vehicle. Anyone wanting to search the vehicle or plant a bomb would have ample time to do so," Kel reprimanded.

"No worries, Mister Paranoid. This place is on the RSO's green list. Relax."

Kel shrugged. He stood and watched the valet pull the vehicle to an adjoining lot, in plain sight of the front of the establishment. *Not good,* Kel thought as he joined his companions.

The Garden's elegant architecture was much like that of the other upscale edifices around the capital—immense fluted stone columns and open breezeway porticos. The valets' immodest dress was unusual in Kel's experience and he said as much to his friends.

"Wait till you see how the costume looks on the women. Brother!" Ramer exclaimed with a wink.

What am I getting myself into? Kel wondered.

They were shown to a table in a private room overlooking a small sunken courtyard, a fountain, and sitting area bathed by colored lighting in the center of the garden. There were couches for lounging arranged in small collections as well, none of them yet occupied.

Now seated, the table and room covered in the dim light of actual candles, four beautiful female attendants dressed in short thigh-length robes draped over a single bare shoulder appeared from behind a curtain and took a position at each of the table's corners.

Kel tried to conceal his surprise, but his looks must have revealed his discomfort. Kel grew up on Pthalo, a vacation world in the galaxy of planets, but he and his parents were working class people; he'd never experienced luxury or treatment as accommodating as this was clearly meant to be. It was a discomforting experience for Kel.

"The food is excellent. You're in for a real treat," Gren said, seeing Kel's unease.

The four attendants waited quietly until a waiter appeared, dressed in a similar though more modest, manner. He welcomed them and asked if they had any special drink requests or if the house wine was sufficient. Kel stayed silent and let his companions do all the talking, ordering the wine and the standard fare for their table.

The man departed and soon returned, leading three more female servants, placing goblets in front of the three gentlemen and retreating.

How many servers does it take? The four others are still here, doing nothing, Kel thought. He didn't want to appear boorish to his friends, and resisted his temptation to ask what their purpose was. He also didn't want to be overheard by the women standing to either side of him only a meter away. He felt like he was being watched from all sides. His companions seemed to be enjoying themselves. *Maybe I need to learn to relax.*

They drank their wine, Kel taking cautious sips, when three different female servers appeared carrying small trays. The women standing at each corner of the table now took an abrupt step forward and reached onto the table in unison, removing the napkin from next to each diner and placing it across their laps, the fourth attendant remaining still behind the empty seat at the table. Kel restrained himself from flinching when the woman nearest him did so, telling himself that he was not being attacked.

The other attendants then placed a plate in front of each diner from their left, and placed several small trays on the table, dishing a small portion from each onto each man's plate until each had several different things to sample. When done serving, the attendants again disappeared.

The food was excellent. Kel had no idea what he was eating but each of the different dishes had distinct but complementary flavors. Soon another course followed, then another. Each additional course was served on its own distinct ware; one course was brought to them on jade-green colored flat stones. The next was placed in the center of the table on a twisted gnarled nest of branches, looking very much like a dwarf tree, and on each branch a small lavender blossom contained a morsel of the chef's creation, the flower every bit as edible as the morsel it held.

As goblets emptied, the corner attendants left their posts to retrieve a flagon from a nearby cart. They cleared the plates and serving dishes, then took small brushes and gently swept the tablecloth in front of each diner.

Kel had never in his life experienced such an elaborate show based around the simple act of eating.

The guys will never believe me, he thought. He started to relax and enjoy the spectacle of the whole thing.

Several more courses arrived and while each was little more than a mouthful at a time, Kel found himself getting full. It was surprising to him. His normal manner of eating was to consume as much as he could, as fast as he could. He hadn't ever considered that there was another way to eat.

Finally, in what Kel assumed must be the end of the dining experience, the attendants brought a selection of sweets and pastries along with strong kaff. Kel had a sweet tooth. He'd never tasted a sweet he didn't like and wouldn't have a second helping of. His mother always chided him for it, worried that he would get fat or develop some incurable health issue. It hadn't happened to him yet, and he saw no reason to change his habits now.

The dessert courses were all light and did not leave him with a heavy or sluggish feeling. *I could come here every night,* he thought at the height of his enjoyment.

"Did you get enough, Kel?" Gren asked, showing great satisfaction himself.

"I should say so. That was amazing. Man, am I going to sleep well tonight," he said, starting to stand along with his friends.

"Ha, ha. We're not done, buddy," Ramer said.

Kel's brow wrinkled as his partners grinned back at him.

"Mandatory after dinner relaxation," Gren said, inclining his head to the courtyard below them.

The attendants then each moved to take their hands, Kel resisting the urge to pull his back, leading the men down the grassy slope to the garden and three shallow couches. *The "Garden" part of Socrates' Garden,* he wondered. The women gestured for the men to sit as they moved to stand behind them, reached forward, then began massaging and kneading their necks. Kel braced himself to not flinch when the attendant behind him did the same, but soon relaxed under her warm touch.

The waiter appeared again, three more servers trailing, bringing thimble-sized glasses of aperitifs. Kel decided to go with the flow. The whole experience was surreal. He sipped his drink, noting its similarities to the liquor that Gavros had shared with him at his estate a few nights before. Kel thought about how the rest of that night had played out, with him killing four men just a few hours later. He silently pondered the juxtaposition of the experiences. He wondered if there was a brutal event awaiting him yet tonight.

Kel squelched the violent images in his head as he listened to Gren and Ramer's small talk, reminiscing about other worlds they'd been posted to and the comforts they'd experienced there. He held back. He didn't have any elaborate tales of opulence or extravagance to share and didn't want to be the one to spoil the mood by bringing up his own stories of hardship and privation. It would be rude to his friends.

"Kel, try this," Ramer said as he lay back on the couch, propping his upper back up on a large pillow at the end of the lounger, resting his neck on top of the shallow arm. The attendant took the cue and moved to the end of the couch to begin rubbing his friend's temples in a circular motion, breaking occasionally to rub his forehead in the same swirling pattern.

Gren had assumed a supine position as well, ahead of Kel's move to follow Ramer's lead. Kel lay back and tried to relax as he saw his friends doing, but it was difficult to close his eyes and trust the masseuse. He settled for staring at nothing in particular, especially trying not to meet the eyes of his masseuse. He readied himself to see a knife appear in one of the hands of one of the attendants to slit the throat of the relaxed, unsuspecting victims. Kel was acutely aware of the location of his pistol, and formulated a plan of action for any eventuality. Just as his lids grew heavy, the massage stopped. All three ladies met, bowed, then left.

The waiter approached, passing the three ladies as they left the courtyard, moving toward them with a small datapad. Gren raised his hand from the elbow to signal the man.

"I've got this one. You can buy next time, Kel."

It had been quite the evening and nothing like Kel would have imagined beforehand. *Is this how diplomats live all the time?* Kel could see a new dimension to the Ex-Planetary service he had not considered previously.

As they walked toward the valet, Ramer pointed at a side street. "The same people have a great restaurant on the other side of the property. Probably use the same kitchen. You should try it. Great place for lunch. They only do the big show here at the end of the week. Pretty nice though, don't you think?"

Kel agreed wholeheartedly. He thought about his life on the ride back to the palace. He felt relaxed and not wanting for anything. He'd been to a lot of places in the galaxy, most of them not nice.

Of course, he reasoned, *had they been nice places, there wouldn't be cause to send a kill team there.*

15

"Kel, now is time to see rest of Meridian," Gavros said. They sat in the general's office, sipping kaff with the major. "I think you can be very helpful to efforts of our regional special reaction teams. Operational tempo proceeds much faster. We gained much information after the last hits. Investigation and Hoplites work together more closely. Yet I am concerned about operations outside of capital. It's time for you to travel and see what you can do to help as you have here."

Major Todalin motioned to Kel to look at his own link. Pulling it from his pocket, Kel opened the file from the major and skimmed the list of organizations and locations he was to tour.

"Your *aspida* and identification give you first priority for all travel. National Police transorbital hopper remains at spaceport most of time. You can use. Todalin will help with details."

The itinerary was ambitious. A copy of the memorandum sent to the commanders of the SRTs to be evaluated described him as a "counter-terrorism operations adviser" appointed by General Kyrgiakos, and as a commissioned officer in the National Police with the rank of major. He was to be given full access and cooperation and reported directly to Gavros.

That's plain enough. It should be smooth, thought Kel.

"The schedule is open," Major Todalin interjected. "If you find you need more or less time with any of these units, feel free to change the itinerary as you see fit. Just inform me and I'll make all arrangements."

Kel had questions of Gavros, what he expected of Kel on these assessments, what Kel's responsibility and authority were to be if he assessed significant problems in how any of the units were operating.

He voiced these concerns and Gavros' answer did not put Kel immediately at ease.

"Use your best judgement," was the given answer and in it Kel saw both trust and ways things could come apart at the seams. *No one likes a visit from the boss's snoops.* That's most certainly how he'd be perceived.

They spent another few minutes discussing the trip, and then Gavros got up, signaling an end to the meeting. The general walked with him to the double doors of his inner office and shook Kel's hand.

"This will be very helpful. Oh, my daughter has received interview appointment from your cultural attaché. She is very excited. I thank you, Kel."

"Only too glad to help, Gavros. I'll report back to you soon."

"The major will help with details. Safe travels, Kel."

The major led him to his own small office near the general's suite. Behind the man's desk were multiple holos and stills of Todalin in Hoplite garb. Some with him dressed as an assaulter, some holos of repeating loops of explosive breaches, some with him posed in sniper gear with various long rifles. The general's aide had been an operator as well.

"I served under Gavros when he was still the commander," the major said when he noticed Kel's attention to the glory wall common for staff officers from time immemorial. "I was a Hoplite the last few years before he got promoted out of the unit. I made team leader my last year there. Those were the best days. We did a lot of anti-crime work back then."

Kel nodded, non-verbally inviting the man to continue.

"It was a good time to leave when Gavros did. I went to investigations for the next several years and learned much. Now, here I am, riding a desk."

From the beginning, Todalin's savvy and professionalism impressed him. This filled in a piece of the puzzle as to how the general's assistant came to be where he was, and why he was so competent. He'd known many operators who found themselves going to staff positions. It was necessary for an officer to further his career. Kel intended to always remain a sergeant. He couldn't imagine a life off the team.

They went over specifics, and Kel began contemplating actions as he learned about his itinerary.

"Corinth, well, it's been pretty quiet out there," began Major Todalin. "The unit trains a lot, but they actually do very little that I know of. As far as I know they're competent, but they don't have many operational successes to be judged by. There's not been much ME activity there.

"The next stop, Eritrea, might be a different experience. ME has not been particularly active there either, but the NP are doing joint operations with the state militia on the southern coast. It's an area where the illegal narcotics trade is based. Jade Lotus especially. They do some seizures of growing sites, processing labs, and some interdiction of traffic. The crime gangs there are quite violent. The team there does a lot of hits and I think you'll see some interesting things."

Kel agreed. It did sound interesting.

"Cyrene is landlocked. It's a small region, mostly urban. They're a large banking center and also home to the world's destination for gaming and gambling. They have a small ME presence and we're hoping to keep it from growing."

Kel was especially interested to visit the next site on the list, Peloponnese.

"As you know, Peloponnese was the region where we've had the most horrific act by ME. The school kidnapping. Gavros and I are not satisfied with the answers we've received about why the job went bad and I have a packet for you with all our internal reviews. I didn't want to load too much on you up front, so take what's useful from the reports."

Kel shook hands and took his leave. He was going traveling.

After checking in with Don and the other members of his team at the embassy, Kel headed downtown to meet with Jacee.

She beamed at his news. "Kel, I can't tell you what an important step this is. You're making real inroads into the Meridian security apparatus. Whatever you're doing, don't start screwing up now. Keep taking what they're offering."

He laughed with her. He liked Jacee and thought she was likely facilitating a lot behind the scenes. It was her detailed knowledge about his activities that still troubled him. Could he trust her completely? For now he intended to share as little information with her as possible going forward. *Self-protection, like Bigg said.* He did not want his actions on the ground to be examined too closely by her or the House of Reason. Politicos were duplicitous. Right now, he was the favored child. Should there be an unforeseen complication, or if Kel was on the scene when something went really wrong, he knew his current status as favored child could be reoriented to blame.

That was just the nature of the game and it was best to plan for all the tiles to fall that way. Still, someone was giving her information from the inside. *Who?*

The next morning as he loaded his gear, Kel heard pattering steps approaching as Eirene rushed out to say goodbye in the courtyard. She pressed a container of the flaky, honey-covered pastries into his hands.

"Goodbye now. You take these. Have good trip. Many thanks, again."

"Come on now, Eirene, you know I had nothing to do with that."

Eirene's husband owned one of the fabrication shops that Pen had contracted with to do some of the vehicle upgrades. She thought Kel had something to do with the good fortune she and her husband were receiving. Kel tried to dissuade her from that idea, but she was having none of it.

"I know you help. You such good boy. I know these things."

She patted his cheek.

"When you return—pretty wife for you. You see!"

He grinned at that. "Why do I need a wife when I've got a good woman who loves me right here?" She giggled like a schoolgirl at that. "Well, thanks for these. I'll enjoy them. See you soon!"

A half hour later, Gren dropped him at the spaceport, Kel showing his NP aspida and identification holo to the gate guards. The guard looked at the items, came to a sharp position of attention and rendered a salute in the manner of the locals, bringing his fist horizontally across his chest before extending the arm fully in front of him.

Gren drove on to the field. "I've never seen them do that before. You some kind of a big shot now?"

Kel kept a straight face. "It's not what you know, but who you know."

Gren dropped him and his gear off at the NP air section, where Kel said his goodbyes and walked in through the entrance to the operations office. Outside there were several hovers and fixed wing atmosphere ships along the flightline, and beyond was the sleek black trans-orbital transport, all marked with the NP seal.

Over at the commercial transport hub, two cargo container ships were grounded. They reminded him of the *Callie*, though both appeared to be quite a bit smaller. He'd have to remember when he returned to ask Ramer if he'd heard anything about his friends and whether their venture had profited them.

Kel found a lieutenant behind the counter and bounced him his orders. It took only a minute before a crew chief came to collect Kel and his belongings and escort him across the duracrete to the ramp of the stubby winged ship. Once onboard he was shown to the passenger compartment while the crew chief took charge of Kel's gear and stowed it.

Kel was settling in when one of the pilots came down the narrow stairway from the cockpit to greet Kel.

"Major Turner? I'm Captain Ateno. I'll be your pilot today. I understand we'll be seeing each other frequently over the next several weeks?"

"Yeah. Just call me Kel. I appreciate the lift."

"The trip to Corinth will only take about an hour once we lift. If you need anything, just let the chief know. We'll tell you over comms when you need to be belted in. Ever take a suborbital ride before?"

Kel assured him he had but didn't volunteer more.

"We'll get going soon. You're our only passenger."

There weren't many of this kind of craft on the planet. It seemed extravagant for them to detail the craft to transport him alone, but he wasn't going to say no. This was another indication of the importance Gavros placed on Kel's pending evaluations. Did Gavros know something he wasn't sharing? *What does Gavros know that makes this trip urgent?*

Over the cabin comms Kel was alerted they were preparing to depart, and soon the craft taxied down the runway and achieved lift, making a few gentle, banking turns as it climbed into the Meridian sky, rapidly gaining altitude with noticeably increasing thrust, the force of gravity pushing Kel into his seat. They soon reached the edge of space. Kel was familiar with the type of craft and its capabilities. The ship was mainly used for hypersonic flight at suborbital altitudes, making travel across the planet rapid, but could also reach a low, extra-atmospheric orbit and had docking rings and airlocks capable of transferring passengers and cargo to larger space-going vessels.

Kel wondered if the Hoplites were trained in zero-gee combat and ship seizure? They had the transorbital craft which would make the capability feasible. If they already had the essential tactics for tubular assaults—the generic term for dealing with passenger craft like buses and planes—they just had to learn to do so in a micro-gravity environment. The docking rings and locks had no gravity-decking, and frequently many exterior spaces where crews spent little time did not have the luxury. Kel would think carefully before broaching the subject with Todalin.

Sharing expertise of that nature might be proscribed. The ME didn't have an orbital capability that he knew of; sharing that knowledge might extend beyond his mandate to assist Meridian in dealing with the current threat.

They spent little time in the upper atmosphere before the craft dipped into a free-fall trajectory toward Meridian's surface. After a while the thrusters kicked in and the craft banked its way into landing.

Corinth lay at a higher latitude than Tiryns, which combined with the northern sea currents traveling its coast, making the region's climate cooler than what Kel had been enjoying in Tiryns.

On the ground he was met by the executive office of the NP Special Reaction Team and driven to their base where he was provided with quarters. The accommodations were more of what Kel was accustomed to—a simple room with a shower.

Later he was introduced to the commander, a colonel, and the rest of the team. They had a forty-man unit, with half of that number being part-time members who regularly had duties in patrol or investigations. They made him feel welcome but were clearly apprehensive about his visit. Kel could understand why.

The colonel politely asked about Kel's orders and what he was expecting to see during his stay with them.

"I'm not here to find fault or to criticize," assured Kel. "General Kyrgiakos has asked me to make an objective evaluation of all the NP tactical units and to determine if there are any gaps in capabilities or training. The escalation of the threat environment from ME warranted the review. He's trying to anticipate any problems and rectify them before they become an issue."

That was factual, but also only part of the answer. Kel was certain that he was being asked to make recommendations about the fitness of the different units. He wanted to stay as positive as possible and not make it seem that any of his observations could turn into a punitive action against the unit commander by Gavros.

Kel spent the next week meeting the members of the unit, observing their training, looking at their equipment and vehicles, and spending time with the assault teams and snipers individually, trying to assess their abilities.

"We are famous throughout Meridian for our art," his hosts bragged after training one day. In his travels he always found a regional pride present as a result of some element unique to his host's home. He was given a tour of the artisan section of Corinth and he agreed, the locally produced works were marvelous. No holo recreations—the effort of two human hands working natural materials had produced all the items. A gemstone that existed only in Corinth was another source of pride and Kel purchased a small stone as a memento. The opalescent green reflected even in dim light and was pleasing to hold. It would go on a shelf to join the other small keepsakes that reminded him of his many travels.

At the end of that time his assessment of the unit was straightforward. They were competent and had no deficiencies in skills. Only one issue stood out: they spent way too much time shooting and not enough time on other skills. Ninety percent of their time spent training as a unit consisted of being on the range just shooting. Meanwhile, they did not have a ballistic kill house in which to challenge themselves. They had no means of practicing live-fire in any structure and didn't think it was necessary for their threat environment.

The XO and commander both confirmed to Kel that most of their time as a unit was spent doing dignitary protection at public events and gatherings. The aristocrats of the family in Corinth spent a great deal of time at sporting events and the seasonal festivals, and that required the presence of the SRT for security at the venues.

They did not serve high-risk warrants for their investigators; the investigators had that capability themselves. They had not had a hostage rescue to perform in the unit's history. While they had responded to major crimes like bank robberies, the investigators did most of the surveillance and anti-crime work and they rarely called for the Special Reaction Team.

Kel added to his report each night in his room and had it ready to bounce to Todalin by the time he departed. He placed the blame for the deterioration of their skills and the reprioritization of the Corinth SRT on the leadership of the local NP at all levels. Their mission had been redefined and no one had dissented.

Kel's final recommendation was to detach a mobile training team from the Hoplites to spend several weeks reviewing skills and recertifying the unit. A kill house would have to be built. Otherwise, Kel's recommendation was that the unit could not be considered capable of performing counter-terror or high-risk missions should the need arise. Any crisis in Corinth, the Hoplites would have to be deployed.

It also gave him some insight as to why he felt Gavros was pushing for this assessment. Would Kel find other major deficiencies revealing that his supposedly best people were unprepared to deal with ME?

Kel next moved south to Eritrea. He took a commercial flight, down the long, coastal region along the same body of water that formed Corinth's western limit. Eritrea contained large undeveloped areas—long stretches of desert in the south and miles of tropical jungle closer to the equator. The travel took him the better part of a day and was much less convenient than the sub-orbital route he'd taken from Tiryns to Corinth.

He was again met by the leadership of the NP Special Reaction Team for Eritrea and taken to their base of operations. Most of the population centers were within a close span of kilometers from the coastline. In the capital, Attica, the city extended in a narrow band from the shoreline up to mountain foothills rising just a dozen kilometers inland from the coast. At night Kel could see small lights high on the slopes where homes held spectacular views of the aquamarine ocean beyond the city. Kel found the region quite beautiful and the temperature pleasant with ocean breezes attenuating the heat reflected off the brown, craggy slopes so close. Several island systems lay just offshore, some of the larger ones visible from the city on a clear day.

Kel had arrived at an interesting time; the SRT were conducting operations with the militia along the southern coastal islands, interdicting the drug traffic that plagued the region.

"It is the curse of our people that wherever the chosen of the gods go, there is always the weight of the

Kurkmen hanging on them," the commander of the SRT explained to Kel.

The area studies emphasized the population of Meridian was one of the most homogeneous of human colonized planets in the galaxy. It had been founded and settled by a single culture and ethnicity, who took pride in preserving the traditions and genetic makeup of their culture. So much so, that the founders purposely sought a planet at the galaxy's edge; isolated and free from interference. There was, however, a distinct ethnic and cultural minority on the planet, the Kurks.

The Kurk culture was as ancient as that of the Meridians, but they had little in common except an ancient mutual dislike.

The Meridians believed in a multitude of gods who controlled the destiny of men—their economics, their social relationships, even natural forces like the weather. Multiple temples to the different gods stood throughout Tiryns. Some folks worshipped many of the gods, while others focused on a single heavenly patron. At the palace, Kel had seen Eirene praying to a small carved statue of a feminine figure set into a small shrine off the kitchen. Kel had seen all kinds of religions and their associated workings, human and alien alike. Some were quite beautiful; others, horrific.

The Kurks had a different religious flavor than the Meridians. Theirs was a monotheistic religion that demanded many daily acts of devotion and condemned followers of other religions to the status of being sub-human.

"Wherever there are drugs, the Kurkmen are never far behind," continued the commander of the SRT. "They cultivate and purify jade lotus in remote jungle valleys along the island chains. They process and purify their product at labs along the southern coast, and then transport their products by sea and air all over the planet.

"We've had good success against them, but sometimes you cut off the head of one monster, and two grow in its place. It seems to be a never-ending battle against the hydra of myth and legend."

Kel had seen the damage that drugs did to communities. He'd found no cure for the unfortunate people who sought to destroy their own mental faculties on chemically-stimulated highs. He didn't believe in the theory of the victimless crime. Wherever those problems existed, misery accompanied the people involved in the drug trade and its victims.

Kel met the team the next morning for the operations order. It was presented in a logical format, one recognizable by Kel. It covered the essentials of the mission and its intent, and went into exacting details of the movement plan and coordination between the NP—who would be conducting the raid on the suspected drug gang compound—and the militia, who would be providing the maritime capability to transport the force for the mission.

Kel was especially interested in the portion of the order detailing plans for actions on the objective. Knowing that the thick vegetation surrounding their target made finding an exact location difficult, the plan was to perform what Kel would have called a tactical reconnaissance to locate the stronghold, and then marshal the forces back together to perform the strike.

He was impressed. It was obvious they had experience in these types of joint operations. After a morning meal break where he got to know everyone better, he mingled with the troops as they checked and loaded equipment onto trucks.

At the coastal base two utility vessels hovered in the bay, sending a fine mist from beneath the repulsors. One of the same type craft was beached on a duracrete ramp, its front ramp lowered to reveal a wide gaping deck. Camouflaged personnel directed NP vehicles onto the deep gunwale craft. After trucks were loaded, the vessel raised its ramp and backed out of the slip, making room for the next vessel to approach and do the same until the dock was empty of the ground transports.

Kel had no idea that the militia had a fleet of amphibious landing craft. The flotilla was accompanied by several smaller attack boats with mounted heavy and medium machine guns. The militia in Eritrea was truly more of a naval infantry unit than what Kel had imagined. There was little in the area study that had indicated this level of sophistication. He would be adding to that document as soon as he returned home.

At dusk, they moved out of the harbor and toward the islands. They would not reach the main island beach until well after dark, a preferred time to provide some concealment to their activities, but also a factor to potentially complicate the off-loading process at the beachhead. "Everything is harder in the dark" was true in all of Kel's experiences. If they could do so in total darkness, it would impress him.

The trip was uneventful and even pleasant. He'd grown up near or on the water and though no seaman himself, the operations of the crew were familiar to him. It was not dissimilar to watching the crew on the *Callie;* bosuns performing their check-and-recheck routine of the vehicles and passengers to ensure everyone's safety while onboard the craft.

He made his way to the observation deck to stay out of the way of the deck operations that would start soon with the landings. Kel could make out the outline of the island's volcanic peaks and soon could see the lights of a small bay, where a mole shielded a beach.

The three landing craft beached alongside each other, and soon the NP were driving their vehicles off the beach, and up a narrow hard packed road beyond the beach zone. The coastal road wound through small fishing villages, then up a series of switchbacks into the higher elevations of the central mountains.

After another hour of slow climb into a thick jungle, the vehicles parked in a glade. The three team leaders gathered their teams in separate areas of the clearing to give one last brief before the teams split up and searched the thickly forested valleys around them.

The jade lotus grew only in densely shaded, perpetually moist areas. The road the SRT had used to travel to this location was the same one drug gangs used to transport the raw or refined product to and from the only available portage. The terrain was rugged and the vegetation so thick that travel by any other means was virtually impossible, especially when it came to transporting thousands of kilograms of the narcotic.

Kel was invited to join one of the three teams; the commander and XO each joined a team as well. Soon all moved on slightly different azimuths out of the clearing. The ground sloped on three sides, leading down multiple gullies and into the valley that their holo-topographic projections said would be present beyond.

Kel had spent a great deal of time in jungle environments. While the flora and fauna differed from planet to planet, the commonality between them all was that the topography was fluid. Last year's terrain mapping might be significantly different from today's survey. Hilltops increased and decreased in height, the course of streams and rivers changed dramatically, while improved roads and trails sometimes disappeared completely. Simply nothing remained unchanged over time in these environments given the effect of perpetual rainfall. Trying to navigate by features recorded on a map frequently led to confusion and missteps. Geo-location was more reliable when available, and Kel was glad that Meridian had such infrastructure.

The men had rudimentary night vision lenses. Few wore them and Kel thought that was good; they did little to help where vision was limited to the man in front of you as you followed them through the darkness.

Like most jungles he'd been in, this one was alive with the chorus of insect and animal life. Wind brushed through the gigantic trees and rain pattered down, soaking uniforms and muffling the tread of their boots through the vegetation.

He reached into his pocket and pulled out protective skins for his hands. Everything in the jungle, plant or animal, wanted to bite, sting, stab, or cut you, especially your hands.

They spent hours moving cautiously and slowly down one wet draw after another, the soil giving way under their feet and forcing them to grab branches and vines to keep from sliding off small banks into patches of even denser brush.

Given that they were essentially policemen, Kel thought the men were adept moving through the jungle. They'd learned many vital infantry-type skills by having to operate in this environment. Competence in jungle patrolling wasn't exactly what he thought he'd be evaluating on this mission, but so far he liked what he saw. It was a difficult capability to have mastered.

ME doesn't have to stick to cities. Once I report to Gavros, these guys might find themselves picked for rural operations everywhere if they can do this well, he noted.

Raised fists were held at head height, the universal signal to halt and remain silent. Kel eased forward, cautiously placing each foot onto the ground and gradually testing its firmness before placing his full weight on the sole, repeating the process until he had made his way to the front where the team leader kneeled, looking through a pair of day-for-night binoculars.

Kel's specs were far superior to anything the man was using. Through narrow voids between the trees, man-sized shapes moved. Dim lighting coming from underneath the structures in the clearing did little to illuminate the surrounding area to anyone with un-augmented vision. Kel clicked a thermal overlay and identified no less than a dozen shapes moving in and around the low structures. As of yet he did not see any armaments.

Kel knelt to whisper into the team leader's ear. "I see a dozen men. No weapons obvious. They don't suspect we're here." To respond the man did likewise, cupping hands around Kel's left ear. "I think you're right, Mister Kel. I'm going to inform the other team leaders and we're going to sit tight."

After using his link to relay what he'd found to the other teams, the man whispered, "The teams are headed to this grid. The commander is with the closest team a little farther up the valley. They're going to get here pretty rapidly, like in the next hour. If we can sit tight, when they get here they can serve as a blocking force for us to assault the objective. The XO's team is probably too far away to wait on. Will you stay put and keep eyes out while I tell the rest of the patrol?" Kel nodded.

The man slowly moved down the line, visiting each member of the patrol to share the information, while Kel kept watch under his superior night vision. The men in the small clearing were still unaware they were being watched.

I'd feel better about assaulting now than waiting to be compromised if anyone gives us away, Kel thought. He was going to make the suggestion at any hint they were detected.

But it didn't happen. They waited silently, the men showing excellent noise discipline until after an hour or so, the team leader reached over to squeeze Kel's shoulder.

"CO's in place about fifty meters downhill from us."

The team could've been a thousand meters away and not been any less visible, the jungle was so thick.

"I'm going to get us on line and we're going to move into the camp with white lights and announce ourselves."

The man again moved down the line giving instructions and the element began to gather in a linear formation parallel to the structures just twenty meters ahead in the small clearing. This was different from a true assault like Kel would execute with his team; they'd seen no arms and were not receiving gunfire. They were obligated to take control of the suspects and identify themselves as police; they would only use force if it became necessary.

The team leader initiated his team's actions by standing up and turning on the white light at the front of his carbine as he yelled, "National Police. You are all under arrest. Do not resist and you will not be harmed."

He repeated this several times as the line of armed men walked forward together on line and into the clearing. White lights illuminated the scene, the faces of multiple surprised men staring back at them, clearly shocked at the appearance of the SRT operators from the surrounding jungle.

Some of the suspects turned to run down the natural slope of the valley, toward the waiting blocking force, whose own lights were now visible and shouting the same verbal commands as they had just done.

A shot rang out from one of the low buildings and the man to Kel's left made a grunting sound before he keeled over. Kel raised his weapon in the direction of the building as the men to his left and right did the same, immediately releasing a torrent of fire. The fury of the projectiles ripped apart the thatched walls of the structure, a corner brace collapsing and a portion of the building crashing to the ground.

Kel got off a flurry of shots but did not see a human target. *Got you.* A body toppled out of the collapsed building, a rifle falling from his hands.

The team flowed forward as the commander's force moved into the clearing from below. Many of the suspects already lay on the ground; others stood with their arms raised, too terrified to move.

The team secured the suspects; those not on the ground were quickly forced down, and all were efficiently restrained at wrists and ankles. Kel's team leader divided his force to start clearing the structures. Kel decided he could be of most use checking on the wounded operator; in the chaos of the first few minutes, he might've been the only person aware of the casualty.

Kel found the man sitting down, his protective vest removed, massaging his chest.

"You all right, man?" Kel knelt to examine.

"Yeah, just knocked the wind out of me. Hurts like hell. Looks like I took one square-on. Did they get him?"

"Oh, yeah. We got him."

"Good. Wish I had done the deed, though."

Kel understood the sentiment. "It happens." He lifted the man's shirt and ran his hands over his chest, abdomen, and back. He then looked at his own hands. Seeing no blood, he again asked the man if he was okay and if he hurt anywhere else.

"Nah. I think I'm fine. Everything feels good."

Kel turned the man's protective vest over and saw where the man had been struck in the center of his vest, the bullet smashing into one of the magazines on the front before contacting the composite material underneath. A small soft area of the plate collapsed under Kel's thumb pressure.

"Your lucky day, man."

Kel moved back into the clearing again to report the injury. The teams had gathered the suspects together and had them lying face down in a close array. The last team made their way into the clearing, the XO with them. Kel hailed him and updated him as they walked together to where the commander and the team leaders stood.

"Glad you could make it," the older commander joked as his XO reached out to shake everyone's hand, including Kel's.

They walked to the rear of the small compound to an open shed where stack upon stack of ribbon-like loose material lay. Raw jade lotus. They moved to the next building to find containers filled with chemicals and table after table covered in piles of a moist, dark resin.

"I'd say that informant earned his pay this time," the XO said to the group. Everyone laughed.

The commander pulled the XO to the side of the group and spoke to him for a few moments before leaving the building. The junior man walked back over to Kel.

"The commander is sending me back to the vehicle staging area and thought you'd like to go with me," he said. "We'll take our injured man out with a few of the other guys to help. We'll head back down the coast and wait there. They'll be here several more hours wrapping up and torching the place."

Kel shrugged. He had no objection and was more than happy to help lead them out; his navigation by link and specs was probably more accurate than theirs. It would be helpful in getting the injured man out by the most efficient route. "Sure. Glad to," was all he said.

They started up the slow grade, one man on either side of the injured operator, two more trailing and carrying the man's weapons and gear, with Kel up front leading the way. The injured man protested that he felt fine until they started up the grade of the jungle floor, then his heavy breathing and grunting betrayed his pain.

They had not traveled very far before a gunshot rang out behind them. Kel paused and looked back. He ignored the sound until he heard another gunshot. He was about to ask the XO if they should return to the scene to assist when he heard yet another gunshot. Then it came to him.

They're executing the karking suspects!

Gunshots continued to ring out at regular intervals and before Kel could say anything the XO spoke, anticipating Kel's question.

"Mister Kel, things are different here in Eritrea. We are in the center of the poison trade of the jade lotus. The penalty for growing, processing, or distributing drugs is death. If you were caught in Argolis doing the same, you'd be arrested and brought before a magistrate, and the punishment would be death as well. Here, we just skip the middleman. Besides, one of those idiots shot at us and hit one of our men. What did they think was going to happen to them?"

Kel nodded and turned his attention back to navigating out of the dark and twisted jungle.

FLASHBACK

Learning Occurs, or, Experience is What You Get When You Don't Get What You Want
Antione

It's the beginning of our second week with the kill team. They've let it slip that's what their five-man team is called. A kill team. We've done a couple of dozen hits together. Some of the missions have us spread thin and it's not unusual for me to roll on to the objective with them. Trumbull is running the squad tonight. They're sitting in a grav sled just around the corner, waiting to be called up. I'm trying not to be distracted, thinking about the trust they keep placing in me as I climb the ladder to the second story window.

There's been a fair amount of climbing lately, sneaking in from rooftops or second stories to seize the upper floors as part of the team work from the ground. They think I have a talent for climbing. I suppose that's true. At least tonight I get to use a ladder and don't have to free ascend another slick exterior. The architecture on Antione is somewhat dated and influenced by what culture I couldn't tell you. For the common folk, they don't like ledges or decorative touches that make for good toe and foot holds.

The K-17 is on my back, and close to my chest is a Collins needler. It's a very compact personal defense weapon, impeller powered and silent. I'd grabbed one out of the locker after asking TA if I could use it. He'd hesitated slightly before shrugging. "Be my guest. To each his own." The last mission I'd had trouble getting my carbine in to play off my back after a particularly difficult climb onto a roof, and thought the smaller weapon would be ideal for what we were doing.

Howard is below stabilizing the ladder for me, pulling it into the wall with his body weight. Somewhere around the corner, TA is climbing and D'antonio is doing ladder duty for him. We're hitting two buildings simultaneously, this residence and an adjacent office where a late night meeting is happening. The men are next door and only the women are moving about the home. These aren't militia. Means there shouldn't be any serious fighting. That's all they've told us about the targets. It should be simple compared to what we've done so far.

Like most second story windows, it's not locked. The panel slides aside and I bring the needler up as I take a look. It's as we guessed, a sitting room and at this late hour, empty. "Hey, I'm in," TA tells me. He's just a few walls away from me. "I'm stepping in now," I tell him. We'll link up inside and secure the women we think are in the bedrooms. "Wait one, I'm almost set."

No sooner do I get my rear foot on the floor than the door opens. Gun! I bring the needler up and pull the trigger. The man reacts by freezing in place. I stitch the guy, the needler pumping out the thin slivers that I know are finding their mark as shredded holes open wider and wider in the man's shirt. The needler stops humming as the charge pack runs dry. The man doesn't raise the rifle in his hands. He looks at me in confusion. I've taken to carrying a vibroblade like my mentors and let the needler hang as I pull the knife and rush forward to plunge it into the man's chest. That gets a response. His knees buckle as I cover his bearded mouth with my other hand and ease him to the floor.

TA is here, helping me pull the body into the room. "You good?"

"Yeah. No sweat," I say as I put the blade away.

"Well quit screwing around. We've got work to do," he says to me, a little annoyed. We move through the upper floor and capture the women, girls really. They are frightened and put up no resistance as we chain and hood them. By the time we're finished, the rest of the team has taken the office and my squad is up, helping to put hooded suspects into the grav sled. We're hovering out of the suburbs now, no one the wiser we were even there.

"Hey," TA asks me as we float along. "What was with that vibroblade kill back there? Getting fancy?"

"Nah, man," I try and explain, more relaxed around the cool guys than the first day. "I shot the guy with that Collins needler and he acted like nothing happened. Nothing. He just stood there, like he knew something was happening to him, but didn't know how to react. That vibroblade was the next weapon I had handy."

TA doesn't laugh. "Yeah. Well, some folks just need a little time to figure out they're dead. Plus, that Collins is a dud. Now you know."

TA tells me we're going to stand down for a day while Zero and Papa Bear are off at a meeting of the minds. We've been doing hits every night, which means we start work after lunch, and with few exceptions, sleep most mornings.

Despite the official word that we're knocking off for the day, I can't sleep. After I down a ration I head to the equipment module. I return the needler to its slot and pick up a bandolier of grenades. I head out the back gate to the makeshift range we've been using; really just a small valley with a hill for a backstop. The basic at the gate salutes me. We're probably the first legionnaires these basics have ever seen in person. Being with our hosts, the word is probably out that all legionnaires are bearded mystery men. No such thing as bad publicity, I guess.

We share the small hover port with a Repub mounted battalion. They pull security on the base and we stay in our own detached part by the hover field with the Talons.

I'm not much older than the two basics on the gate, but they look like children to me. "Call it in that the range is in use, Private," I say as I return his salute, not wanting to disappoint. Don't want any drama from the basics thinking the base is under attack.

I need a little time on the hand blaster, but what's been troubling me is the K-17 carbine they've let me use. Don't get me wrong, the thing is a dream. I'm in love with it. I just don't have a good feel for the energrenade launcher. The trajectory is different with the oddly-shaped energrenades than the conventional M7 launcher that D'antonio stuck with. Maybe he had the right idea. So far I've only used it on a hit once at about 75 meters, so the burst more than made up for my aiming error. TA told me they couldn't give us the program that slaves the ballistic reticle to our buckets, just told us to use the high dispersion setting and the mechanical backup sight on the side.

I range some rocky features out to a few hundred meters and decide to find out for myself what it'll do. I set the output to low and launch one at a jagged outcrop a little over 400 meters away. I hold a little higher on the next and pause to jot a note on my link. I plot a curve using a few estimates and pick a new target 250 meters away, make my best guess, and fire. A few more tries and I think I have what I need.

"Hey Turner. Fun or work?" I hadn't noticed Provo walk up behind me. He was quiet, even in full battle rattle. He moves like he talks. Even. Smooth. "Uh, work, I guess. Just trying to get a feel for the launcher. Other than the quick familiarization you guys gave us, I've only used it once. Kinda been losing sleep over not having the full package to run it like you guys do. Think I got it figured out."

"Oh?" Provo has the first hint of inflection in his voice he's let slip around us. "Tell me what you came up with." I show him. "It's just a mathematical progression. For every 50 meters in range I just add two to my elevation to about 300 meters, then I start adding three. It seems to get me pretty close."

Provo's bucket nods. "Hmm. Just a sec." He shoulders his own K-17. I can tell he's using his HUD as his head rises slightly as though looking at the holo reticle for the launcher. He lets the carbine drop and it hugs his chest as he produces his link and pushes a few figures around. "You know, that's not bad. Very close." Sounds like a compliment to me.

"Thanks. Think I'll get the squad out after lunch and run them through this." Provo grunts. "Glad to hear it. Nothing personal Turner, but I like to be alone. You can have the range back later. Get some rest."

I wish him good training and head out. Behind me, Provo starts working out. Every so often I turn back to watch. Now he's carrying a huge rock, holding it against his side as he fires his carbine one-handed while running.

I turn away. I'm certain he's the kind of guy who doesn't like to be watched.

16

Kel stared at a blank screen as he composed his report the night before leaving Eritrea.

How much of this do I put in writing? he wondered.

Committing to black and white that he'd likely witnessed the sanctioned murder of a dozen suspects in custody was sure to set a series of actions in motion. Kel wasn't sure what his role in that should be. He paced the floor of his quarters considering the quandary.

In the end he wrote a sanitized version for the major but on his return, he would discuss the matter with Todalin and Gavros directly. If they wanted Kel's full documentation of the incident, he would gladly provide it then. If they ignored his revelations, he had other avenues.

He prepared a full version of the events for his friend Don. Let *him* share the information with the military-political brains back at the embassy. The diplomats could decide what they wanted to do with the knowledge of the brutality he'd witnessed in Eritrea. If it involved recommending sanctions or the withdrawal of aid, so be it. In the meantime, he'd continue to focus on the task Gavros had given him; it served many of the goals of his mission here on Meridian.

He took another commercial lift to the center of the continent, reaching the namesake capital of Cyrene.

He again was met by the commander and executive officer of the regional SRT. They drove him into the city center to dine at one of the fine casinos that populated the upscale, modern city. From what Kel had seen so far, Cyrene had every appearance of being a rich, clean, yet traditional Meridian metropolis.

The casino they'd chosen was impressive in every way; the design contained traditional elements as well as risky, modern details that would seem more at home in the core.

The restaurant looked down on the main boulevard; lights from the many casinos and hotels with their fountains and sculptures dotted the landscape. Well-dressed people meandered the many thoroughfares. Kel noted no indication of a crisis occurring.

They kept the conversation light, being in a public place, but they asked Kel about his travels around Meridian and his impressions of life here. He replied with many genuinely complimentary things to say. They answered Kel's questions about Cyrene; there were no surprises. They confirmed that many of the planet's banking and investment firms were based here. It was also the center of gambling and gaming activities which, in a way, seemed appropriate to him.

Make it, lose it, invest it—here it's all done in one place, he decided as he listened.

They took Kel to a luxury hotel at the other end of the strip that seemed quieter and less busy than where they'd just dined. When Kel checked in and brought out his link to transfer payment, his hosts intervened, insisting that the accommodations were complimentary of the owner who had a special relationship with the NP. Several years before, the man's daughter had been kidnapped, and the SRT was part of the successful resolution of the crisis. Now, whenever they had the need, the organization used the hotel at the request of the owner.

The commander explained. "Many times, we have told the man that we cannot accept the gratuity, but he insists. So, when we have a dignitary like yourself come visit, we make the request and he gives us a luxury suite gratis. It lets him show his gratitude and keep his dignity, and we do not directly benefit from his gift. I doubt anyone would see that as corruption. Anyway, we thought you'd be comfortable here. And we don't maintain quarters or barracks on the compound."

The room was indeed luxurious, and in the morning, the owner came to meet Kel himself while he ate breakfast. The gregarious older gentleman lavished praise on "those wonderful, brave policemen" who'd saved his daughter. He gave Kel a brief review of the events of what surely had to have been the worst trial of the man's life—having his daughter held for ransom and threatened with death.

Without knowing who Kel was or what he did, he shook Kel's hand and thanked him for what he and men like him did. Kel politely accepted his thanks and as efficiently as he could, made his way to his room to gather his kit and wait for his hosts to come collect him. Kel was uncomfortable with the display of attention from the man. He wasn't ungrateful, he was simply unaccustomed to anyone thanking him for doing his job. It wasn't the DO way.

The NP compound was concealed and enclosed by excellent physical security; manned checkpoints and gates led into the compound.

After a tour of the facility Kel joined them for their mid-morning physical training session. He followed along with the team as they were led through a series of body-weighted exercises on the grassy training field, then donned their protective gear and grabbed carbines and ran loops around the compound for several kilometers. Kel thought it an adequate workout. He didn't judge them by his personal standards; that would be unreasonable. The group was clearly fit, and many of them were older than Kel by ten or twenty years. This job did not require the kind of physical stamina that being in DO required. He did not believe in using the physical standards of DO as a means of measuring others' ability to do their jobs. It was not helpful.

"Major," one of the team leaders said, despite Kel's insistence to forget the honorary rank. "We have the rest of the day scheduled for some range work. Since you have all your kit, care to shoot with us?"

The team leaders took turns with each of their teams running everyone through a brief refresher qualification. Kel approved. They were an excellent metric for measuring an operator's competence with his weapons, testing the ability to fire at a number of distances and in different positions with varying time requirements for the separate drills with both carbine and pistol. For a team leader, it was valuable feedback on the performance of his subordinates and allowed a near-instant evaluation of an operator's preparedness.

Kel was satisfied to watch the men rotate several relays of shooters through the course of fire before himself joining the last relay to shoot. By this time, he was familiar with the exercise and had already mentally rehearsed his upcoming performance.

Kel enjoyed all kinds of tests of his shooting ability and relished training with his own team on the range. At home they each took turns deciding which drills and standards they would shoot, competing to see who could come up with the most difficult. Some of the drills had unrealistic expectations of accuracy combined with extreme time constraints, but served to challenge the shooter to his maximum ability. It was bad to only shoot drills you could ace every time.

The drill they prepared for now was shot wearing all of their gear. How well one shot 'slick' without their gear had little meaning to a hostage, and Kel approved of this group's training ethic.

The drill was not particularly difficult, and Kel pushed himself to shoot as fast as his sights settled on the target. He was quite a bit faster than even the fastest shooter on the line and found himself waiting for the rest of the shooters to complete the drill after he had already finished.

Speed could be a trap; Kel knew that. Shooting within a time standard but failing to have the requisite accuracy became an exercise in building bad habits. Accuracy could never be sacrificed for speed. Kel had learned the adage, "It's not who shoots first, it's who hits first," early in his life.

After the last portion of the drill was completed, Kel stood by his target as the team leader made his way by each shooter's target.

The men to Kel's left and right eyed his target. Soon the team leader made his way over. There was only an enlarged hole that could be covered by two of his fingers in the center of the circle, and another much smaller single hole in the center of the small box above it.

"Men, cover down on me." The team leader drew everyone to move to the center of the line to look at Kel's target.

"This is our new standard. Good work, sir." The man extended his hand to Kel and Kel returned the gesture with a smile.

"Just call me Kel, gentlemen."

He made quick friends with the SRT after spending the first day of training with them. The next day found them practicing in their kill house. Kel observed the men working in different parts of the huge structure as individual teams from the catwalk. The commander and executive officer joined Kel later, and spent time asking him questions about how Kel's unit did things, and what differences he saw.

These guys really remind me of DO, Kel thought. He'd never worked with any indig who had as well-developed capabilities as he'd seen in the Hoplites and their derivative SRTs. He'd certainly never worked with any I-squared of similar competence; universally they were a nightmare of pointless and even dangerous combat practices. Maybe someday he'd find the exception.

But he had yet to. And he'd pulled ops on a lot of worlds. It was not long into his reverie when the commander and his XO received an alert on their links and disappeared to a small office. Soon, the four team leaders received alerts, one of them motioning for Kel to join them in the office.

"Here's what we know so far," the elder commander said to them all. "We just got alerted by investigations that we may have a warrant to serve tonight. Their surveillance team is on a guy suspected as an accomplice in several recent robberies and with a record of violent crimes. The intel looks convoluted, but the investigators think there may be a connection to ME. The guy has been known to associate with some of the student groups here, and the recent robberies point to another operation to build cash supplies for ME.

"They think he is going to meet another group that is suspected of smuggling weapons into Cyrene."

The team leaders groaned.

"I know, I know, it doesn't sound like they have anything firm on the ME connection. Still, he needs to go down. They gave us an early heads-up, and that's what I prefer. Look on the bright side, it came before we cut everyone loose and had to recall the team from home and beds. Let's get dinner and then settle in for what could be a long wait."

The team leaders departed to brief their men. Meanwhile the XO brought out his link and scrolled through selections for carry-out food.

Kel had been here many times before—getting spun up for a mission to spend hours of waiting and anticipation, only to eventually be stood down, disappointed and tired. Looked like this scenario was as familiar to his hosts as it was to him.

He chuckled. *Because the warrior knows not when the first arrow will fly, the armor is only loosened after the battle is won.* He stole that from a holo he and the guys liked about barbarian raiders. Just because it was fantasy, didn't mean it was without a glimmer of truth. Which is why they liked it. Plus, everyone had cool swords, wore animal skins, and rode into battle on huge six-legged reptasaurs. *If only something half as cool would happen tonight.* He wondered what the rest of his team was doing right now. While they probably weren't in the capital of a casino-state, they were probably doing something more interesting. Luxury rarely meant excitement for an operator who was after combat.

The bounce alert came about three hours later after darkness had fully set in.

The operation order identified that they were to perform a raid on a residential structure for the purposes of securing it for intelligence and evidence collection and to serve the arrest warrant on the named suspect. Anyone else they picked up would get sorted later. The primary suspect had a history of violent offenses, and given the scenario, the threat of weapons was significant.

The holo screen projected the target building—a two-story house in an unremarkable neighborhood, neither exclusive nor impoverished. From what Kel had seen of Cyrene, he doubted there even were slums. The team would perform a rolling assault right up to the breach points, the tactic most likely to catch the suspect unaware and keep the operators safe.

They loaded up, Kel the first climbing up and into the deep bay of the armored vehicle. He would then be the last off, following one of the assault teams to the target.

The vehicles traveled for about thirty minutes. The team leader issued warnings from the cab of the truck, counting down to arrival. Soon the "one minute" order was given. The vehicle slowed as it took a sharp turn, then zoomed forward to skid to a halt.

The heavy doors popped open and the men jumped out, Kel following. Men crouched beneath the windows along one wall, a strip charge placed against a door that led to the kitchen. There were lights on in the house, but no movement visible.

Other operators stood back, weapons elevated.

The door charge ignited with the same type of signature coming simultaneously from the other side of the building, like glowflies talking on a hot summer night.

The men moved forward into the house and gunfire chattered from within. Still outside, Kel raised his weapon, viewing through his specs the second-story windows where he briefly saw movement. It was unlikely that either team had assaulted up the stairs yet, but firing blindly into the space would never be acceptable.

Now a more rapid exchange of gunfire echoed out, followed a microsecond later by flashes through the upper windows, then nothing.

He was already moving by the time he heard, "He's bleeding out!"

Kel pushed into the structure, passing operators, following the sounds of distress until he reached the front room. It was a chaotic scene. Two suspects lay on the ground covered with blood, cuffed, being searched.

At the front entrance an operator lay on his back surrounded by his teammates and the XO. Kel pushed himself through to the wounded man. Two of his teammates knelt at his head, as two other operators worked to place an auto-tourniquet on the man's left thigh, his legs and waist soaked with blood.

The injured man grimaced and groaned but did not yell out. "Hold still, Mychel, hold still, we've got you, you're going to be fine," his friends repeated over and over. Mychel only moaned.

Kel did not intend to interfere with the man's treatment, but instinctively knew that critical time was being lost. *He's not talking. Not good. The chrono's running.*

He got the XO's attention.

"Sir, is there still resistance in the house?" He had to ask a second time to get an answer.

"No," the shaken man said. "Another bad guy dead upstairs. We own the house."

"Okay. I need to see if this man has other injuries. Get his vest and gear off."

At a nod from their XO, the men hit the release points on the gear and began stripping items. Kel removed his own medkit and activated the small palm-sized tool he produced from within. The device glowed blue as he passed it along the front of the man's torso and then down each leg, the materials of the wounded man's uniform and remaining equipment parting to reveal the bare skin underneath. The molecular scissors would not cut skin and could pass through even reinforced materials like a blaster through synthsilk.

As he pushed the rent clothing aside he placed his hands around the bare skin of the man's trunk, back, and limbs, checking his hands for fresh blood. *He's not bleeding anywhere else,* he thought as he took a breath to gather his observations into a relevant assessment. *But he's going downhill. Guy's breathing is falling off and he's turning waxy. He's still bleeding from somewhere.*

Kel inspected the tourniquet on the man's left thigh, as high as it could be placed in the man's groin. It glowed dull green, indicating that it was cinched tight and had not lost compression. Kel re-inspected the entire extremity quickly. While the entrance wound was visible just below the tourniquet, there was hard swelling well into the crease of the man's inguinal region. There could be only one cause.

"He's got a junctional wound. He got hit at the top of his thigh and the bullet penetrated his pelvis. He's bleeding deep internally, not from his thigh. I have to stop the bleeding. We have medical on the way? They need to have a stasis chamber ready."

The confused looks on the men's faces made him realize that they did not have stasis chamber technology. He quickly rethought his request.

"Tell them to have blood or synth-colloid; he's lost a lot of blood. I have something that may help till they get here."

Kel moved to the man's left side and knelt to face toward his legs. He placed his right knee onto the man's lower abdomen and forced the weight of his body through his knee as deep into the man's pelvis as he could go.

The man moaned in response. *If I'm hurting him, he's alive enough to feel.*

"Take that tourniquet off," Kel told the operators at the injured man's feet.

No one questioned his directions, and someone moved to disable the autotourniquet, which turned red as it released its squeeze and fell away.

Kel spread open his medkit as he maintained his body's pressure over the large vessels deep in the man's pelvis. He produced a small injector. With one hand he wiped away the area of the wound, exposing the jagged entrance caused by the bullet, and with a drilling motion advanced the nozzle of the injector tube into the wound. The dying man responded, gasping as Kel did so.

"This is a nano-hemostatic. If I can keep the vessels from bleeding, this might have a chance to get in there and stop it at the source." Kel knew the stuff was not magic. It served no purpose if the bleeding was not halted by pressure or a tourniquet; the strong force of arterial bleeding would simply carry the bioengineered medicine away with the rushing current of pulsing blood, accomplishing nothing.

They remained in that position for many minutes while in the wound, nanites formed a lattice mesh to seal any injured vessel. Kel knew the process took at least five minutes. Waiting was more difficult than action. Time passed slower rather than being compressed by furious activity. Kel's legs went numb as he continued to kneel, the full weight of his body and gear focused through his knees and the balls of his feet.

He removed another item from his medkit. He unrolled the small panel and pressed it into the man's chest. It quickly adhered to the skin and in a moment, displayed a series of numbers indicating the man's blood pressure, pulse, respiratory rate, and hemoglobin oxygen saturation. The letters "O POS" appeared in the last remaining space on the panel.

"Med transport is here," someone said just as men with a grav-litter nudged concerned operators out of the way.

Kel explained the situation to the responding docs, and while they looked confused at his description of the nano-med he'd administered, they didn't argue. Kel slowly eased himself off his patient to stagger back onto his butt, his legs too numb to stand. The medics moved in to slide the litter underneath their patient. They slipped an oxygen hood over the man's face, walked the litter outside, then floated their wounded comrade into the transport speeder and rushed away. An NP vehicle led the way, lights and sirens raging.

When the sun rose they were still on the scene. Kel walked through the house with the commander and XO, as well as a team of investigators and criminalist technicians.

The picture the men put together of what had transpired beyond the small portion of events he had witnessed told him everything.

The assault team breaching from the front received resistance immediately on entrance. The wounded man had been the first through the door. The team pushed through and completed the mission, just as he and his kill team would have. *The fight doesn't stop because you take casualties. The fight doesn't stop until the battle is won. The best medicine is fire superiority.* He would have a lot of praise for the Cyrene SRT to share with Gavros.

It was a shocking scenario. Three armed defenders had been prepared and waiting for the team. Had the suspects been alerted to the raid? Had the mission been compromised in some way, perhaps by the surveillance unit? It was clear they didn't have the surprise they'd hoped to achieve. Right now, everyone had more questions than answers.

"What do you think went wrong, Kel?" He snapped out of his trance. They stood in the front room, the techs capturing holos of the blood-stained floor, the bodies of the suspects still lying where their souls had left them. Kel recognized his interrogator as one of the men that had placed the autotourniquet on the wounded man. He was still covered in the downed operator's blood.

Kel blew out a breath. The butcher shop floor he stood on contrasted with the wealth and luxury of his earlier appraisal of Cyrene hit him like a gut punch. *Death waits everywhere. There is no safe place.* It was an old truth for him.

"Nothing went wrong." *These men need to hear it from me. They need to get ready to fight again.* "You guys did it right." He had the attention of the other men, even the eyes of the techs were on him. "It wasn't bad tactics or bad luck that got Mychel shot. These maniacs were ready for us, and didn't hesitate to shoot first." Expressions had gone from sullen to angry. Hateful even.

Good. Now, I can tell them what they really need to hear. "Nope. It's just this. ME's getting their act together for a real war. So we're going to give them one."

17

The last and most challenging leg of his journey finally arrived: Peloponnese. Again, he would have to gain the confidence of another group of strangers, and he couldn't help feeling that of all the teams he'd visited, Peloponnese was not going to be as welcoming. The tragedy of the hostage rescue gone extremely bad would be a cloud hanging over the entire unit. Kel was sympathetic. Were he in their place, the feeling of being under the microscope would be justified.

No one liked that particular spotlight.

He arrived to find a lone uniformed NP sergeant waiting for him as the sun rose over the airfield. "I'm to take you to your quarters, sir." Kel inquired about the SRT. "I was instructed that someone would meet you in the morning, sir."

They rode in silence. Kel was deposited at the visitor's lodge on the NP base and given a chit to the local dining facility where the recruits in training ate.

Kel took the opportunity to exercise and after cleaning up, made his way to the dining facility to have lunch. He found few people in the hall; apparently the base was between training classes for new policemen. A couple of cadres were present as well as some uniformed officers. No one paid him any attention, and he kept to himself.

He spent the rest of the day quietly, deciding to work out again before the evening meal by taking a long run around the base. He noted little activity as he ran past the different areas on base. Where was the unit he was sent to evaluate?

They probably have their own separate compound. But if true, why had no one from the unit contacted him? *Perhaps they're on a callout.* Kel could understand that and decided not to read anything into the lack of contact just yet.

The next morning came and he worked out before the sun rose in anticipation of his host's early arrival to begin a full day's work.

The sun was high in the sky before a vehicle pulled up. Two fit men got out, their hair worn long, their pistols and brassards exposed, their outfits civilian clothes. Kel tried to remove the irritation from his face.

"Major Turner?" one asked. "We're here to escort you to the SRT compound."

Relax. Show some courtesy, he reminded himself, thinking that finally things would start to develop as he had come to expect. The men were both sergeants, each team leaders on the SRT. They talked as they drove, their compound a short drive out the main gate and across the road, located in another small cantonment. Kel could have walked to the site from his quarters.

"We have some training starting this morning after everyone shows up. The chief thought you might like to see some of the different weapons we have and maybe get a chance to shoot some yourself."

Kel wasn't sure what to say to that.

Who do these guys think I am? Why do they think I'm here? He held his tongue as they pulled into the compound and parked. The two men escorted him into the first building, where he was introduced to a warrant officer who said he was in charge of training for the SRT.

"We thought you might enjoy getting to see a little bit of what we do and some of the gear we use. I hope you're not afraid of loud noises, sir."

What in the nine hells? Kel'd had enough.

"Chief, where is your CO or XO?" It was an effort to keep the frustration out of his voice.

The man looked surprised at Kel's question. "Uh, Major, they won't be here today. They don't normally come out for things like this."

"Chief, 'things like what,' exactly?"

"Uh, showing off to VIPs, sir."

Kel paused to breathe before speaking.

"Chief, what were you told about my visit?"

The man looked confused. "Major, we were told you were a VIP from Tiryns and that we were to show you around."

Kel produced his link and bounced a copy of Gavros' directive to the man. The chief read the directive for himself. He paled as he read.

"Sir, uh, I..."

Kel had lost patience. It was time to throw around the weight that Gavros had given him.

"Chief, I'm not sure what's going on here. I have a feeling you've been left out of the loop. Do you understand that I've been sent here by General Kyrgiakos to evaluate your unit's fitness?"

Now the two sergeants paled with their warrant.

"Sir, I cannot apologize enough. We, I mean, I was not aware that was the purpose of your visit. Let me see if I can straighten this out."

The man nearly ran for the confines of his office and spoke in hushed tones by link, he assumed to the unit commander. The man returned a few minutes later.

"Sir, the commander apologizes for not being able to join you today. He wished me to convey his apologies and promises to see you tomorrow. In the meantime, he'd like you to feel at home and see anything you'd like while you're with us."

Kel was still confused. *What could keep the commander away from something as critical to his unit as this visit?*

"Chief, is there an operation or critical incident occurring at this time that I don't know about?"

The man looked surprised by the question. "No sir, not that I'm aware of."

Enough! I've been here a day and so far what I've evaluated is zilch. Take a deep breath, Kel. "Chief. Then I guess what I can accomplish today is to observe your training. Carry on, with haste."

"Yes, sir," the warrant replied as he motioned the two team leaders to move along.

Kel was anticipating disappointment. He was not wrong.

The warrant officer had told Kel that the plan for the day was to work on pistol marksmanship skills in the morning and proceed to carbine in the afternoon. Kel nodded but said nothing.

He observed the usual mechanics as they practiced their basic marksmanship at different ranges, starting at three meters and working back gradually to shoot a single course of fire at twenty-five meters. The men wore their pistols and no other protective gear. They were practicing 'slick.'

Maybe they're planning to graduate to full gear later? Kel thought.

He watched as the second relay performed the same routine as the first group had done. When they had finished, he heard the chief announce that it was time for lunch.

"Are you coming, sir?" The chief stood by Kel as the shooters left the range in small groups.

"No, thank you, Chief. I'm not hungry. I'm going to go for a run. I'll be here when you start up this afternoon."

The man looked confused but said nothing as he turned to catch up to his teammates.

Kel was waiting on the range when they returned. The men of the SRT straggled to the range, carbines slung on their backs, still no vests or other protective gear on their bodies. Kel stayed back, and watched the group repeat the same performance as before. After setting up, the first group started at a distance of about seven meters from the targets, fired several strings, then proceeded to the targets to check the results. They moved back to the same seven-meter distance again and repeated this sequence. They did this several times. Then, Kel watched as the second group moved to the line and performed the same sequence as the first had done.

After the second relay performed the same drill for the third time, the shooters took down the targets and everyone gathered up their gear.

"Major," the warrant officer said on his way out, "we're going to clean weapons and do some physical training before we end the day. Is there anything else you'd like to see?"

Anything else? What did I just see? "Chief, I don't even know where to begin," Kel said, speaking frankly. "I'd like to meet you and your team leaders in the office. Right now. I have some questions."

Kel studied the men sitting before him. His intuition told him that if he could get these men to trust him, he was going to have all his questions answered and a complete picture of this unit and the actions that had led to the tragedy during the hostage crisis. Taking the role of stern father would not do. He asked himself how he would respond if he were them. Finally, the best of all courses occurred to him. *What would Bigg do?*

He asked the men about today's training, taking the tone he thought his team sergeant and mentor in all things would take, picturing himself as the older, wiser man. "Is this normally the type of training you conduct on the square range?" The men mumbled a bit as they looked at each other, seemingly reluctant to answer.

"Yes sir, I'd say that is pretty typical of our marksmanship training," someone answered. "But sir, you never came downrange with us to inspect targets. Every one of these guys is an excellent marksman."

"I don't doubt it." He was getting closer to what he wanted to know.

"I notice that your team practiced with your pistols out to twenty-five meters, but when you switched to your carbines, you only shot from about seven meters. Why was that?"

The men looked at each other. One of the sergeants shrugged his shoulders and said, "Well sir, we only do entries."

A light exploded in Kel's head. The last piece of the puzzle dropped into place for him. He'd been waiting to hear just such a rationalization.

"I see. May I ask, at what distance you zero your carbines, Sergeant?" Kel already knew the answer.

"At seven meters, sir. It's like I said, we're a tactical team and we only do entries."

Boom. There it was. It all made sense now. Kel knew exactly what had happened several months before during the school hostage crisis.

Bigg had once told him that there was nothing new revealed by the spiral motion of the galaxy. He'd taught Kel that new solutions to new problems were usually old solutions to old problems. In many cases, the solutions were as bad then as when they were reintroduced years later by another well-meaning innovator.

"Everybody is constantly reinventing the wheel. Every generation thinks they've found a new way of doing something, even if it's wrong," Bigg would say when he saw something objectionable about a new product or questionable technique. Having spent three years under Bigg's tutelage, the observation rang truer and truer.

One of those observations was a misconception about fighting inside structures—what they referred to as CIC in Dark Ops. Close Intensity Combat. When Kel was learning the basics of CIC as a young legionnaire, he'd been taught by squad leaders only a few years older than himself. Looking back on his initiation into the art of "room clearing," he remembered hearing the vapid expression about "doing entries."

Initiates in the techniques of room clearing frequently taught that there were different rules when fighting within the confined spaces of a structure. That since the action took place at closer distances, the marksmanship was somehow different.

The fallacy in that argument was twofold. One was that some structures contained spaces that were much larger than the average living room or bedroom. Some structures, like schools, auditoriums, hospitals, and large commercial spaces, contained areas with distances that were as great as those encountered in confrontations outdoors. The other fallacy being that the vital zone of the target presented might be only a few centimeters in size.

The "we only do entries" theory centered around the idea that the operator would only encounter threats at distances of a handful of meters. Kel had heard it before, even in the regular Legion. After getting his first formal training on the correct elements of CIC in the Legion Urban Combat Course, the myths had been easily dispelled. Years in Dark Ops further cemented the truth of combat in enclosed spaces. Physics was physics.

There were many conceptual fallacies he had encountered when trying to unlearn bad training. The Hoplites themselves did not suffer from any of these forms of psychosis, but it appeared that the sickness existed in Peloponnese.

The dots that had just connected were elementary, but he'd need to explain it to the team here.

The difference between the line of sight through the optic mounted on top of the weapon and the line of the bore where the projectile traveled was a critical distance known as the mechanical offset. It was a distance of about six centimeters on the S-5 carbine.

Any weapon's "zero" was simply the point where the bullet intersects the line of sight downrange. At any reasonable distance from which to zero a weapon, from fifty to a hundred meters, that "zero" provides a means of knowing where the projectile would impact the target at a given range.

At distances closer than fifteen meters, because of the difference between the line of the bore and the line of the sight, the bullet would always impact low, about six centimeters below the point where the shooter aimed.

What that in turn meant was that when aiming at very small targets—like the small box that represented the human brain—the shooter would have to apply the offset distance by placing the sight the same amount higher on the target, about six centimeters. It was the very real difference between putting a slug in the hostage taker's brain and hitting the hostage.

It was a difference that mattered. Out of laziness these men had ignored a fundamental concept. He knew for a fact the Hoplites had trained these men in mechanical offset.

Out of laziness they'd tried to get around the need to apply the mechanical offset by 'zeroing' the weapon at seven meters. At close ranges, no differencing in aiming point need be applied. It was the black hole of gunfighting, a gravity well that crushed the light of reason.

But when attempting to shoot at targets at farther distances, the line of the projectile's path rose dramatically. And so slugs had missed terrorists and hit children instead.

Kel's suspicions about the tragedy at the airfield had been confirmed. The deaths of so many hostages during the school kidnapping crisis had all been avoidable. The question still was why this had happened? How had their doctrine and training become so distorted? They knew better. Kel intended to find out.

"Gentlemen. I want to know what happened at the airfield when the hostages were shot."

One of the sergeants leapt to his feet. "You weren't there, sir! It wasn't our fault!"

One of the other men tried to calm his friend. The warrant officer slumped in his chair, putting his head in his hands.

Kel assured them he was not there to lay blame. It was only important that whatever caused the failure be identified and corrected. Kel appealed to their honor as warriors, as sworn protectors of innocent life, to share with him what had happened.

The warrant officer spoke up. "Well sir, it wasn't one single thing that caused us to fail those children."

One of the sergeants muttered just loud enough for Kel to hear. "I knew we shouldn't have protected him. He's never been there for us." Kel thought he knew who the man referred to. The absent commander.

The men went on to describe how the move to the airfield to meet the terrorists' demands had created a difficult situation. Kel could imagine. The rebels executed the teacher. It was as critical an incident as could exist for an operator. The choice to try to ambush the hostage takers at the airfield and remove them with surgical fire had been the commander's directive. Kel could not fault that part of the plan.

The team lay in ambush in an adjacent open hanger. The commander had given orders for the men to shoot only at the hostage takers' heads in order to avoid hitting the children. It might even have worked. If not for the fact that their weapons were zeroed at seven meters. At the distances from where they were engaging, the first shots had missed over the kidnappers' heads by a good margin.

The scene the tearful operators described to him would have been the stuff of nightmares. On hearing the gunshots that had no effect, some of the hostage takers lifted the children in front of themselves for cover. At least one of the gunmen started executing children. The operators attempted to correct their aim by holding at some indeterminate distance low on the targets; the terrorists were all killed, but so were more children. Some of them by bullets from the SRT.

It was as terrible a tale as Kel had ever heard.

And it explained all the mysteries of the Peloponnese SRT.

As Kel calmed the men, he probed about the genesis of their doctrine. It was, as he'd suspected, their commander.

"He insisted we use seven-meter zeroes. He said all that stuff we learned in operator training was garbage, that it was most important to be able to aim without using offset in a hostage situation, and that the stress of the situation would be too great to remember to aim high. He always said that we're a tactical team; we do entries on structures. Only the snipers deal with long-range stuff."

One of the other men spoke up. "Like he would know. He never trains with us anyway."

Kel found himself shaking his head. The whole situation was truly awful.

"What's going to happen now?" the warrant officer asked dejectedly.

"General Kyrgiakos sent me to find the truth. I think I've found it. Now, I make my report." Kel thanked the men for their honesty and promised there was going to be a change for the better.

We only do entries. Kel could have wept.

Kel walked out of the compound and back to his quarters. He needed the time to think as he walked. He got back to the small room and pulled out his datapad, the holo keyboard in front of him as he started to type.

After a few minutes, he thought better of it. He removed his link and opened a visual comm to Major Todalin. The man answered immediately. Kel hadn't thought about it, but it must have been the middle of the night in Tiryns.

"Kel, what's wrong?"

"Major, I'm sorry to disturb you. I know what went wrong with the school hostage crisis, and you're not going to like it."

A few hours later Kel was awoken from a fitful sleep by his link. He activated the visual projection to see Major Todalin's face.

"Kel, stay where you are. I'm coming in on the hop. I'll be there shortly. I'm coming to relieve the commander of the SRT and personally escort him back to Tiryns to meet Gavros. See you in a few."

Kel couldn't get back to sleep.

The major pulled up to his quarters less than two hours later in an NP vehicle. The sun was rising and Kel was already dressed. It was a short ride and the two spoke little. "This could go bad. Once he realizes why I'm here, things could get ugly. I don't want the man to kill himself in front of his wife. I don't want us to get hurt, either. We're going to disarm him, cuff him, and take him directly to the airfield."

Kel accompanied the major to the front door of the man's home, embarrassed to see a middle-aged woman open the door in her house clothes and invite them in as she called for her husband. The major told her they'd prefer to wait outside. The door opened again, the commander standing in his full dress uniform. *He knows what's about to happen,* Kel intuited. It was the first Kel had laid eyes on the man. He looked frail, like a hollowed tree holding out until the last strong gust topples it.

"Theodus, I'm here to take you to Gavros."

Kel reached forward and pulled the man out of the threshold, placed restraints on his wrists, and quickly searched the man for weapons. He met not a hint of resistance. *It's a relief for him!* Kel realized. *He has no fight left. He knows he's done.*

As they drove away, neighbor women poured from their houses to comfort the commander's sobbing wife as she collapsed on the duracrete steps, a sea of teared faces burned into Kel's mind, staring at them as they carried the disgraced man away to his fate.

Kel helped the major place the commander on the hop. Todalin followed him to the hatch and waited while Kel bounced the major the codes to his enerchains.

"I'll uncuff him when we get to headquarters. I don't want to perp-walk him in front of the command staff if I can avoid it."

Kel nodded but remained silent. It was a sad scene.

"Gavros wants you to stay here and do what you can. I'll cancel the next legs of your trip. Plan on spending the next two weeks here. I'll talk to you later tonight."

Kel stayed in place as Todalin turned to move back into the aircraft.

"Major, who will be in charge of the SRT?"

Todalin halted.

"For now, you are. Gavros has already sent orders."

FLASHBACK

If You're Clueless, Just Shut Up and Do What You Do Antione

"What's a NATRO?" Trumbull whispers in my ear. We're crowded with the cool guys under the stubby wing of one of the Talons, all of us out of our armor. There's a hot breeze blowing through the hangar as the sun outside bakes the duracrete.

Zero had just told us the next mission was a NATRO recovery. "Native resource," Zero says. Whether he heard Trumbull's question or just anticipated we wouldn't know, I'm glad he did. I didn't know. Now I'm hoping he'll explain what a native resource is and why we're recovering it.

"Turner," Zero says, pointing at me. "You and your team are going to be in two sleds, waiting to pour on the heat if things go sideways. Provo is going to be the contact," he points to Provo, whose back is to us. His skin and hair color match the locals a little better than the rest of the kill team. His beard is bushy and covers most of his face, growing high onto his cheek bones unlike the others. "He'll be in local garb. He makes contact, escorts the resource back to us, we all get out of there. Simple, understand?" I have no idea what he's talking about. I know the squad doesn't either and will be assaulting me with a thousand questions as soon as the cool guys are out of ear shot.

Papa Bear stands up. "I'll make it simple. Just shoot anyone who doesn't look like us."

"And don't shoot me," Provo's flat voice bounces off the Talon's fuselage and back to us.

"And don't shoot him," Papa Bear parrots. "Let's get the sleds loaded."

It's dark when the Talons land. Under quarter power to float them we guide the sled off the ramp, then power the repulsors up to full as we crowd in the back. I'm the last in and close the rear doors as we float away. Papa Bear is driving and TA sits with him, navigating. Warchief is driving the other sled just behind us and Trumbull has half of the squad with him in the back. The Talons take off to do whatever pilots do to entertain themselves while they're waiting for our call to come pick us up.

We glide along for about an hour before we enter the city. There's some vehicle and foot traffic that makes our presence seem normal, no matter how much I feel like we're the leej in PT gear at the formal ball. This city hasn't been the subject of our bombing as there isn't any big militia presence. The locals clearly know there's a war on though; doors are closed and blackout curtains reveal only brief glimpses of interior light. We stay dark like the other sleds crawling through the streets. The locals preferentially are out during the night hours of high summer. Not even a full-scale planetary invasion can suppress the need of people to do routine things like shop and work.

I listen to the cool guys communicate as TA and Zero in our other ride help navigate our two-sled convoy through the narrow streets. Our vehicles are beat up panel trucks, unremarkable in every way including a body so thin that it wouldn't stop an angry word.

"Alright, time to split up," Zero says. "Papa Bear, take that corner as your spot. We're going to skirt the block and drop Provo off and we'll end up just down the street from you other side of the complex." I was watching the feed from TA's bucket. It's always a little nauseating, watching someone else's feed. Wherever they turn to look, so are you, but it was the only way I could see outside the truck. The one-way film we helped the cool guys apply turned the windscreens into security glass. Nonetheless, we all wore the loose hooded tunics over our armor, same as the locals wore to keep the sun off them. It wouldn't fool anyone for long once they saw our armor and weapons.

"Let's do it," Papa Bear says. "Good luck, Provo."

I check in with Trumbull on the squad channel. "Yeah, we're good," he confirms. "Man, this has got to be the craziest thing I've ever seen. Provo just slid out and is mixing in with the locals. Shouldn't someone be with him? He's in the middle of Antione by himself, surrounded by these nutters. Naked."

TA was listening in on our channel. "Provo? There's nothing he can't do by himself. Most of the time he doesn't even want *any of us* around. He *prefers* being alone." I don't say anything, knowing TA is listening, but what I would tell Trumbull later is how absolutely frelling nuts I thought all these guys were. My mentor TA continues. "All we have to do now is sit tight. Provo will holler if he needs our help. Just be ready to un-ass and blast if he does."

We wait.

I'm getting cramps in my low back sitting on the narrow bench, hunched over my thighs. The other guys are squirming too. I try not to check the chrono, but I do. We've been parked for over an hour. Groups of locals pass by our truck, their voices and laughs minorly dampened by the thin shell of the sled. These people don't feel like they're in danger even though a flotilla of the Republic's biggest war craft sit around their planet. I'd like to tell them to knock off whatever has gotten the House of Reason mad at them before we lay waste to their town, too.

"He's coming out," Zero says, the first to lay eyes on him. "He's got the NATRO and is on the exterior concourse, fourth level." The local we're recovering has been holed up and waiting in his residence, an apartment in the middle of a quadrangular complex, apparently reserved for high level members of the political machine of Antione. It looks like a giant ghetto to me.

Provo's voice through his implant comes up, his sub-vocalizations not much different from his usual speaking voice; flat. "Our charge tells me the secret police are on us. There're two groups of 'em, four or five each, moving into the stairwells. I think I'm gonna need a little help."

"Go-go-go," TA yells as Papa Bear accelerates across the corner to one of the arched exterior entrances. "Turner, with me," TA says as he launches out his door, the sled still gliding forward. I already have the back door open and hit the ground running, leaping out backward to match the direction of travel as I pick up speed to match TA's. We're through the short passage and into the court-yard. "Where is he?" I ask as I pan around, slowing from my dead run. I don't need an answer. A group of males in cheap baggy suits is blocking one of the corner stairwells. The front two raise hand weapons and TA and I are firing before we have time to think.

We don't stop until all of them are down. We pick up speed again and as we get closer, I follow TA's lead and send more blasts into the shapes on the ground. Zero is plowing up the corner stairwell to our left, two of my guys following. Blaster flashes reflect off the walls up the tower of stairs. Whoever was in that stairwell was a toasty critter now.

On the breezeway above, a man brings a weapon to bear at TA's running figure and I send three quick blasts. The first one hits and knocks him down, the next two whiz past to send plasticrete adobe raining. My guys have fallen in behind TA and are bounding up the stairwell. I make my move.

I leap onto the sill and jump, grab the ledge and swing my feet up until I can grab the wall and roll over on to the breezeway deck of the second story. The charred face of the guy I shot from below tells me I can look elsewhere. Nothing. I hop on the parapet and scale the outside of the column to the next level, the decorative ribs giving me a perfect hold. I'm grateful.

They don't see me. Two of the thugs have their backs to me and are trading shots through an open apartment door. Zero must have made his way down a floor to barricade in an apartment. I get toes on the ledge, pull my pistol and hammer them one-handed as I hang onto the column with my other arm. They drop like stones. I holster and swing my legs over. Coming from both directions now the rest of the team runs full tilt to where I cover the dead men.

"Provo, come out," Zero yells. "We're ready to move."

Provo appears, dragging a hesitant companion. "Take him," Provo says to me. I grab the guy and we start down the breezeway to the stairwell. I'm in the center of our conglomeration, protected by a wall of armor as I lift the terrified man by the back of his shirt and belt, levitating him with us down the flights of stairs.

Both sleds pull up as I move to the first, Papa Bear at the controls, and throw the little man into the back, then turn to push armored bodies in ahead of me. Provo hops in last. I run to the next sled where Trumbull and the rest of the squad are leaping into the rear. "We're in," I yell diving in, the doors bouncing and swinging behind me as we glide off. I double check the head count as my guys sound off by name over L-comm. "My squad's up," I say over the team channel, to no one in particular. I have to put a hand on the ceiling for balance as we slide around a corner and pick up speed.

"We've got vehicles in pursuit," Warchief says. The doors are still flailing around, but I see lights behind us. Not good. "Get 'em off us," Zero says. I pull the plasma torch off my side and run it around the frame. The doors fall off and skitter behind us, not deterring the advance of three sleds that float over them. Pabon and Howard are already at my side. "What are you waiting for? Light 'em up," I tell them as I get my K-17 in my hands. They need no further encouragement. They make short work of the thin-skinned vehicles with a few blasts each. Our pursuers fall behind us as the front vehicle stops completely. I drop a grenade into the tube and send it just as people exit from the disabled sleds. We take a violent turn and as I fall into Pabon the last thing I see is the explosion.

A single Talon touches down on the dark plain as we abandon the sleds and race to the tailgate where the crew chief stands waving us frantically on. Somewhere above, the second Talon watches over us.

We're lifting. I'm looking straight down at the ground as we race for the heavens, the ramp closing so slowly I'm fearful I may tumble out of the aircraft if we don't level off soon. We do, and I get off the deck to collapse on a jump seat. My bucket comes off and I scratch with both hands. Provo is standing in front of me and speaks monotone and flat as anything I've ever heard him say.

"Thanks for not shooting me."

18

The suborbital hop home was uneventful and Kel disembarked to see Major Todalin awaiting him outside of the NP flight operations building, a civilian speeder parked nearby. He'd stayed in Peloponnese for the two weeks rebuilding the SRT. Some of the men he was able to save. Some he could not. The guilt and self-doubt proved too much for those.

Gavros greeted him warmly and invited Kel to sit in the familiar circle, kaff and waters waiting on the small table between them. Gavros dismissed his attendants, leaving just him alone with Kel and Major Todalin.

"I much appreciate the timeliness of your reports. I have read them at length. This matter in Peloponnese. That Theodus conspired to hide truth and was so toxic a leader that he incapacitates our SRT, this I cannot forgive.

"Being weak leader and forcing bad doctrine on his men, that is one thing. Concealing from us these errors and forcing his men to participate in lie, that is crime."

Todalin anticipated Kel's query. "He's sitting in confinement. He'll be charged with making false statements to investigators and criminal conspiracy to conceal his crimes, as well as conspiracy to commit negligent homicide."

Gavros interrupted. "There will be justice for those children. The public demands it. In old times a man knew to fall on his sword. There is no disgrace in this." Kel knew he would soon hear that the commander had committed suicide.

Life was harsh in the galaxy.

"Let's talk about your first stop: Corinth," the general prompted. "There seemed to be many difficulties discovered."

"Your recommendations for retraining are good," Todalin said. "I'm not sure how we're going to go about that now. The Hoplites are far too critical in importance and are too few in number. We can't detail anyone for retraining the SRT either in Corinth or to bring them here for a cycle."

Gavros spoke up. "The problem is in command. They have been allowed to become infirm. I am sending one of Hoplites to take command of team. One of the team leaders is senior man. I am giving him brevet rank and sending him to take charge. Current commander is already fired."

Kel knew it was more than just the unit commander who had lost sight of the scope of the mission of their SRT.

Gavros knew what Kel was thinking. "I am making changes in NP command in Corinth as well. This takes longer as there are political considerations."

The large man released a big breath. "Eritrea report was most interesting."

In great description, he talked about the capabilities he witnessed. The SRT had appropriately adapted their mission to the threats they commonly dealt with and had a seamless interoperability with the state militia units. The jungle environment was a difficult one to operate in, and the unit was completing aggressive operations in a harsh environment and doing so with a lot of success.

"Tell me about jade lotus raid," the general prompted.

He gave a summary of the concept of the operation and discussed the excellent organization of the mission and the individual actions of the operators.

"What else?" The general was being patient, but it was clear he wanted Kel to volunteer more.

He knows or he suspects. No avoiding it, I guess, Kel thought.

With a sigh, Kel pulled his link out to bounce his full report on the prisoner execution. "I wanted the chance to talk about this before I gave my formal report, sir." He then told the story.

The two men listened attentively. The general rose from his chair to stand in front of the large windows. He took several long breaths, reflecting before turning back to Kel and the major.

"I was expecting this."

He sat again. "Mister Kel," he'd reverted back to his previous manner of address for the legionnaire. "I don't know what you think of us, of Meridian people. I want you to know I think very highly of you."

Kel remained silent and still.

"This is not right. Abuse of custody is wrong. Executing prisoners is wrong. I want you should hear it from my lips."

The general returned his gaze out the window as he continued to speak.

"The old ways are for old times. The galaxy is small place now." He stared out the window a moment longer before facing Kel.

"I must think on how to handle this revelation you have confirmed for us. I tell you, the law must apply to all. The law must protect all. Many of the troubles we now have is because we have not changed in so long. Now, to remain the same is no choice."

Kel understood the man though his Standard seemed to worsen the longer he continued. He did not doubt the sincerity of what the general was saying. There was a sense of unexpected relief in it.

"Two hundred years ago, pfft, even a hundred years ago, how would we have handled group like ME? I tell you. They would have hung students and dissidents by their necks from the streetlamps. Their families too.

"We try to find way to protect without harming the innocent people in our society. I hope you understand this about us."

Kel was moved. The general cared what Kel thought of Meridian, and what Kel thought of him personally. He'd grown up the son of a mechanic who was a former legionnaire. Kel joined the Legion as a teenager. The only advanced education he had was within the Legion.

The general and Major Todalin were from the highest levels of Meridian society. They were both well educated, both of them having advanced degrees from their world's best universities. It humbled Kel to consider that these men valued his opinion so highly. He understood the enormity of what one of the most powerful men on the planet shared with him.

"I'm just glad to help, sir. I hope I can continue to be of use, General."

Smiling, the big man reached over and slapped Kel's nearest knee.

"I ask you to report, and even the unpleasant truth, you do not keep from me. I was right to trust you. Plus, you do so in best manner. Some things is best to say in person, some things okay for report. Is all Republic adviser smart like you? Maybe I misjudge Republic?"

This made Kel laugh. "I'm not necessarily sure about that, sir."

"And, what I tell you? You call me Gavros."

He made the rounds at the embassy the next morning and after checking in with Pen and Bell, made his way to the Trade section to see Don. They spent several hours together and after discussing his debriefing with Gavros, Don asked him to write a contact report detailing what had been said as well as Kel's analysis of the general's intentions.

"I think we should bring Jacee in on this. Let me get her here." Kel had been curious what Jacee's response to the drug gang's murders was going to be; he'd wondered about it since the incident.

Her response was measured and somewhat surprising to Kel.

"It's not a shock, and it's certainly not new news."

Don nodded his head in agreement as she continued.

"The death penalty or summary execution for involvement in the jade lotus trade used to be fairly common here. What you witnessed confirms what we thought we already knew.

"That's not to say that the House of Reason approves of such abuses. It just means that we know we aren't in a place where the citizens have the same basic protections as those on a Republic world."

Don nodded in agreement.

"If this was a Republic world, you wouldn't be here, would you?" she smiled at Kel. He supposed that was true.

"So, do you see this as affecting what we're currently doing here, or what I am doing here?" Kel asked.

The man and woman looked at each other, Jacee being the one to answer.

"No. Just don't go executing any prisoners yourself, okay?"

Kel felt slightly better. He'd done what he'd thought was right by formally reporting the incident to the diplomats.

"What do you think about Gavros' admission to me? About not wanting to go down the same road anymore?"

Again, the intel-man and the diplomat looked at each other.

"Well, it certainly sounds reassuring, doesn't it? We can't necessarily take what he said to you at face value, but it's encouraging," she said.

Don took his turn answering. "I concur. Kel, he may be the head of the security apparatus on this ball, but he doesn't make policy. It's good to know he doesn't aim to kill suspected criminals or dissidents without some due process, but beyond that..." The man trailed off.

Later that day as he floated around the embassy, Colonel Graviakis bounced him with a request. "We want you to take a more active role with the Hoplites, if you're not too busy."

This is what he'd been waiting for. The time he'd put in to build trust with the secretive police unit was showing real results. He was excited. "Anything, anytime, anyplace, sir. Supporting the Hoplites and the NP is my mission priority." Kel meant it. Of any institution that was directly working to end the crisis, it was them.

"While you were on Gavros' errand, we developed a better picture of ME's organization. Of course, a good deal of that, thanks to you." Kel appreciated the compliment but he didn't need to be stroked. He was ready for action.

"A lot's happened while you were gone. There've been some bad incidents. Can you come to the compound today?"

His heart raced. "Is now too soon?"

Kel understood the problem they brought to him.

"The House Police responded to a call," Todalin reviewed. "It was an ambush. ME mined the path to the front door. Other responding units got the same treatment coming in the rear entrance. They lost four guys. After the site was rendered safe by EOD, they found nothing. It was a trap designed solely to kill officers. Place was clean."

"It's a big escalation in their tactics," Graviakis agreed. "We've got good leads but if this is their new method of operating, coming up with options how to counter them is holding us up."

He sat with the two men and the Hoplite team leaders as they looked at the crime scene holos.

Mines. Improvised Explosives. Using asymmetric means to deter capture. He understood all too well.

"Been there, done that," he said earnestly. "It's not too tough. We get off the ground is all."

Kel stood on the ramp of the dropship as it descended and triggered the hoists. The solution he'd come up with was better than simply fast-roping. He'd gotten the idea watching construction around the embassy. A simple hoist with retrieving sheaves guided a woven cordage that substituted for a rope. It was soft and strong and would be easy on the hands. When he'd watched a hover crane lower construction materials into a narrow alley, a light went on for him.

As they glided to a hover over the roof, he activated the hoist at each side of the ramp and watched the lower sheave bounce onto the flat surface. *My idea, my plan, so my lead.* "Go!"

Kel was first onto the rope, the team leader on the other just a step behind him. They'd practiced with the rig several times until they were all confident the commercial product met their requirements.

He gripped tightly as he felt the rope pass between his boots. The shock of his halt momentarily stopped him before he propelled himself away to make room for those descending above him. The team raced to the access door as he turned to see the two ropes retract and the dropship float away. They'd been over the roof less than a minute.

Rescue vehicles raced forward in the dark and froze to maintain a safe distance, visible through breaks between other buildings. Hoplites spilled out, snipers exited hatches and set up on the flat tops of the armored grav sleds, ready to contain the scene. Even the largest explosive device would not harm the men on the ground, who were poised and waiting. If an escaping terrorist chose to detonate a device, no one else would be taken from the world of the living with him.

Kel tried the door handle. It turned easily. The man next to him saw this and raised the barrel of his gun letting Kel know he was ready. He pulled the door and tossed the stunner in deep, immediately bringing his own weapon up. They both paused to let the intensity of Kel's plasma stunner dissipate—the Hoplites had all seen how effective they were—and pushed in.

They knew that's what we'd do, he thought the split second he recognized what lay ahead. A sandbagged fighting position sat across from them, and a chatter of rounds whizzed past Kel as he moved deeper along the wall and away from the threshold. His trigger finger hammered relentlessly on his weapon, never stopping the barrage of slugs he continued to send against the hidden defenders.

"Frag out!" he heard from the threshold and threw himself to the ground.

Kel kept his head down as the explosion made his teeth vibrate. He snapped his eyes up and jumped to his feet.

"Going long!" he yelled, accelerating forward. As he passed the meter-high wall of sandbags, he released another torrent of shots aimed into the masses he found there. The remains of three bodies, one of them a woman, lay in repose. A large box-fed automatic gun stood between them.

"Bet they wish they'd put a roof on that thing," one of the Hoplites said, admiring the results.

"Who tossed that frag?" Kel asked.

One of the bearded men responded with a raised finger.

"Nice toss!" Kel coughed, dust still hanging in the air.

"The gods were with you my friend," another man said. "I saw you drive into that room as they opened up on us. You had shots on them the whole time you moved."

"They waited for us to enter before opening up," observed another.

"I saw your slugs impacting through their firing port," one of the shorter men offered as he shook his head in disbelief. "That's the only thing kept us all from getting killed. Incredible!" There were nods all around.

Kel was thankful for all the practice the Legion put him through. Shooting accurately on the move was a good skill to have.

"I'd say your gods are looking out for us all," Kel said sincerely. Gods. Plural. *I'll take any help I can get!*

The other teams killed more and captured a few, and now all stood on the roof as the dropship hovered over them. The hoist lowered the two lines and the prisoners were carried forward, restrained at ankles, knees, and arms. The hateful grimaces on their faces now turned to fear as the Hoplites attached harnesses to them.

You don't like heights? You shouldn't start planting explosives. Play stupid games, win stupid prizes, he thought.

Muted protests were drowned in repulsor hums as the ship lifted to take a short excursion to the Hoplites waiting just off site. In a short time, the bird would return and they would likewise take turns riding the hanging lines to a safe landing zone.

Just like I planned, he mused.

As they loaded onto the vehicles, Graviakis pulled Kel aside. "That was very smooth. EOD can spend as long as they need to render the area safe for search."

"Sir, I'm disturbed by the fighting position we came up against. They're anticipating our tactics and are adapting, ready to fight us to produce maximum casualties. That was an assault against a fortified position in there." It was more like an infantry drill than a police action.

Graviakis agreed. "And, you overcame it. We really do need your help, Kel."

Kel supposed it was true. It was a miracle he and the team hadn't been killed. The colonel interrupted his train of thought as he considered how they would modify their tactics next.

"The investigators tell me these are hard core believers," the colonel related. "They won't come up with anything we can act on for a follow up hit too soon."

"Maybe we need to loose Major Todalin on them?" Kel offered.

The colonel laughed. "He is one of the best, you're right about that. Ride with me so we can talk." As the cuffed and hooded suspects were loaded, Kel asked the colonel what would happen to them.

"They'll be processed and remanded to custody, incommunicado for seventy-six hours. We'll put their DNA and biometrics through the system and get as much information out of them as we can. After that, they're allowed to confer with the legal counsel. The judge can release them on the spot at the preliminary hearing if he feels there isn't sufficient evidence to warrant their custody. For cases involving ME, that's unlikely to happen."

That seemed especially true now that the revolutionaries had progressed to using explosive devices to wantonly murder public servants. It was all-out war whether anyone chose to admit it or not. He wondered about the interrogation process, expecting the worst, and the commander seemed only too eager to set Kel straight.

"They can be intense. When I was an investigator, I had partners who were famous for getting people talking."

"Sir, I'm curious. How?" Kel had done very little tactical questioning himself. You just couldn't interrogate some of the alien races, it all got turned over to the locals. When tells were defined by changes in color or in the number of clicks preceding an answer, it was impossible. He was genuinely curious how the process occurred under the auspices of the professionals once the prisoners were processed.

"Interrogations can be a very intense and exhausting three days. There's no sleep for the suspect and not much for the interrogators. Usually the task is split into two teams, taking four- to six-hour shifts working the suspects.

"But, it's still probably not what you're thinking. We don't physically abuse anyone. It may not be expressly prohibited by the law, but it's simply not useful. I learned a long time ago from some pretty smart guys: beat a suspect, he'll tell you anything to stop you from beating him, just probably not the truth."

The colonel left him with a last thought as they hopped up into the gravsled. "Even ME deserve protection under the law. You've heard Gavros say the same. Yes, our laws are outdated, but our methods and how we enforce the laws have changed over time. We want our laws to catch up with our modernized society. Unless ME sets us back." Gavros had tipped him to that being his fear about the Conclave, too.

But with ME's tactics becoming more and more like an invading military force, the government is going to be strained not to respond in kind, he thought.

He's an odd one. At our first meeting Jacee made it sound like he was a strongman. Now I think he's trying to be a reformer.

Kel hoped so.

From the compound he found himself driving to Socrates' Garden. He felt like celebrating. Graviakis had asked him to take the place of the team leader leaving to take charge in Corinth. It was proof that he was making a difference. Now here he was, headed to the Garden.

He found the place easily. This time there were no costumed attendants as there had been when his housemates had brought him. It relieved Kel in a way. He didn't feel like a big production, just a decent meal that he could let settle for several hours. Then get in a vigorous bout of exercise and think about how to solve the Hoplites' next dilemma.

He was escorted to a table on the veranda. As he was led past a line of booths, he saw a woman, partially obscured by shadow, with silver-streaked hair. Was that Jacee? As he drew closer, he could see the back of a man's head opposite her.

Jacee looked up at Kel and shifted her gaze quickly to her companion before turning her attention back as he approached, their contact now unavoidable by proximity.

She smiled brightly as Kel got closer. With another step, Kel recognized her partner. Gavros.

"Hello, Kel! So nice running into you!" Jacee said. Gavros moved out of the booth to stand.

"Hello, Kel. We talk soon." He turned back to Jacee briefly. "Nice to see you, Jacee," and turned to leave before Kel could reply.

It was a surprise to find the two together.

"Hi, Jacee. I heard this was a nice place. Any recommendations?" he said, the best he could come up with in the moment.

Jacee stood to leave. "I think you'll find everything is wonderful. I'd stay and join you, but I have a meeting to attend. Let's do lunch together soon, though. Good to see you, Kel." She gave him a quick hug and walked away.

He let himself be seated on the veranda and had a few moments alone before the waiter arrived. Gavros had made it no secret to Kel that he had little use for the Republic's diplomats. Jacee had a strained relationship with Gavros just a short time ago. That was clearly no longer the case. *Did I have something to do with that?* He didn't want to be narcissistic. He decided to simply file it for later examination. Could he inquire about the discovery with the spy master, Don?

If this was some political machination Don's aware of, he still wouldn't discuss it with me. He again decided to spend no more time wondering about the run-in.

When he next met with Don, there was significant news. "Guess who got a call from the NP?"

"Yeah?" Kel said, inviting the normally reserved man to elaborate.

"I think you've impressed enough people to convince them to accept some more help from the Republic. Their investigative and intelligence division invited me to sit in on their next ME brief. Who do you think green lit that?"

They both knew the answer. It could only be Gavros.

"Hope you make the most of it," Kel advised. "You might only get one chance to wow them. Better make it good."

"Don't worry," Don smiled. "What I'm offering, they're going to love."

The next weeks were as good as his best weeks with the kill team. He pitied the guys for not being here with him. It was one operation after another.

As Kel helped them improve their tactics to fit the changing threat environment, the Hoplites became even more energized to try different methods. When the mission demanded it, they still hit a place hard—through the doors and windows to storm a target. When the best option was unclear, or especially if the threat of IEDs existed, Kel helped them perfect their tactical call-out.

They surrounded a target and began by launching retch gas into the building. Anyone not wearing a protective mask who whiffed the toxin would evacuate from both ends simultaneously. Highly effective. Any revolutionary not completely committed to the cause would give up in minutes. The mess they made, though, was pitiable. Kel didn't envy the patrol officers who had to transport the custodies afterward.

By dropship, by explosive breach, by call-out, Kel and the Hoplites dominated the fight. Most of the time, there wasn't one. When there was, Kel's friends crushed it. As a team leader, he spent most of his time not "on the gun," but directing critical decisions during an operation. He was proud of the Hoplites. Their confidence in Kel's teaching and leadership grew every day and after a month, he realized he felt no differently about them than he did any kill team in Dark Ops.

More captured and dead suspects meant more intelligence and a quicker end to the crisis. Eventually, the pace slowed as fewer targets were identified for them. To Kel, it meant one thing. *We're winning! If this isn't what success feels like, then I don't know what would.*

Things had gotten slow. He paid a call on Don to ask for guidance on where he could suggest the NP direct their attention next.

"I'll have something soon, I think. I'll keep you in the loop." This was a departure for the usually furtive man. *I can hold out hope that RI wants to play with the rest of us*, he mused.

Jacee broke into a bright smile when she saw him, leaning against the reception counter of the foyer of the military-political section offices. He flinched when he saw Minister Sun frowning from his doorway, slamming his door forcefully as Kel passed.

"Something I said?" he quipped to Jacee.

"We've just come from a meeting. The number of operations the NP is carrying out against ME is impressive. For Sun," she tilted her head toward his office, "what some might call impressive is what he screams about to the ambassador as brutality."

Kel frowned. "Who does he think these people are? They're murderers of the worst sort, killing innocent people over politics."

She shrugged. "I know. He's the type that thinks political problems are only solved through diplomacy. What he's really mad about is that you're instrumental in the success and he's not. And, he's voiced concerns about the Republic being implicated in what he calls war crimes."

War crimes! I knew the man was an ass. "There's no blowback for the Republic!" Kel exclaimed. "I'm not even here." *That's why they sent Dark Ops.*

"Ignore it, Kel. Don's bragging on you in our meetings. You're doing great things. The ambassador is pleased. That's all that counts. Keep it up."

19

He was still feeling irritable on the drive to the palace when he received a message over his specs.

Tamford,
Just made planetfall at Tiryns. If you're available,
everyone would love to see you. Great news to share.
Caroline and the crew of the Callie

Kel was surprised. He'd all but forgotten the cover identity he'd used while traveling. But his surprise soon blossomed into excitement. He thought often about the friends he'd made on the *Callie's Dream*, a pleasant gift breaking up what would have otherwise been a dull trip to Meridian.

He'd followed up with Ramer some weeks before, inquiring about how trade was progressing and specifically how the deal he'd brokered for the Yomiuris had panned out. Trade to the core had risen dramatically and the goods were bringing record prices. Ramer suspected the Yomiuris would be back on Meridian for another run. Maybe that was the good news Caroline had mentioned.

He changed course to head to the spaceport. After battling traffic, he came to the familiar landing field and had no problem getting entry through the checkpoint, his vehicle cleared to drive directly to the commercial terminal. There was no missing her; the *Callie's* massive hull dwarfed the smaller craft parked around the field.

As he floated forward, Kel could see the crew hard at work around the open hold, directing loaders and the local freight workers to unload cargo.

Faces became recognizable. Caroline was engaged in her purser's duties and Captain Jim was supervising the off-loading operations with Tan and his wife, Aggie. He ambled toward the gathered group amidst the orderly chaos of containers being marshalled out of the hold and down the ramps onto the waiting flatbeds.

He made his way up the forwardmost ramp to where the captain stood with his purser, rendering a hand salute.

"Permission to board, Captain?"

His answer came by way of the rush of bodies now gathered around him, beaming faces, handshakes from the men and hugs from the women, and lots of backslapping and exclamations of, "Look who's here!" "How you been, Tamford?" and "Are we glad to see you!" Kel grinned, a little lightheaded at being the center of attention. He just now realized how much affection he had developed for the family after such a short time together.

"Oh Tamford, we have the most wonderful news to share!" Caroline gushed.

The captain spoke to the group. "Everyone, let's finish supervising the off-loading. You'll all get a chance to see Tamford later. Promise."

The captain turned to Kel. "That is, if you have time? Spare a few minutes to come sit with us in the wardroom and have some kaff?"

"I'm not going anywhere," he said, still grinning uncontrollably.

The Yomiuris led him up to the wardroom, and a moment later Auntie Meiko popped her head in and walked directly to Kel, giving him a big hug. "Sit and I'll get kaff. No, no—sit!" she commanded. Kel laughed. He had no intention of disobeying.

As they sat and sipped Meiko's brew, the two reviewed for Kel the events after their parting.

"We lifted without a square centimeter of space left on the *Callie*. The vessel you'd contracted for the next leg of the trip to Liberinthine was awaiting our cargo at Orion Station. We were empty in a shift. We took a few small jobs around the mid-core, wanting to be close enough to get word on how the trading finished on the goods you'd commissioned."

At this point in the story, smiles on the husband-and-wife team grew even larger.

"We were back at Orion Station four weeks later, and waiting for us at the broker's were the credits secured as our portion of the contract. Apparently, the futures market drove the prices of all the goods to a near record, so needless to say, we made a significant profit," the captain said.

"What Jim is holding back is that our profit was, well, an answer to our prayers. We didn't tell you all of our troubles, but we were close to having to sell the *Callie*." Her eyes became puffy and she brushed back a tear.

Her husband pursed his lips and placed his nearest hand over his wife's.

"Tam, we're not only out of the red, we're paid up! I mean, in full." She looked around at the ship with pride in her eyes. "We own this old girl outright!" His face returned to the broad smile again. "You were a godsend. I mean it. To think I almost chased you away when we first met. Oba, I hate to think about it now!" They all laughed.

"Thank you, Tam, this is all thanks to you," Caroline added.

He was overwhelmed at their good fortune.

"I did nothing," he said holding up his hands in protest. "Sometimes the universe is little better than a place constantly trying to kill you; sometimes..." He paused. "Sometimes it lets good people see good fortune. I'm just glad it happened to you and your family."

The captain raised a finger. "Speaking of family, we have some other good news to share. We're taking a vacation. We have what looks like a regular run from here to Orion lined up for the next six months or so, like clockwork. The ship will be here for another ten days waiting to load before we depart. It's been months since we've been able to give the kids a prolonged break, and we won't make it back home for a while with all this work lined up."

"So it's time to celebrate our good fortune," Caroline put in. "The man at the chandlery gave me a good line on a vacation spot down on the coast and was able to recommend a place where we can rent several adjoining homes for a week. We're locking up and taking the whole family for a rest. Say you'll join us!"

Kel was taken aback. It was not an invitation he was expecting. "That's very kind. I couldn't intrude..." He barely finished the words when his two friends began objecting.

"Nonsense! After everything you've done for us, you're part of the family," the captain interjected.

"Please say you'll come. At least for a few days?" Caroline pleaded.

Kel considered the offer for only a second more. It felt impulsive, but he couldn't restrain himself.

"Yes. Yes, I'd love to. I have a couple of days of work scheduled, but I can drive down and meet you after that. Would that be all right?"

They both assured him it would be perfect.

"What do I need to bring?"

Caroline laughed. "Your appetite, for one. Meiko is going to stuff you until you can't walk. Other than that, just yourself."

"Oh, you might find this interesting," the captain said. "Our little altercation on Calcarion that you so deftly handled?"

As if Kel could forget.

"The Spacers League is levying a huge fine against the mining consortium rather than shutting down shipping to the planet. The legal-types are still pushing the electrons around on the documents, but the consortium has agreed to the penalty to avoid the embargo. The best part, we get a very large portion of that fine as the aggrieved party."

That was great news. That incident was egregious in every way. Kel still felt angry about the idiocy of the miners. He was glad they were being punished and that his friends would get some additional relief knowing justice had been done.

Kel agree to find them at the grid Caroline gave him. They were planning on leaving with the whole family at the end of the day once unloading had been completed; vehicles had already been rented for the trip. He had just one more item to clear up before they parted.

"About my name being Tamford..."

The next two days couldn't pass fast enough. His friends were not troubled when he told them that they'd known him under a travel identity. Jim Yomiuri shrugged, taking the explanation as sufficient and said nothing more.

He'd packed many light clothes that he thought would be appropriate for the coast and found a pair of short exercise trunks that would serve for swimwear, should the Yomiuris wear such. On Pthalo, swimwear was an encumbrance and generally only seen on visitors from a few select worlds. *Who bathed dressed?* Kel didn't want to assume anything, though. It could be embarrassing for everyone if he showed up to swim with the rest of the family clothed and Kel in his natural swimwear.

He thought about Tara, the Yomiuris' daughter. He'd not seen her in the short visit to the ship the other day. Kel thought that the young Miss Yomiuri had simply kept her attempted visit to Kel all to herself. If there had been an issue, he was certain that Caroline, the girl's mother, would have addressed it in some way, probably by not having invited him to vacation with them. Maybe, Kel thought, he had misinterpreted the moment completely. It was a possibility.

He alerted Caroline that he was on his way and should arrive just after sundown. It would take two hours to drive south to reach the coast and he was looking forward to it; he'd seen nothing of that part of Argolis yet. Eirene assured him it was an excellent destination.

"The gods themselves would vacation there," she told him.

Colonel Graviakis and Major Todalin were both supportive. "Have a good time, Kel," Todalin said. "You should see the beautiful to offset the ugly while you're with us. I'll alert you if there are any important developments."

The colonel spoke. "Besides, it's time we put a new team leader in." Kel was expecting this. "The next senior man is Jakob and it's time for him to step up. Out and up for you. When you get back, I want you to spend more time with the command group." He saw Kel's frown.

"Ha! Look at that face. Don't worry, you're going to be busier than ever."

As he reached the coast, he branched off onto a coastal road that hugged short cliffs and rounded coves while waves lapped their sandy beaches. The white curls of the breaking waves were just visible in the last light of the early evening. Much about this coast reminded him of his birth world. Hotels and guest lodges populated the cliffs, some located on the low estuaries near the beaches themselves. Then he reached a private unlit road, and let his specs guide him on the route down a curvy drive to a sloping beach surrounded by more cliffs. A compacted rock parking area held several multi-passenger vehicles, and a lit staircase led down to a cluster of villas arranged in a semicircle facing the beach.

Kel descended the stairs, hearing laughter and the clink of plates and silverware. Long tables in the center of the courtyard came in view, the family milling about, the small children chasing each other in some game as the adults corralled them toward the tables.

"Kel! You made it!" Caroline yelled and soon he found himself again surrounded by hugs and handshakes from the large family. "Perfect timing. Ochio, go help Kel with his stuff. Tara, go with them and take Kel to his room. Get something comfortable on and come back. Auntie won't like you being late for dinner." Everyone was using his real name. Apparently, it was no big deal; Jim and Caroline must have explained the situation. It made him feel at ease.

Kel had never seen anyone in the family in anything but spacers' coveralls. They were all dressed in shorts or skirts and wore no shoes. Everyone smiled and looked relaxed.

The two Yomiuri youths helped Kel get settled into a private bedroom with a small veranda that overlooked the ocean. The windows and doors were all open, the sound of waves and smell of the water filled his senses from wherever he paused. He changed quickly into some loose clothes and returned, barefoot as well.

"What a beautiful place and thank you for the room. How did you find it?"

Tan spoke up. "Caroline's a wizard."

She seemed to scoff but accepted the praise. "Mister Symopolous at the chandlery was very helpful. I saw a holo of the place and told him to contact the owner right away; he said he could get a better bargain than we could, and I was only too glad to let him. He didn't want any commission, but I did put in an order for supplies for our next jump. Hey, by the way, it was you who turned us on to him. He remembered us from your order. That was quite a surprise. Thank you again, if we failed to say so the other day."

Kel waved them all off and grinned. "Hope you liked the things I chose. I have a better handle on the cuisine and foodstuffs now, having been here so long. I was making educated guesses that day. Hope what we selected was edible."

"Edible? Are you kidding? It was all fantastic. No wonder the core is going crazy for stuff from Meridian," Eric, the first officer and Jim's brother-in-law, interjected. "Good going, Kel. We had no idea your taste was as good as your gun handling."

Everyone laughed, but it embarrassed Kel, and he stayed quiet while everyone moved to sit around the long tables. Kel was ushered to sit with them. Meiko appeared to rub his back as she took his plate. "Guests first," she said with glee. Cheers went up. Tara sat across from him, hiding her face behind her hair, her white smile impossible to conceal. He took some deep breaths to fight the unusual feeling of tears welling in his eyes.

What's with you, man?

The next days were a whirlwind for him. Each day he rose with the sun, appreciating the natural beauty of the water and the waves in the early light. The days were divided by huge meals, the time in between spent together at the beach. Eirene had been right, the place was perfect. The water was the stuff of dreams, blue-green against the white sand. The weather was temperate with gentle cooling breezes abundant.

The children all competed for Kel's attention and he spent hour after hour teaching them games he remembered from his own childhood and learning new ones they taught him. Almost every minute he found himself transporting one of the kids on his back as he waded through the warm bath-like water, bobbing with the waves and taking advantage of the buoyancy of the ocean to entertain his riders. He did so while wading farther and farther offshore, the kids taking turns on his shoulders shrieking with delight.

The Yomiuris wore bathing attire except for the small children. That suited Kel fine. Many times, he saw Tara staring at him. He made every effort to not be alone in her company.

She's a teenager, he reminded himself. *Eighteen is still a kid,* knowing he didn't feel the same about himself as a seventeen-year-old legionnaire. Besides, he wouldn't want anything to spoil the magic of the moments he was living.

The adults stayed up late each night. They built fires on the beach and talked until everyone yawned, stuffed from Auntie's cooking and tired after a day spent in the sun, swimming and playing with the children.

Kel had planned on staying two nights. By the end of the second night, he found the idea of leaving the next morning unbearable and decided he'd stay with them longer. Nothing urgent awaited him back in the capital, and if Major Todalin bounced, he could move out at a moment's notice and be on-station with the Hoplites in two hours or less. He had taken no more than a portion of one day a week for himself the entire mission; many of those weeks not as much as that. He decided to feel no guilt about this time for refit.

One evening while Kel stayed with the kids on the beach as the adults left to clean up and start the evening meal preparations, Kel found himself alone for a moment, watching Tara play in the waves with some of her younger cousins. He felt disoriented, viewing the occurrences in front of him as if through the eyes of another person.

He asked himself a question he'd never before entertained. And it shocked him—*Could I have a life like this if I wanted?*

Their last night together, Kel said his goodbyes to the entire family. He begged off staying another day to leave when the whole family departed. He had work to do. He did his best to avoid Tara's gaze, but failed. There were tears, and some of them were his. This had been one of the best times he could remember.

He rose early the next morning before anyone else stirred and headed north toward the capital, dressed to go to the Hoplite compound and start his new position. It was the best way he knew to fight the melancholy. Work. He was truly sad to leave the Yomiuri family. He promised he would make every effort to communicate with them and their paths would cross again. Kel didn't know how, but he meant to keep that promise.

After Founders Day, it would all be forgotten.

FLASHBACK

Not just Pirates Search for Buried Treasure
Antione

I've checked the squad for the third time. "Yamazaki, think about moving that bipod back to get a better beaten zone on that pig." He gives me a thumbs up. We're standing on the deck of the Talon. The tailgate is open. It's night. The cool guys have helped us rig and shown us a new way to jump, our weapons exposed, laying horizontal across our bellies. They assure us we'll be stable. Not that it will matter much. It's a hop and pop. We're exiting at 4500 meters and will deploy canopies immediately to float silently down, covering about 20 klicks of horizontal flight to the target site.

The intel asset we helped recover was apparently worth the effort. At least, he gave up three sites where the big boss reportedly could have gone to ground. It remains to be seen if any of them are jackpots. It's funny how all these dictator types are secretly scared of their people and have to have safe houses to retreat to in case of revolution. Or invasion.

The cool guys tell us kill teams are hitting the other two sites simultaneously with us. With no small amount of pride Papa Bear tells us we get to hit the biggest and best of the targets. Seems our deeds have not gone unnoticed by the cool guys' bosses, who I guess are our bosses too, and this is their reward to us. I'd feel better if we let the

Repubs roll tanks over the compound. I bring up the notion and Zero shoots me down. There's not enough time.

"One minute. Move to the ramp." Papa Bear is the jumpmaster. He is cooler than cool. I hear the grin he's wearing behind his bucket. "Stand by. Go." He controls the pace and taps us out one at a time. Canopies inflate below as I get tapped. It's my turn. I jump, arch, and pull. I'm under the huge oval and steer to follow the cursor in my HUD, four canopies in front of me. Papa Bear will be the last out. TA is in the lead. I check the rear view and count chutes. We're all good. Now it's just follow the leader as we take the floating voyage across the desert.

Cloudy. Perfect. There's no way we could be spotted from the ground and our sensor signature is nil. I see the compound on the horizon. We're aiming for a spot this side of a low rise. There's bound to be an observation post and sentries on top. That'll be our first stop. I peel off right to flare and land on my feet. My weapon falls into my hands as the container drops off and disintegrates.

We stay on our feet and don't halt but instead move out. I'm at the head of our wedge with my squad, just trailing the kill team. We're trotting. "Hold up," TA says. We come to a halt and get on our bellies and crawl forward on line with each other. "Turner, you're with me and Provo." I crawl forward to where two shapes are on their hands and knees moving uphill and follow in kind. As we get near the top, Provo eases onto his belly and we do the same. "Voices," he says. "They're up there." My anticipation is building. I'm not nervous. I'm thrilled to be on the hunt. Now Provo does the weirdest thing. He stands up casually and starts walking. TA is on his left. I take the right.

We crest the hill and in a small depression sit three militia, rifles resting on the rim, heads down, hands in pockets trying to stay warm. They barely look up as we approach. On low power particle beam the K-17s produce no light. No noise. The three bodies fall backward. "Move up," TA says and we spread out to clear the encampment. The rest of the team barrels in behind us. We own the hill.

Howard and Pabon drag the bodies away as Yamazaki and D'antonio take up residence in the pit. Yamazaki gets behind his medium blaster and moves the bipod towards him as I'd suggested and starts building a range card. D'antonio is doing the same, his M7 grenade launcher and N-16 on the ground next to him as he lays out bandoliers of flying death where he can reach them.

Warchief takes a knee by them. "When we holler, lay waste to those out buildings, then shift fire and discourage anyone else from approaching. We'll tell you if we need anything closer, got me?"

"Let's move," Papa Bear says almost musically. I feel it, too. The rush.

We follow a draw to the backside of the compound. There're no roving guards on the short walls. The buildings are blacked out. It's as though we're the only ones here. We vault each other over the wall and I reach back to help Provo, the last man. Papa Bear and Warchief take Trumbull and Pabon. I go with Zero, TA, and Provo. The palace is laid out like a "U" and there're two entrances, both sealed by durasteel doors. The windows are covered by retractable blast shutters.

"She's here. I know it," Zero says. "Fits the psychometric profile. Thinks she's invincible." Now I'm convinced this is the place and that we're going to find treasure.

"Sensor field emission," Provo says. "They know we're here."

"Do it fellas," Papa Bear says. "Turner, get your guys slaying." I tell Yamazaki and D'antonio to light them up. We're running to the armored doors. I face out, expecting troops or auto turrets to appear any second. "Breaching," Zero says as I feel a tug and I'm following him to hug the wall. I momentarily hear the explosions and blaster impacts in the distance from my guys' work when the courtyard explodes in violet and silver. The doors clank on the ground. TA tosses a stunner and more purple arcs bleed out from the depths before dying and I'm last through the threshold.

"Positive breach," Zero says. "Likewise here," Papa Bear returns. We start working, knowing on the other side they're doing the same. I try and keep up. These guys flow down the hall, toss stunners, take rooms without speaking. I decide my best role is to provide rear security as we keep rolling through.

We round a corner. Blaster fire. I don't get the opportunity to get into the fight. Bodies are stacked ahead in front of another set of reinforced doors. These have been gilded and are surrounded by carved figures in an arch. TA and Provo are laying strip charges around the semi-circular portal as Zero and I face back. I tuck into a threshold and brace my forearm against it, ready to blast anything that moves. Zero is across from me doing the same. TA moves in behind me. "Tuck in. We're lighting." He waits a second and I hear him speak.

"Fire in the hole."

That's a big one. I make the mistake of looking and my HUD flares before going black for a second, then I follow TA out of the room. The entrance is a pile of twisted steel and rubble, dust obscuring the view past into the room. I follow. Stepping over the debris I see a figure to my left

on the ground. I see a gun and don't wait to see movement before I fire. Everyone has their bucket floods lit as
we search. I find a massive fresher suite with tubs and
showers. Provo is standing in the center of the room, not
moving. Everyone returns from their search to join him.

"Nothing. Just the one guy," Zero says. I move to look
at the body of the guy I shot when moving in. Where he
was in the room, he was likely already dead from the
breaching charge blast before I shot him. I roll him on
his back. He's in some kind of garish dress; velvet pajamas costumed as a uniform with gold braid and sewn
on ribbons.

Zero's over my shoulder. "I make that as General
Alach. He's consort to Lady Shah Khan. Papa Bear," he
says on L-comm. "We've got number two down over
here. I think we're close to jackpot."

"Rog. Headed to you."

Provo is still. I see where he's focused, on the canopied bed. The covers are turned down and it looks like
both sides have been occupied. "Help me," he says as he
sprints from the center of the room to the bedside. "Lift." I
squat to help him and we toss the huge piece of furniture
over. The bed concealed a slide and at our feet, a smooth
durasteel surface is revealed.

"She's got a safe room," Provo says. The rest of the
team bust in. TA bends to run a gauntlet over it. "Or, it's a
tunnel system. We need help."

20

Then came Founders Day. The planet-wide celebration of the founding of the planet and the veneration of its original settlers was a weeklong holiday rather than a single day's event. It was preceded by the meeting of the Domestic Conclave at the Pa'artenon outside of Tiryns, the celebration capping the end of the legislative year. Traditionally, any new legislation would take effect after the holiday, an opportunity for citizens to celebrate and relax before starting a new period of taxes and decrees.

Most regular work ceased during the holiday. There were daily festivals and parades, nightly carnivals and feasts, all dedicated to the ancient gods of Meridian. Except Founders Day itself—that was dedicated solely to the Twelve Families who first settled the planet.

The week before the holiday started, an increased presence of uniformed patrol officers and vehicles appeared at every intersection in the capital. Vehicles and occupants were questioned and searched thoroughly before being allowed to proceed anywhere north toward the area of the Pa'artenon.

At the Hoplite compound, hovers and dropships were parked around the cantonment, awaiting directions to carry the operators when needed.

"Most of us are headed north to stage near the Pa'artenon," the colonel told him. "VIP protection. It's like this every year. It'd be a waste to have you hanging around with us flipping tiles and playing cards."

Don had no intelligence to augment what little the NP had come up with. There had been a precipitous decline in incidents over the last month after their many operational successes; no bombings, no tax-collecting hold-ups, no kidnappings. They were breaking ME's back!

"It is a holiday. Take the time. Help out at your embassy," Graviakis suggested. "Everyone's tense. I'm sure your presence will help make them more at ease." Bell had been pestering him about helping with the embassy security during the holiday week, anticipating the potential for trouble. Now there was no reason to put him off.

"All right, sir." Kel couldn't argue the colonel's logic. Despite the general feeling of ease displayed by the Hoplites and the cautious indifference of Don, he wasn't ready to celebrate.

Either ME had been beaten into insignificance, or they were saving their efforts for something larger.

Two days before Founders Day, Kel turned in early. He was going to the embassy compound the following morning and planned to spend the next forty-eight hours on-site, ready to assist with any defense of the grounds and manage any crisis as it occurred. Bell and Pen planned to do the same. The embassy was all but closed for the holiday week, and there would be few personnel on the grounds besides them and the security force.

He had not been asleep long when he awoke, his subconscious registering a deep, rattling vibration and tremor, a millisecond delay before the noise of a detonation followed, betraying the cause. Kel sat up quick.

The explosion was close.

It was starting...

Kel had planned for the defense of the palace for months. He dressed quickly in the dark. The exterior cameras could be viewed through Kel's link. He scanned the feed and saw no one approaching the palace walls. He activated the algorithm to detect active movement on the cameras, which would then feed the image to him on his specs. Two windows popped up—Ramer and Gren each speaking to him in a flurry of words.

"Guys, calm down," he told them. "Get your armor on and grab your carbines. Gather Eirene and the girls and move to Gren's apartment like we planned. I'm going to evaluate the situation outside. I'll bounce you in a few. Whatever you do, don't shoot me. I'll take it personally. I'm going up top to scout. Keep the lights off."

When planning their defense of the compound for his housemates and the ladies, Kel instructed them to rally in the first floor living space of Gren's unit. It was the most central structure, and it had the protection of the thick exterior wall around the grounds, giving it the most layered protection from blast or projectiles. He'd explained to his housemates they were less likely to be injured and more likely to be able to defend against an attack together, rather than spread out throughout the house. He'd had the whole group practice the drill once before and now wished he had done so more often. *There's never enough time.*

They nodded understanding and broke the link.

Three more explosions echoed from different directions and distances across the city. This was more than another isolated bombing. This was the show.

Kel had already donned his own protective gear and grabbed his carbine while moving onto the balcony outside his bedroom, scaling the ladder he'd left there and mounting the roof.

None of the apartments or common areas of the palace were lit. Clouds obscured the moon. He crawled on his stomach to the peak of the roof and brought his carbine out in front of him. The vantage gave him an excellent view of the street and compound, and the long avenue leading downhill.

Through his specs and the more powerful resolution and magnification of the optics on his carbine he made a careful search. From the houses behind him, people stood in bedclothes on their balconies, trying to view the disturbances around them. Kel was somewhat concealed in the shadows cast onto the roof by the large spreading trees overhanging his apartment. Unless someone was observing him with night vision, he would be difficult to spot.

"I don't see any activity on the streets," he said on his link. "Keep scanning the exterior cameras and tell me if you see anything. I'll stay up here." Kel's program would send him the camera images before his friends would be able to report to him, but it gave them something to do.

"Got it, Kel. We're good down here," Gren replied.

To his left at the far extent of his view, at what his carbine told him was 223 meters, two cars were parked on the street. That was unusual. Vehicles usually parked in the interior lots of the estates, not on the street.

Seeing nothing after another few minutes, he climbed down the ladder and was about to join his friends when he heard muffled voices and the thump of vehicle doors.

Kel grabbed his long rifle from its resting place by the bed. He activated the repulsor-pod under the forearm as he moved to the window. He settled behind the big gun and scanned the street through the optic toward the parked cars. Big-B remained rock steady as the grav-pod maintained the height he desired, allowing him to relax as he scanned for motion through his scope.

A flash of movement caught his eye. Four men with weapons dragged two figures through the open gates of the compound, forcing them into the vehicles he had seen earlier. The two central figures appeared bound. He had heard a female making noises of resistance. Kel could now make out the female figure, struggling as she was held from behind by a single captor. Another man stood by the front vehicle, gesturing with the pistol in his hand to put the victims inside. A limp man was being carried under his legs and arms by the other two captors, rifles slung across their backs.

Kel went into a routine practiced thousands of times, unconsciously activating a program of performance with the long gun he had perfected through years of agonizing discipline.

Without changing the grip on his rifle, Kel tapped the right side of the receiver twice, silently activating the electronic ignition of the weapon.

He chose his first target, the man holding the struggling woman. She was shorter than her captor by a half-meter. Kel noticed and accepted the range and environmental information his specs fed him by blinking twice in rapid succession. The distance was close enough that there would be little difference from his 100-meter zero, but he would accept any push toward perfection he could get.

The left lens of his specs erupted with a small projection window containing Bell, his mouth opening to say something as Kel clicked his teeth twice to close the window and lock-out incoming messages.

It never fails, he groaned and concentrated on the target...

He brushed the trigger with the pad of his index finger and applied a light rearward pressure as he felt the tension increase slightly, the trigger moving rearward through its first stage of travel until reaching a firm wall of resistance; another few ounces of pressure and the shot would inexorably and irretrievably leave the weapon forever.

The reticle settled on the man's head. Kel picked a spot of darkness at the inner corner of the man's left eye and pressed the trigger. The man's head disappeared. Kel snapped his eyes to the man bending forward slightly at the waist, his arms wrapped around the legs of the hostage he carried.

Kel was aware of the looks of confusion by the group during the moment following his first shot. He'd seen it many times before. People looked around in desperate confusion, vainly attempting to understand their predicament. He was a god of war. His acts were beyond their comprehension. But it was not time for him to stop and admire his work; it was time to take advantage of the sweet moment of surprise.

Drawing an imaginary line bisecting the circumference of the man's chest, he broke the next shot. The man fell away. He drifted his reticle to the man whose arms wrapped underneath his captive's armpits. When the captor dropped his load and obligingly offered Kel a full view of his chest, Kel sent a round right through him.

The man closest to the vehicle had wisely chosen to abandon his colleagues. He had already gotten in the driver's seat and started the engine when Kel placed a shot through the windscreen. Aiming at the line where the man's neck joined his chest, knowing that the angle of the windscreen would cause a slight deflection of the projectile, the 8-millimeter projectile struck the windshield. Kel did not hesitate to press the trigger once more as his reticle settled on the same spot again, taking advantage of the weakness his first round had created in the barrier, just in case. The unpiloted repulsor hovered lazily on its own volition to be halted by a nearby tree.

The woman hostage crawled to the bound male figure lying close by, surrounded by the other unmoving shapes Kel continued to watch.

After another minute, Kel raised his head from the weapon.

You're welcome, he thought. He'd like to have moved to the scene and assisted the victims further, but he had other priorities.

The alert in his specs flashed. He keyed the icon and was immediately greeted by Bell's face, his voice stressed to a higher pitch than normal.

"We've got trouble, buddy."

"Sorry. Been busy here. What's the situation?" Kel asked.

"It looks like this is the big one. I'm at home with my wife, we're locked down in my safe room. I'm managing what I can from here."

Kel confirmed that he was at his domicile as well, and that his housemates were accounted for and safe.

"So, where's the fire?"

"That's what it is. One of our diplomat's residence is under attack. Seems his guards have left, and there're men trying to get into their safe room. I can't get the NP or anyone to respond. I've tried several times. Stuff's happening all over the city. Judges and city officials have been targeted and there seems to be an orchestrated effort to kidnap or kill a lot of pols. It's all happening now. It's all going down right now tonight. They're responding where they can, but their own people are their priority."

Kel thought he remembered that the home down the street was the residence of one of the local magistrates. The whole area swarmed with the elites of Tiryns. If there was a campaign to kill or kidnap them, this would be an ideal location.

"Kel, I think you're the closest responder. They're only about a half-kilometer from your location."

Without hesitation, Kel was ready to act. He didn't need to be asked the question.

"Bounce me the location. I'll be moving out presently. Who's the diplomat?"

"Chief Minister Sun."

Kel gathered his gear and made his way to Gren's apartment, announcing himself as he moved.

"What's happening?" Gren asked.

Eirene and the house maids looked anxious, the two younger girls hanging on to either side of the older woman's waist like her children.

In few words, Kel updated them on what he'd learned from Bell and what had occurred outside, adjusting his carbine on his chest and moving grenades to different pouches as he spoke.

"I've got to go help a diplomat not far from here. Stay put and keep monitoring the cameras. I'm going to check on the guards. I'll update you when I can."

The two men nodded, their hands clutching their carbines.

"You have to go out there?" Ramer asked. "Do you need help?"

Kel smiled. It took a lot of courage for the trade expert to volunteer to go with him. He respected that.

"Thanks, but it's really best if you two stay here and protect the ladies. Don't worry, I'll be back as soon as I can."

He headed to the courtyard and through the parking area to the small guard house, checking the exterior feed all the while. He half expected another scene like the last. The surrounding neighborhood appeared quiet.

"Guys, it's Kel, do you hear me?" Kel said as loud as he thought necessary to get the guards' attention. He did not want to get shot before even leaving the compound.

"That you, Meester Kel?" He took that as permission to enter.

One of the men peered through the sliding viewport, observing the front of the gate and drive, his subgun around his neck. The other relaxed in a chair, a stim stick in his lips.

"Is all quiet. You kill those men down the street?"

They'd probably had at least a partial view of the commotion a few minutes before. "Yes."

"We thought maybe was you. That is Magistrate Cosmatos. He send my brother to prison once. He very nice man."

Kel was not sure what to make of the man's story but thought it would be worth hearing some other time.

"Let me out the sally port then secure it. I've got to help someone. I'll signal you when I come back using my white light. Several short flashes like this," Kel activated his carbine light several times in succession, "is what I'll use to get your attention. Don't shoot me, got it? You're doing a good job. Thank you."

The men grinned in the dark. "You no worry, Meester Kel. Maybe we get lucky and get chance shoot people too, eh?"

Kel slipped out the narrow reinforced door and waited to hear it secured behind him. He'd considered taking his vehicle part or all of the way to the minister's residence but thought better of it. It would draw too much attention. This was a time for stealth. If intruders were already in the residence, arriving silently would give him an advantage.

He dimmed the night vision feed through his left eye, giving him the ability to see shadows and other cover under natural light, while his aided right eye saw the details as though it were daylight. Trees lining the avenue cast dark shadows against the walls and hedges of the estates. He moved rapidly through the concealed areas, pausing to scan before moving slowly through lit areas until he reached shade again.

The streets were empty. Kel ran at a hard pace down to an intersection and paused to observe the long, open avenues.

People staying put and keeping their heads down inside, Kel thought. *Good.*

He reached an intersection where the corner of a large estate sat, its walls partially obscured by vines. Looking up the rising slope of the street, he saw the front of the minister's residence and confirmed it on his specs. He'd taken time to pull up an overhead of the area. He was close. The front gate hung open, a vehicle parked before it. No motion was obvious, but lights shone from within the front courtyard.

Kel walked across the lit intersection, then broke into a trot. Running across streets was the sure way to attract attention. A slow, deliberate walk better concealed an operator's intentions. He found the narrow drive custodians and workers used to access the rear of the estates. He hugged the left wall as he moved up the sloped path until he reached the rear of the minister's mansion.

The rear of all the properties held garages and servant quarters that abutted each other, forming a two-story wall. There was no way into the grounds save through the rear foot entrance or over the roof. The service door was a reinforced security door, but the garage door was a thin metal, much easier to breach. Kel had considered scaling the two-story façade and going over the roof. He dismissed the idea; it would require more time and leave him exposed for far too long.

From the pack at the small of his back, he withdrew a knife-like instrument with an angled nose at the tip. Kneeling by the garage door, he ignited the plasma cutter. A fine purple glow emanated from the tool, and he drew it horizontally in a smooth motion from the edge of the door and then down, his other hand rising to capture the separated piece of the door as he completed the downward stroke. He extinguished the tool and put it away. He knew the tool emitted little light or noise, but in his heightened state of awareness, he feared his actions were visible from orbit.

Kel laid the piece of thin metal to the side and peered through the square portal he'd created. Bringing his carbine up and activating his low-spectrum invisible light, his night vision exploded with detail of the space: a utility vehicle, tools, and other grounds implements became visible. Kel knee-walked into the space, making his way to the front door, and cracked it open only enough to see a path leading around tall hedges to a courtyard beyond.

Silently, he closed the door and bounced Bell.

"I'm on the grounds," he subvocalized. "What's happening in the house?"

"Wait one, I'll bounce them," Bell said as he moved a hand to open another screen in front of him.

"*Don't* tell them I'm here," Kel urged. That idiot Sun was likely to brag to the invaders that the cavalry had arrived. "Ask him how many intruders there are."

"Understood. I'm going to key you into their link."

Soon Kel saw the face of the plump older man as he conversed with Bell.

"Minister, how are you holding up?" Bell asked.

"How do you think, you fool? My wife and I are in mortal danger. Men are outside this very door who want to murder us. Where are the police? Where are the embassy guards? Where are you? I demand help this minute!"

"I'm trying to get you help, sir. You are in the safest possible place right now. Just stay there and remain calm."

"You don't understand. They're threatening to blow us up or burn us to death if we don't come out. I've been trying to negotiate with them. I've stalled them for thirty minutes already. I can see them doing something to the door."

Kel knew the type; the safe room was a small module the size of a large closet located in the bedchambers. It was spacious enough for two people to sit or lay down, but little else. Once inside, the occupants were protected from a variety of threats and had oxygen and supplies for two days. It would not withstand explosives placed in proximity to the door and would only provide protection from the heat of a fire if the fire suppression system outside was functional. The occupants could be roasted alive or blasted if the invaders were so inclined. In the background, the man's wife sat hugging herself, legs pulled into her chest.

"If you don't hurry, we're going to die."

Bell closed the link.

"Bell, can you get me a camera feed into the residence?" Kel asked.

"No can do. There is no external link."

Kel blew out a breath. "Okay. I'm going dark. Bounce you when I can." He'd gotten all the information he was going to get.

Those thugs have no idea who's coming for them.

He opened the door and moved out along the dark path, carbine at the ready, head erect and peering just over the top of the optic. Reaching the end of the hedgerow, he lowered his carbine to peer around it and into the partially lit courtyard. He took a route along the edges of the garden in as much darkness as existed, heading for the veranda. He was one going against an unknown number. If he was discovered now, the only advantage he had would be gone. The plan for that was always the same. *Shoot everything until it changes shape or catches fire.*

The lights were on in the main house. He took an oblique path through the expanse of sliding doors, scanning as deeply as he could see into the spaces beyond. A wide staircase led from the living area to an upper balcony and sitting area where beyond it were a set of double doors. Loud male voices floated down.

With Tem, Bigg, and Poul, he could have taken this whole structure in minutes. Kel missed his Legion armor. He missed his K-17. As one man, he'd be lucky to make it to the top of the stairs.

Kel made his decision.

He'd made it halfway up the staircase when a man walked out of the threshold in front of him. Surprise registered on the man's face and he reached for the rifle slung across his body. Kel fired a quick succession of suppressed rounds, tumbling him backward as the impacts tore his chest to shreds.

It's on now!

Men ran out in response to the engagement, firing blindly in Kel's direction.

Without thinking Kel collapsed, his right hand reaching into his rear pack for a stun grenade he'd planned to use at the top of the stairs. Instead, he felt the sharp corners of a multifaceted explosive grenade in his hand. As more fire erupted from the doorway, Kel thumbed the lever and chucked it into the room, throwing himself flat again onto the stairs.

Ka-WHUMP.

The blast exploded deep in the room. Kel rushed up the stairs, his rifle raised and leading him forward through the dust clouds and raining debris. He stepped over the body on the landing. Lying in the threshold, the next body he encountered got three quick rounds in the chest as Kel passed him.

A man waited upright on two knees, pistol in hand. Blood seeped from his mouth and nose from the over-pressure of the blast. Kel fired several shots into the man's chest and head, then looked for the next threat.

In the corner a man stood, rifle at his feet. Shocked, the man's mouth hung open, blood-tinged spittle foaming from his mouth. Blood seeped from his ears and his leather jacket was riddled with holes.

Two shots to the brain ended it for that one.

An open bathroom door invited him to toss the un-used stunner past it. He heard no response and moved to the last portal in the room on the other side of the canopied bed.

He cleared a small vestibule to find the security door of the safe room. Kel took a moment to consider his next actions. If there were other intruders in the house, he did not want to bring the minister and his wife out just yet.

After a quick search of the rest of the second floor, he bounced Bell.

"Hey man, I'm in the minister's suite. I think I've got the situation secure, but I could sure use some help. Any word from the NP?"

"*You are?* Was there anyone there?"

Kel coughed. The debris and dust still filled the air. "Yeah. Sun wasn't joking." Kel had found a satchel that contained explosives in the bedroom. The intruders' intent to blow open the safe room door and the occupants inside hadn't been an empty threat.

"No. No word yet."

"All right. I'm going to call for help myself. I'll get back to you."

Kel keyed his link for Major Todalin. He was pleasantly surprised to get an immediate response.

"Kel, you all right?" the major asked. "You look like you've been busy. What's going on?"

He gave the major a brief recap of his night so far and requested help to evacuate the minister and his wife.

"Yes. Yes, of course. Stay put. I can send units to your location within the next thirty minutes. I'll send someone to the magistrate's as well."

"Major, do you have any armored rescue vehicles available?"

"No. We don't. We're stretched thin. The Hoplites are all north. We had to send them all up to the Pa'artenon region. There were some attacks on a few of the residences. I don't have any other tactical assets to send your way, but we can get armed escort vehicles to you. Stay put."

"Don't send them in hot! I'm in here with the minister and his wife. Please have them bounce me as they get close."

He knew the major would have relayed the situation, but some things bore repeating, like "don't shoot the good guy on the scene."

Some thin-skinned gun speeders would be better than nothing, he thought.

It was time to contact the victims. Kel bounced the minister using the source he'd received from Bell earlier. Sun's pink face filled Kel's specs, eyes wide with panic.

"They're trying to kill us! They're going to blow us apart! Help, please!"

Kel felt sympathy for the man. His grenade would have been indistinguishable from any other explosion from inside the safe room.

"Minister, it's Kel Turner. I'm just outside your safe room door. It's all right, the intruders are dead. I'm here to rescue you. You and your wife are safe."

"Oh, my word. Sweetness, do you hear that? We've been rescued finally. Is it safe to come out?" the man asked Kel.

Kel assured him it was and moved to meet the man. The safe door cracked open, and the minister's face appeared through the slit.

"Mister Turner, I'm very glad to see you. Are the police with you? I need to get my wife somewhere safe."

Hearing the man act in a chivalrous manner toward his wife made Kel feel regretful about how he'd previously judged the diplomat. No matter what else, Sun was still a man trying to protect his wife.

"It's just us for right now. Why don't I help you both downstairs? There's been some damage up here and I think it best we move out of the house, perhaps to the courtyard."

He took the arm of Mrs. Sun and helped her through the coaming of the safe door. "The bodies of the men who tried to hurt you are outside. They're not a threat anymore, but I don't want you to be alarmed. It's not gonna be pretty, minister." It sounded stupid, but it was the only thing he could think of to say.

Of course these poor people are alarmed, he chided himself.

He was not wrong. At the sight of the dead men in her bedroom, the woman shrieked, leaned on her husband, and broke into sobs. Kel ushered them out of the devastation to the veranda outside. He gathered a throw off one of the sofas and placed it on the shoulders of the overwhelmed woman as her husband tried to console her.

The minister told Kel what happened. They'd heard the explosions around the city and were awake when the minister tried to check in with their gate guard. The man had deserted them. The feed gave him time to react to the men entering the compound with weapons. He acted quickly to take himself and his wife to the safe room, locking themselves in seconds before the intruders reached their bedroom. Any more of a delay and they would have been hostages or worse.

"You did well, Minister. You saved your and your wife's lives. That was quick thinking."

"I tried to reason with them over comms while we waited for someone to rescue us. The National Police. Bah! Our treaty specifies that they are responsible for the security of diplomats from the Ex-Planetary mission. It's a treaty, for goodness sake! That idiot Bell did nothing. I begged him to come rescue us. I am absolutely going to have him reprimanded if not imprisoned."

"He couldn't have helped you, minister. It wouldn't have been—"

Kel was interrupted.

"It was you and your Kyrgiakos friend at the National Police that caused this!" the minister said, his face flushed red. "I've heard about the stunts you've been pulling around this planet with those stormtroopers. You are the ones who have driven the dissidents to such desperate acts! Couldn't you at least have gotten here before they tried to blast us to death? It was only the protection of the safe room that kept those animals at bay—even then, that was only because I insisted that all minister-level diplomats have safe rooms, since we're a target for kidnapping and terrorism. If not for my forethought, we'd be kidnapped or dead already."

Kel's reassessment of the minister's character had come full circle.

"Actually, Minister," Kel said, chagrined, "the intruders never got their bomb planted. The explosion you heard was the grenade I threw into your bedroom."

The man's eyes widened as he took this in. His face turned bright red.

"What if you'd *killed* us?" he demanded.

Kel couldn't help the guffaw that escaped.

"Well, Minister, it was a chance I was willing to take."

21

"Good hunting, Meester Kel?" the guard asked, grinning so widely Kel could make it out in the darkness. The NP sent two speeders and two repulsor gun-sleds to the residence. The minister's estate was now a crime scene and had been locked and sealed for investigation. Bell arranged for the diplomats to stay with the ambassador and his wife at their heavily guarded residence.

"The best," Kel replied.

He thanked the officers as they departed and received a salute from the young lieutenant who'd escorted him. He'd given a preliminary statement to the lieutenant. He'd heard no more from the minister on their short ride to the palace.

Kel found his housemates and the staff sitting in the kitchen, Eirene cooking for them all, dim candles lighting their faces.

"Oba, what happened? You look like hell," Gren said, rising to give Kel his seat at the small kitchen table.

"Oh, you know. Making friends again."

Eirene clucked at him and handed him a plate heaped with food.

In between bites, Kel got on the link with Bell. "What's the threat assessment for the other embassy staff? This thing may not be over. How are you and your wife?"

The RSO was no longer in his safe room and was moving about his own residence. Kel could see two of the ambassador's protective detail with him.

"We're fine. I checked in with Pen, he and his wife are fine, too. As far as the developing situation, it's hard to say. We got caught unprepared. I've been on the link to the security company we contract with for the residential protection service. They've agreed to double the numbers of guards on all the residences. I've also got the promise of the House and Transit Police to detail officers to security at points around the region of the Hills. A lot of their officials live around here, too. Seems they got caught unaware and have been hearing about it from their own pols."

Kel thought about the magistrate and his wife who'd been assaulted down the street. He wondered how they were. He could imagine how busy Gavros must be right now, trying to juggle the security of the entire capital.

"We all know it's obvious where embassy personnel reside," Bell admitted.

It was true. If ME had monitored the travel patterns of high-value targets like the top diplomats, locating their residences would not be hard. The embassy was also staffed by local Meridian hires; if any of them were sympathetic to the ME cause, their knowledge could all be exploited. It was a problem Bell dealt with daily as the RSO.

"That's good work, Bell. More rent-a-cops on the residences is the right move. More cops on the streets will help, too."

"I'm not as concerned about the embassy. The compound is almost empty this week. Getting overrun while the diplomats and ambassador are on the grounds was my nightmare scenario. I'm not so worried about that now. I'm going to head in at first light. The protective detail leader has things well in hand at the ambassador's. Maybe you should consider staying put at the palace? I mean, it puts you closer to most of the staff and their families if something like last night happens again. Whaddya think?"

Kel preferred not to perform any more one-man rescue missions, but he understood Bell's reasoning.

"Okay."

The night was only a few hours old. Kel checked the time. A little after midnight.

"It could be a long night and a long few days yet. I'll stay on station here and wait it out."

"I'll bounce you when I know something. Out." Bell disconnected and left Kel with his thoughts. He'd better get his ammo topped off and check his gear. Grabbing the frag grenade from his pack instead of the stunner had worked out, but had certainly been making the best out of a bad situation. He vowed not to repeat the error.

As he stood in his closet inspecting his choices in accoutrements, Kel's specs flashed. It was Don.

"Kel, I've got trouble." *Must be bad if he's calling me. He's got his own mercenary force,* he thought, remembering the thugs hanging out in Don's courtyard.

"You and Stefania all right?"

"Stefania and I are fine here. No, it's... do you know the ship's chandlery, Symopolous and Sons? I know you do."

"Yes, I know them."

How does Don know I've used the chandlery before?

"He's one of ours."

Those words spoke volumes. Symopolous must be an Expanded Horizons agent. At least, that would be Kel's best guess.

When Kel had been read into some of the programs used by Republic Intelligence to facilitate information gathering from around the galaxy, one of those programs he was made aware of was Expanded Horizons.

EH took mid-level Republic military officers, usually from the intelligence branch, and offered them an opportunity to work for RI as a contract agent, gathering and sending information to RI through the cover of a legitimate business located on various worlds of interest.

The cover they worked under was non-official and not associated with the Republic. RI gave them a cover identity and a financial stake to get their business started. The venture was always an actual business, and it had to be profitable. The asset would spend a career running the business, usually some type of import/export venture. It gave them plausible reasons for dealing with customers from all over a planet and the galaxy. In the course of their work, they sometimes developed important intelligence, giving indicators of trends, financial stresses, or crises that presaged trouble the Republic needed to know about. Sometimes they served more concrete functions for support of covert activities within their area of operations, smuggling goods, weapons, even people, as directed by RI.

Always the business generated profit, and the profits were funneled back to RI to finance black ops. The asset also made a profit. Rational self-interest and patriotism motivated a person to spend their life on a world not of their choosing, trading in goods and secrets for the Republic. Earning a financial profit was a powerful motivator.

Kel had heard a rumor about the program once from Bigg. A DO operator had been recruited to Expanded

Horizons on his retirement. After years of living under-cover and having established a booming business, the asset had been recalled to take another assignment. He flatly told his handlers to get karked. What would they do in response? Send someone to kill him? He continued funneling profits to RI and lived under his cover for the rest of his life. But as a result, no DO operators, or leejes in general, would ever be recruited into the program again. They were too difficult to control once given autonomy. At least, that was the rumor.

Questions popped into Kel's mind.

"How's he in danger? He runs a shop by the space-port. Was he blown?"

"No, he's not *blown*," the man replied, answering Kel's question as to whether the asset's cover had been revealed. "This is random. He's at the chandlery. He lives in a small flat upstairs of the offices. It looks like some-one's been probing the spaceport. The NP have a heavy presence there, and there's been some fighting. George thinks it's crime gangs who are taking advantage of the situation and are robbing and looting. Warehouses are on fire and he's seen some armed gangs in vehicles cruising the area. It could be crime gangs, it could be ME. Point is, he needs help."

"Okay, then why doesn't he report it to the security forces for them to respond? It's crime, right?"

Don nodded. "He's tried. They took his report and have promised to send help, but it hasn't materialized."

"Okay then, I'll make a call to my people at the NP and—" He didn't get to finish his offer.

"*Don't*. They'll want to know why the chandlery is im-portant enough for you to take an interest and you can't tell them he's one of ours. That'll blow his cover for sure, understand?"

Kel understood now.

"I'm loading up with my guys and coming to you. I need your help with this to protect not only George, but an important operation. Will you help me?"

Kel blew out a breath. "Yes. I'll be waiting for you at the gate. I assume we'll roll in your Panther?" The armored grav-sled would be the logical choice.

"Already moving, Kel."

Ten minutes later Kel slid out the sally port as the Panther pulled up, the rear compartment doors unfolding as one of Don's mercenaries hopped out, extending an out-stretched arm toward the portal. The man had full protective gear on and carried a heavy blaster. The only blasters Kel had seen on the planet were those in the embassy arms room. Apparently, RI placed no restrictions on themselves when it came to protecting its people.

Kel noticed National Police seals had appeared on the sides of the vehicle since he'd last seen it parked at Don's residence.

Another of Don's similarly geared-up mercenaries sat in back, the driver in front and Don in the seat next to him, also wearing full protective gear and helmets.

Kel moved to the troop seat right behind Don and heard the rear door grind closed as he braced for the impulse of movement.

"George says they're pillaging the warehouse across from his. He thinks it's only a matter of time before they hit him." The intel-man diverted his attention to his specs and spoke. "We're on the way. Stay in your flat. The security doors will slow them down for quite a while. We'll be there in twenty minutes. If you have to, escape and evade. Try not to get into a fight. Hold on."

He turned back to Kel.

"He's freaking out."

They drove all out, Don talking on his link to each of the Transit Police checkpoints, clearing their passage and confirming a clear route ahead. Don had his datapad projecting a holo of the route. He monitored a column of information beside it, swiping at lines of code hanging in the air, bouncing into comms of the approaching checkpoints.

They encountered no delays and in twenty minutes of driving, slowed as they neared the spaceport. Normal traffic would have made the trip take twice as long. Don's masterful spoofing got them there in record time. They started the series of 90-degree turns through the maze of streets leading to the rows of warehouses and business surrounding the spaceport.

Don pulled up a holofeed from the front of Symopolous and Sons. There were three feeds showing slightly different but overlapping views. In the distance, fires raged from some of the warehouses. Across the street the gates and security fencing had been pulled down from the front of the business. A large truck with chains dragging from its rear end, the one that had presumably breached the business across the street, was making a turn and backing up to the front of the chandlery. Men with rifles stood around, gesturing and laughing, others gathering the chains and guiding the vehicle backward.

"It's definitely going down. Is your man still inside?" Kel asked.

"Yes. He's staying put. I tried to get him to leave out the back. He thinks he'll be spotted," Don said. "What's the plan?"

"Stop them before they can get inside. Tell your man George to stay put on the second floor and get behind cover."

He scooted forward to get the driver's attention. "Halt about 100 meters down the street and angle the nose of the vehicle to them like so," Kel said, jamming the fingers of his knife-hand into the other palm at an acute angle. "It will give us cover and keep the Panther from getting struck head-on by fire."

Using armored vehicles correctly was more complex that it appeared. Pulling directly in front of a group of shooters in hopes of engaging them from within the relative safety of the vehicle was a plan of failure. The firing ports along the vehicle's sides were nothing more than blaster magnets for the opposition. It took very little enemy fire directed into firing ports to kill the occupant. Kel didn't have time to teach them how to fight with an armored vehicle. He just didn't want them to drive right up to the front of the building and create a disaster.

The driver made the last turn and raced forward for a few seconds before coming to a complete stop, angling the vehicle's nose as instructed.

"Use the Panther for cover and light them up," Kel said as he jumped out of the vehicle's rear port. The fires in the background made everything like daylight in his specs. The security gate over the entrance lay on the ground, the truck that had pulled it off surrounded by armed men.

Shots pinged off the Panther from the direction of the chandlery. More shots bounced off the flexible skirt below the vehicle's chassis, spalling off the pavement. Hard objects pelted Kel's legs, and his nanotubule undergarment squeezed, stiffening in response.

The first man he saw with a weapon, Kel fired at, sending two controlled shots into the man's torso. The man crumpled backward through the front of the building's breached entrance.

Kel shifted to get a better angle on the truck as blaster discharges came from the other side of the Panther to pepper the truck and the assailants ahead. Kel dashed behind the Panther to move up with the mercenaries, still blasting away with the K-17s.

"Hold up, stop firing!" Kel yelled several times to get their attention. "They're all down. Get the next threat. Let's move up and check the building." The mercs had been firing indiscriminately. Their charge packs would be near depleted and the weapons would shut down from overheating when used so ignorantly.

He banged on the side of the driver's compartment, motioning him to pull forward. As the driver idled forward, the men kept pace with Kel, keeping the Panther between them and the chandlery as they moved slowly toward the scene of carnage.

Kel put his fist up as they reached the front of the building, signaling the driver to stop the Panther. Peering around the nose through the destroyed entrance, shots rang out from within the deep cavern of the building, the flash of the muzzle causing bright spots in his visual field as he quickly retreated behind the vehicle.

"Right, at least one left in there, maybe more." As he said that, one of the mercenaries with the heavy blaster took Kel's spot at the front of the vehicle and fired a burst into the building. "Who's got a stunner? Launch one into the building then we'll go in after it."

Kel heard no response and looked from man to man, but only got blank stares.

"No one has a stun grenade for your carbine?" he asked again.

Shrugs, all around.

Kel reached into his pack and this time found a stun grenade. The stunner could be thrown by hand or, when detached from its activator, be fitted in the launcher underneath a carbine. Kel gestured for the man in front of him to hand over his K-17. The man begrudgingly did so.

Kel loaded the stunner into the short tube and leaned around the front of the vehicle again, pausing only momentarily to sight through the optic before launching. Its vapor trail into the building turned into a streak of plasma as it erupted in the familiar purplish light, arcing widely and illuminating the front of the store.

"Let's go." Kel handed the man his weapon back as he rushed forward, the three mercenaries with him as they activated the white lights on their carbines, flooding the space with blinding light. A gunman lay on the open floor of the entrance. Kel advanced cautiously forward as one of the mercenaries rushed ahead of Kel, firing a blaster bolt into the man's chest where he lay.

"Hey!" Kel yelled. "We can cuff anyone who's stunned!"

The man looked at Kel, paying him no mind before turning to join the other two mercenaries, moving deeper into the building. Kel joined them.

"Got two here!" one of the men yelled from the rear of the building.

"Another here," the man to his right called.

"Cuff them so we can interrogate them—"

Blaster fire shrieked from both directions before Kel could finish.

Don appeared over Kel's specs. "All clear in there?"

"Dammit, Don! Your mercs are executing stunned men." He was furious.

"I'm coming in."

Don and the last mercenary made their way into the building while Kel waited for them at the entrance. Don looked at his driver and said, "Start cleaning up."

Don moved to ascend the stairs. "George sounds pretty relieved. Let's go get him."

"Don. Stop. Your men just murdered all the suspects. What gives? There's no one to interrogate. They just murdered a bunch of guys."

"They're doing what I told them to do. Now, let's make sure George is okay."

At the top of the stairs was a landing and a security door at its terminus. Don waved at the eye above the door. After a second, the door receded and bright light flooded the landing. George Symopolous stepped out.

"Nice of you to make it. Mister Turner, I can promise you a significant discount next time you need my services."

Well, that's just peachy, Kel thought. *And how is that going to help me from prison when they convict me of murder?*

The sun was rising as Don's mercenaries worked to cover the front entrance with sheets of plate steel they'd brought from the yard on a lifter. A plasma welder sparked as the makeshift gate was tacked into place over the front entrance.

Bodies from the building had been brought out to join the other blaster-charred corpses stacked in the street. A loader appeared from the yard and made its way to the front, driven by Symopolous.

He pulled to where the bodies lay and got out of the loader. "I've got the mass converter fired up. Let's load them."

The mercenaries moved to lift the bodies, one at the feet, one at the head, and stacked them in the scoop of the lifter.

Kel grabbed the spy master's arm. "Don, what in Oba's name is going on here? This is a crime scene. The NP needs to process this place. There could be intel we need. They could be ME."

Don stopped watching his men load the bodies and glanced at Kel's hand.

"No."

"No?" He let go like he'd been suddenly burned.

Dawn was here and a pall of smoke hung over the city.

"No," hissed Don. "We need to clean this scene and get rid of any evidence that there was an incident here."

The loader reversed course and turned, heading back behind the fence and around the back of the building into the yard, the grisly cargo in its scoop. The mercenaries followed on foot.

"We can't leave anything that would draw attention to the chandlery."

Kel's face betrayed his confusion as Don continued to explain.

"Look, these gunmen could be part of a crime gang taking advantage of the chaos to loot. They could be ME, looting to fill their coffers. Doesn't matter now. What matters is that this operation is not compromised. There will be no police investigation. Knowledge of our involvement in the rescue of Symopolous would compromise the operation.

"See, it would have been easier if the police had responded. They didn't. So, I had to. In a way, we got lucky. Now, thanks to you, the police don't need to come at all. We'll save them time."

Kel's head was swimming. He stood by and watched the loader return. Symopolous and one of the mercenaries attached the chains from the back of the truck to the loader's bucket and towed the vehicle around the back, no doubt to be mass converted into atoms like the bodies.

The warehouse was deserted and Kel's curiosity urged him to investigate as the work to clean the scene proceeded. He'd done business here when he first arrived and noticed nothing out of the ordinary—samples of stores, shelves of mechanical parts and tools, riggings and lines. All normal. A security door focused his attention. The pad was bio-locked but less than a minute with his link spoofed the code and allowed him entry. *DO's intrusion package is as good or better than anything RI has. At least, that's what Tem says.*

He recognized the artwork from his trip to Cyrene. Paintings sat stacked against the wall and sculptures lined the floor space. Several clear cubes stuffed with gemstones ready to be packed in grav containers lay on a desk. The stones were not rare or valuable. The one Kel purchased was as large as any of these. Despite their beauty, they weren't worth a great deal.

He moved to the dark room at the rear and stopped. The scent was unusual, dank but sweet. It reminded him of the jungle of Eritrea.

"See anything you like?"

He startled at the voice of George Symopolous.

"I can give you a killer deal if there is. Let me know. Come on, let's button up. Don's out front waiting."

Kel smiled and made bland pleasantries as he passed the man. Neither man mentioned how Kel had gotten in the room. The smell stayed with his brain even in the smoky air outside. It was the smell of the thick resin processed in Eritrea. Then he understood.

Jade Lotus.

He'd tried stimsticks once as a recruit. He never picked up the habit.

For the first time in his life he found himself wishing he had a smoke.

Few other incidents occurred after that night. Most of the subsequent events were minor and likely copy-cat crimes as opposed to terrorism coordinated by ME. The emergency was declared over at the end of the holiday week.

Kel checked in with his friends at the NP. The entirety of the Hoplites had been detailed to protecting the dignitaries once the crisis kicked off. They were now off alert status and ready to start responding to other events as needed. Todalin invited Kel to the headquarters, saying that Gavros wanted to talk. He looked forward to it. Kel had been far busier than the Hoplites during the past week. The previous day he had met with two separate groups of NP investigators, detailing each of the two incidents he'd been involved in on the Hill. They visited both crime scenes and Kel had walked them through the events. They had no information to share with him about the perpetrators, but Kel had expected that; it was an ongoing investigation. He was certain Gavros and Todalin would have some knowledge to share with him.

He would keep the events of the rescue of George Symopolous to himself. He'd made the decision that it was best to forget the incident entirely. He would simply live with it, as dirty as it made him feel. What else could he do?

He had been used by Don. If he attempted to shine a light on the incident, the only risk would be to himself. *And what would it achieve anyway?* he asked with disgust. *I used to think RI was one thing, then another. Now I'm right back where I started. They can't be trusted to do the right thing for anyone but themselves.* There were rumors of another, deeper part of the intelligence service whose reputation was even more frightful. Even Bigg wouldn't talk about what he knew of them.

He now knew why Bigg had warned Kel to watch himself around the pols.

The events on Argolis and especially in Tiryns had become clear. The local casts reported scenes of the devastation from around the capital. Many police sub-stations were attacked, largely unsuccessfully. Several banks had been robbed and government offices bombed. Reporters discussed the attempted kidnappings on the Hill and shared images of burned warehouses near the spaceport. In the end, while property was damaged, few lives were lost. The security forces had performed well during the crisis. Reporters lauded the many instances of the Transit and House Police winning confrontations against the ME, showing holos of the crime scenes complete with terrorist bodies riddled with bullets.

It seemed the ME had gambled on the success of a large coordinated attack on the capital, and had lost.

The government announced that it would address the crisis publicly. Kel was as anxious as anyone to hear the statements from the National Police and the head of the Domestic Conclave. He joined his friends in Bell's office to watch the official government news conference.

A still holo of the Pa'artenon filled the background for a moment until Gavros' uncle, Conclave Chairman Kyrgiakos, took to the podium. He reminded Kel of Gavros, though slightly larger in the waist and with more gray at the temples. The chairman had a less pronounced accent to his Standard than did Gavros as he spoke.

"Citizens of Meridian, chosen of the gods, I come before you today to say that a great crime against our people has been perpetrated, in a most cowardly way, by terrorists who wish to destroy our very way of life.

"The past year has been a trying time for our people.

"I can assure the members of our great society that the Domestic Conclave has dealt a heavy blow to these monsters, and that the safety and security of our citizens is our only concern.

"I urge all citizens to remain calm and to have faith that you can continue life as normal, safe in the knowledge that the terrorist threat is soon to be eradicated."

He made a few more pronouncements before he stepped down without taking questions from the press. It was conspicuous that the chairman had made no mention of Meridian Eleftheria, nor had he made any mention regarding the loss of life or destruction of property that had occurred.

What did he mean "soon to be eradicated?" Kel pondered. *Have they caught a break I haven't heard about yet?* Tomorrow he'd meet with his NP friends. Maybe they would know the significance of the statement.

Gavros took the podium next, addressing specifics of the events of the past week that his uncle had only hinted at. Afterward, he took a few questions from the press, a reporter from the Spiral News Network in the crowd. The presence of a galactic reporter was noteworthy. Gavros gave a "no comment" answer to most of the questions, particularly when queried about the size and scope of ME, and the connection between the group and previous incidents around the planet during the past year. It seemed to him the information blackout by the government was lifting.

"I've never seen a media event like that here before," Bell said after the link closed. "That was a first for Meridian."

"Yeah, no kidding," Pen added. "I've been here two years, and I don't remember seeing anyone from the Conclave, much less the chairman, making any statements publicly that made it seem like life on Meridian was anything less than perfect."

"You've been here to see some real history being made, man," Bell told Kel, laughing.

"I certainly have."

Kel met with Gavros the next day. Todalin sat with them, sipping kaff as Kel gave the men the highlights of his two interventions during his busy night on the Hill. He felt comfortable speaking to the two, having associated with them so much the last five months. He knew he could tell his part in the two incidents without being perceived as self-aggrandizing. He told the story chronologically, answering questions as they had them, the men nodding as he described his actions in both episodes.

Concluding his tale with the walk-through of the crime scenes by the investigators, he stopped. The continued silence transformed Kel's feeling of comfort into anxiety. Gavros looked at Todalin, and him at Gavros. Both said nothing as they looked back to Kel.

The guilty flee when none pursue! his father had always said. *They know about the rescue of Symopolous,* he panicked. *They know about the Panther marked as one of their vehicles. They know about the cover-up!* Kel's dread built as he waited for the next words.

"Kel," Gavros began, searching for words, "I think we are very grateful to you. But we have problem."

Kel's heart pounded in his ears.

"The magistrate and his wife have contacted me. They are very grateful. We have not told them it was you who saved them. It is policy to never reveal identity of Hoplite operator for reason of safety. I can only tell them it was National Police who save them. Magistrate is powerful man, very popular. He insist on hero's recognition of my man who save his life. I tell him we appreciate but cannot do. So, you see my problem."

Kel tried to keep from showing the relief on his face. Of all the things he expected the general to say, that was not one of them.

"Especially, you are Republic operative. It would be hard to explain. So, I hope you can forgive me. We are in your debt, but we cannot make public recognition of your courage."

The general and Major Todalin looked visibly strained, as if telling Kel something truly dreadful, like his mother had died.

Kel couldn't keep it in any longer as he exhaled loudly. "Gentlemen, please believe me when I say that being publicly recognized is the last thing in the galaxy I hope ever to happen to me."

They sat longer, the general and the major now carrying the conversation forward.

"When my uncle spoke yesterday, you saw, yes? When he spoke, he made statement to whole world that threat is over. He and Conclave have made known to me this very simple thing: I will end the threat."

The large man looked strained.

"I have been commanded to do whatever is necessary to make ME disappear, and to do it now. I fear if we do not, what Conclave may do next will be bad time to everyone. And whatever happens then, I will be spectator from my estate. We have maybe a few weeks to finish this. I think we are close. Please, help us finish."

The Hoplites had effectively been tied up doing little more than protective detail and ground security work for the visiting Twelve and their families during the crisis. The investigators, however, had been hard at work. They had in fact made excellent progress in mapping out the organization of ME and had enough intelligence built from the forensic evidence of the last few days' attacks to guide them to new targets.

The plan was to start a new cycle of DARK ops tonight, and Kel was invited.

22

In addition to the Hoplites Kel sat with, another group of men were seated toward the rear of the small auditorium. They had protective vests on over their civilian dress clothes, and sat clustered, distinct from the operators. Kel thought he recognized one of the men, an investigator who'd accompanied the team on one of Kel's last operations with the team. It seemed the investigative cell had finally become integrated with the Hoplites' operations.

More Hoplites were filing into the front sections of the room, their hair shaggy and wearing full kit, rifles slung around their necks as they took seats. Colonel Graviakis stood with Gavros at the front, waiting for everyone to settle into place.

Kel scanned the dim room, noting a familiar face among the men of the investigative cell. Don. He was dressed casually, wearing his own protective gear, and whispering with the NP man to his left. After a moment, he sensed Kel's gaze and gave him a nod. Kel nodded back.

He had never before seen the intelligence officer in the presence of the National Police. Don told him he'd made some inroads thanks to Kel. Now he knew what he'd meant.

Jacee and Gavros. Don and the NP. Me. I was their way in. A picture was forming that too rapidly dissociated into broken fragments as the colonel began speaking, a holo of the target site appearing behind him.

They loaded onto dropships there at the compound. The sorties were crowded, operators jammed shoulder-to-shoulder in troop seats, others sitting on the deck of the craft. He imagined the other ships looked about the same. They were headed west to the city of Ithaca. The target was an estate with grounds laid out in a multi-family compound. They would not have their armored rescue vehicles, and Graviakis' plan was to land the four ships with assaulters directly within the grounds, each team assigned a building to secure. The fifth ship with the investigative cell and Gavros would remain on-station and airborne until the compound was secured.

The threat brief anticipated no resistance and the mission was simple: secure any suspects, render the compound safe for search by the investigative cell. "We are looking for intelligence connecting the residents to ME," was all Todalin said. Gavros remained silent.

Kel was hearing this all for the first time, as were the Hoplites. *We've only been hitting the small guys. This is a darned estate! Whoever these people are, they're movers and shakers, someone big in Meridian society. They have evidence they're supporting ME? No wonder this has been kept quiet.*

This time Kel was joined to the Hoplite command cell, his temporary gig as a team leader over. The assaulters cleared the ramp as soon as the bird touched down, Kel following the men out the tail of the aircraft. Across the grounds, other ships landed, sprouting their own armed men.

They followed their assault team into the large mansion in front of them, uniformed house staff in shock as the Hoplites laid hands on them, restraining and corralling them into the large common room.

The team leader reported the building cleared, and all occupants secured. Kel stayed quiet as other team leaders reported on their own targets. Soon the teams had searched the grounds and secured a perimeter. With no assigned role, Kel listened to the message traffic. The general and the intel cell were landing presently and ground vehicles from the local NP would be arriving soon to take custody of the captured suspects.

Outside, the last dropship landed, Gavros leading the way off the ramp as he was followed by members of the investigative team, Don in their midst. Gavros caught Kel's eye as he passed, winked, and continued in with the many followers. Kel fell in with them, noticing the difference in the altitude here as compared to Tiryns, the cool night air chilling him.

What will we find? he wondered. *Could it really end here?*

By morning, Kel had part of his answer. Gavros and the command group toured the mansion's rooms, noting the people in custody. Single families resided in several of the homes, the men separated from their families and brought to the main house.

Don moved from room to room, accompanied by two of the investigators. A small grav container moved with them to each stop. Kel joined the general as he followed Don and his group into one of the large rooms on the main floor, and there sat an older man in silk lounging clothes secured to a high-backed wood chair.

"Hello, Dimitrios," the general said as he walked toward the man, a Hoplite standing on either side of the chair. The man met Gavros' eyes.

"It's okay. You don't have to say anything. I know," Gavros said, quirking a smile as the restrained man looked away.

"Meester Don, you have what you need?" Gavros said.

"Yes, General. This won't take long."

Don moved forward with his two assistants. The grav case opened to reveal several small machines and data-pads of a sort Kel couldn't recognize by type or function. They looked vaguely medical. Kel had the sinking feeling he was about to witness something awful.

Instead, Don removed a small slate and placed it under the palm of the restrained man. A bright blue glow blinked and was gone, faster than the bound man could protest. Don put the slate on one of the devices in the grav container.

Kel caught Todalin's eye. *What's going on?* Kel asked, furrowing his brow.

The major gave the slightest shake of his head; he either didn't know or couldn't say.

Kel had learned in the Legion to hurry up and wait. Tonight, they had hurried; now he would wait.

He sat on a wall watching the sun rise as the investigators wrapped up their work. The colonel approached from one of the other buildings, Don with him, his assistants still in tow and their grav container with them. They paused at the entrance, shaded by the portico, and were immediately joined by Gavros and Todalin. Kel stayed where he was, listening as the colonel looked at Gavros and said only a single word.

"Kanellis."

Gavros nodded. "Epirus then."

"Yes, Gavros." The colonel issued over his comms, calling in the team leaders for a briefing by the colonel. They were returning to Tiryns.

Kel rode with the same assault team back to the capital. As the ramp opened, Kel realized they had not returned to the Hoplite compound but landed at the spaceport. As he walked down the ramp, he noted the NP air operations office and several official transport vehicles parked outside.

The dropships were all down now and deplaning the troops rapidly. Two of the Hoplites and several of the investigators stood with the high-value target, Dimitrios, dressed in his silk pajamas and restraints, staring at the ground. They escorted their prisoner to a windowless vehicle and drove off the flight line.

Kel joined the rest of the Hoplites as they gathered around Graviakis. Don and one of the investigators stood to one side speaking to Gavros and Todalin. Gavros in turn spoke to Todalin, nodding his head in Kel's direction before turning to join Don to ascend the ramp of the sleek black plane. Todalin smiled as he approached.

"Kel, Gavros has asked that you stay behind. We all appreciate what you've done, but it is best you don't accompany us for the next part of the mission."

It was a punch in the gut. "Can you tell me what's going on? Are you going to Epirus?" Kel had heard them mention Epirus earlier. It was an island continent in the southern hemisphere some distance the other side of the planet. He knew the Kanellis family was the predominate power broker there, the other name he had overheard the men disclose after Don's procedures. Todalin moved closer to Kel and lowered his voice so Kel had to strain to hear him over the noises of the airfield.

"Yes, that's the next target. Gavros suspects there may be things about to happen that is best the Republic not be intimately involved in."

Kel saw Gavros and Don ascend the stairs and disappear into the hop.

"You know who he is, right?" Kel asked, tilting his heads toward the intel-man as he passed through the aircraft hatch.

"Yes. Look, Gavros doesn't want there to be any blowback on you in case things go wrong, understand? Gavros is trying to protect you."

Kel wasn't sure he understood but was willing to accept what his friend was telling him.

"Sure. Okay. I'll see you when you get back."

Todalin nodded at Kel. "We can only take about half of the unit. We declared an emergency and borrowed one of the commercial lifts to get as many of us there as we could. Go back with the rest of the team. We'll talk soon. Promise."

Todalin extended his hand. "You got us a long way in a short time. We're all grateful. You're one of us. You know that, right? You've always got a home here."

Kel returned the man's strong handshake. "Thanks."

It felt to Kel like he was saying goodbye for the last time to his friend the major. He watched the men load onto the two planes and depart. Kel got into a truck with the rest of the Hoplites as they returned to their compound. Everyone was sullen and quiet during the ride. They all felt as he did; they were missing out on the action and jealous of their absent teammates still on the hunt, following the trail of intelligence developed in Ithaca only a few hours before.

Kel was unloading his kit into his vehicle when he got a bounce alert on his specs.

Report to my office as soon as
you can. Jacee.

Kel drove directly to the embassy and made his way through the layers of the maze that was the embassy until he reached the military-political section. Jacee was waiting for him at the reception area, her hands folded in front of her.

Had he gotten himself into trouble for some reason? He tried to keep his imagination under control and not think about the possible reasons for the summons. But Jacee wore a bright smile that put him at ease.

"Kel, you are a busy man, and don't you look great!"

Kel had learned she was a flirt. It made him chuckle.

"I know I look like I haven't slept in a while."

"Let's get some kaff and have a sit in my office."

Kel was hesitant. "Jacee, can we just sit down? I'm anxious to know why you called me."

She nodded as her smile turned into pursed lips. "Okay. Let's do that."

He followed her into the office, allowing her to hold the door for him as he found a chair and collapsed into it. He felt fatigued for the first time. He hated suspense. She closed the door and took the chair across from him, their knees almost touching.

"Kel, you're going home."

Kel sat upright. He wasn't due to leave for another four weeks.

"Home? Jacee, what have I..."

She leaned forward and patted his knee.

"You have done nothing wrong, let me assure you. In fact, I think your work here has been nothing short of extraordinary. I know this is unrated time for you, but my report to your command says more about you than I know you'd say about yourself. That should mean a lot for your career. I mean it—job well done, Legionnaire."

Kel shrank into his chair again, still confused.

"I've also updated the Planetary Security Council on the recent developments, and I have mentioned you by name in my report."

Kel started to protest. Identifying him by name as Dark Ops was not something beneficial. It could jeopardize his ability to function if his name was compromised through a leak in official senate proceedings.

"I know your concern. You're a covert operator. Don't worry. The council already knows who you are."

Kel shrugged. He still didn't understand what was happening to him.

"Jacee, if I haven't done anything wrong, then why am I going home early?"

Jacee smiled at him as though he was a child who'd just asked his mother where the sun went at night. He felt even more so as she answered his question.

"Sweetie, your work here is done, and I've got a special request from someone who thinks highly of you. Gavros asks that you accompany his daughter off-planet and see her on her way to Liberinthine."

She took her link out of her pocket and bounced something to Kel.

"That is a first-class ticket on the commercial liner, the *Antarean Princess*, which hits orbit tomorrow and will depart for Orion Station in three days. Gavros has asked that you get her there on your way to Victrix."

Kel frowned. "My mission is being terminated a month early because Gavros needs a babysitter for his daughter?"

Jacee sighed. "No. Look, there are developments I can't talk about right now. Let's just say getting you away from Meridian is beneficial and the timing to help Gavros is fortuitous. Look, Kel... it's Gavros who has requested we get you off the planet now."

Kel paused. "Gavros... requested?" *I thought Gavros liked me.* His confusion was worsened rather than abated by her revelation.

Jacee looked weary. "Sweetheart. Listen to what I'm saying. Gavros trusts you. The reason we are where we are now is because of that. Gavros wants you off the planet. He also trusts you to watch over his daughter. Accept that. Maybe later it will be clear to you." She stood and moved to the door to open it.

He was being dismissed. He rose and moved to the door. As he did so, Jacee held her arms open to him, and he embraced her. She gave him a crushing hug that surprised Kel.

"You're one of the good ones, Kel. I loved a legionnaire once more than anyone in the world." Tears welled in her eyes. "Don't let them... don't let Dark Ops... don't let them change you."

Kel walked off the floor and back to the elevators feeling less anxious, but just as confused as when he had entered her office.

He let his housemates and friends at the embassy know he was leaving prematurely. He started packing and spent time getting the embassy arms room in order, returning his S-5, the ammo, and other devices he had not yet used and got them cleared off his account by Bell.

"Bounce me a receipt on that, man. I can't have sustainment cell tracking me down in a month, saying you're billing me for equipment I never turned in to the embassy." Bell laughed. "We're getting Marines, you hear that? Better late than never, I guess."

Bell had been a good friend and was good at his job. Kel told him as much as he shook his hand for the last time.

Eirene was tearful on the news of Kel's imminent departure. Kel gave her a big hug every morning and night his last few days at the palace. He would miss her, too.

He did not want to leave without saying goodbye to his Hoplite friends. He'd worked as closely with them as his own kill team. More so than the end of most planetary security missions, he'd feel their absence. He'd bounced Todalin the last two days but received no response. Finally, on the day before his departure, a message came.

Sorry we can't get together.
Mission tempo high. Will explain
as promised when I can. T.

He'd spent time weekly composing what would be his after-action report. Now he stared at the blank section under the heading "Analysis and Recommendations," trying to make sense of his last week. He found himself unable to come to a conclusion about the ultimate effect he'd had on stabilizing the situation on Meridian. Kel headed into the embassy a last time. He bypassed everyone he'd already said goodbye to and went directly to the office of the man he hoped could shed light on this situation: Don.

The intel-man answered the chime almost immediately.

"Hey, Kel, glad you came by. Come in."

Kel followed the man into the windowless office and sat without being invited. Don closed the entrance and then went to his desk to activate the security field as he'd done many times before.

Kel could feel the tension between them, and frankly... he didn't mind it.

"Don, I didn't want to leave without saying goodbye, and also wanted to give you my after-action report."

Kel bounced the document and put his link away.

"I'm a little weak on my results and recommendations section. Can you help me?"

Don smiled at Kel without pulling up the report on his own link.

"What's on your mind, Kel?"

"I'm tired of being in the dark." Kel let it all out. "What was the purpose of the last hit in Ithaca? What happened when you went to Epirus? What does the Kanellis family have to do with anything?"

Don nodded silently, looking at a point in space in front of him, not meeting Kel's eyes.

"You don't want much, do you, Leej?"

Kel was asking for Don's help to fill in the hole that was the last week out of five months of his life spent on Meridian. He was hoping for some accommodation, but found he was losing his cool.

"I think you owe me something, Don. I was there from the beginning. Tell me you would be where you are now without me." It was against Kel's nature to make a case for his own accomplishments. In this instance, he knew what he was saying was true.

"Not to mention, I think I've helped you with more than just the ME mystery," Kel said, the Symopolous operation still heavy on his conscience.

Don appeared unperturbed, then shrugged.

"Okay. I'll give you that. You ask a question, and if I can answer it, I will. Shoot."

Kel thought. Now he wasn't sure where to begin, but one thing stood out to him.

"What was with the medical exams on the hit in Ithaca? What were you doing?"

Don narrowed his eyes and fought back a slight smile.

"You've been read-in to quantum bio-energetic signatures?"

He shrugged. Kel had not been officially read-in, but he knew a little bit about the theory. It was a topic of discussion when the subject of fraud or financial malfeasance came up. Supposedly, if you lied on your itemized expense forms after a mission, the treasury investigators could tell where you spent misused funds by traces of your distinct personal energy field betraying your movement and habits associated with the crime. While there certainly were some mysterious tools in the toolbox of the House of Reason's financial enforcers, Kel doubted the existence of such hocus-pocus.

"When you started having success with Gavros and his people, I was able to build on your success. Again, thanks for that. I was able to make the case that we had methods to assist in their analysis. The packet Gavros gave you with all the NP intel was the first step in building that bridge. You know he intended that to get to me, right?

"After you gained more of their confidence with your Dark Ops magic, they also brought me into their confidence and gave me access to the detained suspects and forensics you all had gotten. I was able to start building a database—DNA, bio-sigs, quantum fingerprinting, the works."

Kel was beginning to follow.

"The bio-signatures and the like by themselves don't tell you who did what. But in connection to the overt patterns of the perpetrator's activities, they can help to establish a lot of other relationships. When it all came together, it proved our early hypothesis correct."

Kel noticed he'd said "our."

"Once the link analysis was complete to include all the quantum-bio data, the one group it identified as having the most connections to the acts and the greatest distance from victims was the Kanellis family. That's why Kanellis, and that's why Epirus."

Kel stayed silent as he considered this.

"Okay. That makes sense and I'm glad you were able to help. So, what's happened on Epirus and what is Gavros doing now?"

Don smiled. "I told you I'd answer what I could."

These questions Don was not going to answer.

"Do you know why Gavros wants me gone?"

Don remained silent. That told Kel that Don knew something, but he wasn't going to answer that either.

"Well, I guess we're through then." Kel stood and extended his hand toward the spy-master. "It was nice working with you, Don. A real education."

Don took his hand. "I wanted to tell you. This is my last hurrah. I'm retiring."

"That's great news. I'd say you've earned it. Where are you headed?"

"Oh, I'm not going somewhere to head into senescence; I'm staying right here. Stefania and I are getting married. I wish you were going to be here; you'd be high on the guest list. I mean that."

Kel shook the man's hand again.

"Don, that's great news. Congratulations. You've got a great girl there. What are you going to do with yourself, stay home and raise the babies while she goes to medical school?"

Don shook his head. "No. It turns out I'm joining a business firm that is poised to take advantage of the soon-to-be booming market for export goods from Meridian. I'm joining George at the chandlery."

"You're joining Symopolous and Sons? The ship chandlers?" he repeated back, trying to hide his disbelief.

"Yes. We're poised to make a killing. Remember what I told you once, Kel? There's more to life than duty. Take it from me. Find a nice girl and build a life for yourself. Don't wait until you're as old as I am."

Kel could only stare at the man, speechless.

"Hey, you're a good man. The best. If you ever grow up and leave the Legion, Symopolous and Sons could use a dependable man like you. The offer stands in perpetuity. Think about it."

Kel reflexively smiled and said his final goodbye. He didn't remember what he said or how he'd phrased his departing pleasantries. The last thing he heard as he left Don's sanctum was:

"Take care of yourself, dark operator."

When he was behind the controls of his speeder, heading back to the palace for his last night, he thought about what he'd learned.

Don used me to help his mercenaries kill the men robbing his future business partner, a front for Republic Intelligence. Then we erased the crime scene. Was he preserving a covert operation or protecting his future interests? Or both?

Kel knew he would ponder that question for a long time.

Pen took him to the spaceport the next morning, reversing the circumstances of their first acquaintanceship a handful of months before. Kel took one last look around Meridian before walking into the commercial terminal to start his return to Victrix. He knew there were things about Meridian and the people he'd come to appreciate that he'd miss.

He doubted he'd miss being used like a sharp instrument by the pols and spies.

He checked in under his Tamford Nielsen alias and soon found the young Miss Kyrgiakos at the boarding station, her dark features and brow looking much like Gavros. She seemed to recognize Kel as he neared.

"You're Father's friend!" she said in perfect Standard, making Kel miss the general already. He heard the man's voice in his head, using broken Standard in the amusing ways he did. He'd caught himself thinking in Gavros' speech before. There was no one like him, Gavros once told him. He was right.

"He said you'd help me find my way once we got to Orion Station. He's been so busy lately, I barely got to see him at all before I left. I've never been anywhere off Meridian before. Is it nice on the station? I guess I'll only be there for a night. I hope I get to see the whole thing. What's Liberinthine like? Can you tell how excited I am by how much I'm talking? I tend to do that. I'm so glad I'm going to have company for the trip. How do you know my father? He said you worked at the Republic embassy, is that so?"

Kel found he didn't have to worry about responding. She asked question after question, starting the next before Kel had begun answering her last. They made the lift to the cruise liner and Kel and the young lady were escorted to their first-class cabins. They were luxury accommodations, not at all like the cramped cabin he had occupied with the crew of the *Callie*. He'd fantasized that he would find a way to coordinate a ride back to the midcore with the Yomiuris, that maybe the timing would work and they'd be heading to Meridian on one of their new round trips. He was sad that didn't happen. He'd gladly trade his first-class suite for the small stateroom on the *Callie* to be with the family again. He'd begun to think of them as more than acquaintances.

It was a five-day journey to Orion Station. Kel would meet his young companion for meals, but after the first day was relieved to see she had found friends her own age to associate with, spending her time in the lounges and promenades with a trio of young ladies from Meridian. One of them was a distant cousin, also headed to Liberinthine for schooling. Kel enjoyed watching them together, overhearing their conversations about subjects Kel couldn't fathom the importance or meaning of.

Gavros' daughter was happy and starting the adventure of her life. She seemed to be without fear or concern. Kel could never remember feeling that way. Always, he worried about being seen as capable, and feeling honorable in all his actions. The young lady seemed unconcerned with how others perceived her and just enjoyed life as it came at her. Kel admired that, in a way.

He spent the rest of his time in his cabin, refining his report and exercising. Both were helping him regain a sense of balance and to put a conclusion to his mission on Meridian. By the time of their arrival at Orion Station, he felt at peace. Reviewing the report again, he admitted to himself he'd accomplished a lot in a short period of time. In fact, it seemed the crisis there might be ending.

His mind swirled with emotions. Impatience to re-unite with his team, excitement, optimism. Everyone but Tem would be there; Tem would likely have anoth-er month or so in the six-month PS mission cycle of his own assignment. He wanted to swap stories with his best buddy. He doubted Tem would have anything that would compare to Kel's memories of luxurious living and travel. He couldn't wait to rub Tem's nose in it. Kel had taken ho-los of everything he could and saved images and short vids of some of his experiences, like the surreal dining at Socrates' Garden. He could imagine Tem's gaping ex-pression viewing that one.

He escorted his young companion to her hotel near the commercial space line that would carry her the rest of the way to Liberinthine the next morning. She hugged Kel and thanked him.

"When you message your father, please send him my best," he said as they parted, telling her to bounce him if there was any issue with her departure. Kel would be on the station for another week awaiting his ship to take him to Victrix's orbit.

In the military quarter of the station, Kel checked in at the navy base to see if there was availability of transient quarters until his ride on the frigate *Lepanto* would occur. Kel hoped there would be no issue that kept the ship in station for long. He was patient by nature and training, but without a mission, he knew he would be feeling antsy un-til his journey was actually underway.

He wasn't a diplomat. He was a legionnaire. The soon-er he could resume the military way of life, the better.

He'd hardly touched any of the mission funds. Virtually all his living expenses had been paid by the Ex-Planetary mission of the embassy. He would have an uncomplicated travel voucher to itemize on his return and would likely get to keep the funds of his daily living rate. Paying into the house meal fund for Eirene to feed them was his main expense, and that was a fraction of what he had been allotted for his meals. He stood to make several thousand credits on top of the paychecks he'd banked while he was on Meridian. Maybe there was a new rifle in his future? The numbers in his bank account were already being drained in his imagination.

He stayed in civilian clothes and on his first day found a barber to shave his head. He wasn't going to bother with a bio-cosmetic recoloration of his hair; he'd let it resume its natural color as it grew back. He shaved his beard but kept a mustache. It seemed a small vanity.

The next day he wandered off the base to enjoy the sights of the concourse and soon found himself in a bar with holos running over all the tables and booths, and ordered a sandwich and a beer. He'd worked out hard that morning and thought he deserved a break in his dietary routine to celebrate.

He sat by himself awaiting his food as he swiped through the programs on the holo, when he came across a feed from the SNN. The sound was muted, but what caught his eye was a picture of the Pa'artenon and the large letters floating behind the talking head of the announcer—

Government coup on edge
world Meridian...

Kel ran his hand in the air over the volume bar to hear what the announcer was saying.

"A period of major unrest on Planet Meridian has been capped this past week by a coup removing its hereditary governing council. This coup was led by a man some are calling the most powerful individual on the planet, the head of their police force, General Gavros Kyrgiakos."

Kel froze.

"We have a report sent earlier this week by reporter Nesta Sedaren, still on Meridian as we speak."

The shot from the studio gave way to a reporter on location outside the NP headquarters' front gate.

"Meridian. An idyllic planet on the galaxy's edge. A place locked in time and tradition for humanity's rediscovery. A burgeoning trading partner with the Republic. Also, a world living under the despotism of a ruling class, a hereditary council composed of twelve families, the descendants of the original colonists who've ruled the planet with an iron fist since its inception."

The reporter moved slightly, allowing the holo to show a platoon of NP recruits marching past the headquarters.

"But for the past year, a popular uprising known as Meridian Eleftheria has waged a campaign of terror and disruption across the planet in protest of the despotism of the political system and repression of the Meridian peoples.

"We've covered the conflict and the response of the government forces to the crisis. After the events of the Founders Day attacks in the capital of Tiryns, the government reported the capture and arrests of dozens of subversives that culminated in a raid on the stronghold of the Kanellis family, one of the ruling families.

"The Conclave traditionally has controlled the press on the planet, and has allowed little in the way of independent reporting by off-world newscasters. The government today announced the arrest of the Kanellis family leaders and the indictments against the family for conspiracy to support terrorism and the gravest charge—treason against the Domestic Conclave."

The report transitioned to Gavros' uncle behind a podium at the Pa'artenon.

"We are shocked and saddened by this grave act of treason against the people of Meridian, and we promise a return to order. If found guilty under our laws, the terrorists and their families will be punished."

The reporter returned.

"Just yesterday the Domestic Conclave issued the official accusation against one of the members of the twelve families as the perpetrators of the crisis that had almost consumed Meridian, promising a return to normalcy.

"However, sometime during the night, this man," a picture of Gavros filled the screen, "the general of the largest security force on Meridian, the so-called National Police, Gavros Kyrgiakos, took control of the government in a bloodless coup and has named himself protector of Meridian."

Gavros appeared outside of the Pa'artenon. Kel strained to see, wishing for a wide-angle holo, but could see Hoplites in the background, their faces covered under their protective gear. Todalin and Graviakis were standing to either side of Gavros in the background.

"The abuses of the Domestic Conclave and the twelve families is at an end. The people of Meridian deserve justice. I promise a return to our true traditions, to a representative government, and a better life for all Meridian with equal justice under the law. Be patient as we work to build a better future for our world and our children."

The speech sounded polished and practiced, with little of his normally broken Standard.

The reporter continued.

"What remains to be seen is what these promises will mean from a man who has seized power by the use of the state security apparatus, and whether they will use their powers against the people to enforce this new vision for the world. Reporting from the galaxy's edge on Meridian..."

He looked down to notice his server had brought his food. But he was no longer hungry. He waved his link over the reader to pay for his meal, gathered it up and left, slipping into the crowds filling the concourse outside, no destination in mind.

The trip back to Victrix was slow and numbing. Kel took his meals in his stateroom, invoking his option of isolation as a DO operative. The trip took days and he filled the time furiously exercising in his quarters until exhaustion drove him to a fatigue-filled sleep.

They established orbit around Victrix. It took a half a day for a dropship to be prepared to take him to the spaceport near the secretive DO compound. He had no sooner gotten secured for the trip into the atmosphere when an alert appeared in his specs. The message was dated a week before. It had likely followed him from Orion Station and caught up to him in the hours since they had left hyperspace. It did not contain a holo, only text.

The dropship lifted out of the frigate bay, and Kel figured he had at least thirty minutes to kill. He opened the message from the unidentified sender.

*Kel, I am sure you have
heard of the events that have
transpired on Meridian since
your departure. I promised
I would contact you when
I could. This is the first
opportunity I have had to do
so.*

The message was from Major Todalin.

*Gavros was concerned about your well-being and
wanted to protect you. We identified the link between
ME and the Kanellis family on the Ithaca mission.
We had suspicions for several months but Gavros
could not act against one of the families until he
had proof. Your assistance allowed us to get the
information we needed, and the cooperation of
the Republic Intelligence officer and his technology
confirmed it.
One of Gavros' first concerns was for your safety. He
feared if we had to move forward to overthrow the
DC and you were still accompanying us, that there
would be negative repercussions for you with your
House of Reason. As it turned out, he was right. The
DC responded to the treachery of the Kanellis clan by
ordering a secret trial and executing dozens of the
family. We wanted no part in that, even though the
evidence supports their guilt and complicity in the
terrible crimes of the past year.
We are working closely with the Republic embassy to
ensure the support and assistance of the Republic,
but with or without the support of the House of
Reason, Gavros and his supporters have committed*

*to change on our world. That meant ending the rule of
the Twelve Families.*

*Gavros has taken the temporary title of Protector of
Meridian. He has promoted Graviakis to General of the
National Police. I have been promoted and am returning
to command the Hoplites.*

*Gavros is grateful to you, Kel. We all are. Gavros has
made you a Knight of the Order of Achilles. You have
the full rights of a citizen of Meridian. We all meant
what we said. You are one of us. There is a place for
you among us today if you desire. Whatever path you
take, remember that you are our brother.*

—Todalin

Kel read the message several times. There was an
attached document in the indecipherable Meridian language. It had the appearance of something ancient, from
a holo-action-drama set in another time. A rough, angu-
lar script filled the face of it. The only words he could read
were his full name "Kelkavan Turner" contained in the first
two lines of the many that followed. A holographic gold
seal sat at the bottom.

The flight ended and Kel found himself squinting in
the bright sun reflected off the spaceport duracrete as
he waited the microsecond for his specs to darken. He
gathered his gear and grav container and followed the
ground marshal off the flight line and through the small
military customs checkpoint, only to be waved through
without delay.

He found an autonomous sled waiting outside, loaded
his things, and directing it to take him to his team room. It
was noon. All he wanted to do was to be in his gear cage
surrounded by his teammates. He needed that now more
than anything he could think of.

Kel made his way to the door, the familiar "3" in bold face above it. Kel had sent no word ahead that he had returned. He thought someone would be in the team room at this time of day. He placed his hand on the plate, his bio-signature recognized, and the door slid aside to reveal Bigg, Poul, and Captain Yost sitting in a small circle. Their shocked looks of surprise made him grin.

I'm finally home, he thought, relief flooding through him.

Everyone leapt to their feet, shook his hand, and crushed him with hugs. He gave the same back. But then he noticed no one was smiling. Poul's eyes were puffy and red. Dread grew in the pit of his stomach. Somehow, he knew what they were about to tell him.

"Bigg, what is it? Is it... Tem?"

Bigg nodded. "He's gone, Kel."

FLASHBACK

I Don't Believe in Destiny,
but I Do Believe in Friendship
Antione

I'm standing at the panel with TA as we reach down to lift out the frail figure hugging the floor, trying to find air. We'd breached the tunnel system and flooded it with gas. She hadn't planned on that. We heard the sound of her gagging and pried open the panel concealing the last room. It was a small chamber with a bed and fresher. The old woman didn't look as regal as the jade and gold gown she wore as she sputtered and coughed, thick phlegm running out of her nose and mouth. We had to get her to the surface and get an oxygen hood on her before she died.

We step out into the daylight, carrying her between us as hands reach out to relieve us of our package. The Repub medics put her on a gravstretcher and start to work. An SNN reporter is there with specs running. A green clad basic colonel walks over and steps in front of him blocking his view. TA grabs me and we fade into the green crowd and out of the compound, where the rest of the team waits.

Repubs are everywhere, dismounted and in mechs roving over the landscape. A dozen Talons are parked on the ground and more circle above. We weave our way on a path to where an individual in black armor waits by a Talon with a much larger armored man. Papa Bear and

Zero join them as the rest of us get on the Talon. Yamazaki and D'antonio are there waiting in the pax compartment.

Papa Bear and Zero walk up the ramp and the tailgate closes as we lift. I know the cool guys are talking to each other on their own channel, but I'm not included. "Was that the head honcho? The big whale?" Trumbull asks me. "Seems that way," I reply, still kind of in shock.

"So, what," Pabon asks. "Does that mean the campaign is over?"

"Not by a long shot," TA interjects. He's monitoring our squad channel. Again. "A lot more people have to die first. But this may help. At least, we can take a little break."

Papa Bear's laugh fills my ears. "Colonel and Nail say we get some down time. I could use it, I don't know about you youngsters." Youngsters? I wonder how much older Papa Bear is than me. I've never considered him as old. The man amazes me.

I'm shaking the synthsilks I tried to get the filth out of in the sonic fresher when Papa Bear and TA walk into our squad area. The rest of the guys are passed out on their cots. "Turner. Let's talk," Papa Bear tells me. I slide the skins on and join them. They walk me over to where the team racks out and TA pulls up a floaty for me to rest on as he and Papa Bear take their own.

"We're moving on," Papa Bear says. "We have to kick you and your squad back to recon. Get us back the gear we loaned you and there'll be a Talon to take you to your unit this afternoon." He stands and extends his hand. I do the same. It's a shock. I'm crushed. Deflated. I knew this couldn't last forever, but I didn't think today would my last day with the cool guys. It must show. Papa Bear shakes my hand vigorously and releases my paw from his huge mitt to thump me on the chest as his guffaw fills the hangar.

"Hey, don't look so down. You did a great job. Me and the whole team appreciate it. TA wants to talk to you about a few things. Be seeing you. Stay safe, Turner." With that, he walks away. I'm numb where he thumped me. It's how I feel inside, too.

"Sit down, Turner." TA's still here. I ease the floaty under me and it pushes back as I relax onto it. "What I'm about to say to you is very important. Confidential. Understand?" I nod and frown at the same time. *What could he be getting ready to lay on me now?* I expect it'll be more of the same about how everything I've done is secret and I can't ever talk about it, along with the inevitable threats. I'm sure.

"I can't tell you when, but you're going to be getting a bounce and some orders. It ain't gonna be next week, I can tell you that. Might take a year. But you're going to be getting an invitation to a sit down." *A "sit down"? I guess he means a meeting. An interview?* My heart races. I think I know what he's saying.

"We all agree. You're the kind of guy we want with us." Now I feel the butterflies. This can't be for real.

"In the meantime, keep learning. Keep working. Don't stop trying to be the best leader you can to your men." He pauses but I remain silent, transfixed on what he's telling me. "Our unit, well, it ain't for everyone. You may decide not to stay. That'll be up to you. But we all think you deserve the chance." Now he stands and extends his hand to me. "By the way, my friends call me Tem."

I shake his hand as the electricity races through my body. "Mine call me Kel."

"See you soon, Kel."

I know he means it.

23

The ceremony was the next day. A few of the other teams were on Victrix to participate; many more were elsewhere, serving the Republic.

They wore their dress uniforms. This was the only time they wore a uniform of any type, when they had to memorialize one of their fallen. From his years in DO, the Legion dress blacks now carried the connotation of death and sadness; the pride of the accomplishments displayed on his chest a remote memory.

The colonel stood at the podium, a holo of Tem in the background. Images of Tem and the team from missions across the galaxy danced around the central still of his face, showing him at work and at play with the team. A holo of the team and their I-squared after the last raid on Kylar hovered for several seconds, Kel marveling at the team's wide smiles after the last hit on the donks. It had been a great day. One of the best.

The colonel then began to speak.

"I call the roll of Team Three."

"Captain Braley Yost."

Braley rose to stand at attention. "Here."

"Team Sergeant Matthew Biggetti."

Bigg rose as well. "Here."

"Sergeant Poul Radd."

Poul rose. "Here."

"Sergeant Kelkavan Turner."

Kel took his turn to stand. "Here." Kel knew what was coming next and took deep breaths as he braced himself.

"Sergeant Temostecles Armsmear."

"Sergeant Temostecles Armsmear."

"Sergeant Temostecles Armsmear."

After the third unanswered call, large, hot tears rolled down Kel's face. He remained at attention.

"A brother has gone ahead of us to prepare the way for his Legion comrades, never to be forgotten," the colonel said. "Until the glorious day his kill team shall be reunited for all eternity."

Kel made his way to Bigg's house. He'd visited rarely, always wanting to respect Bigg's time with his wife. The team was always deployed, and it seemed wrong to interfere with what precious little time they had together as a couple, especially when he got to see Bigg almost every day.

The walk was lined with beautiful tropical flowers and native plants, trimmed and manicured by Mrs. Biggetti. Kel knocked on the door of the small house before entering. Inside he heard his friends, collected together to celebrate Tem.

He walked in to see that most everyone had changed into civilian clothes, the exception being the colonel, who was making the rounds and shaking hands with the operators. Poul stood on the back deck with a drink in his hand, alone. Kel headed over to him, avoiding words with his other DO comrades. He felt morose. Brittle.

He stood next to Poul, staring out at the small backyard and carefully sculpted topiaries. Bigg, he knew, was not around enough to be the one to maintain such a garden.

After a few minutes of silence Kel broke their reverie.

"I still don't understand what happened to Tem."

"There's not much to understand," Poul answered. "It was the kelhorned zhee."

"But, how did it happen?"

"What do you mean, how did it happen?" Poul said, exasperation in his voice. "Anywhere there's zhee, there's going to be dead humans, or Kylar, or koobs. Hell, they'll probably start waging a holy war on microbes who don't convert. They're a plague on the galaxy. That's what happened."

"I know. What I mean was, where was he? What were the circumstances?"

Poul shrugged. "We only found out the morning before you got back. There's not a lot of detail yet. It just happened a week ago. We've gotta wait until we get more info. Not even Bigg had more for us. If someone knew more, they'd tell us."

Poul turned toward him. "I'm sorry, man. I didn't mean to snap at you. I know how tight you guys were. I'm just..."

Kel put his hand on the large man's shoulder. "It's all good. I know. We're going to make it right."

"KTF."

"You know it. KTF."

Later that afternoon as the other operators paid their respects to the members of Kill Team Three, Bigg motioned Kel to follow him to the second floor where the team sergeant opened the door to a small study. A desk was positioned underneath a small window, and a couch and large leather chair filled the rest of the room. Every square centimeter of wall was covered with holo-stills and plaques from Bigg's many Legion assignments and destinations. Images of all the alien races and human worlds on the edge that Bigg had served.

Kel knew that Bigg had been in the Legion for decades. Everyone in DO treated Bigg like he was the ultimate legionnaire. He'd seen the colonel stand to greet Bigg whenever they were in the same room, and everyone in Dark Ops listened when he spoke. Someone had told Kel once, "There's two kinds of people: those who Bigg knows and those who don't matter."

Mrs. Biggetti came in behind them and placed glasses of iced kaff in each of their hands. She bent to kiss her husband on the cheek and brushed Kel's shoulder with her hand as she left, closing the door behind her.

"Tough day, Kel, huh?"

Kel nodded. "Yeah. A real kick in the teeth."

"I'm sorry I haven't had the chance to check up on you. Having to get everything together so quickly for Tem's memorial has been tough. I'm glad you were here. It would've been rougher without you. Thought it'd be another month before you'd be back, though. Everything all right?"

Kel couldn't hold back. He told him everything. He told Bigg every step he'd taken and what had happened. How he'd been used by Don and Republic Intel. About his relationship with the Yomiuri family, how he'd begun to think about a life outside the Legion for the first time, and about being made a knight and offered a place on Meridian.

He talked until the evening sun changed the colors within the room, the light casting its last rays on the wall behind Bigg. For the first time Kel could focus on one of the plaques on display there, lost in the noise of the many mementos and images.

Kel moved closer to inspect the keepsake in the fading light. Plaques commemorating an operator or kill team's time with a unit, be it indig or I-squared, was the norm. It was a military tradition that spanned almost all cultures and races.

On the large wooden plaque was mounted a zhee kankari. All forty centimeters of it, gleaming silver steel with curved razor edge. Underneath it was a small plate inscribed in Standard:

> *In acknowledgment of your*
> *assistance, from the faithful of the*
> *Guardians of the Gran Pasha.*
> *Eternal damnation to the Unclean.*

Kel spun around. "Bigg, you trained the filthy zhee!" he shouted, his tone accusing. He couldn't help it.

Bigg nodded. "Twenty years ago, the zhee were a potential ally."

Kel plopped back onto the couch. He couldn't understand this.

"The zhee are monsters. They killed Tem. What are we doing?" he asked to no one.

Bigg took a deep breath.

"Today's enemies are tomorrow's friends and vice versa. You know that. That's how it's always been."

Kel looked up at his hero.

"We are the foot soldiers of the House of Reason and their galactic games," Bigg continued. "You've been put through the wringer by the spies and the pols and now you've gotten a punch in the gut because your brother got killed by the zhee. I understand. Sometimes I forget, but there was a time when I could have taken a different path, out of the Legion, out of Dark Ops, and forged a normal life. But I met Marisol. She didn't mind the life of a DO operator's wife. I didn't feel I had to give up the Legion to have more in my life. You're at the age when guys realize there could be a life for them outside the Legion."

Bigg understood. Those thoughts about his purpose in life had been filling him with doubt since he reconnected with the Yomiuris. The end of the Meridian mission and now Tem's death had just made those longings come to the forefront even more.

"Son, all I can tell you is this: you can love the Legion, but the Legion will never love you back. We do what we do because it is our calling, and we do it for each other. Whatever you decide, you have my support."

Kel walked back to his quarters in the last light. He left the room dark as he crawled into bed. There was so much to think about. He suddenly remembered something his father had told him the night before he had shipped out to the Legion as a youth of seventeen, so many years before: "Don't quit today. Quit tomorrow. Then, tell yourself—Just get through today, you can quit tomorrow."

He thought about his best friend Tem, dying alone without another legionnaire or even a human to help him. He thought about the last five months of his life and what he'd seen and who he'd met.

He thought about vigilante miners, ship captain's daughters, and middle-aged women who cared how well he ate. He thought about watching brave men he barely knew but held a bond with walk into harm's way time and time again to do what was right. He thought about politicians and spies and their conniving ways, and he thought about Gavros, and Bigg.

Finally, Kel slept. He would awake the next day rested but would not remember any of his dreams from the night before. The last thing he remembered as he drifted .

off was hearing the waves crashing against the cliffs of Pthalo, a world he didn't consider home anymore.

THE END

Kel Tuner will be back in book two of the Galaxy's Edge: Dark Operator series. To find out when it releases, subscribe to the Galaxy's Edge Newsletter at www.InTheLegion.com

ABOUT THE AUTHORS

DOC SPEARS is a veteran of the United States Army.

JASON ANSPACH & NICK COLE are the co-creators of Galaxy's edge. You can find out more about them and Galaxy's Edge by visiting www.GalaxysEdge.us or by joining the Galaxy's Edge Fan Club on Facebook.

HONOR ROLL

Galaxy's Edge would like to acknowledge and give its sincere thanks to those who supported the creation of *Dark Operator* by subscribing to become a Galaxy's Edge Insider at www.GalaxysEdge.us.

Artis Aboltins

Guido Abreu

Garion Adkins

Elias Aguilar

Bill Allen

Tony Alvarez

Galen Anderson

Jarad Anderson

Robert Anspach

Jonathan Auerbach

Fritz Ausman

Sean Averill

Nicholas Avila

Matthew Bagwell

Marvin Bailey

Kevin Bangert

John Barber

Logan Barker

Robert Battles

Eric Batzdorfer

John Baudoin

Steven Beaulieu

Antonio Becerra

Mike Beeker

Randall Beem

Matt Beers

John Bell

Daniel Bendele

Edward Benson

David Bernatski

Trevor Blasius

WJ Blood

Rodney Bonner

Thomas Seth Bouchard

Brandon Bowles

Alex Bowling

Ernest Brant	Thomas Cutler
Geoff Brisco	Alister Davidson
Raymond Brooks	Peter Davies
James Brown	Walter Davila
Jeremy Bruzdzinski	Ivy Davis
Marion Buehring	Nathan Davis
Matthew Buzek	Ron Deage
Daniel Cadwell	Tod Delaricheliere
Charles Calvey	Ryan Denniston
Van Cammack	Douglas Deuel
Chris Campbell	Isaac Diamond
Zachary Cantwell	Christopher DiNote
Brian Cave	Matthew Dippel
Shawn Cavitt	Ellis Dobbins
David Chor	Ray Duck
Tyrone Chow	Cami Dutton
Jonathan Clews	Virgil Dwyer
Beau Clifton	William Ely
Alex Collins-Gauweiler	Stephane Escrig
Jerry Conard	Steven Feily
Steve Condrey	Adolfo Fernandez
Michael Conn	Ashley Finnigan
James Connolly	Kath Flohrs
James Conyers	Jeremiah Flores
Jonathan Copley	Steve Forrester
Robert Cosler	Skyla Forster
Ryan Coulston	Timothy Foster
Andrew Craig	Bryant Fox
Adam Craig	Mark Franceschini
Phil Culpepper	David Gaither
Ben Curcio	Christopher Gallo

Richard Gallo	Joshua Hopkins
Kyle Gannon	Tyson Hopkins
Michael Gardner	Ian House
Nick Gerlach	Ken Houseal
John Giorgis	Nathan Housley
Justin Godfrey	Jeff Howard
Luis Gomez	Nicholas Howser
Brian Graham	Mike Hull
Gordon Green	Donald Humpal
Shawn Greene	Bradley Huntoon
Erica Grenada	Wendy Jacobson
Preston Groogan	Paul Jarman
Brandon Handy	James Jeffers
Erik Hansen	Tedman Jess
Greg Hanson	Eric Jett
Adam Hargest	James Johnson
Ian Harper	Randolph Johnson
Jason Harris	Scott Johnson
Jordan Harris	Tyler Jones
Revan Harris	John Josendale
Matthew Hartmann	Wyatt Justice
Adam Hartswick	Ron Karroll
Ronald Haulman	Cody Keaton
Joshua Hayes	Noah Kelly
Richard Heard	Caleb Kenner
Colin Heavens	Daniel Kimm
Jason Henderson	Zachary Kinsman
Jason Henderson	Rhet Klaahsen
Kyle Hetzer	Jesse Klein
Aaron Holden	William Knapp
Clint Holmes	Marc Knapp

Travis Knight	Mark Maurice
Ethan Koska	Simon Mayeski
Evan Kowalski	Kyle McCarley
Byl Kravetz	Quinn McCusker
Brian Lambert	Alan McDonald
Clay Lambert	Caleb McDonald
Jeremy Lambert	Hans McIlveen
Andrew Langler	Rachel McIntosh
Dave Lawrence	Jason McMarrow
Alexander Le	Joshua McMaster
Paul Lizer	Colin McPherson
Richard Long	Christopher Menkhaus
Oliver Longchamps	Jim Mern
Joseph Lopez	Robert Mertz
Charles Lower	Pete Micale
Steven Ludtke	Mike Mieszcak
Brooke Lyons	Ted Milker
John M	Mitchell Moore
Richard Maier	William Morris
Ryan Mallet	Alex Morstadt
Brian Mansur	Nicholas Mukanos
Robert Marchi	Vinesh Narayan
Jacob Margheim	Bennett Nickels
Deven Marincovich	Trevor Nielsen
Cory Marko	Andrew Niesent
Lucas Martin	Sean Noble
Pawel Martin	Greg Nugent
Trevor Martin	Christina Nymeyer
Phillip Martinez	Grant Odom
Joshua Martinez	Colin O'neill
Tao Mason	Ryan O'neill

Tyler Ornelas	Jaysn Schaener
James Owens	Landon Schaule
David Parker	Shayne Schettler
Eric Pastorek	Andrew Schmidt
Zac Petersen	Brian Schmidt
Dupres Pina	Kurt Schneider
Pete Plum	William Schweisthal
Paul Polanski	Anthony Scimeca
Matthew Pommerening	Aaron Seaman
Nathan Poplawski	Phillip Seek
Jeremiah Popp	Christopher Shaw
Chancey Porter	Charles Sheehan
Brian Potts	Wendell Shelton
Chris Pourteau	Brett Shilton
Chris Prats	Vernetta Shipley
Joshua Purvis	Glenn Shotton
Max Quezada	Joshua Sipin
T.J. Recio	Christopher Slater
Jacob Reynolds	Scott Sloan
Eric Ritenour	Daniel Smith
Walt Robillard	Michael Smith
Joshua Robinson	Sharroll Smith
Brian Robinson	Michael Smith
Daniel Robitaille	Tyler Smith
Paul Roder	John Spears
Chris Rollini	Thomas Spencer
Thomas Roman	Peter Spitzer
Joyce Roth	Dustin Sprick
Andrew Ruiz	Graham Stanton
David Sanford	Paul Starck
Chris Sapero	Seaver Sterling

Maggie Stewart-Grant
John Stockley
Rob Strachan
William Strickler
Shayla Striffler
Kevin Summers
Ernest Sumner
Carol Szpara
Travis TadeWaldt
Daniel Tanner
Lawrence Tate
Tim Taylor
Robert Taylor
Daniel Thomas
Steven Thompson
Chris Thompson
William Joseph Thorpe
Beverly Tierney
Kayla Todd
Matthew Townsend
Jameson Trauger
Cole Trueblood
Eric Turnbull
Brandon Turton

Dylan Tuxhorn
Jalen Underwood
Paul Van Dop
Paden VanBuskirk
Patrick Varrassi
Daniel Vatamaniuck
Jose Vazquez
Josiah Velazquez
Anthony Wagnon
Humberto Waldheim
Christopher Walker
David Wall
Andrew Ward
Scot Washam
John Watson
Ben Wheeler
Jack Williams
Scott Winters
Jason Wright
Ethan Yerigan
Phillip Zaragoza
Brandt Zeeh
Nathan Zoss